"JAKE," SHE CALLED. "WAIT."

As Molly hurried, she stumbled and lost her balance on the platform shoes. She toppled forward, letting out an involuntary shriek of panic. Jake, only steps ahead of her, turned to see what had happened. Molly pitched, flailing frantically toward him.

He caught her against his chest, stumbled backward, and sat down hard on the boardwalk with Molly sprawled over him.

"Oh my God," she said in a tone of absolute mortification.

She smelled good, Jake thought, slightly disoriented. The scent of suntan cream and warm female skin surrounded him, heady as an opiate. She felt good, too. One of her hands was clutching his thigh, and the other was clamped onto his shoulder. She was lying across his lap and between his legs and he found the position very agreeable.

Strange woman, Jake thought. Sexy…but she had "trouble" written all over her…

Also by Melanie Craft

Trust Me

MAN TROUBLE

Melanie Craft

NEW YORK   BOSTON

Cover design by Diane Luger
Cover illustration by Sandy Haight
Cover photograph by T. O'Keefe/Photolink
Book design by Giorgetta Bell Mcree

Warner Books

Time Warner Book Group
1271 Avenue of the Americas
New York, NY 10020
Visit our Web site at www.twbookmark.com

Printed in the United States of America

First Paperback Printing: May 2004

10 9 8 7 6 5 4 3 2 1

To Kira

MAN TROUBLE

CHAPTER 1

"The captain's boy be no boy at all," snarled Delancey. "And I'll prove it to ye!"

Angeline gasped, stumbling as the first mate's thick hand jerked her forward. "No!" she cried. "He's a liar—"

"Liar, am I?" With one cruel motion, Delancey ripped her tunic from collar to hem, exposing the tight wrapping of bandages that she had used to disguise the curves of her bosom. She struggled, spitting and swearing at him, but he made short work of that last protective layer of cloth. A rumble of astonishment ran through the crew at the sight of her milk-white breasts.

Delancey leered at her, close enough for Angeline to smell his stinking, rum-laced breath. "What do you say now, wench?"

"Very brave, Professor Shaw," said a voice just behind Molly. "Are you finally throwing caution to the winds, or are you just getting sloppy?"

Startled, Molly jumped, her leg knocking against the underside of the cafeteria table. Next to her laptop, a cup of lukewarm coffee sloshed into its saucer. Her fingers hit the key combination to activate the computer's screen saver, and the page of text was instantly replaced by a bucolic scene of blue water and gently cruising tropical fish.

Outside the student union, the view was somewhat different. It was snowing again, not an unusual event in Belden, Wisconsin, in early December. Through the tall windows, Molly could see a row of bicycles lined up haphazardly in a rack. They were frosted with white and slumped together as if huddled for warmth.

"Carter," she said, without turning around, "didn't your mother ever teach you that it's rude to read over someone's shoulder?"

Carter McKee came around the table and sat down opposite her. He was a small man, with rumpled brown hair, a rumpled brown jacket, a blue bow tie, and a crooked grin that made him seem more like a naughty schoolboy than a journalist.

"My mother taught me to salsa dance," he said, picking up Molly's coffee cup. He sipped, grimaced, and quickly set it down again. "She also taught me to mix a mint julep, and to rationalize the kind of behavior that might otherwise make me question my morals. I don't recall anything about shoulders, though."

"You're a snoop."

"Me?" Carter said innocently. "You'll feel terrible for saying that when you realize I was being helpful. Think what might happen if one of your students strolled by and saw his history professor madly typing 'milk-white breasts' into her laptop."

"I wasn't typing *madly*," Molly said. "I was typing *steadily*. That's different. You make me sound like some kind of crazed spinster."

"Either way, I assumed that the mysterious Sandra—"

"Shh!"

Carter lowered his voice. "I simply assumed," he repeated, "that the mysterious Sandra St. Claire didn't want to be unmasked by a nosy freshman in the Belden College Student Union."

"You've got that right," Molly said. "We both know what would happen to me if the administration found out about this."

Carter's grin returned. "That would shake things up in this fossil pit."

"Not funny! This is my career we're talking about."

"What, you think that your dean wouldn't be happy to learn that one of his elite faculty members wrote the novel that the *New York Post* just called . . . what was it? A sleazy saga?"

"Swashbuckler," Molly said grimly.

He chuckled with delight. "That's it. 'A sleazy swashbuckler, soaked with sin and shipwrecked by schlock.' I love it."

Molly groaned. "Do we have to talk about this?"

"Not the greatest review," Carter said. "But you have to agree that it was an impressive use of alliteration."

"There's something very bizarre about having the *New York Post* accuse *me* of writing sleaze," Molly said.

Carter shrugged. "Don't tell me you were hoping for a Pulitzer," he said. "You want credit for your brains, write an academic book."

"I did! *Maritime Wives*: a feminist analysis of the role of sea captains' wives on eighteenth-century merchant ships. I lifted it straight from my dissertation, and it sold forty-two copies, ten of those to my mother. I didn't make a dime." She paused, reconsidering. "No, actually, I probably did make a dime."

"I have a copy," Carter said. "Your mother gave it to me. But I thought that money wasn't the point with you professor types. Aren't you supposed to survive on the fruit of knowledge and the milk of reason?" He quirked an eyebrow at her. "Or something like that?"

"That's after I get tenure," Molly said. "Which will never, ever happen if anyone links me to *Pirate Gold*. They'll take away my library card. I'll be out on the street, holding a sign that says 'will deconstruct social theory for food.' "

Carter looked exasperated. "Why do you need tenure? You wrote a best-selling novel, for God's sake. Quit. Go buy a castle somewhere and write another one. Enjoy your life. What's so great about this place?" He gestured contemptuously around the half-empty cafeteria.

"Are you serious? You know how hard it is to get a teaching position at a top college, and this isn't just any top college. This is *Belden*. I was lucky to be hired." She paused, then couldn't help adding, "And despite what everyone says, I earned it."

"Are people still grumbling about that? It's been three years. They should drop it."

"Academics never drop anything," Molly said. "There are feuds on this campus that go back to the 1940s. When I'm seventy, and hobbling across the quad, they'll be whispering, 'There goes that Shaw girl. She had a very *influential* father.' "

"That," Carter said, "is a chilling thought."

"I agree. Which is why I'd like to distinguish myself in something other than the trashy novel field."

"I meant that it was chilling to think that you might still be here when you're seventy."

"My father is seventy," Molly said. "And he's still here."

"Exactly," Carter said. His sour expression betrayed his opinion of Molly's father, who—she knew from experience—returned the sentiment. "And how is the great Stanford Shaw these days?"

"Fine," Molly said. Her father, currently Belden's emeritus professor of history, was the top god in the college's academic pantheon. He was the author of *The Chronicles of Civilization*, a dry nine-volume series considered to be among the finest scholarly works of the twentieth century, and although he no longer taught regularly, he was a regular sight on campus. One glimpse of his noble white head was enough to raise the heart rates of impressionable freshmen, and to give everyone else the uneasy feeling that they were not living up to their potential.

"Everyone here is holding their breath, waiting for me to fail," Molly said. "I'm damned if I'll give them that satisfaction. I would rather be run through with a cutlass."

"Cheers," Carter said. "I salute your determination. Just one question, though."

"What?"

"Do you like it here?"

"What do you mean?" Molly felt an upwelling of anxiety in her chest. "I spent my whole life working to deserve this job. Why wouldn't I like it?"

Carter shrugged. "Just asking."

"No, you weren't. You were making a point. I can tell by that smug look on your face. But you can forget it, Carter. I am not a trashy novel writer. I'm a professor and a historian. I have an excellent academic reputation, and I'm not going to throw all that away just because my *hobby* accidentally turned into something huge!"

He gazed at her, unfazed. "But do you like it here?"

Molly scowled at him. "You know," she said, "every historical detail in *Pirate Gold* was one hundred percent accurate. You could learn as much from that book as from an introductory text on the eighteenth century. Just because there was a little bit of sex in it . . ."

"A lot of sex."

"Well, a reasonable amount of—"

"Molly," Carter said, "it was a lot. And then there were the kidnappings, and the keelhaulings, and the torture scenes, and that rather . . . stirring . . . episode in the waterfront bawdy house with Andre DuPre and the two ladies of the evening . . ."

"Oh, all right," Molly grumbled. "Whatever."

"Don't try to explain to me why your novel has academic merit," Carter said. "I don't care. But I'd love to know why you want to stay at a place where you have to hide the fact that your book was on the *Times* best-seller list."

"I like it here," Molly said. "I *like* it here. Okay? Satisfied?"

"If you say so."

"I do! I have an office. I have students. I like teaching."

"So come and live in Chicago, teach at the community college, and quit panicking when someone reads over your shoulder."

"Leave me alone!" Molly exclaimed, too loudly. People turned to look, and she blushed, avoiding the curious stares. On her laptop screen, the tropical fish meandered through their virtual ocean, electronically bright and perpetually placid. "I really don't want to talk about this."

He held up one hand. "I didn't drive an hour north in this weather just to argue with you. I do have another reason for being here."

"Good," Molly said. "What?"

"My new project." Carter picked up her coffee cup again and began to fiddle with it, turning it round and round in his fingers. He flashed her his most charming smile. "It's big. Very big. But it hinges on a couple of things. One thing, actually, in particular." He took another swallow from the cup and made the same face.

"Carter," Molly said, "would you like me to get you some fresh coffee?"

He shook his head. "No, listen. This is important. The project hinges on you."

"Me?"

"I need your help."

"What, as a consultant? You're doing some kind of historical piece?" It seemed out of character. Carter's writing style was aggressively commercial, the kind of work more likely to be published in *Esquire* than in *American Antiquity*. It was hard for Molly to imagine being any help to him on the type of project that he would consider "big."

"Not exactly," Carter said. His ears were turning red. He frowned. "I'm not sure how to put this."

Molly hadn't seen him look so uncomfortable since their senior year in high school, when he had tried to talk her into telling Kara Swenson that he had already asked Becky Lipinski to the prom.

"Out with it," she said. "What's this project?"

"Okay," he said. He put down the cup and stared meaningfully at her. "Two words. Jake Berenger."

Molly nodded. "And?"

He looked disappointed by her lack of reaction. "You do know who he is," he said reproachfully. "The hotel mogul? The resort developer? The *billionaire*?"

"Of course I know who he is," Molly said. "I read the papers. But what's so new about this? You told me a year ago that you were doing a profile on him. You said that the *Miami Herald* wanted to run it in their Sunday magazine. Last I remember, you were busy interviewing all of his former girlfriends."

"Not all of them," Carter said. "That would have been physically impossible if I wanted to publish in this decade. Anyway, it was getting redundant. They all said some version of the same thing. 'Jake was always a gentleman, but I could tell that underneath it all, deep emotional wounds were preventing him from ever trusting me with his heart.' " He rolled his eyes. "Yawn. Spare me, please, from the pop psychobabble of a bunch of models."

"You never showed me the article," Molly said. "How did it turn out?"

"It didn't. He wouldn't talk to me. Not in person, not on the phone, not even by e-mail. And then I found out that he never gives interviews."

"Never? But he's always in the papers. There are pictures of him everywhere."

"Yes," Carter said. "People take pictures of Jake Berenger. People write stories about Jake Berenger. But he never gives interviews. He may be the world's most publicly private person."

"How strange," Molly said. "Doesn't the head of a major corporation have to talk to reporters sometime?"

"Oh, sure, he does the earnings reports," Carter said. "Very tightly controlled by the Berenger corporate PR office. But he's never done a single personal interview, not that every magazine and newspaper on earth hasn't been trying to get to him. Word on the street is that he hates the press." He chuckled evilly. "Can't imagine why, when we love him so much."

"Too bad. I hope you didn't waste a lot of time on him."

"It wasn't a waste. There's no shortage of market for articles about this guy. The fact that he won't talk only makes people more obsessed with him. But there's only so far you can go with an outside-observer piece. The usual tabloid trash about the girls, the race cars, the wild parties . . . you know the tune. I think I can do better. A lot better. I'm going to write"—he paused, for dramatic effect—"a book."

"A *book*?"

"The one and only authorized biography of Jake Berenger. He doesn't know it yet, but he wants to work with me. I can feel it."

"He sounds like a shallow playboy. Why don't you pick someone more worthy to write about?"

Carter grinned. "He's worth one point one billion dollars, on a good stock day. That's worthy enough for me."

"You're unbelievable," Molly said.

"Share the wealth, Molly! This book will sell. It'll get my name into the mainstream. When they write about him, they'll quote me. If I can make this happen, it'll be the coup of the decade."

"Great. All you'll need to do is get a man who never even gives interviews to agree to help you write a book. Or did you forget about that small detail?"

"No," Carter said. "I didn't forget."

"So . . ." Molly prompted. "How do you plan to succeed where a hundred other hungry journalists have failed?"

"The approach," Carter said. He nodded. "Yes. I truly believe that it's all in the approach."

Molly smiled. "Oh, you're going to ask him *nicely*?"

"In a sense, yes. When you want to break through someone's armor, you look for the weakest spot, don't you?"

"I guess so."

"Right," Carter said. He had a determined look on his face. "Okay. Molly, when we were in college, and your car broke down on our way home from the Dells, who walked eight miles in the snow to get help?"

"You did. You were very brave."

"And who covered for you when we were sixteen and you were dating Greg Ackerman? You couldn't admit to your father that you had a crush on a football player, so you told him that you were studying at my house every Saturday night. And then you went home slobbering drunk that time, and Stanford was sure that I'd done it to take advantage of you."

Molly frowned. "I wasn't slobbering."

"He's hated me ever since," Carter said. "But most recently, who convinced you to send *Pirate Gold* to my agent in New York, when you were barely willing to let it out of a locked dresser drawer?"

"Carter, I agree that I owe you a favor," Molly said. "But I don't see how I can help you with this Jake Berenger project. What do you want from me, a letter of recommendation assuring him that you're a decent guy? That you won't do a hatchet job on his life story?"

"You could include that when you talk to him," Carter said thoughtfully. "It might help."

Molly stared at him. "Hold it. Talk to him? Are you saying that you want *me* to ask Jake Berenger if he'll do this book?"

"That's the plan," Carter said. "But first, you'll need to seduce him."

CHAPTER 2

"Jaaake! Where are you?"

The call came plaintively through the warm Caribbean air, echoing down the hallway of the villa. It was a sweet, girlish voice, and to Jake Berenger, it was every bit as melodic as the evening lockdown bell at San Quentin. He pushed aside the pile of paper on his desk and closed his eyes briefly.

"Darling," said his mother, who was sitting in a leather armchair nearby, studying fabric samples for the renovation of the Gold Bay lobby, "did I just see you cringe?"

"Yes," Jake said. "And before the week is out, you may see me snap completely."

Oliver Arias, Jake's number-two man and Berenger Corporation's Chief Operations Officer, was too discreet to laugh, but a faint smile hovered on the edges of his mouth.

Cora Berenger began to protest, but Jake held up a warning hand as he heard light footsteps approaching the library. The door to his suite of rooms had been closed, which would have suggested to most people that he did not want to be disturbed, but he knew from recent experience that it took more than subtle suggestion to discourage Amanda Harper.

Moments later, she appeared in the doorway. Twenty-one years old, golden-haired, with the face of an angel, the body of a centerfold, and the soul of a pit bull, Amanda was the only daughter of Harry Harper, Jake's longtime friend and mentor. Unfortunately, the same steely determination that had made her father a major player in the oil business had expressed itself in Amanda as one single-minded goal: to have and to hold Jake Berenger.

"I found you," Amanda said. She was wearing a lime-green bikini under some kind of gauzy white minidress, and she smiled at him, tilting her head so that her hair swung forward in a shining curtain.

"You did, indeed," Jake said.

"It wasn't very hard. You're always in here. How can you work on such a beautiful day? Why don't you come down to the beach? You're supposed to be on vacation."

"Funny thing about the world," Jake said, "it doesn't seem to care that I'm on vacation. And I thought that I was doing well, working only six hours a day instead of ten."

Amanda laughed uneasily, and Jake could tell that she wasn't sure whether he was joking or not. He wasn't. *You want me, little girl?* he thought. *Be careful what you wish for. This is what you'll get.*

She, like everyone else who didn't know him, had bought into the tabloid version of his life. She wanted it for herself, but she didn't know that she was chasing a phantom. If you believed what you read in the papers, his world consisted of glittering parties, jet-set events, and an endless procession of beautiful women. The reality was somewhat different. The parties were choreographed publicity stunts designed to keep the media buzzing about the Berenger hotels; the jet-set events were corporate sponsorships carefully chosen to flash the Berenger logo in the eyes of their most elite customers, and the women were models or actresses who saw the chance to appear on his arm as a useful promotion for their own careers. It was a mutual use situation, and Jake had learned that there was no shortage of available flesh as long as the champagne was flowing and the flashbulbs were popping.

He heard his mother sigh, as if she'd read his thoughts. It had been her idea to invite Amanda to spend the winter holidays at Gold Bay with their family. The official reason given was that Amanda's parents were enjoying a twenty-fifth wedding anniversary trip to Europe, but Jake knew his mother well enough to guess that she had an ulterior motive similar to Amanda's.

"Oliver," Cora said briskly, and Oliver looked up nervously from his sheaf of papers. He, like everyone else who worked for Berenger, held Cora in a regard that mixed awe, adoration, and terror. Gold Bay was the crown jewel in the company treasury, and it had been Cora's baby from the beginning. She was the managing director of the exclusive resort, and she ran it with an efficiency that would have impressed the U.S. Army. In keeping with that theme, Jake teasingly referred to her as his five-star resort general.

"It seems a shame," she continued, "to send you back to New York tonight without giving you a little time to enjoy the fresh air and the sun."

"Oh, no," Oliver said. "I'm—"

"Oh, yes," Cora said. "I insist, dear. In fact, I have a wonderful idea. You should take a drive over to the west side of the island and see the site we've marked out for the new golf course. We've only just broken ground, but you'll get a sense of the layout. The views are stunning." She smiled. "Amanda, would you be a sweetheart and go with Mr. Arias? I'm sure he'd enjoy the company."

"Now?" Amanda asked with a clear lack of enthusiasm.

"Now," Cora said firmly. "Oliver needs a break. My son will work us all to death unless someone intervenes."

Amanda began to pout. "But—"

"Jake and I have a few more things to discuss, but we'll see you this evening, at dinner. All right? Good. Now, go ahead, you two."

Cora waited until they heard the sound of the hall door closing behind Oliver and Amanda before she spoke again. "Well," she said in a tone that made Jake wonder if he should have gone with the others, "I've been waiting for a chance to ask what got into you this morning at breakfast. It's the first time I've ever seen you read the newspaper through a meal. You know how I feel about that."

"Sorry. But it was preferable to the company."

"Oh? I had no idea that I'd become so tedious, darling."

"You know I'm not talking about you," Jake said. "Every time I looked up, there was Amanda, staring at me over the orange juice. Those blue eyes blinking, those glossy lips pouting . . . I'm sure it works on the boys at school, but I don't want to play."

"You've hardly given this a chance!"

"Why should I? It would be a waste of my time, and hers. She's a pretty little package, and I'm sure that she'll meet another nice businessman, marry him, and spend the rest of her life shopping and doing token charity work. Frankly, though, if I wanted a pet, I'd buy a collie."

"Jake!"

"Oh, come on, Ma. You should know me well enough to know that I could never take Amanda seriously. She thinks Watergate was a spa."

"She's young."

"Exactly."

"She'll grow up, get more worldly."

"I don't give a damn about worldly. I'm talking about character. Amanda has always had everything handed to her on a silver platter. She's never worked or struggled for anything in her life."

"You're being deliberately difficult," Cora said. "How can you complain about Amanda's character? What about all of the other women you've dated?"

"What about them?"

"Darling, they've hardly been a lineup of Nobel laureates. I fail to see how Amanda Harper is any more deficient in character than Skye Elliot, or Tamara Thomas, or . . . or . . . who was that woman who kept writing to you?"

Jake grinned. "Kristy Kreme?"

"That's the one. She said she was a dancer, but I've never heard of a ballerina with a name like that. I think she was a fraud."

"I wouldn't know. I never actually met her."

"My point," Cora continued, "is that if you insist on running around with shallow women, couldn't you at least pick one from a good family?"

"No. Harry is my friend, and I'm not going to date his daughter. It wouldn't be ethical."

Cora regarded him with barely controlled frustration. "Why on earth not?"

"Because Amanda—and her daddy—would expect too much from me. I'm not going to settle down, and I'm sure as hell not going to cut back on my work schedule. The women I date don't want Prince Charming, they want a good photo op. That's as committed as I intend to get."

"How interesting," Cora said. "I think you may have forgotten to mention that to Skye Elliot, darling."

Jake exhaled sharply. His mother was the only person on earth who could needle him with impunity, but sometimes she went too far. "I didn't forget," he said. "Miss Elliot has selective hearing. She knew exactly what she was getting into when she had her publicist call me. But she tried to change the rules in the middle of the game."

"She fell in love with you. As your mother, I can hardly

blame her for that. But what she's doing now is unforgivable."

Jake's mouth turned up slightly, humorlessly. "Hell hath no fury . . ." he quoted and shrugged. "I was always completely honest with Skye."

"I'm sure that you were," Cora said, and sighed. "My dear, life is not just a series of photo ops. You're forty years old, and I want more for you. I want you to be happy. I want you to fall in love."

Love? Jake felt a sourness in his stomach, as if old dreams had fallen there to rot. He remembered being in love. It had been a long time ago.

"I am happy," he said.

"Not like you were. When you were in school, you were—"

"A child. And then I grew up."

"Too fast. You had no choice. This was never the life you wanted. I remember when you didn't care about business, or money—"

"I learned to care a lot about money once we didn't have any," Jake said. "Funny how that happens."

But Cora was caught up in her sentimental reverie. "You would have finished school, married Karen . . ."

"And lived happily ever after?" Jake's voice was suddenly harsh. He preferred his mother in her executive guise. "I doubt that. Hindsight suggests that it wouldn't have worked out anyway."

Cora looked hurt, and Jake felt a stab of guilt. She meant well, and it wasn't her fault that her misty-eyed memories brought up emotions that he preferred to keep buried.

"It doesn't matter now," he said, trying to soothe her. He gestured around the luxuriously furnished room. "It all worked out in the end, didn't it?"

"It's not the end yet," Cora said tartly, and Jake grinned, remembering from whom he had inherited his temper.

"Oh, Jake," she said. "I don't suppose you'd reconsider this business with Amanda? She's a nice girl."

"No."

"She's pretty. And she wants children."

"Not interested."

"If you'd spend some time getting to know her, you might become interested. And it would be good for you to get the Skye episode behind you. Publicly, I mean. You need to show the world that you've moved on. Amanda isn't high profile, but right now that's an asset."

"I don't care," Jake said. "I'm not going to date Amanda Harper, publicly or privately. Give up, Ma."

"Hmm," Cora said. "We'll see. Regardless, you need to do something about Skye. That girl is unstable, and she has the newspapers eating out of her hand. She's a talented actress, I'll give her that, but that's just what makes her so dangerous. She'll say anything to hurt you, and believe me, those reporters won't bother to confirm it before they print it."

"So what?" Jake shrugged. "You know my take on that. Publicity keeps us hot, and even scandal sells rooms. There's nothing Skye can say that can do us any damage."

"Don't be so sure. It would be much better if you spoke to the press yourself . . ."

"No."

"The journalists are beginning to resent you for shutting them out. I can see it in the way they've been writing about you."

"I don't know why you read that junk."

"Because someone needs to keep an eye on these things, and I'm the only one who can make you listen! I see trouble, Jake. You're giving the reporters the impression that you think you're above them, and they're passing that feeling on to the readers . . . our customers."

"That's ridiculous. You know why I don't give interviews. It has nothing to do with snobbery."

"I know that," Cora said. "But they don't."

"Too bad. I don't talk about my personal life to the press. Not now, not ever. That's where I draw the line."

"I'm not sure you still have the luxury of drawing a line," Cora said. "The Berenger board is concerned about you, Jake. They say that your public image has become too frivolous. The world is calling you a playboy, and the analysts are questioning whether you're still an appropriate figurehead for the company. And now, this trouble with Skye . . ."

Jake had heard enough. "Damn it!" he said, slamming his hands down on the desktop. "Everything I do is for the good of the company. Everything. I built it, I run it, and until the economy took a dive, I didn't hear any of those sanctimonious pricks on the board complaining about the value of their stock. If things are rough these days, it has nothing to do with my personal life. The whole hospitality industry has taken a hit. Berenger is doing better than most, and it's specifically because of my hard work."

"I agree," Cora said. "But you can't fight human nature, my dear. Bad economy or not, when the stock is down, people want someone to blame. Right now, they're looking at you, and I want you to be careful."

CHAPTER 3

"Okay, Carter," Molly said. "Just tell me one thing."

"Sure, what?"

"Have you gone *completely insane*?"

They were back in Molly's apartment, the spacious bottom floor of an old clapboard house near campus. Carter's declaration had pushed the conversation to a point where Molly had decided that it would be better continued in private.

"I mean, listen to yourself," she continued. "Are you seriously telling me that you want me to go with you to one of Jake Berenger's resorts and spend a week swanning around in a low-cut dress, trying to catch his attention so that I can then use my feminine wiles to persuade him to let you write his biography?"

"Yes," Carter said.

"Yes, you've gone insane? I thought so."

Carter shot a nervous look at the chef's knife that she was using, and Molly realized that she was gripping it in a way that suggested that she had intentions beyond chopping parsley. She put down the knife and wiped her hands on her apron.

"Why me? If you really do want to go through with this . . . bizarre plan, why don't you hire some local model to go with you? I'm flattered that you haven't noticed that I'm not exactly the glamorous type, but—"

"Packaging," Carter said dismissively.

"What?"

"Packaging," he repeated. "That's all it is. Your infrastructure is as good as any other female's. Better, actually."

"My *infrastructure*?"

Carter looked uncomfortable. "You know what I mean. The whole . . . girl thing." He raised his hands and waved them vaguely along the outlines of a female form. "You're actually very good-looking, Molly, or you would be, if you didn't try so hard to hide it."

"I'm not trying to hide anything," Molly exclaimed. "That is such a typically male thing to say. I suppose you think I should show up at faculty meetings in high heels and a miniskirt. Don't you think that it might be a little difficult for me to discuss my teaching load with the department head while he's staring at my thighs?"

"Maybe so, but you weren't always like this."

"Like what?"

He didn't even blink. "Frumpy."

"What!"

"The pearls, the glasses, those baggy beige sweaters, two at a time—"

"They're called twin sets! They're cashmere. They're classic. Grace Kelly wore them."

Carter shrugged. "I'm just giving you the male perspective. I don't know where you got the idea that dressing like your own grandmother would make the people at Belden take you seriously, but it seems like a wasted youth to me."

Molly stared at him, unable to speak. She knew that she should be outraged that he would dare to say these things to her. She tried to work up some righteous indignation, but it came with difficulty. Mostly, she just felt deflated and foolish. Carter had called her bluff. She didn't particularly like the way she looked these days, but she didn't think that she had any choice about it. There had been mornings when, sick of her usual drab uniform, she had put on something more daring—daring, for her, being a snug sweater and a skirt hemmed above the knee—only to lose her nerve before she set foot out of her front door. It had gotten even worse in recent months, since *Pirate Gold* was published. She felt as if she were always seeing herself through two sets of eyes: her own, and those of some sour-lipped critic who saw any attempt at vanity as proof that she was an intellectual fraud.

"In my opinion," Carter said, "you're seriously conflicted, Molly. This trip might turn out to be as helpful to you as it is to me."

"I doubt that very much," Molly muttered, but the vigor had gone out of her voice. She felt tired, suddenly, and she sighed. "Carter, please. Don't ask me to do this. I can't. My feminine wiles are gone . . . they dried up and blew away while I was in grad school. Anyway, your plan can't possibly work. Jake Berenger just broke up with *Skye Elliot*—"

"Aha!" Carter said triumphantly. "You do read *People* magazine. I knew it. You probably have a subscription. Where do you hide them? Under your mattress?"

"My point," Molly continued, ignoring him, "is that if the man's last love interest was an Academy Award–winning actress who also happens to be one of the most beautiful women on the planet, then what are my chances? He won't even look at me."

"He will," Carter said, so positively that Molly was intrigued, in spite of herself.

"Oh?" she asked. "Why?"

"I told you," Carter said. "It's all in the packaging. Marketing makes the world go round, Molly, and Jake Berenger will notice you because we have done our market research."

Molly looked blankly at him. "Huh?"

"It's simple. Look, he's a market of one. So we study him to find out exactly what's been selling. Then we design the perfect package, create buzz, do some strategic product placement . . ."

"Wait a minute. I don't like the sound of this. What am I, a can of soup? I'm not a product. And you're not selling me, to Jake Berenger or anyone else."

"Wrong," Carter said. "Selling you is exactly what we're doing. That's what seduction is all about, right? Convincing someone that they want you? That they have to have you? Sounds like sales to me. Am I wrong?"

"Yes! It's not that cold-blooded."

"Oh, come on," Carter scoffed. "What do you think attraction is? You subscribe to the Cupid theory, with a little naked guy flying around shooting arrows of love into people?"

"Of course not," Molly said. "But I think that when two people are attracted to each other, it's because they've recognized qualities in each other that are personally meaningful—"

"Exactly," Carter said. "And let me tell you what qualities Jake Berenger considers meaningful. Hair: pale blond and long. Eyes: blue. Height: five feet eight. Body: slender but curvy, about one hundred and twenty-five pounds. Age: twenty-six . . ."

"*What* are you talking about?"

"Patterns. Statistics. I collected all of the information I could find on all of the women he's dated over the past ten years and gave it to a friend who's handy with computers. What I just told you is what the statistical analysis program told us. We took every detail that seemed relevant, fed it into the program, and it gave us, to an inch and a pound, Jake Berenger's ideal woman."

"How charming," Molly said. "If you're trying to get me to seriously dislike this man, just keep on talking."

"Oh, I could," Carter said. "I was only warming up. How about a tendency to prefer women who wear the color pink?"

"*Pink?* This is becoming a bad cliché. Plus, pink makes me look blotchy. This is never going to work, Carter! My hair is brown, I don't have blue eyes, I'm only five-foot-four and I might be slender, but I'm definitely not curvy—"

"Details," Carter said. "We'll deal with all of that later."

"Not unless I agree to go along with this. Can you explain to me how I'm supposed to charm such a shallow, ridiculous man?"

"Acting. This isn't about *you*, Molly. It's not about the two of you falling in love. It's about creating a fantasy character, just like when you write a book."

"It's deception. It's not honest."

"It's an adventure," Carter said. A wheedling note crept into his voice. "Do you want me to beg? I will. Please, Molly. Please come with me, your old buddy, and help me reach the heights of success. You know, those same heights that I helped you reach?"

"But I don't know *how*—"

"Yes you do. Read your own book. Spend a week forgetting the Respectable Professor Shaw and become Sandra St. Claire. If you can write like her, why can't you live like her for a week?"

Molly didn't answer. She had just remembered a game called "Spies" that she had invented and played as a child, with the help of a red-haired girl named Kristin, her best friend at the time. The game had involved a clandestine meeting in Molly's attic, where each girl assigned the other a "secret identity" consisting mostly of a made-up name. They had never done more than run around acting mysterious and giggling a lot, but Molly still remembered that exciting sense of possibility, the feeling that she could do or say anything, with the justification—however questionable—that it wasn't really her.

Acting, Carter had said. He was right, wasn't he? It wouldn't really be *her* out there, in a pink dress, batting her eyelashes at a hotel tycoon. Whether she failed miserably or succeeded, it wouldn't matter. Whatever happened on a Caribbean island, hundreds of miles away from Belden College, would be as harmless and as meaningless as a game of Spies.

"Well," Carter said gloomily, "if you aren't willing to help a friend in need, then so be it. I understand, really I do."

"Carter . . ." Molly began.

"No, no." He put up one hand. "Don't worry about me. I'll just keep on with my pathetic existence as a B-grade journalist, struggling to survive, barely making ends meet . . ."

"Carter," Molly said again, more forcefully this time.

He ignored her. "I'll just give up on all my dreams of ever bettering myself, of ever achieving the success that you—"

"Carter, shut up! You win. I'll do it."

"You will?" His grin was sudden and blinding.

"Yes. But let's clarify one thing. When you say that you want me to seduce Jake Berenger, I'm assuming that you mean that in the old-fashioned sense, right? Because if you're asking me to sleep with him, I can tell you right now that you have the wrong woman."

"Molly," Carter said, looking mildly scandalized. "Please. What kind of person do you think I am?"

"I'm not going to answer that. So we understand each other on that point?"

"Oh, sure. Definitely, I mean. Sleeping with him won't be necessary, anyway. Someone told me recently that the power is all in the chase."

"Who said that?"

"Ah," Carter said smugly. "My secret weapon. Our guarantee of success."

"You've lost me again."

"Another trick that I've learned in my long and illustrious career," Carter said, "is that when you need expert help, what do you do?"

"You call an expert?"

"Bingo." Carter reached for his battered leather satchel, pulled out a paperback book, and handed it to her.

Molly looked down at it. On the cover was a perfectly groomed platinum-haired woman who appeared to be in her early forties. She was smiling, knowingly and glamorously, at the camera. "*How to Meet and Marry the Rich*," Molly read aloud. "*A Guide for Girls Who Want It All*. By Elaine McKee Culpepper Von Reinholz Newberg? Carter, what on earth? Elaine McKee? Isn't that your . . . ?"

"You remember my sister?" Carter asked. "She writes, too. In her case, it tends to be autobiographical."

CHAPTER 4

Billionaire Gets the Boot

"I had no choice but to break it off," says a pale and fragile Skye Elliot, speaking to this reporter of the recent end of her well-publicized relationship with resort magnate Jake Berenger. "Jake and I just don't have the same values. I wanted to make a home for us, but he only cares about life in the fast lane. The parties, the drugs . . ."

Drugs? "Oh, I never saw *him use drugs," she says. "But with that lifestyle . . ." Her cerulean eyes have a haunted look, hinting that the celebrity tycoon has a darker side.*

"He told me to give up my work as an advocate for Third World children so that I would have more time for him. I just couldn't do it."

Tears spring to her eyes. Gratefully, she accepts a tissue from her manager . . .

Jake folded the *Daily News* in half and tossed it across his desk toward Oliver Arias. "Well," he said, "we expected this, didn't we?"

"It's going to get worse," Oliver said darkly. "It's going

to be a feeding frenzy. I think we should sue. I'll talk to the lawyers."

"Don't bother," Jake said. "We're not suing."

"What?" Oliver's face was flushed with outrage. He shook the paper at Jake. "These are *lies*. She wants to destroy you. She's calling you a drug addict! We need to act fast."

"Actually, what she said was that she'd never seen me using drugs, which is certainly true. She's too smart—or the *Daily News*'s lawyers are too smart—to give us anything to hang a libel suit on."

"It's the principle of the thing. We need to make a statement. We have to fight back."

Jake shook his head. "We can't. It would be gasoline on the fire. There's nothing that the media would love more than a public mud-slinging match, and I guarantee that between Skye and me, the one with the teary cerulean eyes would win."

"But—"

"Take a deep breath," Jake advised, "and forget about it."

"We have to issue a statement! The reporters have been calling all morning, reading us things that she's said about you, asking if you want to refute them."

Jake shrugged. "They're playing chicken with me, trying to get a reaction. If they don't get one, they'll give up. We've been through this kind of thing before."

"No, we haven't," Oliver said. "Not a personal attack from someone who actually seems credible. I don't like it, Jake. This is very bad. The stock is down again—"

"So I keep hearing," Jake said coolly. "And meanwhile, my so-called playboy lifestyle is on hold, and I'm doing my damnedest to get things back on track." He stopped, hearing defensiveness in his own voice. His mother's warning about the rumblings of mutiny on the Berenger board had been on his mind for the past few days.

A dry smile touched his mouth. Skye was either remarkably clever, or just very lucky. Knowing her, his bet was on lucky. She had stumbled across the only way that she could really do him damage—by publicly painting him as unfit to be the head of Berenger Corporation. Luckily, her media appeal was limited to Hollywood magazines and scandal sheets like the *Daily News*, a category not taken too seriously by the Wall Street investment community. His image could afford to take a few hits, and the story would eventually die. He hadn't gotten this far in life by panicking every time someone slung a little mud in his direction.

❦

"She's perfect," exclaimed Elaine McKee Culpepper Von Reinholz Newberg, clasping her manicured hands in delight as she looked Molly up and down. "Yes, absolutely perfect."

Molly blushed, unexpectedly flattered. It was Saturday, one week after Carter had driven up to Belden to propose his scheme, and they were now sitting on brocade-upholstered chairs in the parlor of Carter's sister's penthouse condominium, on Chicago's near north side.

"I admit," Elaine continued, "that I had doubts about your judgment, Carter. But this is going to work out beautifully. This project will test the *limits* of my ability. We are truly beginning from ground zero."

Abruptly, Molly tuned back in. "I beg your pardon?"

Elaine patted her arm. "Oh, my dear. My clients are usually much more advanced. They're models, pageant winners, girls who already know how to dress, how to flirt, how to interest a man. All they need from me is a little guidance, a little reassurance that there is nothing whatsoever wrong with setting one's sights on a man who is—as I like to say—economically advantaged. They are already halfway there by the time they come to me, and it's no challenge at all, really. But you . . . my goodness! If I can take a history professor with no apparent fashion sense and limited social skills, and turn her into the kind of woman who would interest the most eligible bachelor on *earth*, then I will have proven to myself and to the world that my techniques are foolproof. You will be my triumph."

Her eyes took on a faraway look. "I'll use this as the feature case study in my next book."

Molly's mouth had dropped open in shock, and she was having trouble breathing through the sudden constriction in her chest. "You . . ." she began, ran out of air, and had to take another breath. "Book? About this? Oh, no, you won't. You're not putting this into any kind of book!"

Elaine looked surprised. "But . . ."

"Absolutely not!" Molly exclaimed. "Carter, tell your sister to swear that she'll never write a word about this, or I'll walk out of here and never speak to you again."

Elaine's eyebrows shot up into two exaggerated arches. "Fiery!" she said.

"Oh, God," Carter mumbled. "Listen, you two. Can't we just . . ."

"Passionate," Elaine continued, appraising Molly with a sharper eye. "I wouldn't have guessed that by looking at you, dear. But that's a good thing. We can work with that."

"Carter!" Molly shouted.

Carter looked uneasily at his sister. "You heard her," he said. "Sorry."

Elaine looked hurt. "Names and all identifying details would be changed," she said. "Naturally."

Molly glared at her. "Publish a single word about me and I'll have you killed," she said, and turned to Carter. "And let me warn *you*," she added, "that my 'limited social skills' are connected to a limited tolerance for this project."

"Oh, all right," Elaine interrupted. "Fine. I won't put you in the book, although it does seem like a waste, considering the size of my investment. If I'd known that I couldn't use the material . . ."

"What investment?" Molly asked.

"Never mind," Carter said quickly. "We'll all be putting our time and effort into this, and I am deeply grateful for your collective generosity, in all of its incarnations—"

"Shut up, Carter," Molly said, and turned to Elaine. "Is that what you meant? Investment of your time?"

"Yes," Elaine said. "My time, and my money. You don't think that Carter can afford a week for three at a Berenger resort on his salary at the *Tribune*, do you? My dear, this is not a Holiday Inn. Gold Bay is *the* most important spot in the Caribbean, and one of the top resorts in the world. And let me add that getting a reservation there, at the last minute, in the height of the holiday season, was just about impossible. I had to call the Princess Von Faxon Westenburg, my ex-sister-in-law, whose daughter Chantal works at Sotheby's with the son of a Berenger senior VP of marketing."

Carter looked pained. "It's a loan," he explained to Molly. "Against eventual royalties. My sister was more forthcoming than my publisher, who is sadly lacking in optimism."

"I couldn't possibly turn down such a fascinating project," Elaine added. "It was made for me. I am the sort of person who needs to be needed."

"Good for you," Molly said. "But I'll be paying my own way." She had no intention of taking charity from Elaine, and it was a pleasure to be able to refuse it. On the more practical side, covering her own expenses also meant that she had no obligation to anyone but herself. She still had her doubts about Carter's scheme, and this meeting was doing nothing to allay them.

Elaine looked surprised. "Rooms at Gold Bay are *extremely* expensive."

"Then I suppose that your brother and I had better keep out of the minibar," Molly said coolly. If Elaine McKee Culpepper Von Reinholz Newberg thought that she could intimidate a member of the Belden College faculty, then she was in for a shock. The woman might have perfect nails and a two-hundred-dollar haircut, but she had certainly never read Plutarch.

Molly frowned. Something that Elaine had said, just a few moments ago, was nagging at her, but she couldn't quite put her finger on it now. It had seized her attention like a bee sting, but the conversation had quickly moved on, distracting her with talk of princesses and Sotheby's, and loans to Carter . . .

"Wait a minute!" she exclaimed, alarmed. Now she remembered. "Did you just say something about a week for *three* at Gold Bay?"

Elaine's matte-red lips curved into a delighted smile. "Yes, indeed," she said. "You don't think that you can do this alone, do you? I'm going with you."

Judging from Carter's expression, Molly guessed that this was news to him, as well.

"Ahh," Carter said. His face had turned an odd shade of gray. "Elaine, that's very nice of you, but we had talked about you giving Molly just a couple of quick lessons, remember? The short course?"

Elaine shook her head. "The short course," she said, sliding a meaningful look in Molly's direction, "will not be long enough."

"Won't Mr. Newberg miss you?" Molly asked, doubting

it. So far, there had been no sign of anyone who answered to that name.

"Leonard and I separated six weeks ago," Elaine said. "He is currently in Bermuda, visiting his offshore corporation. I don't expect a reconciliation. Not before Christmas, at least."

"Oh," Carter said. "I'm sorry to hear that."

"Yes, thank you, it's very sad," Elaine said briskly. "But life goes on, and I hate spending the holidays alone."

CHAPTER 5

The Gold Bay beach was half a mile long, curved in a crescent-moon shape that hugged the blue water and gentle waves of the bay. At eight A.M. it was still deserted save for a few dedicated joggers, and Jake, who was taking his morning reconnaissance walk.

Behind the beach was a lush garden of palms and flowering vines, and tucked into this water-hungry landscaping was a row of thirty cottages, strung like pearls around the neck of the resort. They were the best suites at Gold Bay, each with two bedrooms, a living room, a caterer's kitchen for private parties, and a large deck overlooking the sand. The trees and vines had been carefully arranged to give the occupants of each cottage the feeling that they had no neighbors, but to allow them an unobstructed view of the ocean and the action on the beach.

Room service to the cottages came by way of an electric golf cart equipped with coolers and warming trays. There was a complimentary morning delivery of fresh juice, pastries, coffee, and the morning paper from the guest's home city, all of which would appear at a time previously arranged with the cottage's private butler. Breakfast was rarely requested before eight, but Jake noticed that a cart was arriving at Cottage Five, and wondered who the early bird was.

A yoga-obsessed supermodel, perhaps. Ingrid Anderson, a Victoria's Secret catalog veteran, had arrived three days ago with a bald man in flowing white robes who had signed the register as Rama Guru. For the past two mornings at nine A.M., Rama and Ingrid, both wearing thong bathing suits, had done the Sun Salutation on the pool terrace, to the awe and delight of the rest of the guests.

Jake strolled up the beach, a little closer to the cottage, looking curiously to see if Ingrid and Rama were there. But he saw only a smallish mousy-haired woman sitting in a chair on the deck, wrapped in one of the thick white terry-cloth Gold Bay bathrobes. The bulky robe was too big for her, and made her look as if she were being eaten by a polar bear. He nodded to her, in casual greeting, and was startled to see her eyes widen as if he had just given her the finger. Without a word, she jumped to her feet, stumbled over the hem of the robe, regained her balance, and then fled back into the cottage.

Jake stopped, taken aback. He waited for a few moments to see if she would come out again, but the cottage was now as silent as its neighbors. The curtains moved slightly, and while it was probably just the wind, he had the sudden feeling that she was standing there, hidden behind the fabric, peeking at him.

Weird, he thought, wondering what could have spooked her. If the sight of a man in swim trunks frightened her so much, she was in for a seriously terrifying vacation. He shrugged, lifted a hand in a brief wave toward the curtain, and continued on down the beach.

"My dear," said Elaine McKee Culpepper Von Reinholz Newberg, "what on earth are you doing?"

Guiltily, Molly jumped. Her heart was still hammering so hard that she could hear the beat of the blood in her ears, and her cheeks were hot. She released her grip on the curtain, and turned, feeling foolish.

"Nothing," she said.

Elaine raised her eyebrows. She was wearing black satin mules, a red silk nightgown with a matching robe, and diamond earrings. Her hair was pinned into a neat chignon, and her makeup was perfect. It was five minutes after eight A.M.

They had arrived at Gold Bay late the night before, after a six-hour snow delay at Chicago's O'Hare airport. Commercial travel took them only as far as Antigua, where they were met by a Gold Bay helicopter that whisked them and their baggage over the last stretch of ocean to the resort's private island. Molly had been surviving on minimal sleep in the days prior to the trip, working nights to get two hundred freshman final exams graded before she left town, and by the time they arrived at Gold Bay, she was so dazed with fatigue that her brain had barely processed the scene around her. She had tumbled into bed after a brief discussion with Carter and Elaine about the fact that they were three people in a two-bedroom cottage. Elaine had explained that it would be perfect for Molly and Carter to share the room with the twin beds, and although her logic was dubious, Molly had been too tired to argue.

She slept as deeply as she had ever slept in her life, and woke at seven with a fuzzy awareness of warm, jasmine-scented air and the sound of breaking surf. Carter was still snoring gently, an unidentifiable blanket-covered lump in the other bed, when Molly opened the bedroom door and slipped out of the shuttered darkness into the dazzling morning sunshine.

"You look as if you've just seen a ghost," Elaine said.

Molly shook her head. "Worse," she said. "I saw Jake

Berenger." She felt like an idiot, which was a bad beginning. Without her glasses, anything farther away than twenty feet had the colorful cloudiness of an Impressionist painting. When the vague shape of the person walking toward her had suddenly resolved itself into a tanned man with an unmistakable face, Molly had been as shocked as if a photograph had suddenly come to life and winked at her. She had reacted instantly, without thinking.

"Jake Berenger?" Elaine said skeptically. "Where? Here? Are you sure?"

"Yes. He just walked by. He . . . waved to me." Molly winced at the thought. He had known that she was looking at him from behind the curtain.

"How odd," Elaine said. "I can't imagine why he'd be wandering around at this hour. He saw you, then . . . like that? Good heavens. Well, not to worry. He won't remember you."

"Thanks," Molly said coldly. "I feel much better now." But she knew that it was true. Even if she had been sitting on the deck wearing a see-through negligee and singing "I Feel Pretty," Jake Berenger probably would not remember her. He was handsome, she thought wistfully. He had wind-tousled black hair and a chest with muscles that curved like dunes on the Sahara. There were not a lot of men in Belden, Wisconsin, who looked like that, or so she assumed. It was hard to be sure when everyone spent seven months out of the year wearing parkas.

The doorbell chimed, and she stiffened sharply.

"Breakfast," Elaine said, looking curiously at her. "Are you always this jumpy, dear? I had problems with my nerves during my first marriage, and Valium did me a world of good."

"I don't . . ." Molly began, and then stopped herself.

There was no point in answering. "I'm going to get dressed," she said.

Elaine nodded. "Good. Do your best to wake Carter while you're in there. Otherwise, he's likely to sleep until noon, and we have no time to waste."

Molly succeeded in waking Carter during the awkward process of rooting around in the dark bedroom, searching first for her luggage and then for clothes to wear. By the time she'd managed to dig out a pair of shorts and a T-shirt, he was stirring and grumbling in his bed.

By the time she emerged from the bathroom, Carter's bed was empty. She found him in the living room with Elaine, wearing plaid pajamas and clutching a coffee cup with both hands. His hair was sticking up in random tufts, and his eyes were puffy.

"Good morning," Molly said.

He acknowledged her with a squint. "You are," he said in a creaky voice, "a morning person. So is Elaine. It seems obvious to me that the two of you should share a room."

Molly smiled and poured herself a glass of juice. Breakfast had arrived in the form of a large wicker tray bearing starched napkins, a pitcher of juice, a white Limoges coffeepot, and a linen-lined basket filled with steaming croissants. In the corner of the tray sat a tiny crystal vase holding one huge red hibiscus flower. There were more flowers on the table, a complex arrangement of tropical color massed into a bunch that reached Molly's eye level.

"How beautiful," she said. There was a white envelope tucked into the bouquet, and she plucked it out.

"It may be beautiful, but it isn't ours," Elaine said. "It was misdelivered. You'd think that a resort of this level would have better service. It's appalling, really. I've already called the manager."

It took Molly a moment to decipher the elegant script on the back of the envelope, but when she did, she felt as if all of the air had suddenly rushed out of the room. She stared at the small rectangle of paper, speechless.

"I can't imagine why the bellman thought that Sandra St. Claire was here with us," Elaine continued. "Where does he think she is, under a chair? In a closet somewhere? I suppose that he mistook me for her. I've never met her, but I've heard that she's very beautiful."

"Funny you should say that," Carter began, but Molly wasn't listening. Quickly she tore open the envelope and pulled out the card. *Dear Miss St. Claire*, it said, *it is my pleasure to welcome you to Gold Bay. Please do not hesitate to call me if there is anything I can do to make your stay with us more pleasant. Sincerely, Terry Wong, VIP Guest Services Manager.*

"What," Molly said, very softly, "is going on here?"

"Because, in a sense, you could say that we do have Sandra St. Claire in a closet," Carter continued. He seemed to be fully awake now, and very pleased with himself. He was practically giggling, but the delight on his face faltered when he saw the look on Molly's.

"You told them about me?" Molly asked in the same soft voice. "You *told* them?"

"No, no, no," Carter said quickly, holding up his hands as if he feared that she might attack him. "I didn't tell them about you. Well, not exactly. I told them that Sandra St. Claire was here, with us, but I didn't tell them that *you* were Sandra."

"I beg your pardon," Elaine said. "*Who* is Sandra?"

"She is," Carter said, pointing to Molly.

"I am not!" Molly exclaimed.

"Yes, you are," Carter said. "It's all part of the plan.

You're going to be Sandra St. Claire for the week. We discussed this, don't you remember?"

"No!" Molly said. "Was I in the room when we discussed this? There is no way in *hell* that I would have agreed to pretend to be Sandra! What were you thinking, Carter?"

"Profanity is a no-no," Elaine interrupted. "A gentleman might be able to get away with a potty mouth, because it can make him seem rugged and macho, but a lady cannot afford to sound like a sailor's parrot."

"We discussed it," Carter insisted. "I said, 'Spend a week forgetting the Respectable Professor Shaw, and become Sandra St. Claire.' Or something like that. You agreed. Remember?"

"Well . . ." Molly sputtered. "Yes, but when you said that I should become Sandra, I didn't know that you meant that I should *become* Sandra."

Carter gazed at her with innocent eyes. "What else could I have meant?"

"I thought that you were telling me to become her in . . . in a spiritual sense."

"Oh, no," Carter said. "We need an actual Sandra. It's critical. Jake Berenger only dates high-profile women. I have the statistics in my suitcase."

"Carter, dear," Elaine said, "if you're suggesting that Molly impersonate Sandra St. Claire for the week, I have to say that I think it's a very bad idea."

"That makes two of us," Molly said.

"I've heard," Elaine continued, "that Miss St. Claire is part of the international jet set, which means that someone here at Gold Bay is certain to know her. If you're caught, you'll find yourself in court. Or worse."

"Much worse," Molly said firmly. Six months ago, she would have been unsettled to hear someone speaking of her pseudonym as if Sandra were a real person, but by now she was used to it. When *Pirate Gold* had begun its surprise climb up the sales lists, her publisher's massive PR firm had quickly joined the party, releasing fictional interviews, "leaking" information, and planting gossip to create a Sandra St. Claire mystique. The media had eagerly reported these delicious tidbits, embellishing freely, and somewhere along the way, Sandra had taken on a life of her own.

It was not unlike the bigfoot phenomenon. Sandra St. Claire fan sites popped up on the Web like mushrooms after a rain, all claiming to have "official" and "exclusive" information about the mysterious author. Was she or was she not a member of the Greek royal family? Was her name a rough anagram of Carla Andresi, the glamorous Italian socialite? Sandra sightings abounded in the press, and Molly had collected a folder of clippings from breathy gossip columns recounting the parties where Sandra had been seen, the boutiques where she shopped, and the restaurants she favored. A busboy at Spago Beverly Hills reported that she had come in on four consecutive nights, each time with a different man, and each time had ordered nothing but champagne and caviar. She was notoriously camera-shy, but she was widely described as a stunning blonde, and Jean-Luc Valmont, celebrity colorist and owner of the eponymous salon, made a point of telling the press that he would never violate Miss St. Claire's privacy by confirming that she was his client.

At first, Molly had been horrified by the buzz. There had been so much interest in Sandra that it had seemed like only a matter of time until the reporters were at her door, and she had developed a bad case of insomnia from the anxiety. But as the months went by, and her life at Belden plodded on in the usual manner, she had slowly relaxed. Neither her agent nor her publisher had ever tried to persuade her to come forward, which, she soon realized, was in their interest as much as her own. The gossip and speculation had pushed *Pirate Gold* to the top of the best-seller lists, and it would have been foolish to do anything to destroy the lucrative Cult of Sandra.

Still, Molly didn't believe in pushing her luck, and at her request, the PR firm had backed off, releasing word that Sandra was staying home to work on a sequel. The restless eye of the media soon focused elsewhere, and Molly started sleeping through the night again.

Despite the royalty checks that kept arriving, and her covert collection of press clippings, the commotion had been so removed from Molly's daily reality that even she had begun to think of Sandra as a separate person. Not a stranger, of course. More like a twin sister prone to outrageous and embarrassing behavior. The mental division was soothing, and although Molly was aware that the Psychology department would have a field day with her coping strategy, she didn't spend much time worrying about it. It had all settled down into an odd but manageable situation.

"Carter," Molly said, and found that her voice was shaking, "I think that I've been very agreeable about helping with this project. I agreed to come on this trip. I agreed to put on a blond wig, blue contacts, a tight dress, and a bra with pads so thick that I would probably survive a shotgun blast to the chest. I agreed to spend a week of my life acting like a simpering idiot in order to convince a playboy billionaire to pay attention to me. But I never *ever* agreed to be Sandra in public! I won't do it. What if someone figured out that it was me?"

"Not possible," Carter said calmly. "If nobody here has ever seen Sandra, then how could they know that you're not really her?" He frowned. "That didn't come out right. I meant—"

"I *know* what you meant," Molly said.

"Excuse me," Elaine said. "But I simply don't see how you can be so sure that no one here knows Miss St. Claire."

"I'm sure," Carter said. "Trust me, I'm sure."

"Hmm," Elaine said, and then shrugged. "Well, have it your way, then. I'm beginning to see that it was a good decision not to include this project in my book. I personally believe that lying should be limited to minor issues like one's age and natural hair color."

Carter started to speak, but was interrupted by the sound of the phone.

"Goodness," Elaine said. "That's probably the manager returning my call about the flowers. How annoying."

She picked up the receiver. "Yes? Oh, yes, hello. Well, I'm afraid that we had a bit of a misunderstanding . . ."

Carter's hand closed on Molly's arm. "Molly, listen," he said in a low, urgent voice. "This is the reason why I didn't hire a local model for this project, like you suggested. We need someone with a famous name, someone with cachet. We need Sandra. Otherwise, the project is doomed."

"You tricked me," Molly said. "You knew that I wouldn't have agreed to come here and play Sandra. You brought me here under false pretenses."

"It's true," Carter said, suddenly drooping like a scolded dog. "It's true, and I admit it. I am a terrible person, but I'm desperate, Molly, don't you see? You're my only chance, and I thought that if I could just get you here, I might be able to convince you that it wasn't really so different to put on the costume and call yourself Sandra instead of . . . Fifi, or Trixie, or whatever name we would have picked. It's the same adventure, just a little more exciting."

"Exciting for you, maybe," Molly said. "You're asking me to risk my reputation and my career in order to help you with yours."

Carter gazed at her with soulful eyes. "Isn't that what friends are supposed to do?"

Molly groaned. "I don't believe this."

"How dangerous could this be? Nobody here will guess that you and Sandra are the same person. And there are no paparazzi allowed on the island, so you won't even have your picture taken. All you'll do is cement the perception that Sandra St. Claire is a tall, voluptuous blonde. What better way to make sure that nobody ever links her to Molly Shaw?"

"What about the fact that I happen to be sharing a cottage with her?"

Carter shrugged. "I doubt that anyone other than the staff will notice. But if someone does, you can say that you're an old friend of Sandra's, and you're working with her as a historical consultant on her next novel."

Molly didn't answer. She looked away, folding her arms against her chest. Elaine was finishing her conversation with the Guest Services Manager, smiling as she spoke.

"Well," she said briskly, hanging up the receiver and turning to Molly and Carter. "It took a bit of creative improvisation to get us out of that mess. Carter, in the future I'd appreciate it if you'd remember to share your plans with me, so that I don't make a fool of myself again. Now, have you and Molly worked out whether or not she intends to go ahead with this?"

"I don't know yet," Carter said. He looked hopefully at Molly. "Could you possibly—"

"I don't know yet, either," Molly said crossly. "I'm still thinking about it."

"Perfectly reasonable, dear," Elaine said. "But you'll need to think fast, because Sandra has been invited to a VIP cocktail party tonight at Jake Berenger's villa."

CHAPTER 6

"I find that spending more than two weeks aboard a yacht becomes very confining, don't you?" asked Fiona Carrington. "I mean, being waited on hand and foot is lovely for a while, but eventually one just wants to brush away the stewards, march into the galley, and make oneself a simple cup of tea."

"I wouldn't know," Jake said. "I don't own a yacht." He didn't drink tea, either, but that seemed like a minor point.

"No?" Fiona's eyes opened wide and she gestured in surprise, sending the remains of her latest cosmopolitan sloshing dangerously against the rim of her cocktail glass. "How extraordinary, for a man in your position. But surely, you charter?"

"Nope," Jake said. It was not the first time that he had shocked the glitterati by admitting his lack of desire to own or rent one of the white behemoths that the Brits referred to as "gin palaces." Over the past decade, he had been a guest aboard the yachts of his customers and business colleagues, visits that had done the job of convincing him that this particular display of wealth was not something to which he aspired. The least offensive boats were maritime replicas of British bankers clubs, complete with Victorian paneling, crystal chandeliers, dour oil paintings, and fireplaces. It was when the owners and their decorators got creative that it really became frightening. The *MariJo* had a fiber-optic ceiling over the grand staircase, displaying a rainbow of constellations that rotated gently to the strains of "Starry Night." The *Princess Tiffany* had a full disco and a room of slot machines that only accepted special coins imprinted with a portrait of the owner. The *Sea Serpent*, whose owner was a Saudi prince known for his skill at the Vegas tables, had a master suite covered entirely in snakeskin. During the obligatory tour, Jake had been shown the enormous adjoining bathroom, encrusted with gold and mirrors. Embedded in the Lucite toilet seat was a hand of cards. It was, Jake had realized, a winning poker hand: a royal flush.

"Where do you spend your vacations, then?" Fiona asked.

"Here," Jake said.

"But that would make it so difficult to get away from your work," Fiona said.

Jake nodded. He saw no problem with that.

Fiona leaned toward him.

"You must be . . . desperately . . . in need . . . of relaxation," she said meaningfully. She inhaled, and her cleavage rose toward him like a quivering bowl of strawberry Jell-O. Alarmed, Jake stepped backward, and felt hands seize him from behind.

"Jake!" Amanda slid one arm around his waist and placed another one on his chest, attaching herself to his side in a proprietary manner. "Y'all looked so friendly over here. I thought I'd better come and say hi."

"Quite," Fiona murmured frostily.

The two women looked each other up and down, and it occurred to Jake that a boat might not be such a bad thing. It didn't need a custom-built casino, or 400-thread-count sheets, or gold-plated bath taps. It just needed to be able to float, and to anchor far, far away from shore. Most importantly, there needed to be no women on it at all.

"*Who* is *that*?" Amanda said suddenly, focusing on a point past Fiona's shoulder. Jake followed her gaze. Despite the crowd on the terrace, it wasn't hard to guess who she was talking about. They were not the only ones staring.

A woman was standing in the frame of the open French doors, facing the crowd. She had paused there like a living portrait, arranged with one foot forward, one hip thrust slightly out, shoulders back, and hands raised elegantly as if she were welcoming everyone to her own soiree. She had platinum-blond hair styled into a shining, shoulder-grazing curtain, and her eyes were concealed behind smoky silver sunglasses. She wore a candy-pink dress that was tight enough to display a very ample chest and a tiny waist. Her legs were long, her heels were high, and she seemed to be planning to stand in the doorway indefinitely.

Just behind her were a frosty-looking woman and a small, brown-haired man wearing a rumpled seersucker suit and horn-rimmed glasses. As Jake watched, the small man poked the extraordinary blonde in the back and whispered something in her ear. The blonde unlocked herself from her pose, stumbled slightly, collected herself quickly, and strutted out onto the terrace.

Fiona muttered something under her breath that ended with ". . . real, then I'm the bloody Archbishop of Canterbury."

"Pink is *so* last season," Amanda added in a similar tone.

Jake said nothing. He was no expert on real versus fake, and he had always liked women in pink. The stranger was the sort that the paparazzi would love, and she was exactly the type of woman he was known to take to very public places. But in light of his current situation, she was about as appealing as a loaf of moldy bread. The last thing he needed in his life right now was another flashy diva.

His mother had been chatting with a Palm Beach real-estate agent, but as Jake glanced over, he saw that Cora had excused herself and was headed for the blond stranger. To Jake's surprise—and instinctive alarm—she greeted the woman warmly, as if they knew each other. He hoped that this was not the next of his mother's attempts to manage his personal life. Did this Jayne Mansfield clone also come from a "good family"?

Apparently so, because Cora was now beckoning him over. With a sense of moving from the frying pan into the fire, Jake walked over to join them.

"Darling," said his mother. "I knew that you wanted a chance to personally welcome our latest celebrity. Sandra, this is my son, Jake Berenger. Jake, dear, this is Sandra St. Claire."

"How do you do?" the blonde said, extending her hand. Jake took it, shook it, and—as he had done many times before—tried to look as if he knew who this person was.

Cora's eyes narrowed slightly. She had an uncanny ability to read his mind. "Sandra tells me that this is a working vacation for her," she said pointedly. "How exciting to think that her next *best-selling novel* might be written at Gold Bay."

The older blonde cleared her throat, and Sandra jumped. "These are my friends," she said quickly. "Elaine Newberg and Carter McKee."

"Charmed," said Elaine Newberg, offering her fingers to him. She looked vaguely familiar, in a socialite sort of way.

"Have we met?" he asked.

Her smile was approving. "No," she said, "but you may have seen me on *Oprah*."

Jake doubted that very much. "That must be it," he said. "You're a novelist, too?"

Elaine laughed a silvery laugh. "Good heavens, no," she said, "I am a relationship consultant. I specialize in teaching women how to leverage their natural potential in order to maximize their worldly success."

Jake looked blankly at her. "Great," he said.

Elaine patted him on the arm. "One should always say 'yes' to success," she said. "Men understand this instinctively. Women must be taught."

Carter McKee was squinting at him with the pop-eyed intensity of a scientist observing a new species of beetle. "I heard that you windsurf," he said suddenly. "Sandra does, too. She loves it. She has a lesson scheduled for tomorrow morning."

Sandra's glossy pink mouth opened suddenly, and then closed again. Jake noticed that her hands had clenched into fists at her sides. She wasn't the chatty type, it seemed. She was shy, perhaps, which would explain her strange awkwardness and the affectation of sunglasses at dusk. Then again, no shy woman would wear a dress like that. She didn't look like someone who loved to windsurf, but then, she didn't look like someone who wrote books, either.

"How advanced are you?" he asked her.

"I don't know," Sandra said in a voice as tight as her dress. She looked at Carter. "How advanced am I, would you say?"

"You show great promise," Carter said. He looked at Jake. "Her lesson is with Rico. Tomorrow. At ten A.M."

Jake frowned at the man, wondering who he was. Sandra's agent? Her husband? He was a strange-looking candidate for either position. "Rico is a good teacher," he said, resisting the urge to glance at his watch. It was still an hour before the close of business in Los Angeles, and he needed to make a call to the architect who was designing the new golf course. He nodded to the group and made his excuses.

"Enjoy your lesson tomorrow," he said to Sandra. "The bay is calm in the morning, but there should be some good wind by ten. I'm usually out there myself at about that time."

Sandra nodded. "Somehow, I'm not surprised to hear that."

"Molly! Be reasonable," Carter implored, following closely on Molly's heels and stopping every few feet to pick up glittering bits of Sandra St. Claire as they were shucked off onto the cottage floor. The silver stiletto sandals had gone first, followed by the sunglasses and the dangling earrings. "I really think that 'total failure' is too strong a term."

"Okay," Molly said, stopping. She reached up to yank on the blond wig, which was secured to her scalp with no less than thirty metal pins. "How about 'utter fiasco'?"

"Negativity is a no-no," Elaine said, bringing up the rear. "Whiners are never winners, my dear. Let's focus on the good. We've accomplished an introduction."

Molly exhaled hard. Her heart was pounding, and for some strange reason, she felt as if she were about to cry. "I knew it," she said. "You can dress me to look like Jake Berenger's ideal woman, but he still won't find me attractive."

"You don't know that for a fact," Carter protested. "Maybe he was just . . . preoccupied."

"Ha! It's me, don't you understand? It's me. I tried to warn you, Carter. I don't know how to do this."

Carter looked horrified. "Are you crying?"

"No!" Molly said hotly. She wasn't. Her eyes were still

watering from her earlier attempt to put on the blue contact lenses. She had never worn contacts before, and in the process of inserting them, one had rolled under the bathroom sink and the other had become cemented to her eyeball. She still had one blue eye and one brown eye by the time they were due to leave for the party, and they had been forced to use a pair of Elaine's sunglasses as camouflage.

"It's going to be fine," Carter insisted. "Trust me, this can't fail. It's science."

"I don't think you know what you're talking about," Molly said. "And what was that crazy thing about windsurfing? I don't know how to windsurf! I trip over my own feet on solid ground. If I go out there tomorrow, I'll look like an idiot. Again!" She felt a sense of desperation that bordered on panic. Why had she ever agreed to come on this trip? She had known all along that it was a terrible idea. At least it wasn't too late to quit and go home. Carter could take his stupid plan and his stupid project, and find someone else to—

"That does it," Elaine said suddenly. "Carter!"

Her brother looked wary. "What?"

"Go somewhere else. No, I don't mean into the other room. Go to the beach."

"But it's dark," Carter said.

"Then go to the gift shop," Elaine said. "Go to the hair salon. Go anywhere, but don't come back for an hour. Molly and I are going to have a talk, and I intend to tell her things that are not meant for male ears."

"But I—"

Elaine gave him a look that Molly didn't see. She did see Carter's response, though, and it was immediate. He stepped backward, toward the door. "I feel a sudden craving for fresh air," he said. "And scotch. I think I'll go to the bar."

When he was gone, Elaine turned to look at Molly. She

shook her head. "Wrong," she said, sounding irritated. "All wrong. I should have known better than to let Carter tell me that this was a simple matter of physical appearance. Do you know what your problem is, my dear?"

"Yes," Molly said. "My problem is that I'm stuck on an island with two people who want to tell me what my problems are. Beyond that, I don't care."

"Oh, but you do," Elaine said. "You care very much. Why did you agree to come on this trip?"

"To help Carter," Molly said.

"But you've already convinced yourself that this project is doomed. That's no help to Carter, and it's no help to you, either."

"That's totally unfair," Molly said indignantly. "I'm doing my best. It's not my fault that I can't—"

Elaine sighed. "You have no idea how fortunate you are that I'm here. Now sit down, and let me take that wig off." She moved to stand behind Molly, pulling out the hairpins with careful hands, collecting them into a neat pile. "There is a terrible mountain called 'I Can't,'" she said, "and a beautiful valley called 'Can't I'! The time has come, my dear, to decide where you would rather live."

"Excuse me?" Molly said. Her scalp was beginning to tingle as the pressure of the pins eased.

"I want to teach you something that has nothing to do with enhanced bosoms and the rest of that scientific foolishness of Carter's," Elaine said, and then lifted one finger warningly. "Now to be sure, I am not discounting the importance of good grooming. We all have a personal obligation to be our best selves. But I can tell you right now that charm does not come from the chest."

"Tell that to Jake Berenger," Molly said.

"Nonsense. It's you and Carter who need to be told. If this plan is so brilliant, then why wasn't it an instant success? Why aren't you out there, right now, sipping champagne with a handsome billionaire? I'll tell you why. All of the bleach and the padding in this world won't help you if you don't know how to sparkle from within."

"You have got to be kidding," Molly said. She stood up, lifted the wig off of her head, and dropped it on the couch, where it fell into a sullen lump like a yellow Pekingese. "Look, I know the old cliché about needing to love yourself first, but I'm perfectly happy with myself, and this conversation is really not necessary."

"Oh?" Elaine said. "Happy? So happy that ten minutes ago you were almost in tears? Why were you so upset?"

"I wasn't upset! It was the contact lenses. My eyes—"

"I'll tell you why," Elaine continued. "For reasons known only to you, you have been afraid to try to be an attractive woman. But that shameful brother of mine actually managed to convince you that his silly disguise would magically turn you into a femme fatale. It didn't work out quite that way, did it?"

"No," Molly said. "It definitely didn't. And now, if you'll excuse me, I'm going to bed."

"Your worst fear seemed to come true," Elaine continued dramatically. "You thought that this *proved* that you weren't attractive to men, *even when you tried.*"

Molly gritted her teeth. "I'm feeling very jet-lagged," she said. "Good night."

"My dear," Elaine said loftily, "I cannot help you if you refuse to listen. I am trying to tell you something very important. All of this"—she gestured at the shreds of Sandra—"means nothing. You haven't tried yet. Trying means putting your heart into the attempt. You have not been brave enough to try *at all*, and so you have no basis whatsoever for judging yourself a failure."

Molly scowled at her. If Carter's sister thought that it

didn't take effort and bravery to put on the Sandra outfit and face the world, then she could go to hell. "I did my best," she said coldly. "When Carter comes back, tell him that I'll give his plan one more chance. One. That's all. And if tomorrow turns out to be another disaster, then I officially quit."

CHAPTER 7

Jake knelt to clamp the mast onto his windsurfing board. It was quarter to ten in the morning, and he had spent the past hour on the phone, having a heated "discussion" with the two most senior Berenger Corporation board members: Walter Cronin and Stanley "Skip" Leavenworth, both stuffy white-haired fogies, one the retired CEO of a major development corporation, the other a retired CFO of a major bank. Walter had called in a huff, with Skip conferenced in, to read Jake selected passages from that morning's *Wall Street Journal*, which had featured an article headlined, "Wall Street Questions Value of Berenger Bonds." In it, a prominent analyst was quoted as saying, "Berenger Corporation has borrowed a great deal of money by issuing corporate bonds over the past few years, but Jake Berenger seems more interested in playing with Hollywood blondes than in paying interest on his bonds."

"Jake," Walter had said officiously, "you do understand what this means . . . ?"

"That it was a slow news day?" Jake asked. He took exception to Walter's tone. He was not a misbehaving trust-fund grandson, and did not appreciate being lectured like one.

"This is becoming a serious image problem, Jake," Walter said. "We can't afford to lose more investor confidence. We'll be discussing this at the next board meeting."

He let the mast fall to the sand, straightened up, and ran a hand over his forehead, exhaling hard. Walter's pompous tone still echoed in his ears. *A serious image problem, Jake.*

Yeah, Jake thought. *No kidding, Walter. Thanks.* Apparently, he had misjudged the severity of the situation. Cora had been right to worry. *Always listen to your mother,* he thought. *Wear a warm sweater, eat your vegetables, and don't underestimate the subversive power of the fucking tabloid press.* Titillating articles in the *Daily News* were one thing, but when the sniping reached the level of the *Wall Street Journal*, it meant that his bad press was going mainstream.

The glare from the sand was making his head ache, and he realized that he had left his sunglasses at the villa. He had bolted out of there after the phone call, trying to avoid Amanda, who had been pointedly and repeatedly mentioning her intense desire to learn to scuba dive. He dragged his board higher on the sand, getting it away from the surf. There were usually a couple of extra pairs of glasses in the boathouse, and he could borrow one from Rico for the next hour.

"Where did you find a pink wet suit?" Molly asked Carter. Her cheeks were burning, and she was glad for Elaine's silver sunglasses, because they allowed her to pretend not to see the stunned stares that followed her as they walked across the pool terrace and down the wide steps toward the beach. One man actually dropped his newspaper as she passed his chair. His wife, in the next chair, picked it up and whacked him with it.

"I know a girl who works for Mary Kay," Carter said. "They gave them away as prizes last year. She said that I could have hers. She's more of a dry-land kind of person."

"So am I," Molly said. "How am I supposed to take a windsurfing lesson dressed like this? The wig? The shoes? The chest? What if my stuffing comes loose? If I move too much, one of these pads is going to slip. I don't think this is going to work."

"You're right," Carter said reluctantly. "Okay. I'll figure something out."

"Aren't you supposed to have this figured out already?" Molly asked. "Isn't this supposed to be *scientific*?"

They passed the pool bar, where a busboy was clearing empty glasses from the tables. He looked up, saw Molly, and clutched his heart. She lifted her fingers in a tentative wave, and he waved back, smiling beatifically at her.

"Creativity is the eternal flame burning at the heart of science," Carter said. "Many a scientific breakthrough has been the result of a spontaneous burst of divine inspiration. I am hoping for one of those myself, at the moment."

"Right," Molly said. "Keep me posted." Everyone was still staring at her. Had it been like this last night at the cocktail party? The contact lens fiasco had ensured that she hadn't seen much at all.

"Hurry," Carter said. "We need to catch Jake before he goes out on the water."

"I can't hurry in these shoes," Molly protested, but Carter had seized her by the arm and was pulling her along the path. She clomped after him toward the boathouse.

The path became a low wooden walkway that continued down the sand toward the water. The boathouse was built alongside it, a small building with a thatched roof, it housed racks of scuba gear. On the sand next to the walkway was a collection of brightly colored water toys, from surfboards to kayaks to—Molly saw with trepidation—windsurfing equipment.

Jake was standing by the wooden counter, talking to a young man wearing the white polo shirt and bronze-colored swim trunks of the Gold Bay waterfront staff. Carter released Molly's arm, and she tried to breathe evenly and slow down her pounding heart.

As they drew closer, the young man took off his sunglasses and handed them to Jake. It was obvious from Jake's body language that he was about to leave, and Molly's anxiety increased. She couldn't go out on a windsurfing board. Looking like a fool was bad enough, but she was not a strong swimmer, and encumbered by the too-tight wet suit, the padding, the surgical tape, the wig, and the contacts, she was likely to drown.

"Now what?" she asked Carter in an urgent whisper. "What am I supposed to *do*?"

"Go say hello to him," Carter said.

"Say hello? That's your burst of divine inspiration?"

"No," Carter said, scrunching up his face. "I'm still waiting for that. Stall him. I'll think of something."

Molly steeled herself and straightened her spine, lifting her chest and throwing a little hip into her walk as she approached the men. "Well," she said breathlessly, attempting a sultry voice. "Hello there, Jake. Are you heading out? I was looking for Rico. For my lesson."

"You found him," Jake said, indicating the young man. "Sandra St. Claire, this is Rico Martinez, our waterfront director. Rico was the 1997 world windsurfing champion. He's also an Olympic bronze medalist. You'll be in good hands."

"Lucky me," Molly said. She hoped Carter was thinking

fast. It was a good sign that Jake had remembered her name. He had recalled it instantly, in fact. Surely he didn't remember every guest he met . . .

"Nice to meet you, Sandra," Rico said, and shook her hand. "Welcome. You're obviously serious about windsurfing."

Obviously? Molly blinked at him, wondering what would make such a thing seem obvious. Was it the wet suit? It certainly wasn't the sandals. She smiled cautiously. "Uh," she said. "Yes. Of course. How did you know?"

Rico gave her an odd look. "You're signed up for a lesson every morning this week," he said.

"What?" Molly exclaimed in horror. Rico and Jake both looked surprised, and she cleared her throat. "I mean, is it only mornings? I thought I'd booked an hour in the afternoons, too."

"I don't think so. And the schedule's already full," Rico said. "Sorry. I'll let you know if I get any cancellations, but an hour a day should be enough to improve your skill level pretty significantly by Sunday."

Molly barely heard him. She had just realized that Jake was looking at her. Or, more specifically, that Jake was looking at her in a way that men never looked at the Respectable Professor Shaw. His eyes, slightly narrowed, were moving up her body in a slow assessment that made her skin prickle. It had begun at her feet, slid slowly up her bare legs, moved over the curves of her waist, then lingered on the area of the lowered wet suit zipper and the globulous thrust of her cleavage. His eyebrows quirked suddenly, and Molly tensed, holding her breath. Was this the moment when Carter's magic formula started to work? Maybe Jake really had been distracted last night, and he simply hadn't noticed that she was, in fact, his ideal woman. *See?* she said silently to him. *Blonde! Busty! Pink! You can't resist me. It's scientific.*

She glanced over to see if Carter was watching, but he was pretending to be deeply absorbed in examining the various types of kayak paddles.

"Do you have eyes, Sandra St. Claire?" Jake asked suddenly, and to Molly's shock, he reached out and lifted off her sunglasses. Her startled gaze met his, and in the sunlight, she could see that his dark irises had flecks of gold in them.

"Yes," she said nervously, blinking at him.

He nodded, and handed the glasses back to her. "I wondered. Here. Don't take these out on the bay, or you'll lose them."

He turned away.

"Thank . . . you," Molly said to his back. He was leaving. What was she supposed to do? It had all looked so promising just a moment ago, but now he was about to disappear, and her only method of pursuing him was liable to kill her. Helplessly, she turned to look at Carter, who was widening his eyes in a meaningful way and jerking his head spastically toward Jake's retreating form. Molly took this to mean that she should follow him.

"One minute," she said to Rico, and clunked quickly down the boardwalk after Jake, hoping that Carter's urgency meant that divine inspiration had finally arrived.

"Jake," she called, "wait."

At that moment, something very strange happened. As Molly hurried forward, she suddenly felt a large, flat object thrust between her knees. Surprised, she stumbled against it, then lost her balance on the platform shoes. She toppled forward, letting out an involuntary shriek of panic.

Jake, only steps ahead of her, turned to see what had happened. As if she were watching the scene in slow motion,

Molly saw his face register surprise, and then alarm as she pitched, flailing frantically, toward him.

He caught her against his chest, stumbled backward with the force of her momentum, and then sat down hard on the boardwalk with Molly sprawled over him.

CHAPTER 8

"Oh, my God," said Sandra St. Claire in a tone of absolute mortification.

She smelled good, Jake thought, slightly disoriented. The scent of suntan cream and warm female skin surrounded him, heady as an opiate. She felt good, too. One of her hands was clutching his thigh, and the other was clamped onto his shoulder. She was lying across his lap and between his legs, and aside from a sharp pain in his tailbone, he found the position very agreeable. He wasn't sure how they had ended up like this. It had happened very fast, and he had only a flash of memory of turning and seeing Sandra careening toward him, her mouth and eyes round with shock. He recalled her slight stumble at the cocktail party last night. She was not a very good candidate for the high heels that she seemed to favor.

"Oh, my God," Sandra said again, pushing against him as she struggled to disengage herself and sit up.

"You've lost your shoes," he said. She had fallen entirely out of them, and they were lying several feet away on the boardwalk.

"Good," she said under her breath, and then gasped, and quickly raised a hand to her hair. She touched it tentatively, as if afraid that something terrible had happened to it on the way down.

"Still there," Jake remarked dryly. Every gleaming blond strand had somehow remained perfectly in place.

"What?" She looked alarmed, and then anxious. "What do you mean? Why wouldn't it still be there?"

Strange woman, Jake thought. Sexy, in a klutzy and neurotic sort of way, but she had "trouble" written all over her. And she took her hair a bit too seriously for his taste. "A joke," he said, getting to his feet. He offered her his hand. "Never mind. Are you all right?"

She nodded. "I think so. I—"

"Sandra! Sandra, are you hurt? I saw what happened."

It was her friend, the little man in the bad suit who had accompanied her to the party last night. He had appeared out of nowhere, and was now hovering over her like a worried hen. For some reason, he was holding a kayak paddle. Sandra looked at him, and for just a moment, Jake thought that he saw fury on her face.

She ignored the man, took Jake's outstretched hand, and began to stand up.

"Are you *hurt*?" the man repeated.

She shook her head. "No, I—"

"Are you *sure*? Because that fall might have done something terrible to your *weak ankle*."

With startling suddenness, Sandra collapsed back onto the ground. "Oh, dear," she said woodenly. "Yes. I think I may have sprained my ankle."

"I was afraid of that," her friend said.

"Which ankle?" Jake asked, frowning. They both looked fine to him, although the expression on Sandra's face suggested that she was in pain. She pointed to her right foot, and he knelt to examine it. There was no sign of bruising or swelling, but it was possible that she had pulled a tendon when she flew out of her shoes. It was also possible that something very strange was going on. Was this some kind of setup for a lawsuit? The scene had taken on a theatrical quality, and it made him suspicious.

"She'll need a doctor," the little man said to Jake. "You wait here. I'll get help."

"Hold it," Jake said. "Who *are* you?"

"You remember Carter," Sandra said, from the ground. "Carter McKee. He was at your party last night."

"Yes," Jake said, although he hadn't remembered the man's name. "And you're Sandra's . . . ?" *Don't tell me you're her lawyer.*

"Cousin," Sandra said at the same moment that Carter McKee said, "Brother."

Sandra narrowed her eyes at Carter. "He's my cousin," she said. "First cousin, so he's been like a brother to me. He's a writer, too. He specializes in biographies."

"I'll get help," Carter said again. "Don't leave Sandra alone. She's prone to fainting spells."

He rushed off. He was headed for the pool terrace, but Jake knew that the closest phone was just behind them, in the boathouse.

"I'll call the infirmary," he said. "It'll be just a minute."

Sandra sighed. "No, wait," she said. She sounded embarrassed and annoyed. "Don't bother. I'm fine."

Jake watched curiously as she rose to her feet and brushed herself off. "It's not as bad as I thought," she said, demonstrating by standing on the foot in question. "See? Carter overreacted."

"That's good," Jake said. "Still, you should have it checked."

"I will. But I'm perfectly able to go and find the doctor on my own. You don't need to worry about me—you'd rather be out there on the water, wouldn't you?"

"Not at all," Jake said automatically. She was right, but only a cad would have admitted it. This hour—now swiftly disappearing—was his only free time for the rest of the day.

"You're very gracious," Sandra said. He could see that she didn't believe him. "I'm sorry that I fell on you."

"No problem," Jake said. He hadn't really minded that part. "But you might want to rethink your shoe strategy."

She laughed, unexpectedly. It was a quick gleam of a grin that crinkled the corners of her eyes and gave her face a sudden wry humor that contrasted with her flashy clothes and makeup. She was pretty, he thought, surprised. He had found her physically attractive when he first saw her, but this was something more subtle, and more interesting.

"You were running after me," he said, remembering. "Why? What were you going to say?"

Sandra gazed at him for a moment. "Would you believe," she said, "I have no idea."

"You belong to me, Angeline," said Lord Percy. "Never forget that." The softness of his voice was belied by the coldness in his eyes, and Angeline shivered, remembering the tortured screams of the horse thief echoing within the crumbling walls of the abbey. "You are my wife, and that pirate will never soil you with his filthy hands. I'll see both of you dead first."

Molly had come right back to the cottage after saying good-bye to Jake, without waiting for Carter to return with the doctor. She had ordered lunch from room service: fresh fish cooked in spiced coconut milk, served with tropical fruit salad and champagne. The butler had brought it on a tray, and she had eaten it in this very chair, on the deck outside the cottage, and then spent the next hour napping in the sun.

She was not actually writing a sequel to *Pirate Gold*, of course, and had no intention of doing so, despite the frantic pleas of her agent. She didn't have time. In the past two years, her only academic output had been two journal articles and a textbook chapter adapted from her book about eighteenth-century seafaring women. That wasn't enough to earn tenure at Belden, where "publish or perish" was an imperative. If she wanted to survive, she needed to focus her thoughts and her energy on a real project.

Unfortunately, her thoughts had not been cooperating. *Pirate Gold* had begun as a movielike daydream that ran through her head whenever she was tired, bored, or in a faculty meeting, and merely typing the words "THE END" at the bottom of page 642 had not stopped the flow of the story.

It wasn't her fault. She had gotten attached to her characters, and the idea of cutting them off and not thinking about them anymore made her feel like a murderer. Anyway, she enjoyed the daydream. It relaxed her. Just because she allowed herself to indulge in the story—and occasionally wrote down some of the better passages—didn't mean that she was writing another novel. She had no intention of making this kind of thing a way of life. It could be somebody else's life, certainly, but it wasn't hers.

She dozed off again and woke to the sound of Carter's voice.

"*There* you are," he said. He sounded petulant. "Where have you *been*? I looked everywhere for you. I even came back to the cottage, but I didn't see you out here, so I left again. Where's Jake? Why didn't you wait for me to come back?"

Molly kept her eyes closed, hoping that he would think

she was still asleep and go away. After the excitement of the morning, she just wanted to be left alone.

"Molly! It was a brilliant plan. It was divine inspiration. What happened?"

He was not going to go away. Molly opened her eyes. "Let me get this straight," she said, sitting up. "Your idea of divine inspiration is sticking a kayak paddle between my knees and tripping me? I could have broken my leg! Or was that also part of your plan?"

"I knew you'd be fine," Carter said hastily. "And it worked, didn't it? It was perfect! It was genius. We had Jake right where we wanted him, on day *two*. Do you know what this means? We're *ahead* of *schedule*!"

"You're out of control, Carter," Molly said. But despite her irritation, she had to admit that the morning had not turned out to be the disaster she'd feared. Amazingly, she was sure that she'd seen a spark of interest in Jake Berenger's eyes when he looked at her. It was far from the instant magic that Carter had predicted, but it was enough to boost her confidence. He may not have fallen madly in love with her, but he hadn't ignored her, either. It was possible that she was not a complete loser at the flirting game. Of course, the Sandra suit had had everything to do with it, but still . . .

"Why didn't you wait for me to come with the doctor?" Carter repeated. "Jake would have waited with you. He wouldn't abandon a woman in distress. It was a perfect plan."

"No, it wasn't," Molly said. "Maybe your own personal fantasy is to have a pneumatic blonde landing on you like a leopard out of a tree, but I'm sure that Jake is used to being chased, and he's probably very tired of fending off women. Did you see the look he gave me when you started fussing about my ankle? He was suspicious. It was the wrong strategy. We need to slow down."

"Slow down!" Carter exclaimed. "We can't slow down. This is my only chance, and we have less than a week."

"I know," Molly said. "But if you make this look too obvious, it's not going to work. You don't want to ruin your only chance, do you?"

Carter stared at her. "How can you be so sure?"

"Instinct," Molly said.

"You told me that your feminine wiles dried up and blew away while you were in grad school."

Molly smiled. "It seems," she said, "that I have a few left."

Molly took the rest of the afternoon off of being Sandra, and ended up in the Gold Bay gift shop, looking for something to read. She was also—though she would never have admitted it to anyone—curious to know if the shop carried the recently released paperback version of *Pirate Gold*.

It did. She sidled over to the book rack, feeling as self-conscious as a teenager buying pornography. She lifted one of the hefty paperbacks, running her finger over the raised gold lettering of the title, and stared down at it. It was very thick, she thought, oddly pleased. The size and weight of the book made it seem like a tiny brick. And the cover art was really much better than the other books on the rack . . .

"Excuse me, Professor Shaw?" said a female voice behind her. Molly jumped and dropped the paperback. It thudded to the floor, landing on its spine with the pages fanning out.

"Oh! I'm so sorry," said the owner of the voice, a young woman in a Gold Bay uniform. "I didn't mean to scare you.

I'm Jennifer Martin, the assistant activities director. I've been hoping for a chance to say hello. I wanted to tell you that I totally enjoyed your book!"

Molly's mouth dropped open in horror. She stared at the young woman, unable to speak. It was happening, just as she'd feared. There was no way to keep this kind of secret from the resort staff. They were everywhere! The butler had figured it out, or else one of the housekeepers had found the Sandra wig hidden in her closet. If Jennifer Martin knew the truth, then surely everyone knew. It was only a matter of time until the media heard about it, and her whole life was ruined.

Molly tried to take a breath, but her throat had closed up. It was just like the recurring nightmare that she'd had right after the publication of *Pirate Gold*—the one where she walked into her freshman lecture class and found every seat occupied by the trustees of Belden College, all wearing British judicial wigs, and pointing accusingly at her. In the dream, her father had been in the crowd, and he had refused to acknowledge her.

"Here, let me get that," Jennifer Martin said, bending to pick up the copy of *Pirate Gold*. She handed it back to Molly. "Well, it's good to see that even professors do a little light reading on vacation."

"What?" Molly croaked.

Jennifer pointed to the paperback. "I thought it was good, but I don't know if you'll like it." She widened her eyes. "Did you know that Sandra St. Claire is here this week? I've been looking for her, but I haven't seen her yet."

Molly was having a very hard time processing the conversation. "I'm sorry," she said weakly. "I thought you said that you read . . . my book?"

Jennifer nodded enthusiastically. "In my senior seminar at Vassar. The class was called Heroines of Herstory. You know, herstory, instead of history? It was a feminist class. The professor was Linda Titlebaum, do you know her?"

"Yes," Molly said. She and Linda had gone to graduate school together. She took a deep breath, let it out slowly, and felt the mantle of doom lifting, miraculously, from her shoulders. A silly smile crept over her face. "You read my book," she said, and the smile became a grin. "*My* book. You read *Maritime Wives*. In school. That's wonderful."

"Actually," Jennifer said, "I had a great idea. I was thinking that since you know so much about Caribbean history, maybe you could give an evening lecture for the other guests."

"A lecture? Would people actually come? They're on vacation . . ."

"Oh, totally!" Jennifer exclaimed. "Vacations aren't just about getting a tan anymore. Our guests love having a chance to expand their minds. Usually, we fly people in from the University of Miami. We don't get a lot of professors coming here as guests."

Molly was not surprised to hear that. She still had not recovered from the shock of learning how much it cost to rent their cottage for a week. Elaine had not been exaggerating when she'd spoken of the high cost of a Gold Bay vacation.

"I don't have my notes with me," she said. "I'm not sure that I can just . . ."

"I know it's a lot to ask," Jennifer said apologetically. "And I'm sure that my boss would be glad to offer you ten percent off of your room charge as a thank-you gesture."

"Deal," Molly said immediately. "When do you want me to do it?"

"How about tonight? Tuesday is normally our lecture night. We were scheduled to have a discussion of yoga theory, by Rama Guru. He's a very famous swami to the stars, and he's a guest this week, too. But he had to cancel, because he accidentally ate a salad with bacon bits, and now his chakras are unbalanced."

"I . . . could probably put together something for tonight," Molly said. "Could you give me a little more of an idea of what you want? Are there any general guidelines that I should follow?"

"Pirates," Jennifer said immediately.

"Pirates?" Molly repeated.

"Totally! People love pirates. It would be really exciting to have a lecture about some of the horrible things that the pirates did. The ones in this area, I mean. I'd like to keep it local. Also, maybe you could talk a little about Bonny Mary Morgan? She lived on this island, but you probably know that."

"No," Molly said, "I didn't. Are you sure?" It was the most interesting thing she'd heard in days. Mary Morgan was the most notorious of a very small group of eighteenth-century women who could technically be called pirates, meaning that they had either crewed on or—in Mary's case—captained pirate ships. The few known female pirates had all dressed as men, and their shipmates had generally believed them to be teenage boys. Mary had been special, though. She had become a feared and revered pirate queen, commanding her own ship while dressed in a feathered hat and fine silk petticoats, an affectation that had inspired her nickname. Molly remembered reading that Mary had also owned a sugar plantation on an island near Antigua.

Jennifer nodded. "I heard about Mary from the woman I replaced. She was a total history buff, and she knew everything about this place. It used to be called Cane Island, back when the government of Antigua owned it. The ruins of Mary's plantation are still over on the west side of the island, near the mangrove swamp."

"I can't believe it," Molly said. "Could I go and see the

site?" She had been fascinated by the story of Bonny Mary since she had first read about the seafaring hellion, and the lurid stories of Mary's life had influenced parts of *Pirate Gold.*

Jennifer looked dubious. "There's not much to see," she said. "And it's kind of a mess over there right now, with all the construction. But the views are nice. If you really want to go, I could arrange a guide for you. It's only a fifteen-minute drive from here."

Molly nodded eagerly. She knew from her research that very little had been written about Bonny Mary's life, and it had just occurred to her that a biography of the female pirate, set into an analysis of Mary's historical and cultural milieu, could be just the academic project that she needed.

"Would you schedule the guide for tomorrow morning at eight?" she asked. She could go and take a quick look at the ruins and then make it back in time for Sandra's ten A.M. windsurfing lesson, or whatever else was due to happen in that time slot. She had no intention of windsurfing, or of putting even one toe in the water while dressed as Sandra. She had made that very clear to Carter, but his grudging agreement didn't do much to ease Molly's mind. If she knew him, which she did, it was a sure bet that he would have something equally catastrophic planned.

CHAPTER 9

"This carpet has been an utter disaster," Cora Berenger said. "The company representative sold me on the durability of their new fiber blend, but they forgot to mention that it stains like a sponge. Look at that. And that." She pointed to various shadowed spots on the low pile of the lobby carpet and shook her head, exasperated. "Totally unsuitable. Thank goodness we didn't use it in any of the guest rooms. I will never trust a carpet salesman again, as long as I live."

"Sounds like a principle to live by," Jake said. It was nine P.M., and they were standing in the middle of the reception lobby, with Cora's charts, plans, and fabric swatches, discussing the renovation scheduled for July.

"I have half a mind to replace it all with sisal," Cora said. "But I'm not sure it would work in the library lounge. Darling, come with me and let's go look. They have a lecture going on in there right now, but we'll be quiet and just peek in. I want your opinion, so do your best to come up with one."

The library lounge opened onto the rear terrace of the main building. It had been decorated in a style that reminded Jake of a British colonial club from the turn of the century: ceiling fans, wicker furniture, and potted palms that brightened up mahogany walls and shelves lined with leather-bound books. The glass doors lining the far wall were all open, letting in the warm evening breeze and the faint sound of the surf.

There was a group of about thirty people in the room, sitting in chairs that had been arranged to face a smallish woman standing behind a lectern. She was speaking with animation, clearly warm to her subject, and she had the audience's rapt attention. Not a head turned to look back as Jake and Cora entered the room.

". . . they were ambushed near the coast of Tortola by a heavily armed privateer sloop with a commission from the British king to take pirates, alive or dead," the woman was saying. "The firefight shattered the *Lady Fortune*'s boom and crippled the ship. When the privateer captain ordered them to surrender and prepared to board, Mary took a pistol in one hand and grabbed a cutlass with her other. 'Fight like men,' she cried to her crew, 'else we'll die like dogs!' "

The woman shouted this last bit with theatrical zeal and slashed one hand through the air in front of her as if brandishing an invisible cutlass.

"My goodness," Cora said. "Such enthusiasm."

She began to scrutinize the carpet, but Jake kept listening to the lecturer. He wondered who the woman was, and why she looked familiar. If he had met her before, he couldn't imagine where. She had a heart-shaped face and delicate features that were almost obscured by shapeless mousy hair and glasses with thick cat-eye rims, the kind that proclaimed her to be a "Serious Intellectual." The effect was enhanced by the fact that they kept slipping down to rest, schoolmarmishly, on the tip of her nose when she consulted her notes. Absently, she pushed them back up, only to have them descend again. She was not unattractive if you liked earnest, scholarly women in dowdy clothing. Jake didn't. He stared at her. He had seen her somewhere before, he decided. He was sure of it. Where?

"They fought fiercely," the woman continued, "but they were outnumbered, and the privateer captain knew that the king had put a price on Mary's head. She was taken to Antigua in chains. Sources say that during the trial, people lined up ten deep outside the courthouse, just to get a look at her. The crowd moaned in horror when they heard the sentence. Death. She was to be hanged by the neck until dead."

Her voice dropped, emphasizing the words, and a ripple of excitement moved through her audience. *She has them in the palm of her hand*, Jake thought, impressed.

"Everyone knew that she was a criminal, but they didn't seem to care. She was a celebrity. It didn't hurt that she was also young and beautiful. It's hard to know now which of the stories about her were true and which were just gossip and speculation, but we do know one thing for sure. The game wasn't over, because Mary still had an ace up her sleeve. Any guesses as to what it was?"

"Her crew broke her out of prison?" asked a thin, balding man, who—judging from the expression on his face—did like earnest, scholarly women.

The woman shook her head. "No. Anyone else? I'll give you a hint. It wasn't something that your average pirate could have done."

"She slaughtered all of the prison guards!" cried a teenage girl excitedly. "And escaped!"

"No," said the woman, smiling. "Mary's trump card was that she was pregnant."

The audience murmured with interest, and she continued, "Not only pregnant, but bearing the child of John Whittaker, the governor of Antigua. He had been her lover for several years, which probably had something to do with her amazing ability to identify the ships carrying the richest cargo."

"Way to go, Mary," said the balding man.

"He used his connections, probably to save his own neck as much as hers. She was eventually granted amnesty by the crown on the premise that she had repented of her 'Lewd and Wicked Behavior.' She settled on a small island near Antigua, where she raised her son and spent her remaining years running a profitable sugar plantation."

"Aren't we near Antigua?" asked another man. "Is her island around here somewhere?"

The woman beamed. She had obviously hoped that someone would ask that question. "As a matter of fact," she said, "we're on her island right now. This is where Mary Morgan retired. I've been told that the ruins of her sugar plantation are over on the west side of the island."

There were excited questions from the audience, but Jake had abruptly stopped listening. He stared at the woman. Ruins of a sugar plantation? The west side of the island? This island? *His* island?

"God *damn* it," he said through his teeth. The "ruins" that this cursed woman was referring to, as reverentially as if they were some kind of Heritage Trust site, were the very same pathetic piles of rocks currently being removed by his workmen in preparation for construction of the new Gold Bay golf course.

"I haven't seen the site yet," the woman continued, "but I'm taking a drive out there tomorrow morning at eight. If anyone is interested, you're welcome to join me."

Jake saw several enthusiastic nods in the audience, and his mouth compressed into a thin line. *Over my dead body*, he thought. First, he had no intention of letting a bunch of tourists crawl all over his construction site. Someone was bound to get hurt and hold him liable. Second, the last thing that he needed was to have some little old lady from the Pirate Protection Society decide that Mary Morgan's sugar mills had critical historical value and start lobbying to protect and preserve them. If that happened, he was facing either a PR disaster or the loss of several million pre-invested development dollars. Or both.

He seized his mother by the arm, and—ignoring her surprised protest—walked her out of the lounge and into the lobby.

"This is a joke," he said angrily. "Who the hell is that woman, and who booked her to speak here?"

Cora looked astonished by his vehemence. "I have no idea," she said. "Why? What's wrong?"

Tersely, he explained, watching her eyes widen as she understood.

"Good heavens," she said. "I wasn't even listening, can you believe it? I was thinking about the carpet, and I didn't hear a word. Where on earth did she get the notion that those old ruins belonged to . . . who was it? A famous woman pirate? I didn't even know that there were female pirates, did you?"

"No," Jake said. "I didn't. I've never heard of Mary Morgan, and neither had anyone else, until that damn woman showed up. She has some cockeyed plan to take her lecture group on a tour of the ruins tomorrow morning, and I don't have to be psychic to tell you exactly what will happen when they get there, all dewy-eyed with the thrill of history, and find our bulldozers sitting on Mary's lawn."

"That won't happen," Cora said firmly. "I'll take care of it. I'll also find out who asked her to speak. The activities staff is usually very good, so I'm sure that it was just a miscommunication."

"That was one hell of a miscommunication," Jake said. "Your activities staff appears to be totally clueless. I can't believe that we paid to fly in a historian to find a pirate on my golf course. This could end up being the most expensive lecture in history."

Cora patted him on the arm. "You're overreacting, darling. Don't worry about it. I'll talk to the historian myself and explain the situation. I'm sure that she'll understand."

CHAPTER 10

"I spoke with that professor," Cora said the next morning at breakfast.

It was just after eight o'clock, and they were sitting at a small table on the terrace of the villa, enjoying the early morning sunshine and the view of the ocean, spread out below them like a rumpled blue blanket.

"What professor?" Jake asked, buttering a slice of toast. The breeze was warm and light, and it rustled the pages of the *Miami Herald*, which had come in by ferry at dawn.

"Dr. Shaw," Cora said. "You know, the woman who gave the lecture last night. Her name is Molly Shaw."

"Her name is mud," Jake said. "Did you cancel her field trip?"

"Darling, I didn't *cancel* it. You can't just order these academic people around. You have to reason with them. I spoke with her after the lecture, and she was very agreeable."

"Good. And did you find out which genius on the activities staff brought her here?"

"They didn't bring her here—she's a guest. She was very kindly filling in for a last-minute cancellation."

"A guest? They must be paying professors pretty well these days. Where is she staying?"

"Cottage Five," Cora said. "With Sandra St. Claire, can you believe it? Apparently, she's helping Sandra with the research on her new book."

"That's it," Jake said abruptly. He put down the toast and picked up his coffee cup. That was why the woman had looked familiar. She was the one he had seen the other morning, sitting on the deck of Cottage Five in a big white robe. The one who had fled from him as if he were a marauding Mongol. "Strange woman," he said, drinking his coffee.

"Not at all," Cora said. "She was very nice. She's an associate professor at Belden College in Wisconsin. I liked her. You might even like her."

"I like her just fine as long as she stays away from my golf course," Jake said.

"Well, actually, she was planning to go over to the site this morning. She's there right now, I think."

"What!" Jake put down his cup with a sharp clatter of china, and Cora winced. He stared at his mother. "You just said that you spoke to her. You said that she was agreeable. What do you mean, she's there right now?"

"Darling, calm down. I could hardly forbid her to take a car and go exploring! She's going alone, though, with a staff guide. She agreed that it would be a bad idea to take the lecture group, because of the safety issues. I thought it was a reasonable compromise."

"Great," Jake said grimly. "Just great."

"It's for the best. This way, she'll see that there's hardly anything left of the old plantation—"

"And blame me for it. Publicly, no doubt."

Cora sighed impatiently. "We've barely touched the site. It was a ruin when we leased the island. It'll be obvious that there's nothing worth preserving, so stop worrying and eat your eggs. You've been under a lot of pressure, and I think your nerves must be strained, because you're blowing this out of proportion. This isn't . . . Jake! What are you doing? You haven't finished your breakfast."

"I have a very bad feeling about this," Jake said, tossing his napkin onto the table.

He had seen—even if his mother had not—the glow of excitement and passion on Dr. Molly Shaw's face last night when she spoke about Mary Morgan. That had not been the face of a nice, reasonable, or agreeable young woman. That face had belonged to the kind of woman who might very well chain herself to one of his bulldozers and then call the *Daily News* to tell them all about it.

The old plantation was on the western side of the island, on the low, gently rising slope of the mountain, reachable only by a dirt track hacked out of the tangled rain forest greenery. It was obviously not a popular destination, which surprised Molly. It had taken her less than ten minutes of exploration to become convinced that the site had enormous potential. On a previous trip to the Caribbean, years ago, she had visited the Betty's Hope project on Antigua, an old sugar estate that had been restored and turned into a historical museum. The same thing could—and should—be done with Mary's property.

What remained of the old estate was almost too good to be true. To the uneducated eye, the plantation was just a decaying pile of rubble, long since picked clean of anything with any market value, but to a historian or an archaeologist, it was a treasure trove. It was incredible to think that Mary Morgan had lived and worked on this very ground. The stories of her life had such a mythological quality that she seemed like a fictional character rather than a real woman who had gone about her daily business right where Molly was now standing.

Molly had been assigned a young male "guide," another shiny and well-scrubbed Gold Bay staffer with a complete lack of knowledge about anything that had happened on the island before the resort was built. He looked only slightly older than the students in Molly's senior seminar, and knew much less about history.

"Over there," said the guide, "you can see the outline of the old house. Where it used to be, I mean. There's nothing left, now."

Molly sighed. There was indeed an outline—a depression in the earth still dotted with partially buried stones and knee-high chunks of wall, but it covered an area far too big to have been the great house for any eighteenth-century plantation. Not even the governor of Antigua could have built a house that size. The young man wasn't completely wrong, though.

"Based on the location," she said, "I think that we're looking at the perimeter wall that encircled the great house. The house itself would be inside there, and much smaller."

"Oh," said the guide. "I thought you said that she was really rich."

Molly ignored him. She had tried to convince him to wait in the car, but he had stuck doggedly to her side, and she was beginning to suspect that he had been given instructions to do so. Last night, Cora Berenger had mentioned something about construction in the area, and the terrible condition of the ruins, and their concern for her safety. She had insisted that Molly go with a guide, as if Molly were a doddering old crone who couldn't make it over a pile of rocks without the help of a man. It was ridiculous, in Molly's opinion. She hadn't seen any sign of construction, and the ruins were in much, much better shape than she had dared to hope. The island's remote location and lack of steady habitation had saved the site from being dismantled by locals looking for cheap stone and metal to use in newer buildings. The two windmill towers were still standing, in various stages of decay. In one, the huge iron gears and crushing rollers were still there, though they had long since fallen into a rusted pile, half buried by dirt. Buildings that Molly assumed to be part of the old sugar and rum factory had mostly collapsed, but they were sitting on solid foundations, and were obvious candidates for excavation.

"There isn't much to see," the guide said. "I guess you're probably pretty disappointed."

"Not at all," Molly said. "This is even better than I had hoped. Look, why don't you go back and wait in the car? I just want to take a peek over there, past those trees, where I think the main house must have been. I won't be long."

The guide looked alarmed. "Oh, no," he said. "You can't do that."

Molly frowned. "What do you mean? Why not?"

"Too dangerous."

"It's a grove of trees," Molly said. "What's so dangerous about that?"

The guide shook his head. "They told me that you shouldn't go near the old buildings. They aren't stable. It's not safe."

"Nonsense," Molly said. She walked through a gap in the crumbling perimeter wall, heading for the trees.

"Wait," the guide said anxiously, following her. "No, really. Ma'am, I'm sorry, but I'm just doing what they told me, and they specifically said that you shouldn't go near the old . . ."

"I'm not going to *climb* on anything," Molly said, still walking. "There's no danger at all. I just want to see how much of the main house is still there. The trees are blocking my view."

"You can't." He surprised her then, by taking hold of her arm. She stopped and raised her eyebrows at him. He looked very unhappy, but also very stubborn. "I'm really sorry," he said again, "but you're not supposed to go over there. It's not safe."

He was still gripping her arm. Molly stood silently for a moment, reading the discomfort on his face. Something strange was going on. He definitely didn't want her to go into the trees, but she couldn't imagine why. Was there something inside there that she wasn't supposed to see? If this were one of her own novels, it would be something thrilling, like a secret excavation for a buried pirate treasure. But she had never heard of a treasure connected to Mary Morgan. Bonny Mary may have financed the start of her plantation with stolen doubloons, but she had died a prosaic businesswoman, with her fortune in sugar and rum.

"I can take you up to Falcon's Point on the way home," said the young man hopefully. "The view is amazing. We take guests up there all the time, and they get great photos."

"Okay," Molly said slowly, watching him, and saw the relief on his face. "Yes," she continued, "I definitely don't want to go over there if it isn't safe. That wouldn't be very smart, would it? We should head back. I'd love to see the view."

They walked back to the car, an open-air Jeep, and Molly kept up a steady chatter about how much she was enjoying the comforts of the resort and how beautiful it all was. Just as she had settled into the passenger seat, and the guide had started the engine, she said, "Oh!"

He looked at her, and she smiled at him. "I'm sorry," she said. "I'm afraid that I'll need to make a rest stop before we go."

She could see that he didn't understand. "You know," she said coyly, "a *rest stop*. To the little girls' room."

Comprehension dawned, and he suddenly looked terribly embarrassed, as men in their early twenties did when confronted with female bodily functions. "Oh," he said. "Sure."

Molly fluttered her eyelashes at him. "I'll just be a few minutes," she said. "I'm going right over there, behind those bushes by the windmill. Please don't look. I'm very shy."

Idiot, she thought as she left the car and ducked behind the ruins. That had been almost too easy. The boy—he was less than ten years younger than she was, but to her he was definitely a boy—would wait there for her until she'd had a chance to slip over to the area of the main house and have a quick look around. It probably wouldn't be the first time that he had wondered why women always took such a long time in the bathroom.

When Jake reached the end of the dirt road that led to the ruins, he was briefly pleased to see one of the open-air Jeeps idling there, as if it were about to leave. But then he saw that there was only one occupant in the car, the young man that Cora had sent to babysit the professor.

The staffer was slouched in the driver's seat, looking bored. Jake pulled up next to him. The young man looked over, then straightened up hastily when he saw who had just arrived. His mouth opened slightly, in alarm. Jake was familiar with this reaction.

"Where is she?" he demanded.

The young man—Jake had no idea what his name was, and wasn't close enough to read his tag—turned red and began to stammer.

Jake cut the engine and swung down from the driver's

seat, and the young man quickly did the same. "Where is she?" Jake repeated. "You had very specific instructions to stay with her, and I sure as hell don't see her."

"She's . . . uh . . . she's over there, sir," the staffer said, pointing to a clump of bushes a short distance away. His name, Jake could now see, was Brett. "I was with her the whole time, and then we were about to leave, to go to Falcon's Point, like Mrs. Berenger suggested, and then she . . . uh . . . had to go to the bathroom, so she went . . . over there."

Jake narrowed his eyes. There was not even a flicker of life in the area near the windmills. "When did she go over there? Just a minute ago?"

Brett was looking very unhappy. "Uh," he said. "No. It's been . . . kind of a while, actually, sir. I was just thinking about checking to see if she was okay, but I didn't want to bother her . . ."

"Oh, for God's sake," Jake muttered.

"Do you want me to go get her?"

"No," Jake said. It was very obvious that this had become a situation that he would need to handle personally. And carefully. "Take your car back to the resort. I'll collect the professor. Believe me, I have no problem with the idea of *bothering* her."

Jake did not even trouble himself with stopping near the windmills to see if the professor was still back there in the bushes. He headed straight for the wooded area behind the crumbling wall of rock. Brett had been instructed to keep her out of there, and the professor, being no fool, had seen right through whatever excuse he had used. From the small access road, none of the early construction work was visible, but if you went through the grove of trees and walked around to the far side of the ruins, the story was suddenly very different. Cora had assumed that letting the professor get a quick look around the untouched parts of the site would be enough to placate her, but she should have known better.

Through the trees, Jake saw a flash of navy blue, a color that did not occur naturally in the island flora. He exhaled impatiently. "Dr. Shaw," he called.

The navy blue shape stopped.

"Stay right there," he said. At least he'd caught her at it. She would be embarrassed and on the defensive, which would give him the upper hand.

He skirted the last of the ruins and came through the back of the grove of trees. She was standing there, on the edge of the newly cleared area, her hands on her hips.

Spread out before them was a vista of disturbed ground waffled with bulldozer tracks and dotted with orange construction flags. Some of the earth-moving equipment was already in place, but the real work was not scheduled to begin for several months, in April, when the spring tourist season had passed.

She turned as he approached, and he saw her eyes widen at the sight of him. She had expected Brett. He didn't know if she recognized him or not, but it didn't matter. *Welcome to the majors, lady*, he thought. *I sent the babysitter home. You're dealing with Daddy, now.*

But before he could say another word, she attacked. She glared at him, and he could have sworn that she bared her teeth. "You!" she exclaimed. "Good, this will save me a trip to your office. Okay, Mr. Celebrity Billionaire, suppose you tell me what the bloody hell is going on here?"

Jake flinched. He was accustomed to hearing women curse like men, and never thought twice about it, but hearing this kind of language issuing from the lips of someone who looked like Molly Shaw made it seem much more serious.

"Do you really think I'm that stupid?" she continued. "You sent me over here with a kid to herd me around like a senior citizen on a bus tour, and that might even have worked if you had picked someone with enough sense to do a *good* job of lying to me. Leaving aside the whole issue of what you're doing to Mary's estate, I am frankly offended, Mr. Berenger, that you would send such a nitwit to be your watchdog. Only a complete moron would have believed that kid. Do I *look* that stupid to you?"

No, Jake thought. *Unfortunately, you don't look nearly stupid enough.* He was wondering how he could have considered her mousy. Her hair was pulled up into a ponytail, exposing an unexpectedly pretty face. Her skin was pale except for her flushed cheeks, and something about her appearance reminded him of his fourth-grade teacher. She was the proverbial girl next door. Gone homicidal.

"Anytime that you feel like jumping in here with an explanation," she said, "feel free."

Jake gritted his teeth. If he played this right, he had a chance of calming her down, charming her, and defusing a potentially disastrous situation. He could practically see the headlines now: "Berenger Sued Over Preservation of Feminist Heritage Site."

Damn her, he thought. *Damn her, her pirate, and women in general*. At this point, there was only one thing to do. He smiled at her, and lied. "Dr. Shaw, it sounds to me as if Brett gave you the wrong impression. You've got nothing to be upset about. We're not doing anything to Mary Morgan's estate."

"If you're not doing anything to this site, then why, may I ask, did Brett have instructions to keep me away from here?"

"Because the ruins aren't safe," Jake said. "We don't bring guests back here because the walls of the old house haven't been stabilized. It wouldn't be very good PR for my resort if you were accidentally squashed like a bug, would it?" He paused for a moment, enjoying the thought.

"Hah," said Molly Shaw scornfully.

Jake raised his eyebrows at her, and she continued. "You called me Dr. Shaw, so I presume that you know who I am. I *specialize* in the eighteenth-century Caribbean, Mr. Berenger. This is my *field* of *expertise*. From the looks of your construction zone, you're about to bulldoze over whatever is left of the workers' village and the old cane fields. When is the rest of the estate scheduled for demolition?"

"Workers' village?" Jake said. He had a feeling that he knew what was coming, and he didn't like it at all.

"Slaves," Molly said coldly. "African workers and tradesmen. By all accounts, Mary Morgan was a modern thinker who ran a liberal operation, and she was known to have provided a good life for her workers, under the circumstances. My guess is that she knew from her years onboard ship that her success depended on the loyalty of the people around her, so she did her best to earn it. There was a thriving village here, and I believe that you're about to flatten an important part of Afro-Caribbean cultural history."

"Great," Jake muttered. "Berenger Sued Over Preservation of Feminist AND Minority Heritage Site." This was getting worse by the minute.

"Didn't you have a historical analysis done on this area before you started building on it? What *are* you building? A football stadium? It looks huge."

"It's a golf course," Jake said grimly, "and no, I didn't have an analysis done. We leased the island from the Antiguan government, and it came without restrictions. There are hundreds of these old plantations all over the West Indies, and they've been knocking them down for years. There's a windmill tower over in St. John's that's been turned into a burger joint. We're not talking about priceless cultural resources here."

"This is *not* just a random plantation," Molly said. "This belonged to Bonny Mary Morgan, who was a famous female pi—"

"I know who she was," Jake said. "I was at your lecture last night."

She looked surprised. "You were? I didn't see you."

"I was standing in the back. You told some very thrilling stories, but you didn't mention any sources to back them up. Your lecture sounded more like a paperback novel than a scholarly presentation—"

Molly inhaled sharply, and he was surprised by the expression on her face. She looked as if he'd just slapped her. *These academics take themselves way too seriously*, he thought. He continued. "It made me wonder if you have any proof that this estate actually did belong to your female pirate. Do you? Have proof?" He waited, mentally crossing his fingers.

"I can find proof," she said.

He grinned, not missing the sudden apprehension in her eyes. She didn't have it, and she wasn't sure that she could find it. Things were suddenly looking much better. "So," he said, "this is all just speculation."

"It is not! Mary gave up piracy and retired to a small island near Antigua, where she ran a sugar plantation. There are very few islands that fit that description."

"*Very few* means more than one. For all you know, your progressive feminist pirate never set foot on my island, and this estate actually belonged to some macho male colonist who abused his family, was cruel to his workers, and deserves to have the remains of his rotten life bulldozed."

"Mary Morgan lived here," Molly Shaw insisted.

"So you claim," Jake said. He was now feeling almost cheerful. "Bring me some proof, and then we'll talk."

"I will," Molly said ominously. "You'll see. But regardless of that, this is a very well-preserved site. You should restore it and turn it into a museum. It would be a wonderful addition to the resort."

Jake suppressed the urge to laugh. She was serious. It was almost endearing. "Professor," he said, "I realize that this will shock you, but the average Gold Bay guest doesn't care very much about the eighteenth-century Caribbean. If my customers had to decide between visiting an old ruin shined up to look like a museum, or playing eighteen holes on the most beautiful golf course south of Miami, do I really need to tell you which they would choose?"

Molly Shaw glared at him, and Jake mentally checked himself. He did not need to make an enemy out of this woman, if there was any other option left. Without proof that the estate was special, she would have no leverage with the press, but even so, it would be foolish to antagonize her. He didn't want to do anything that might lead to the project being tied up in court.

"This may also shock you," he added, "but I'm not your enemy. If you can find me solid evidence that this plantation did belong to Bonny Mary Morgan, then I'll take it to my board and try to convince them to rework the plans for the golf course."

It was a deceptively magnanimous offer. If she had the proof and the will to start a public fight, then Berenger would have no choice but to rezone the golf course and exclude the sugar estate. They couldn't afford the negative publicity. But with luck, Molly Shaw's pirate would turn out to be nothing more than a colorful local legend, and she would admit defeat, go away quietly, and the project would proceed as planned.

Molly was frowning slightly, as if trying to figure out whether he was trying to trick her. Finally, she nodded. "Okay," she said. "That sounds fair. When is construction supposed to start?"

"Immediately," Jake said, lying again. He saw no reason to hand a single advantage to this woman. He had never had any problem with lying, as long as it wasn't to his family or his shareholders, and Molly Shaw did not fall into either category. "But I'm willing to push the start back another week, or even two, if necessary. Would that give you the time you need to settle this?"

She looked stunned. "It might," she said. "I'll start checking the records right away. Thank you. That's . . . very kind."

"My pleasure," Jake said, trying to look noble.

She was still staring at him, as if he'd grown a second head—a nicer one, this time. "I didn't expect . . . I mean, you don't seem like the kind of person who would care about . . ."

"Anything but money?"

She flushed slightly. "I didn't mean that."

"I feel very strongly about the preservation of important cultural heritage sites," Jake said, glad that they were alone in the wilderness and nobody had this moment on tape. "But my own personal feelings have to take a backseat to the needs of my company and my shareholders. I have a duty to them. If we can confirm that this was Mary Morgan's estate, then I'll do my best to negotiate an acceptable compromise."

He was rewarded with a smile so genuine that he actually felt guilty. Incredibly, Molly Shaw was beautiful when she smiled. Her eyes crinkled at the corners and her whole face seemed to light up. She suddenly reminded him of someone else, someone who he couldn't place. An actress, maybe. Someone he had met socially, but didn't know well.

"I never would have guessed that someone like you would care about local history," she said.

"Well," he said, and shrugged modestly, "I was at your lecture, wasn't I?"

CHAPTER 11

There was chaos in Cottage Five when Molly walked in the door at ten-thirty. Carter had been pacing up and down the length of the sitting room, and he stopped in his tracks when he saw her.

"Do you know what time it is?" he cried, waving his arms. "Where have you *been*? You were supposed to be here at ten. That was the *plan*. Remember?"

"I'm sorry," Molly said. She had no intention of telling him that Jake Berenger had just dropped her off outside the reception lobby. It would have cheered him up, but the astonishing encounter felt private to her, and she didn't want Carter—or anyone else—to know about it. The feeling made no sense, considering that the point of this whole trip was for her to get close to Jake.

No, she corrected herself. The point was for Sandra to get close to Jake. What Molly Shaw did had nothing to do with anything, and therefore, it was her own business.

"The *plan*," Carter said, sounding aggrieved, "was to put Sandra on the beach with Elaine while Jake was windsurfing, so that he could see her when he finished. And then she was supposed to invite him to lunch. It would have been perfect. The moment was right. But now we don't have time to get you ready before he quits at eleven."

"Jake isn't windsurfing," Molly said. "I just saw him over by reception."

Carter's eyes rounded with delight. "You did? He's late, too? Was he going to the beach?"

"How would I know?" Molly asked crossly. Jake hadn't exactly detailed his plans for the day during the short drive back from the ruins. They had made polite small talk. He had asked her about her work, and Molly had launched into her usual litany of papers published and grants received. It was the kind of answer designed to impress another academic, but Molly had suddenly realized that she sounded as pompous as . . . well, as her father. Jake had feigned interest, but the truth was undeniable. In the car with that man, in that bright and steamy tropical landscape, her carefully cultivated scholarly image felt as colorless and desiccated as an old bone. *I'm not boring*, she thought, frustrated. *Not really*. She knew it, but Jake Berenger didn't. And for some reason, that bothered her.

"We'll give it a try," Carter said decisively. "We've got nothing to lose. Elaine has the perfect spot on the beach. I'll go and send her back to help you get ready. Today is the day, I can feel it."

They arrived at the beach shortly after eleven, with Molly transformed into Sandra, to find Carter holding their place and practically quivering with excitement. He reported that Jake had taken his board out onto the water, and if he stayed out for his usual hour-long session, he was due back in about twenty minutes.

Due to the amount of padding and tape involved in being Sandra, Molly was not able to wear a bikini, so Elaine had improvised by dressing her in a pair of tight white shorts and a white push-up bustier, covered by a gauzy pink button-down shirt open at the front and knotted at her waist. A folded pink and white Hermès scarf served as a headband to help keep the platinum wig in place, and since Elaine's silver sunglasses had become part of Sandra's look, Molly was wearing them, as well.

The only problem was with her "shoe strategy," as Jake had put it. In the soft sand, neither the platform sandals nor the stiletto heels were functional, depriving Molly of the four inches of height that Carter considered scientifically essential.

"Tiptoes," Elaine said cheerfully as they prepared to go for a stroll on the beach. "Up, up, dear."

"Huh?" Molly said.

"Did you ever see Brigitte Bardot clumping around St. Tropez like a flat-footed elephant? I don't think so. Did Marilyn Monroe shuffle like a waitress on the late shift? Never. Tiptoes. Light and playful. Frolic a little. Smile, dear, we're being watched."

Molly smiled. "Are you seriously telling me," she said through her teeth, "that you want me to walk up and down this beach on my *toes*?"

"Lifting the heels elongates the leg and raises the derriere," Elaine said. "It also tones the calf muscles, which is something that we ought to discuss, dear, just as a point of interest to you. A regular exercise program can do wonders for both physique and mood."

"Thanks, dear," Molly said. "I'll make a note of that."

There were several bright sails visible on the bay, but they were all too far out for Molly to be able to identify Jake. It was interesting that he was so committed to his daily hour of windsurfing. She wondered whether it was the sport itself that he loved or the hour of solitude. Despite everything she'd read and heard, he really didn't seem to be the shallow playboy type. He was smart, with a sense of humor, and he had utterly astonished her with his willingness to give her time to confirm the provenance of the plantation ruins. If she had been wearing the Sandra suit, his kindness might have been suspect, in light of his reputation as a womanizer. But, she thought, with a small twist in her heart, it was safe to assume that Jake Berenger had not developed a sudden passionate attraction to Molly Shaw.

So why had he been so agreeable? Did he actually—as he had claimed—care about the island's cultural heritage? It was hard to believe, but she could find no other explanation. He had been willing to listen to her. And to help her, at his own expense. She knew very little about commercial construction, but delaying a project of that size—even for a week or two—had to be costly. His generosity was extraordinary. *How*, she thought, *can a man like that be as bad as the press makes him sound?*

"My goodness," Elaine said. "The sun is very hot today." She was wearing an enormous straw hat that prevented Molly from walking within two feet of her, oversized square sunglasses that covered half of her face, and a black bathing suit with a chiffon wrap tied strategically around her hips. "As a rule, I prefer shade, and so should you, my dear. The sun is not a woman's friend. I know a doctor in New York who is an absolute genius—not to say that I've had any work done, but I make it my business to know these things, and he tells me that it's not just a matter of wrinkles. It's about texture, you see, and too much sun will make you look like an old boot . . . Good heavens!"

She stopped in her tracks.

Molly followed her gaze, and saw two people approaching from the opposite direction. One was a tall and stunningly beautiful young woman, thin as a whippet, wearing a red bikini made of three microscopic triangles. Next to her walked a bald man in flowing white robes. Molly glanced around and saw that she and Elaine were not the only ones staring.

"I don't believe it," Elaine said through her teeth. "Him! That crook! How dare he. I've heard the rumors, of course, but I didn't believe them. I couldn't imagine that any client of mine would ever . . . oh, this is very bad."

"That woman was a client of yours?" Molly asked.

"Yes. Ingrid Anderson. She's a well-known model. I introduced her to her husband two years ago."

The couple was getting close, and Molly looked askance at the robed man. "That's her husband?"

Elaine looked offended. "Certainly not," she said. "Her husband is an investment banker. *That* man is a bedsheet-covered charlatan."

This didn't clear anything up for Molly, but she couldn't ask for more information, because the odd couple was now right in front of them. Elaine pulled off her sunglasses. "Ingrid!" she exclaimed. "Darling! How wonderful to see you."

The young woman looked alarmed. "Oh," she said. "Baroness Von Reinholz."

Elaine patted her fondly on the arm. "It's Mrs. Newberg now, dear. I haven't used my title since I remarried. How are you? I see that you have a new"—she looked the robed man up and down with a cold eye—"friend."

"*Namaste*," said the man. "Peaceful greetings." He put his hands together in the prayer position and bowed.

Elaine's lips formed a tight smile. "Indeed," she said.

The man extended his hand to Molly. "And what is your name, my child?"

"Sandra," Molly said. "Sandra St. Claire." She had been squinting at him from behind her sunglasses, trying to guess his age and ethnicity, and having no luck with either. He had a sculpted face, darkly tanned skin, pale blue eyes, and no discernible accent.

"Sandra," said the man. His fingers held hers, and his eyes lingered briefly on her chest. "My earthly incarnation is known as Rama Guru. I would be honored if you would know me, Sandra."

"Uh . . ." Molly said, taken aback.

"The Spirit is One," said Rama Guru. "In the Light, we are One. Would you like to know the Way to the Light, Sandra?"

"*That* will do," Elaine said sharply. "It's a very kind offer from Mr. Guru, I'm sure, but we have time commitments, so we'll have to say good-bye. Ingrid!"

Ingrid Anderson jumped. Elaine patted her again, as if she were calming a skittish horse. "Come and see me, dear. Alone. Three o'clock. Cottage Five. We'll have tea and some girl talk."

"Okay," Ingrid said. She didn't sound enthusiastic.

"I bid you peace," said Rama Guru. "And the courage to Seek."

Elaine glared at him, took Molly by the arm, and marched her down the beach. Her posture was ramrod-straight, and her lips were pressed together.

"Who was that weird guy?" Molly asked as soon as they were out of earshot. "Where is he from?"

"California," Elaine said grimly, as if that explained everything. She looked out at the bay and then stopped walking. "Ah," she said in a more normal tone. "Let's turn around. I believe I see Jake coming in."

Jake let his sail drop into chest-high water, and jumped off the board. He floated on his back and raised his face to the sun. It was a perfect day, and he would have paid a million dollars—in cash—for the chance to spend another hour on the water. But God was not taking bribes, and neither was his mother. She was giving a luncheon party for the Koppelsons, old friends from Palm Beach, and he was due back at the house at noon. It was currently ten minutes to twelve.

"Christ," he muttered. He knew exactly what awaited him, and it involved fruit salad, poached fish, and an interminable period of time in a seat next to Bunny Koppelson, who was always on some kind of weird health-food diet that she wanted to talk about.

Cora had been laying on the guilt for the past few days, telling Jake that he was neglecting his duties as a host to Amanda. She had suggested that he redeem himself by escorting Amanda to the party, and Jake had made the mistake of pointing out that since he had not invited Amanda to stay with them in the first place, he did not—in his opinion—have any duties as a host. He should have known better than to argue. Cora had then given him a choice: Show up at lunch, or teach Amanda to scuba dive. She added, with the kind of smile that Jake knew much too well, that it was entirely his decision.

He wondered what the professor was doing at the moment. Frantically making calls to the Antigua Historical Society, no doubt, looking for some sort of title deed to the old plantation. He wasn't worried. They were talking about the 1700s, after all. He didn't know much about historical research, but he seriously doubted that such specific records from the colonial West Indies would be easy to find, if they still existed at all.

He dragged his board up onto the sand and shook his head like a dog, tossing the water out of his hair. A beach attendant trotted up and handed him a bottle of cold mineral water and a towel. The latter was not really necessary, as the sun would dry him before he even reached the boathouse, but he approved of the prompt attention.

"Mr. Berenger!" said a female voice, and Jake turned. Standing there, in huge black sunglasses and a hat the size of an extra-large pizza, was a woman he had never seen before in his life. Actually, he had no way of knowing, as he could only see the lower twenty-five percent of her face. But the girl next to her was very familiar. He remembered the sweet smell of her perfume, the feeling of her legs entangled with his own, and her hands pushing against his bare chest.

"Sandra," he said. "Rico told me that you canceled your lessons. Is your ankle bothering you?"

"Oh," she said. "No. Well, only a little. I felt a tiny twinge in it this morning, and I thought it would be better to let it rest."

"No doubt," Jake said. He absolutely could not imagine her on a windsurfing board, and if her coordination on land was any indicator of her skill level on the water, then she was likely to be doing more swimming than sailing, anyway.

The woman next to Sandra took off her glasses, and Jake realized that she was the one he had met at Cora's VIP cocktail party the other night. Elaine something. "What a pleasant surprise to see you here, Mr. Berenger," she said. "Don't you usually go out at ten?"

"Usually," Jake said. He took a drink from the bottle of water. "But I'm running late this morning." He looked at Sandra and remembered something interesting. "Are you sharing your cottage with a history professor?"

Sandra looked as alarmed as if he'd said "ax murderer." "I . . . uh . . . what?" she said.

"Molly Shaw. She's in Cottage Five with you, isn't she?"

"Yes . . . how did you know that?"

"My mother told me. She talked to Professor Shaw after the lecture last night."

"Lecture?" Elaine repeated.

"Molly gave an informal talk," Sandra said shortly. "About pirates, or something. I wouldn't know. I didn't go."

"I thought she was a very good speaker," Jake said.

Sandra looked surprised. "You did?"

"Yes. Have you known her for a long time?"

"No. She's my research consultant, that's all. We hardly know each other. I almost never see her. We talk by phone. She lives in Wisconsin, and I . . . don't."

"Nice of you to bring her along on your trip," Jake said. That solved the mystery of how a college professor had been able to afford Cottage Five.

"She needed a break," Sandra said. A sudden smile twitched the corners of her mouth. "She's very hardworking. She's considered a rising star in her field, in fact."

"Really," Jake said. He frowned.

Sandra's smile grew. "Molly is utterly devoted to Caribbean cultural heritage, and her help has been invaluable to me on my current project. I'm writing a novel based on the life of Bonny Mary Morgan."

Jake choked on his water and began to cough violently.

"Goodness!" exclaimed Elaine. "Mr. Berenger, are you all right?"

Jake nodded wordlessly. He had to clear his throat several times before he could speak. "Excuse me," he said, finally. "Do you mean that you and Molly Shaw are writing a book together?"

"Yes, indeed," Sandra said sweetly. "Molly is helping me with the research. She has an amazing ability to find information about *almost anything*. You'd be amazed by how many documents still exist from the eighteenth century."

"Really," Jake said again.

"Of course, I can't be bothered to sort through it all. It's much too boring and complicated for me, but Molly is a research *genius*. You'd never guess by looking at her, but she's actually very witty. And exciting. Not boring at all."

"I thought you said that you hardly know her."

"Oh," Sandra said. "Well, that's true. But I'm getting to know her now, on this trip. You'll have to meet her sometime."

Jake said nothing. *Great*, he thought. *Just great*. Not only did he have to deal with a "rising star" with a sadistic plan to sabotage his golf course, but now her friend, a best-selling novelist, wanted to immortalize Mary Morgan in print. This was becoming a complete nightmare.

"Is that why you're here?" he asked. "Because Molly Shaw thinks that Mary Morgan lived on this island?"

Sandra nodded. "That and the spa. I absolutely adore your spa. My international jet-set friends and I agree that any resort that offers both a rich cultural heritage *and* a five-star spa is tops on our list of destinations."

Elaine cleared her throat impatiently. "Sandra, dear," she said.

Sandra looked startled, as if she'd forgotten that her friend was there. "Oh," she said, and smiled charmingly at Jake. Her eyes were as blue as the bay on a clear morning, and he wondered if she had any idea that she was colluding to ruin his life. Probably not, considering that Molly Shaw had not even told her about their encounter at the ruins that morning. His impression was that Sandra St. Claire was a nice and slightly ditzy woman; some sort of literary savant who churned out salacious prose while the "brilliant" Molly Shaw worked the strings behind the scenes like an evil puppeteer.

"Sandra," Elaine said again. "My head."

Sandra nodded. "Jake," she said, "Elaine and I had a plan

to take a picnic lunch up to—what is it called? Eagle Point?"

"Falcon's Point," Jake said.

"That's right. It's all packed and ready to go, but poor Elaine has a terrible headache, and now she'd rather go home to bed. I just hate to be alone, and I was wondering if—by any chance—you might like to have lunch with me?"

CHAPTER 12

Molly looked over at Jake, who was in the driver's seat of the open-air Jeep, and suppressed a mild attack of panic. She hadn't actually expected him to say *yes*. He had seemed about to refuse, in fact. She could have sworn that she had seen the shape of the words of a refusal touch his lips before he paused, narrowed his eyes as if he were making a mental calculation, and then—shockingly—accepted.

Could it be that there really was something to Carter's so-called scientific plotting? He had also given her detailed instructions about how to manage the lunch, and how to bring up the topic of interviews, publicity, and biographies in a seductive and appealing manner, but Molly—convinced that things would never reach that point—had barely listened. And now here she was, alone in a car with Jake, and she had no clue of what to do next.

There seemed to be one main road that circumnavigated the island, rising and falling in elevation as it cut through the varied terrain. Narrower, less-trodden tracks branched off of it, with rustic wooden signs pointing the way to the sightseeing spots. "Falcon's Point, 5 kilometers," proclaimed a crooked arrow pointing to their turnoff. The road began to climb, winding through the forest as it rose along the low slopes of the old mountain in the center of the island. It had been a volcano once, thousands of years ago, but the slopes had been softened by time and overgrown with tropical rain forest. Molly could feel the air becoming heavy and damp as the elevation increased, and commented on it.

Jake nodded. "The winds generally come from the east, and we're moving up into the rain shadow of the mountain."

They reached a cleared area beside the road, and he pulled the car over and cut the engine. A steep flight of wooden steps led up into the greenery and disappeared.

"Go ahead up the stairs," Jake said, getting out of the car. "I'll grab the picnic things and follow you."

"I can help," Molly said.

"No," he said immediately with a glance at her shoes. She was wearing the obligatory platforms, and it was not hard to guess what he was thinking.

"Okay," she said grudgingly. It annoyed her to be thought of as a tottering fool. On her own feet, she could have bounded up the stairs two at a time, carrying the basket. As it was, though, she found that she was grateful for the wooden handrail.

At the top of the steps, tropical vegetation gave way to open blue sky, soaring high above a plateau that overlooked a vista so huge and magnificent that Molly stopped in her tracks to stare.

They were on the southern slope of the old volcano, close to the top. From here, looking southwest and down, Molly could see Gold Bay. The resort was as tiny and bright as a jeweled brooch pinned at the throat of the island. To the east, the mountain slopes crumbled away into a rocky cliff that dropped hundreds of feet to the ocean below. To the west, the slope was long and gentle, with green treetops slowly melting into scrub brush, which flattened gradually into the salt marsh. In that direction, somewhere along the edge of the forest, was the ruin of Mary Morgan's plantation. The area would have been cleared of trees in Mary's time, and the location had obviously been chosen to place the cane-crushing windmills in the path of the prevailing easterlies.

She heard the sound of Jake coming up the stairs behind her and turned. "It's incredible," she said. "How did you find this place? And why are we alone here?"

"Most of my guests don't want to travel so far from the daiquiri service," Jake said. He put down the picnic basket. "Frankly, I'm surprised that you did. You don't seem like the outdoorsy type, Sandra."

Molly hesitated, wondering if that was a good thing or a bad thing. Should she agree or argue? Based on the costume Carter had created, it seemed most logical to agree. If Jake liked outdoorsy women, Carter would have dressed her up as a lumberjack. "That's true," she said. "I do prefer a refined environment. There are too many . . . uh . . . yucky bugs in the wilderness. But I was told that the view was worth the effort, and I am actually quite . . . adventurous, Jake."

She saw his eyebrows lift slightly as he heard the invitation in her voice. *There*, she thought, suppressing a grin of triumph. Carter would be proud. She wasn't so bad at this. It just took a little bit of practice, like teaching a freshman lecture class. She hadn't been any good at that at first, either.

"Do you come here often?" she asked coyly.

"Occasionally," he said. "I first saw this place twelve years ago, when we were scouting islands for the resort. When they brought me up here, that did it. I looked out there"—he gestured toward the arc of Gold Bay—"and I saw the resort, in my mind, almost as clearly as you can see it now."

"How fascinating," she breathed.

His smile was polite, but distant. *Uh-oh*, Molly thought, alarmed. *Not good. I'm losing him*. Flirting was apparently like a tennis game, and a weak return would not suffice. Not with this man, at least. He was too easily bored by an amateur.

"And when you looked out there," she said in a teasing voice, pointing toward the western slopes, "I'll bet that in your mind, you saw an enormous golf course, didn't you?"

Jake stopped short. For a moment he didn't move, and Molly's heart thudded in her chest. *Damn*, she thought, chagrined. She wasn't a clever flirt, she was an idiot. He had taken her tone for sarcasm. It would have been better to stick to silly platitudes.

He turned back to look at her, and stood silently for a moment, staring at her. His eyes moved over her face, lingering on her mouth. "Sandra St. Claire," he said slowly, "you are full of surprises, aren't you."

Molly looked nervously at him, but he was expressionless. *Well*, she thought, *at least I have his full attention.*

"So," he said, "you and your . . . friend . . . the professor have been talking about my development plans?"

"She mentioned it to me."

"Really," Jake said. "When?"

"This . . . uh . . . this morning," Molly said.

"Just a little while ago, at the beach, you told me that I should meet Molly Shaw. But obviously you already knew that I had met her."

"Hmm," Molly said uncomfortably. Had she said that? She had forgotten. Jake was staring at her as if he were an inquisition judge. "Well, I guess that's true. It slipped my mind."

"Since Professor Shaw found out about my golf course only this morning," Jake said, "and I know for a fact that she didn't get back to the resort until ten-thirty, that means that you and she must have had your conversation less than one hour before you and I met on the beach. I wonder how it could have slipped your mind in such a short time." He looked inquiringly at her, eyebrows slightly raised.

Molly's knees felt weak. *Buck up, girl,* she told herself sternly. *This is no time to get waffly.* "I have occasional problems with short-term memory loss," she said haughtily. "As a result of an accident I had. As a child."

"I'm very sorry to hear that," Jake said.

"Thank you. I'd rather not talk about it, if you don't mind. It upsets me."

"Of course," Jake said. "I understand completely." He was still staring at her, eyes narrowed, as if he were considering something. She gazed right back at him, doing her best to appear dignified and slightly miffed. Her heart was beating so loudly that she wondered if he could hear it. *Okay,* she thought, *now what?* She had not expected to get herself into a situation where she would be wishing for Carter to show up and do something drastic. Where were he and his kayak paddle when she needed them?

But then Jake surprised her. He shrugged and motioned toward the picnic basket. "So," he said, "hungry?"

Molly blinked. It was an abrupt change of manner. Did he actually believe her? Did blond hair and an impressive cleavage have the power to addle a man's mind so completely that he would lose all logical reason? Maybe the clichés were true. Or—more likely—did he simply not care that her story was absurd? She was here, they were alone, and she was quite plainly throwing herself at him. Maybe for him, that was all that mattered.

"I'm starving," Jake said. He picked up the blanket she'd brought, shook it open, and spread it out on the ground under a tree. "What did you bring?"

"The usual," Molly said vaguely. She had no idea. The Gold Bay Bistro staff had packed the basket under Carter's direction, presumably based on his scientific calculations as to the exact composition of Jake Berenger's Ideal Picnic.

She sat down next to him and opened the basket, leaning forward as Carter had instructed her, displaying everything that the white bustier was able to display. "Champagne," she said, pulling it out and setting it on the cloth. "And cold roast chicken, crusty bread with butter, vegetables with dip, strawberries, and . . . graham crackers?"

"I love graham crackers," Jake said.

"Oh! So do I. Isn't that a funny coincidence?"

"Yes," Jake said, "isn't it."

He helped himself to a piece of chicken and began to eat it with his fingers, like a medieval warrior. Molly broke off a chunk of the bread and nibbled on it, feeling anxious, trying to recall Carter's instructions about seductive ways to bring up the subject of books—biographies in particular. She couldn't remember anything he had said, and decided to wing it.

"Jake," she said casually, "I heard the strangest thing about you yesterday. Someone at the resort told me that you never give interviews. Is that really true?"

One corner of his mouth curved up. "Yes," he said.

Molly affected surprise. "But why?"

"Personal reasons."

"Aren't you worried that you'll be misunderstood by the public if you always let other people speak for you?"

He laughed suddenly and put down the chicken, wiping his fingers and mouth on a linen napkin. He didn't say anything, but simply sat there and watched her, as if she were a one-act play.

"It just seems to me," Molly continued, "that by refusing to talk to reporters, you give them too much power. They can interpret your life however they please, and I'm sure that they're sometimes wrong."

"Wrong?" Jake widened his eyes in a parody of shock. "The press? That's impossible. After all, those things that you see written about me—that I'm a reckless playboy, a serial womanizer . . . that I care more about my sex life than my company . . . it's all in print, isn't it? And they wouldn't print it if it weren't *true*, would they?"

Molly frowned. He was behaving very strangely, and she wasn't sure what to do. She persisted. "Haven't you ever wanted to tell your own story? In your own words?"

"No," Jake said. He smiled at her, but there was something hard in his expression that Molly found unsettling. "Why do you ask? Could it be that *you* want to tell my story, Sandra?"

"Me?" Molly said, surprised. Things were moving more quickly than she had expected. "No, not me, but I do have a fr . . ."

Jake dropped his napkin and moved so quickly that Molly had no time to react. Her chunk of bread went flying, and the unopened bottle of champagne fell over and rolled away as he seized her. His strong arms were around her, and they fell backward, onto the blanket, with Jake on top.

"Sandra," he said ardently, "from the moment I met you, I've been trying to control myself, but I can't do it anymore. I want you."

"What?" Molly gasped. He was crushing her. Even through the ample padding between her chest and his, she could feel his wide, firm muscles. His arms were hard around her, and she felt like a doll in his grasp. One of his hands was behind her head, his fingers sliding up her nape. Horrified, Molly was almost unable to breathe. Did he feel the pins, and the lump of her own hair, tucked beneath the cap of the wig?

"It's true. I want you more than I've ever wanted any woman. I need you. I must have you."

"Have me?" Molly squeaked. "What do you mean, have me?'

"You know what I mean," Jake said dangerously. "I want to make love to you. Here. Now."

"Oh, my God," Molly said in a panic. She squirmed and found herself unable to move. She was absolutely pinned beneath him, and he was insane with . . . lust? It was unbelievable. Carter's calculations had succeeded beyond anyone's wildest imagining. She could scream, but who would hear her?

And then Jake's mouth came down on hers, hard and hot and demanding, and the logical part of Molly's brain stopped working. She inhaled sharply, her mouth opening under his as a shock of sexual hunger coursed through her. His lips were rough, slightly chapped, and he tasted salty and male—very male, in a way that was both new and deeply, instinctively familiar.

Jake made a slight sound, as if surprised, and the forceful kiss slowed and deepened. His mouth moved against hers as if he were suddenly in uncharted territory, exploring her, testing her response. Molly raised her only free hand and cupped his face, feeling the coarseness of stubble under her fingers, and the fine strong edge of his jawbone in her palm. He kissed like an expert, teasing her mouth, tracing the soft fullness of her lips with his tongue, sending shivers of desire down her spine.

Molly clutched at him, responding with reckless abandon, losing herself in a way that normally only happened in front of her keyboard. She didn't know how she could feel so physical and so detached at the same time, as if she weren't real, as if nothing were real but the heat of Jake's body, and the swirling passion inside her.

Her other hand, pinned under his thigh, dug into the hard muscle there, feeling it flex under her fingers as he shifted his weight. His mouth left hers and she moaned softly as he began to kiss her neck, brushing his lips against the delicate skin behind her ear, trailing a line of fire down her throat.

"Sandra St. Claire," he murmured. "You are . . . unbelievable."

The word snapped Molly back to reality. His breath was warm on her chest, and he was getting closer and closer to a region that was definitely unbelievable. Her head was still swimming, and she wanted nothing more than to stay there, for the kiss to go on and on. Jake wanted to make love to her—to Sandra, that was—and if it hadn't been for the limitations of the costume, Molly would have had no objection.

But she did not have the luxury of making that choice. It took all of her strength to slide her hands between the two of them, and all of her willpower to push against his chest instead of knotting her fingers into his shirt and holding him there, against her.

"Jake . . ." she said breathlessly, turning her head, trying to break away. "Stop, please. Could we . . . could we discuss this?"

He laughed suddenly, low in his throat, startling her. She looked up at him, and felt a fluttering in her stomach at the sight of his face, so close to hers. His eyes were hazel, fringed by black lashes, but they narrowed as he gazed down at her.

"Discuss it?" he said. "Absolutely. Sandra, I'm completely in your power. Anything you want from me . . . anything. Just ask. It's yours. What do I have to do to make you mine?"

"I . . ." Molly faltered. "I . . . um . . ." This was the kind of thing that men said in the sort of novels that made *Pirate Gold* seem erudite. She couldn't believe that it was happening to her. Was this the time to bring up Carter's book? Jake had asked, after all, but it didn't seem very graceful to segue straight from a mind-blowing kiss into a business proposition.

He bent his head and began to kiss her again, tasting the hollow of her throat. "Tell me," he said, his breath warm against her skin. "Tell me what you want, and how far you're willing to go to get it. What is it? Money? Jewelry? Or . . . could it be? An interview for whatever pathetic tabloid newspaper you work for?"

"Wh-what?" Molly stammered. "Newspaper?"

He released her with a suddenness that left her collapsed on the blanket like a deflated balloon. Shakily, she lifted herself onto her elbows and saw Jake staring down at her in disdain. "Sandra," he said coldly, "or Molly, or whatever your name actually is, let me ask you the same question that you asked me this morning at the ruins. Do you *really* think I'm *that* stupid?"

CHAPTER 13

Sandra St. Claire went pale under her makeup, and her rouged cheeks seemed to pop out like smears of rosy paint on a white wall. She looked horrified, as well she should, Jake thought. Had she seriously expected to fool him for more than a few days? It only took one extended period in the company of each character before it became obvious that the dowdy professor and the bombshell novelist were the same woman. She had changed her hair, her eye color, and her clothes, but her personality had leaked through each disguise and betrayed her.

He couldn't believe that it had taken him this long to figure it out. He hadn't had a clue until fifteen minutes ago, when she'd had the cheek to bring up his golf course. Did she really think that he was so stupid that she could amuse herself by toying with him? Apparently so, but she had underestimated him. His morning encounter with Molly Shaw was still fresh in his memory, and something about Sandra's voice, just now, had made the connection in his mind. For a moment he hadn't believed it. It was simply too bizarre.

But then, when he had turned and looked at her, *really* looked at her . . . then he had known. It was the mouth. Naked, on Molly Shaw, or covered in frosted pink gloss on Sandra St. Claire, the mouth was absolutely the same.

"Lady," Jake said, "I have seen some amazing stunts by the press, but this is by far the craziest. You should be very proud of yourself."

"I'm not from the press!"

"Bullshit. I assume that you couldn't decide which character would be more likely to get to me—the mousy professor threatening my development project, or the tarted-up bimbo offering sex, so you decided to hedge your bets and try both. I'm impressed that you managed to convince your publisher to foot the Gold Bay bill. Your boss must have a lot of faith in your powers of persuasion."

For good reason, he thought grudgingly. He was still stunned by his own response to the kiss that had been intended only to taunt her. But she had responded with a passion that seemed too raw to be an act, and he had abruptly lost control of himself. She felt exactly right in his arms, an unreliable impression, as he was still trying to sort out which parts of Sandra St. Claire were real and which were removable. Either way, whatever he had been holding had felt very, very good. It was lucky that she'd given him the moment that he needed to recover himself. If she hadn't pushed him away when she had, it would have been easy to take that kiss to its natural conclusion, and God only knew the trouble that would have caused.

"So," he said, "which paper is it? One with a big budget, obviously."

"I *told* you," she said. Her face had gone from white to red. "I'm not from the press. I have no intention of writing a single word about you, and I wouldn't even demean myself by buying a magazine that considered you important enough to write about!"

"How charming," Jake said. "Thanks. You're reminding me more of the professor all the time. Is Molly Shaw your real name?"

"Yes," she said. "You knew who I was before you kissed me. How dare you! You were *mocking* me!"

Jake laughed. He couldn't help it. She apparently didn't see any irony in accusing *him* of mocking *her*. She was sitting there straight-backed, outraged, glaring at him as if she were a nun whose bottom had just been pinched, and Jake was glad. She deserved a dose of her own medicine. He didn't appreciate being the only fool in a group of two.

"Actually, Ms. Shaw," he said, "if you want to get technical about it, I didn't know who you were when I kissed you, and I still don't."

"You know what I mean," she snapped. "When did you figure it out? Just now? Or have you known since this morning?"

Jake shrugged. No point in easing her mind. Let her work herself into a lather, worrying that he had been laughing at her all day. The more upset she was, the better his chances of getting the truth out of her. "If you're not from the press—which I find hard to believe—then who the hell are you? A history professor? A novelist? Or just a girl with a wig collection who likes to travel?"

"I'm a history professor," Molly Shaw said. "I told you. I specialize in—"

"The eighteenth-century Caribbean," Jake said dryly. "Yes, I know. You told me. At length." His tone of voice conveyed his opinion of her stuffy curriculum vitae. She bit her lip and looked away.

"And Sandra St. Claire?" he asked. "I know that she exists, because I've seen her book in the gift shop. Did you have a specific reason for impersonating her, or did you just feel a sudden urge to liven up your life by pretending to be someone else?"

None of it made any sense to him. Only a lunatic would behave like this, but his instincts told him that Molly wasn't crazy. Quirky, yes. A little volatile, sure. But sane. So what the hell did she think she was doing?

She sat silently, staring into the distance. Her lips were pressed together, and he saw her blink hard, several times.

"Well?" he asked.

Molly turned sharply to face him. Her eyes were wide and bright with suppressed tears. "I *am* Sandra St. Claire," she said in a tremulous voice.

Oh, shit, Jake thought, a sinking feeling in his stomach. Had he misjudged the situation? He had never actually met a lunatic, after all, so how would he recognize one if he did? He remembered that on the news, the neighbors of the serial killer always said some version of the same thing. *He seemed like such a nice man. So normal. Who would have guessed that he was burying bodies under the rosebushes?*

Molly Shaw took a deep breath. "I am Sandra St. Claire," she said again. She sounded as if she were talking to herself, as much as to him. "And I am *not* boring."

"Of course you are," Jake said soothingly. "Sandra, that is. Not boring. Definitely not boring."

"I'm serious," she said. "I wrote *Pirate Gold*. But it's a secret."

Jake nodded pleasantly. She was definitely a nutcase. He tried to remember if he had seen anything sharper than a butter knife in the picnic basket. He didn't think so, but he wasn't sure. She was small, and he could overpower her if he had to, but it would not be pretty if she got her hands onto something with an edge.

She sighed. "I shouldn't have told you. The press was after me for months, but they never found me, because I never told anyone. Only Carter. And now, you."

Great, Jake thought. *Carter. And now, me*. Who was Carter, and what had happened to him? He had an uneasy moment until he remembered that Carter was her friend, the little man in Bermuda shorts. He was not buried under anybody's rosebushes. That was a good sign, at least.

"If the truth gets out, I'll lose my job," Molly Shaw said urgently. "My life will be ruined. So, please, would you promise not to tell anyone about this? It has to be completely confidential. Completely."

"Absolutely," Jake said immediately. "Your secret is safe with me. And we should probably be getting back to the resort now, don't you think?"

Mercifully, there was no sign of Carter when Molly returned to the cottage, disheveled and miserable. She didn't know how she would explain that the project was over, that it had failed horribly, and that it was all her fault.

She collapsed onto the couch and dropped her head into her hands. If only she had never gone to the plantation ruins! Who would have guessed that Jake would show up there? But he had, and that encounter had ruined everything. If he had never met Molly Shaw, he would never have seen through the Sandra disguise. She still didn't know when he had figured it out. On the beach? Was that why he had accepted her invitation to lunch? Or had it been up at Falcon's Point, when she stupidly mentioned his golf course? What had she been thinking? Her ego had inflated as quickly as her cleavage, and this was the price of arrogance. She had actually begun to believe that she had a knack for the flirting game. She should have known better.

It didn't matter, either way. Jake knew the truth, and he was laughing at her. He had kissed her, not because he was attracted to her, and not because she had successfully seduced him. He had done it because he had guessed the truth, and wanted to humiliate her before he confronted her. And the way he had kissed her . . . and the way she had kissed him back . . . her breath caught in her throat, just thinking about it. He had used some kind of unethical playboy billionaire trick to coax that response out of her, damn him. He didn't kiss like a normal man, and Molly thought that she had kissed enough normal men to know something about it.

She thought of Greg Ackerman, in high school. In retrospect, he had kissed like a Labrador retriever, but he had been on the football team, and he had eyes like Paul Newman. If a series of clandestine Saturday night make-out sessions qualified him as a boyfriend, he had been her first. In college, she had given up her taste for handsome jocks at about the same time that she had declared her history major. After that, she had dated a series of scholarly types, and had brought the very best ones home to meet her father. But of all the earnest academics that she'd kissed over the years, not a single one, not even the few that she'd slept with, had made her feel as if she had been turned inside out and then stuffed back into her own skin. She wondered what it meant. Was there something unusual about Jake Berenger, or should she simply have been kissing businessmen all along?

The doorbell chimed, and Molly lifted her head. Now that the heat of the moment was fading, she was starting to think that it had been really stupid to confess her secret to Jake. He had sworn on his honor not to tell anyone that she was Sandra St. Claire, but still, it would have been much safer to let him think that she was just a lunatic pretending to be a famous novelist. Why had she told him the truth?

It wasn't a real question, because she already knew the answer. Even if Jake Berenger would never be physically attracted to the real Molly Shaw, at least he would know that she was more than she seemed to be. He might not think much of her academic credentials, but he could never again dismiss her as frumpy, stuffy, or boring. Well, frumpy, maybe. But not stuffy. Or boring. *I wrote a best-selling novel*, she thought with sudden, defiant pride. *How about that?*

The door to Elaine's room opened, and Molly hurriedly straightened her clothes and smoothed the wig.

"My goodness," Elaine said when she saw Molly sitting on the couch. "You're back. And your makeup is ruined. Why? No, no, tell me later. I'm expecting Ingrid for tea. I told her to come alone, but if I know that *guru* of hers, he'll find a way to join us." She paused, one hand on the doorknob. "It's good that you're here, actually. Do me a favor, dear, and play along."

Molly had no time to protest before Elaine flung open the door.

"Ingrid!" Elaine cried. "How delightful to see you." There was a chilly pause. "And Mr. Guru, too . . . what a surprise. I'm amazed that such a spiritual person as yourself would be interested in afternoon tea."

"The Spirit is always within us," said Rama Guru, escorting Ingrid into the room. "Even at teatime. *Namaste*, Sandra. I see that our karma has brought us together again."

"Indeed it has," Elaine said, looking speculatively at Rama Guru, who was looking at Molly. She smiled. "Well. Shall we all have tea?"

Molly excused herself to make a quick trip to the bathroom to repair her lipstick. When she came out, Ingrid was sitting silently on the couch next to Elaine. Elaine was gazing coldly at Rama Guru, who was perched on the ottoman, his legs crossed in the lotus position. A napkin was spread over his lap, and he was eating a scone with jam. One cucumber sandwich sat on Ingrid's plate, but she had not touched it.

"Sandra, dear," Elaine said, "have a seat. There." She

pointed to the chair closest to Rama Guru. "I'll pour you some tea. Ingrid was just telling me that she's moved out of her home in New York, which seems like a shame. You've always been fond of New York, haven't you, Ingrid? And you have so many ties there."

"One must strive to be free of earthly ties," Rama Guru remarked. "Only then can one know the joy of Ultimate Unity."

"What an interesting notion," Elaine said. "Some of us consider earthly ties to be quite valuable. Especially ties to husbands. Ingrid, I hear that Michael has taken your departure very badly."

Ingrid poked at her sandwich. "Gurudev says that one must choose one's own path."

"Does he. How nice to hear that Mr. Guru is so supportive of independent thinking. Where did you say that you're living now, dear?"

"Malibu. At the Temple of Light colony."

"I see," Elaine said.

"It's really beautiful," Ingrid added. "It has a private beach. I asked Michael to come with me, because I thought that he should join me on my spiritual journey, but he said no."

"Yes," Elaine said dryly. "I imagine that he did. It could be rather difficult to run a major brokerage house from the Temple of Light in Malibu. That sort of return address does tend to shake client confidence a bit."

"There are so many closed minds," Rama Guru said sadly. "So many seekers after false joy. Money can never be the Way to the Light."

Ingrid was nodding in agreement, and Elaine fixed her with an inquiring stare. "Really? Ingrid, I don't understand. I thought you were still working. What about the Revlon campaign? And didn't I just see you in the November issue of *Harper's Bazaar*?"

"Oh, it's not *making* money that's a problem on the Way to the Light," Ingrid said self-righteously. "It's keeping it, hoarding it. That's the kind of thing that divides you from others and makes you lonely in your prison of wealth. That's why it's better to share it with Gurudev and the other seekers at the Temple. That way, we're all One. Michael just doesn't understand that kind of joy."

"Yes, I'm sure that he finds the whole concept totally incomprehensible," Elaine said. "It's amazing, really. Who would ever have guessed that the Way to the Light would be right down Pacific Coast Highway?"

Molly piled her own plate with tiny sandwiches, and she had eaten her way through the smoked salmon, the cucumber, and the egg salad by the time she heard enough to deduce what was going on. If Elaine had facilitated the marriage between Ingrid and the forlorn Michael, then a lurid divorce would not be good for her reputation. She was determined to recover her client.

Poor Ingrid, Molly thought. She was beautiful, but not exactly bright, and now she had two pseudo-gurus fighting over her like dogs over a meaty bone. Given the choice, Molly had to side with Elaine. At least she wasn't trying to rob the girl. And if Michael really did love his dim-witted wife, maybe Elaine's intervention would do some good.

". . . has been working on her next novel," Molly heard Elaine saying to Rama Guru as she tuned back in to the conversation. "She's already received a very large advance for it. Sandra, dear, did you ever expect to become so rich at such a young age?"

Molly stared at her, confused. Nothing that Elaine was saying was true. She wasn't working on a novel, she had no advance, and although she was making a nice bit of money from *Pirate Gold*, she wasn't anywhere close to rich. What was Elaine doing? She didn't know, but she guessed that she was about to find out.

She smiled at Rama Guru. "I never expected to become so rich," she said. "It's a . . . uh . . . miracle of karma. Lucky me."

Rama Guru gazed warmly at her. "Sandra, you have indeed been blessed. But you are also in terrible danger."

"I am?" Molly widened her eyes. "Oh, dear."

"Your blessings mean the Spirit has chosen you, my child. But this wealth is a test, and unless you take great care, it will prevent you from ever finding the One True Path to Joy."

"Oh, no," Molly said. "I'd hate for that to happen. Whatever shall I do?"

"It is possible that I can help you," Rama Guru said solemnly. "Tell me, my child, exactly *how* blessed have you been?"

Molly glanced at Elaine, who gave her an almost imperceptible nod. "Very blessed," Molly said. She looked at Elaine again. Elaine was still nodding. "Very, very blessed," Molly continued. "You could say that I have recently received millions and millions of blessings."

Elaine smiled with satisfaction and sipped her tea.

Rama Guru's eyes were fixed on Molly. "Sandra, I can feel the Spirit within you. But you are lonely, are you not, my child? It would be my honor to help you find the Way of Truth."

"What a kind and generous offer," Elaine exclaimed. "Sandra, dear, I think that you should discuss your loneliness with Mr. Guru. Go and take a walk on the beach. Together. Now."

Duh, Molly thought, annoyed with herself for taking so

long to figure out Elaine's plan. She was trying to get rid of Rama Guru so that she could work on Ingrid, and Sandra was the bait to lure him away. Well, fine. The more that Molly saw of Ingrid's guru, the more she disliked him. She was beginning to think that it was her ethical duty to help Elaine deprogram—or at least reprogram—the girl.

"It's true," she said, looking at Rama Guru with what she hoped was a pathetic expression. "But I can't talk about my pain in front of other people. Only with you. I feel a special connection to you. Is it okay for me to say that?"

Rama Guru nodded. "Of course, my child." He looked thoughtfully at Ingrid, then back at Molly. He smiled and stood up, apparently having decided that potential gain of Sandra was worth the risk of leaving Ingrid unguarded for a short time. "Come," he said, "together, we shall walk."

CHAPTER 14

"A *lunatic*?" Cora Berenger repeated, staring at Jake. "What do you mean, the professor is a lunatic? Darling, *you* sound like a lunatic. You're raving. And you have pink lip gloss on your shirt." She raised her eyebrows at him. "The Kopplesons were very sorry to miss you at lunch, but Amanda was thrilled to hear that you'll be teaching her to scuba dive."

Jake exhaled sharply. "Listen," he said. "This is important. Remember Molly Shaw? The professor who you thought was such a nice girl? Well, your 'nice girl' has been dressing up in a wig, and"—he gestured graphically—"padding! And going around the resort telling people that she's Sandra St. Claire."

Cora was sitting on the terrace of the villa, under the shade of a bougainvillea-covered trellis, drinking tea as she watched her son pace back and forth in front of the table.

"Good heavens," she said, putting down her cup. "You're serious?"

"Yes."

"The woman who we thought was Sandra St. Claire has been Molly Shaw all along? Are you sure?"

"Positive."

"But . . . how odd. Why would she do a thing like that?"

Jake stopped in his tracks. "Why?" he repeated. "I told you, she's a lunatic. She believes that she actually *is* this novelist. She was dressed up as Sandra when I figured out the truth, and she got very upset when I confronted her. I had to soothe her—"

"Soothe her?" Cora inquired. Her eyes moved over the pink smudges on his shirt. "How did you manage that? And how exactly did you figure out that Sandra was Molly Shaw?"

"That's beside the point," Jake growled. "I managed to get her back to the resort without a serious incident. She's in her cottage now, and I don't know what the hell we're supposed to do about this. I'm a developer, not a shrink. This is outside my field of expertise."

"Darling, I'm finding this all a bit hard to believe. I talked to Molly Shaw for quite a while last night, and I thought that she was a nice, intelligent, and perfectly sane woman."

"So did I," Jake said darkly. "They're tricky, these crazy people. They fool you. You should have heard her. She told me this nutty story about how she really is Sandra St. Claire, but nobody knows the truth, and the media has been after her for months, but they never discovered her true identity, and it's all a big secret that I can't ever tell anyone."

"Hmm," Cora said thoughtfully. "Interesting."

"It isn't *interesting*," Jake exclaimed. "It's sick. We can't let this woman prance around Gold Bay telling people that she's a famous novelist. I see a mess coming, and it's the size of a train wreck. What happens when the real Sandra hears about the vacation she never took? And what if Molly Shaw gets tired of playing with her wig and high heels and really goes wacko? We know that she's mentally unstable, and that makes us legally liable. We need to get her out of here. Fast. But quietly."

"Darling, sit down," Cora said. "Watching you going back and forth like that is giving me a headache. I feel like I'm at a tennis match. Have a cup of tea."

"I don't want a cup of tea," Jake said. "I hate tea. What I *want* is to get this crazy woman out of my resort before she causes me serious trouble."

"It's possible that she isn't crazy."

Jake sighed. "You weren't there," he said, "so you don't understand, but take my word for it, she's—"

"Do you know anything about Sandra St. Claire?" Cora asked. She reached for the tea strainer, held it above her delicate porcelain cup, and poured slowly from the antique silver teapot.

"You mean the real one?"

Cora smiled mysteriously. "If there is a real one. I did a little research when I saw Sandra's name on the reservation list. Sit down, and I'll tell you what I know."

There was total silence in Cottage Five on Thursday morning, when Molly finally told Carter what had happened with Jake. She had delayed as long as she could, but Carter had awakened her with grand plans for Sandra's day, and she had been forced to confess the truth.

It was an agonizing, drawn-out silence, so heavy with gloom that it seemed to darken the sunshine around them. Molly stood, wrapped in her bathrobe, twisting her hands together as she waited for Carter to react. He sat on the couch, staring at her with the expression of a prisoner who had just been condemned.

"Carter," she said finally. "Say something. Please."

His mouth opened, closed, and opened again. "I don't

understand," he croaked. "What do you mean, Jake Berenger found out that Sandra St. Claire is you?"

"I'm sorry," Molly said anxiously. "It was an accident."

"Sorry? Accident? Last night, you told me that the picnic went well."

"It did go well," Molly said. "Relatively speaking. Jake was very nice about the whole thing, once he understood that I wasn't from the press. He said . . . uh . . . he said . . ." She stopped. She couldn't actually recall what Jake had said after she'd confessed to being Sandra. Her memory was still fuzzy from the trauma.

"I knew he was smart," Carter said hollowly. "I knew that. I could have told you that it would be too risky for him to spend time with both Molly *and* Sandra. Especially in the space of a few hours. You should have told me. We could have changed the plan. Why didn't you tell me?"

"I'm sorry," Molly repeated. "I don't know why I didn't tell you. I just didn't think it would be a problem. Sandra is so different from me, and I didn't think Jake would ever guess—"

"Different!" Carter exclaimed suddenly, throwing his hands in the air. He looked accusingly at her. "Sandra *is* you. She's not different at all! Sure, she has different hair, and wears different clothes, and actually talks to men instead of typing dialogue, but she *is* you, Molly. It's obvious if you look closely. He wasn't supposed to get a close look at *both* of you!"

Molly burst into tears. "Stop yelling at me!" she yelled at him. "How was I supposed to know that he would figure it out? You should have warned me—"

"I didn't think I needed to warn you, because it was so *obvious*! I never thought you'd be stupid enough to—"

"Children!" The bedroom door slammed behind Elaine like an exclamation point, and she appeared before them, imperious as an Olympian goddess, the robe of her black and red negligee swirling around her like smoke and fire. "*What* on *earth* is happening here?"

Molly and Carter stared at her, dumbstruck. Her hair was hidden under the giant pouf of a satin shower cap, and her face was covered with a shiny, viscous substance. Attached to her forehead, her cheeks, and her chin were six flat white discs the size of quarters. A thin wire protruded from each disc, joining below her chin into one thick wire that ran down to a small white box that she held in her hand.

"Well?" she asked impatiently. "I'm afraid that I wasn't able to hear the exact details through the walls of my room."

"What's that stuff on your face?" Carter said finally. He looked horrified, as if he had just discovered that his sister was a cyborg.

"Conducting gel," Elaine said. "Electrical stimulation of the facial muscles for twenty minutes every morning firms the jawline and softens wrinkles. *Except* when one's relaxation time is interrupted by one's travel companions screaming at each other like chimpanzees. Would someone kindly explain this to me? Why is Molly crying?"

"I'm not crying," Molly said. She wasn't, anymore. Elaine's sudden appearance had shocked the tears right out of her. She sniffled, wondering how Carter had managed to upset her so much. Everything felt different these days—more intense, and more real, which made no sense to her. Her real life was at home, in Belden, and she would be back there soon. She sighed, thinking about it. Even that life was starting to feel like just another role to play. *Sandra is you*, Carter had said, as if he were speaking to an idiot. *Fine*, Molly thought. *Sandra is me. I am she. And who am I, again?*

The tension between Molly and Carter hadn't improved by the time that they sat down to breakfast. After breaking the momentum of the fight, Elaine had returned to her bedroom and reemerged a short time later as her usual well-groomed self, a relief to Molly, who couldn't shake off the mental image of Carter's sister looking like a mutant clone in a science fiction movie. It was chilling, although she had to admit that Elaine's jawline did look firm.

Carter settled into a brooding silence, punctuated only by resentful glances at Molly, who was trying to ignore him. She was reading the letter that had arrived that morning from the director of the Museum of Antigua and Barbuda. She'd phoned him the previous day, in an attempt to gather information about the plantation ruins. Many of the original documents from colonial Antigua had been relocated to the Public Record Office in London, but Molly had hoped that the museum's own collection might contain something useful.

The only lead was a map of Cane Island from 1798, the height of the sugar trade. There had been several estates on the island at that time, the director wrote, and Molly had apparently visited the ruins of a plantation once called "Dyer's Fortune." He knew of nothing in the museum's archives that connected the old estate—or the island—to Mary Morgan, although he, too, had heard the stories.

He had enclosed a copy of part of the old map, and Molly recognized the signature shapes of the western coast and the salt ponds. Two crosses marked the location of the two windmills, and next to them the name "Dyer's Fortune" was written in spidery script.

"Hmm," she said, frowning. It was a common sort of name for an old colonial plantation, similar to "Betty's Hope," on Antigua. She had been hoping for something more definitive, like "Morgan's Rest" or "Bonny Mary's House." Still, the use of the word "fortune" was provocative. During her pirating days, Mary's ship had been called the *Lady Fortune*. Was it just a coincidence, or could there be a link?

"What's that letter?" Carter asked.

"Just some research on the old sugar estate," Molly said absently. She needed more information—the kind that was probably buried in an archive in England. But her contact at the National Maritime Museum was on vacation, and wouldn't be back in the office until January second. And her friend at the British Library hadn't returned her call, which suggested that he was also missing in action. It was only a few days before Christmas, after all.

"Sugar estate?" Carter repeated. "You mean, that place where you talked to Jake and ruined my chances of—"

"Carter!" Elaine said sharply. "Please."

"I was simply going to ask why Molly is doing research on an old sugar estate. And why Jake Berenger was there, too. I think I have a right to know, considering that this was what shattered my only hope of ever—"

He broke off at Elaine's warning look. Molly sighed and explained the story of Mary Morgan, the golf course, and the plantation ruins. As Carter listened, his expression slowly shifted from gloomy to pensive to hopeful.

"This could be good," he said. "If that plantation did belong to Bonny whatshername, and we can find proof, then Jake's golf course is in trouble. We could go to the press with an exposé about Berenger Corporation ruthlessly bulldozing over a local heritage site. Yes! We can use this."

"Use it how?" Molly asked suspiciously.

"In case you haven't noticed, Jake isn't in any position to take any more negative publicity. And relocating a golf course can't be cheap. I'll bet he'd be willing to negotiate . . ."

"Are you saying that we could threaten to cause a scandal unless he agrees to help you with your book?"

Carter nodded eagerly. "Right!"

"Wrong!" Molly exclaimed, appalled. "I can't blackmail Jake Berenger. Even if I were willing—which I'm not—there are two serious problems with your idea. First, I don't have proof that the plantation belonged to Bonny Mary. And second, Jake could just as easily blackmail *me*, now that he knows . . . the truth." She glanced warily at Elaine, who sat nibbling on her croissant.

"Don't mind me," Elaine said. "Molly, dear, I've known for days that you really are Sandra St. Claire. You two aren't nearly as clandestine as you think you are."

"Oh, terrific," Molly said. She tossed the papers onto the table and took a deep breath. "Elaine, I'm sorry for everything rude that I've ever said to you. I'll do whatever you want in exchange, but please, promise that you won't—"

"Don't be silly," Elaine said. "Of course I won't tell. I am not the sort of person who ruins other people's lives for fun. Or profit, despite what my ex-husbands might say. Discretion is essential to my work, and although you aren't exactly a client, I consider you a friend."

"You do?" Molly asked, taken aback.

"Yes," Elaine said. "Although, as a friend, I have to say that I can't understand why you prefer to keep teaching at that stuffy college rather than taking the credit for—"

"Okay, okay," Molly said. "Thank you. You sound just like Carter, and he already knows my position on this."

Carter nodded. "She doesn't want to talk about it," he explained.

Elaine shrugged. "Suit yourself."

"Molly, listen," Carter said urgently. "This thing about Jake knowing that you're Sandra isn't a problem. He won't use it against you if he thinks that you've got something to use against him. It'll be a standoff. You have to make him think that you have the proof, and then mention my book. It's not blackmail, it's just . . . a business discussion."

"I'll try to talk to him," Molly said reluctantly. She dreaded the thought of seeing Jake again, but she felt that she owed it to Carter. "But I'm tired of lying. I'll tell him that I'm still working on linking Mary to the ruins, which is true. And I'll bring up your book, and try to persuade him to work with you. That's the best I can do. All right?"

"I guess so," Carter said. "Call the manager's office and tell them that you have information on the old plantation, and you have to see Jake today."

"Not so fast," Elaine said. "Molly can't meet with him until tomorrow. Or Saturday."

Carter looked alarmed. "But we leave on Sunday morning. If he'll see her today, then why not—"

"Tomorrow," Elaine said firmly. "If Molly is going to be meeting with Jake Berenger, then I owe it to her—and to myself, as a professional—to make a few adjustments first."

"Adjustments?" Molly asked.

"Yes," Elaine said. "Molly, dear, you and I will be spending the rest of today at the Gold Bay salon and spa."

CHAPTER 15

"I am so, so excited to finally learn to scuba dive," Amanda said over breakfast on Friday. "Jake, you are so totally sweet to offer to teach me."

Offer? Jake thought dryly. He didn't need to look at Cora. He could feel her warning look burning into the side of his face.

"I've wanted to learn ever since I was really little," Amanda continued. "I used to be crazy about those Thoreau specials on TV. I still watch them sometimes, on the Discovery channel."

Jake frowned. To his knowledge, Henry David Thoreau had never scuba dived in Walden Pond. True, Amanda had a college degree and he didn't, but he was fairly sure about that.

"I think you mean Cousteau, darling," Cora said. "Jacques Cousteau? The famous underwater naturalist?"

"Oh, right," Amanda said. She laughed. "Oops. I always get those French guys mixed up."

Jake bit down hard on a piece of toast and said nothing. It wasn't that he didn't like Amanda. He did. He had known her since she was a toddler, and he had always liked her, more or less. But having her force-fed to him was making him surly, and everything that used to seem cute about

Harry's daughter had now become irritating. It was a serious tactical mistake on his mother's part. She should have known better, but she was obviously getting desperate to marry him off. For a normally sensible woman, Cora Berenger was unreasonably pigheaded about this issue. Her rightful place, as she saw it, was as the grand matriarch of the Berenger dynasty, and if her errant son would only get with the program, things would work out as Fate had intended.

"I'm going to go get ready," Amanda announced, standing up. "Can I wear a bikini? I didn't bring anything else. For swimming, I mean. I don't need a wet suit, do I?"

"Nope," Jake said. "We'll manage."

"Good," Amanda said. "I only asked because when I was at the beach the other day, I saw you talking to that woman, Sandra St. Claire, and she was wearing a wet suit." She wrinkled her nose. "It wasn't very flattering. It made her thighs look big, don't you think?"

"I didn't notice," Jake said. He hadn't been looking at her thighs. At the time, he had been more focused on what he now knew to be a large quantity of foam rubber, and the whole subject of Molly Shaw aggravated him. After the fiasco at Falcon's Point, he had called Sonny Carmichael, the chairman of Leighton House, publisher of *Pirate Gold.* Sonny was a family friend and a Berenger client, and Jake hoped that he would be able to clear up this mystery. So far, he hadn't heard back from Sonny, and he had spent the past thirty-six hours bracing for some kind of lunatic explosion. Molly Shaw didn't know it, but the Gold Bay security staff had been directed to keep a close eye on her.

"Oh," Cora said suddenly, as if she'd just remembered something.

"What?" Amanda asked.

"Nothing, dear," Cora said. "Go and change into your swimsuit. Jake wants to get started right away."

Amanda disappeared into the house, and Jake looked inquiringly at his mother.

"Sandra," Cora said. "Or Molly Shaw, I should say. Amanda just reminded me. Sonny called this morning, and our professor is legitimate."

Jake stared at her. "Are you serious? Molly Shaw was telling me the truth? She really is Sandra St. Claire?"

"You wouldn't believe what it took to get the information out of Sonny," Cora continued. "He said that he didn't call back right away because even *he* didn't know who Sandra really was. He had to call her editor, and then the company's lawyers, and then he told me that if we weren't such old friends, and if he didn't trust me so completely, he wouldn't dream of saying a word. And *then*, after all of that, he made me swear on my life not to tell anyone. You're also bound by my oath of silence."

"She must be making a hell of a lot of money for Leighton," Jake said, reluctantly impressed. "And they must be hoping for more. But what's with all the secrecy?" He remembered the anxiety on Molly Shaw's face when she asked him—begged him, in fact—not to betray her. She had said something about losing her job, hadn't she? It made no sense to him.

"I haven't a clue," Cora said. "Perhaps you should ask her yourself. She called my office yesterday, and left a message saying that she urgently needs to speak with you about the old sugar plantation."

"What about it?" Jake asked apprehensively. That wasn't good. After Wednesday, he had relaxed, assuming that the dramatic story of Mary Morgan the Pirate Queen was just another invention of Molly Shaw's twisted mind. But Molly's mind was beginning to sound less twisted, and if

Mary Morgan was actually real, then trouble still loomed on the horizon.

He exhaled in frustration. Trouble, indeed. Molly Shaw was causing him no end of it, at a time when he didn't need any more complications in his life. "Invite her to the house this afternoon," he said. "Early. I'll find out what she wants, and deal with her."

If nothing else, it would be interesting to see who showed up, calling herself Molly Shaw. The dowdy professor? The bombshell blonde? Or someone else entirely?

"I still don't feel like . . . me, exactly," Molly said, staring at her reflection in the vanity-table mirror. It was Friday morning after breakfast, and Elaine was busily sorting through the Sandra St. Claire clothes, picking out pieces that could be adapted to fit into Molly's new, improved wardrobe. The rejects were tossed unceremoniously onto the floor. Out went the pink wet suit, the tight white bustier, the fuchsia cocktail dress, the white hot pants, the double-D bras, and all of the platform heels. Also cast aside were most of the things that Molly had brought in her own suitcase, including a shapeless beige cardigan sweater, two boxy men's T-shirts, a long India-print skirt, and a pair of old Birkenstock sandals, which Elaine had handled with a grimace, as if she were disposing of a dead rat.

The survivors were laid on the bed: the pink and white Hermès scarf, the gauzy white button-down shirt, a peachy pink cocktail dress, a simple silk camisole, and the silver sandals. From Molly's own collection, Elaine included a pair of faded jeans, a simple white cotton sweater, and a pair of loose navy linen pants.

"Don't worry," Elaine said briskly. "You'll be fine. It always takes time to adjust to change. And this was a rather dramatic change."

Molly had to agree. The previous afternoon, under Elaine's direction, a stylist at the Gold Bay salon had layered Molly's hair into a softly tousled style that fell just below her shoulders. Shorter pieces in the front accented cheekbones that Molly hadn't realized that she owned. After the cut, she had been handed off to a woman who took one look at her and said briskly, "Highlights. Butterscotch and gold. Here, and here. And here."

Elaine was nodding approval, but Molly balked. "Just a minute," she said, "does that mean blond? I don't want to be blond."

The colorist looked shocked. "But you're perfect for it. Lightening your hair would lift your whole look."

"No blond," Molly said stubbornly. "Do something else. How about auburn?"

"No, no, dear," Elaine said. "Not with your skin tone. Red wouldn't suit you. If you don't want blond, we'll do a lighter brown, nothing drastic, just a little warmth, a little depth, as if you've been out in the sun." She turned to the colorist. "Caramel," she said decisively. "Not butterscotch."

"I feel like a sundae," Molly said, trying to cover her nervousness. She couldn't believe that she was allowing Elaine to do this to her, but for some reason that defied logic, she trusted Carter's sister.

It had been a good decision. Her hair—blown dry to a bouncy smoothness—shimmered like amber satin. She had been running her fingers through it since they left the salon yesterday. It was amazing to think that this stuff was attached to her own scalp.

Sandra's makeup palette had also been edited to suit Molly. Out went the frosted blue eye shadow, the sticky pink lip gloss, the liquid bronzer, and the shimmery white highlighter. The new kit consisted of undereye concealer, taupe eye shadow from Elaine's own supplies, a smoky eyeliner pencil, mascara, sheer cream blush, and a peachy lipstick selected by the spa makeup artist.

Like a child with a new toy, Molly had gotten up early that morning and gone through the whole ritual again, alone in the bathroom. It took fifteen minutes to smooth out her hair with the blow dryer and a round brush, and ten more to apply the makeup, but the results were almost as astonishing as they had been the first time.

She wasn't beautiful, but she had never expected to be beautiful, so it was no disappointment. She was polished, though, in a stylish way that made her feel like a new person. She didn't look like a clone of Elaine, or a toned-down version of Sandra, or even a scrubbed-up version of her former self. She looked entirely different. And pretty. Actually pretty.

She was still stuck with her glasses for the moment, but they didn't look all that bad. With her new makeup and her streaky, tousled hair, they gave her a sort of sexy, intellectual look. She smiled at her reflection, hesitantly at first, and then with more confidence. There was a lump forming in her throat.

"Good heavens," Elaine said from behind her. She was holding up Molly's favorite bra, which was several years old, a faded beige, and stretched-out from a few too many spins in the dryer. It was comfortable, though, and Molly was fond of it.

"Out," Elaine said, tossing it onto the reject pile.

"You can't throw that out," Molly protested. "I need it. What else am I supposed to wear under my clothes?"

"For now, nothing," Elaine said. "It worked for Marilyn Monroe, and frankly, dear, wearing nothing would be preferable to wearing . . . that. You're small enough to get away with it, especially in this environment. When we get home to Chicago, I'll take you shopping. Among other things, it will be my pleasure to instruct you on the art and science of lingerie."

CHAPTER 16

"Would you like another cup of coffee, Dr. Shaw?" asked Cora Berenger's butler.

"No," Molly said. "Thank you." She had accepted the first cup mostly to have something to hold in her restless hands, but after sitting for ten minutes on the Berengers' terrace, waiting for Jake, she had slowly sipped the whole thing down.

The villa was made of local stone, and it seemed to rise organically from the low cliffs just uphill from the resort—far enough removed for privacy, but close enough to be at the Gold Bay beach after a fifteen-minute walk. The resort wasn't actually visible from the villa, but Molly knew that it lay just beyond the jetty of rock coming out from the cliffs to the right. The house was high enough so that the crash of waves against the rocks below was softly soothing, and to the left rose the green slopes of the mountain. The terrace was large, built for entertaining, and connected to the house through three large sets of French doors, all standing open to admit the ocean breeze. Crimson bougainvillea climbed the stone walls of the villa, reaching and twining over the top of a wooden trellis that shaded one side of the terrace. This was where Molly had finally settled down to drink her coffee.

She felt as far removed from her apartment in Belden as she would have felt in the middle of an Egyptian bazaar.

It was another five minutes before Jake appeared. "I apologize for keeping you waiting," he said. "I was on a business call."

"That's okay," Molly said. "I've been enjoying the view." She regretted the words as soon as they left her mouth. The last thing she wanted to do was to remind him of the last time that they had been together, discussing a view.

Jake nodded. From his manner—polite and slightly distant—he hadn't noticed her accidental reference. It was as if that day had never happened, and oddly, Molly felt both relieved and disappointed.

He looked her over with a clinically curious eye. "So, Professor, you've changed again. Is this the real Molly Shaw?"

"Uh . . . yes," Molly said. "I think so."

"You think so?"

"I'm not wearing a wig, if that's what you're asking. And from now on, I'll probably look more or less like this."

"And Sandra?"

"Sandra is retired."

"And her alter ego? The mousy scholar?"

"In a sense, she's retired, too," Molly said. It was a testament to Elaine's abilities that Jake thought that her premakeover self had also been a disguise. "But that one is a little more complicated."

"Okay, Ms. Shaw," Jake said. "I used to think that I was a smart guy, but you have me completely stumped. What the hell have you been doing at my resort? Was this some kind of publicity stunt for your book? Didn't you know that we don't allow press on the island?"

"Oh, my God," Molly said. "Publicity? No. I wasn't looking for press. Just the opposite. I told you."

"You told me that you're not a journalist, and you have no desire to write about me. Fine. I like that in a woman. But if you aren't *from* the press, and you aren't looking *for* press, then . . . ?" He looked inquiringly at her, as if to say, *fill in the blank.*

Molly sighed. She hadn't planned to tell him the whole truth, but she was getting the feeling that it would be a good idea. At least it would make things less convoluted, and maybe restore a little of her credibility. Jake did have a sense of humor, so he might find the whole thing funny. "Well," she said, "actually, I was looking for you."

He nodded. "I guessed that. But like I said, if you wanted to have Sandra photographed with me, you picked the wrong place. There aren't any paparazzi hiding in our bushes. Or does your little friend Carter have a secret camera?"

"No," Molly said. "My litt—I mean, my *friend* Carter is a journalist. He was the one who helped me get *Pirate Gold* published, so I owe him a favor."

"Which was to do what?"

"Try to convince you to work with him on a project. He wants to write your biography. He's a very talented writer, and I know he'd do a great job. He did a profile on Donald Trump for *Esquire* magazine. Here's a folder of some other work that he's published . . ."

She stopped. Jake was shaking his head in disbelief.

"Are you telling me," he said, "that the blond bombshell getup was designed to catch my attention so that you could persuade me to work on a book with your friend?"

Molly grinned gamely. "Yes. Can you believe it? It's kind of funny, isn't it? Funny?"

"That's one word for it," Jake said. He wasn't smiling. "Why did you pick that particular character for the job?"

"We did some research on you, and she seemed like your type."

"Did she," he said dryly. "Interesting. I can see why you would think that, but you don't know me, do you? Any more than I know you."

"I guess not," Molly said. It didn't look as if he intended to laugh this off.

"And the mousy professor? What was the goal there?"

"Oh," Molly said awkwardly. "No goal. That really was me. I had my hair cut at the Gold Bay salon yesterday. They're very good."

"Apparently so," Jake said. "But I'm still not clear on the Mary Morgan bit. I was told that you came here to talk to me about the ruins."

"I did. I wanted to tell you that I have more information. From the museum director on Antigua. It's an old map, and I thought you would be interested."

"I assumed that the Bonny Mary story was also fictional."

"Fictional?" Molly echoed, surprised. "No, of course not. Why would you think that?"

"Let's see," Jake said. "Why would I think that something you told me wasn't true?"

Molly felt her face reddening. "Actually," she said, "almost everything I ever said to you was true. I just looked different when I said it, but I suppose that men like you are easily confused by that kind of thing."

He didn't answer, and she continued. "There are plenty of documents confirming that Mary existed. I was also telling the truth when I said that I think she lived on this island."

Jake exhaled slowly. He motioned toward the table. "Fine," he said. "Sit down and show me what you have."

Molly looked suspiciously at him. He certainly wasn't wearing the expression of a man who *felt very strongly about the preservation of important cultural heritage sites*, as he had claimed the other day. He looked more like a man who wished that she would disappear and take her heritage site with her.

She pulled out the copy of the old map and put it on the table, turning it to face him. "Here," she said, pointing. "Do you recognize the coastline? The salt ponds? Those two crosses represent the two windmills. The name of the plantation was Dyer's Fortune."

"And?" Jake asked.

"Mary's ship was called the *Lady Fortune*," Molly said.

He nodded. "What else?"

"Um . . . that's it," Molly said.

"That's it? That's all you have?"

"For now, yes. But I have friends at the British Library and the Public Records Office, and I'll be checking with them as soon as they're back at work after the holidays. It's possible that the name Dyer is connected to Mary's family in some way."

"Time is getting short," Jake said. "We had agreed on two weeks, which will be almost gone by the time that the holidays are over."

"I know, but I might need a little longer to find the information."

"Or to confirm that you can't find it," Jake said. "I'm afraid that I have to draw the line at two weeks."

"But—" Molly began, dismayed.

Jake shook his head. "I wish I could give you more time, Professor, but I can't afford to. I'm sorry, but the project needs to move forward. Every day's delay costs my company money . . . money that belongs to the Berenger shareholders."

"But this is important," Molly exclaimed. "I'm not just going to stop searching after two weeks! What if I turn up the proof after you've bulldozed half of the site?"

Jake looked coolly at her. "That's a good question," he said. "What if you do?"

She thought of what Carter had said, and met Jake's gaze, steeling herself. She had no intention of trying to blackmail him into doing Carter's project—friendship only went so far. But she was willing to fight a little harder on Mary's behalf. "It wouldn't look very good for your company—in the press, I mean—to be caught destroying Bonny Mary's plantation, would it?"

His mouth curved slightly. "I agree. That might be a problem for us."

"Then you have to give me more time. You don't have any choice."

"Don't I?" Jake asked. "Because it seems to me that it might be a problem for *you* if the press found out about your novel-writing habit."

Molly gasped. "What?"

"I think that we understand each other."

"Are you telling me that if I try to go to the press with any information that connects Dyer's Fortune to Mary Morgan, you'll expose me as Sandra St. Claire?"

"Yes," Jake said. "And let me add that you started this fight. You just threatened me, Professor. I've done my best to be reasonable and helpful, to the limits of my ability. Whereas you have been conning me, my staff, and my guests. You've been using unethical methods to try to manipulate me into working with your friend—"

"Unethical methods!" Molly exclaimed. "You kissed me, just to humiliate me! What do you call that, morally upstanding?"

Jake grinned. "You didn't seem to mind at the time."

"I was acting," Molly said coldly. "I found the whole experience very unpleasant."

"Then I'm impressed. You're a hell of an actress."

Molly glared at him, nearly speechless with fury. With shaking hands she gathered up her papers and clutched them to her chest. "That's it," she said through her teeth. "This discussion is over."

He was chuckling as he watched her. "So soon? You were off to a good start, Professor. Blackmail can be very effective when it's done right. But then, you have a habit of starting games that you can't follow through, don't you?"

Berenger Chief Battles Wall Street Critics—
and Rumors of Personal Chaos

Until recently, Jake Berenger, the flamboyant chief executive of Berenger Corporation, seemed to have it all. But even the mighty can fall. With Berenger stock languishing at an all-time low, the once-celebrated playboy billionaire is now dogged by rumors of serial womanizing and drug use. Mr. Berenger was unavailable for comment, but a company spokesman claimed that the accusations were without merit.

"I'm getting very tired of that term," Jake said darkly, tossing the printout down onto his desk. It was late on Friday afternoon, and his office had just faxed him an article due to run in Saturday's *Washington Post.*

"Playboy billionaire?" asked Cora. She had been reading over his shoulder. "You were the one who courted that image, dear. Isn't it a bit hypocritical to get angry at the press now that it's suddenly working against you?"

Jake leaned back in his chair, crossed his arms against his chest, and scowled at her.

She gazed right back at him. "Well," she said, "don't worry. You won't have to suffer with it much longer. The stock is down almost two dollars since the *Wall Street Journal* article, which means that—technically—you aren't a billionaire anymore."

"Thanks," Jake said coldly. "That's great to hear. If you have any bright ideas about how to instantly repair my public image and get the stock price back up, I'd love to hear them. The best our PR department can do is to tell me to start promoting the Berenger Foundation. They say that our charitable donations have been too discreet, and I need to spend more time being photographed with sick children. How's that for hypocritical?"

"Over my dead body," Cora said, looking appalled. "That can't have been their only idea. These people are supposed to be good."

"They are, but they're not magicians. We're falling back on the usual strategy . . . trying to place positive articles while doing as much damage control as possible. I've been cutting costs for months, and rearranging our sales department, so our margins should be better this quarter, which will help. A market upswing would also be nice, but that one's out of my hands. It's going to take time."

Cora sat silently, tapping her fingers against the arm of the chair. Her lips were pressed together, and he could see that she was thinking hard. Finally, she exhaled. "Your PR team is wrong," she said. "This is not the time for the 'usual strategy.' This is an emergency situation. We need to be proactive."

"Believe me," Jake said, "I know. I've even been reconsidering the interview issue. But it's not going to help me to start talking to the press right now. If I suddenly show up on

TV, everyone will ask the obvious question: Why? And under the circumstances, the obvious answer is that I'm in trouble and I'm trying to save myself. If the street starts speculating about internal problems at Berenger, things are going to get a lot worse."

"I agree," Cora said. "Now isn't the time to start giving interviews. You'll need to do it soon, but not yet. First, we have to give the press a better story about you. Then, when they have something new to focus on, we'll put you on TV."

"You sound like you have something in mind," Jake said.

"I do," Cora said. She smiled at him. "It should make you very happy to hear that the era of the playboy billionaire is over. We're going to announce your official engagement to Amanda Harper."

Jake started to laugh. "For a minute," he said, "I thought you were serious."

"I am," Cora said indignantly. "And I haven't suddenly gone senile, so stop looking at me like that. It's a good idea. A splashy public engagement to a nice girl like Amanda would be the perfect way to handle your image problem. Everyone loves a reformed sinner. I can see the headlines now: 'Playboy Tamed by True Love.' "

Jake was beginning to think that he was the only sane person left on the island. "Let me make sure that I understand you," he said. "You want me to use Harry's daughter to patch up my reputation? Am I the only one who sees an ethical problem with this?"

"Yes," Cora said. "Because there is no problem. I'm not suggesting that we lie to the Harpers. Harry will love this idea. It's just the kind of stunt he'd come up with, and Amanda is hardly shy. She'll adore all of the attention—she's her daddy's daughter, after all. She's young enough to enjoy the drama of a scheme like this."

"And I'm old enough to know better," Jake said. "Forget it."

"All we need are a few months of you looking devoted and domestic. It will stop the rumors, make Skye's accusations look like sour grapes, improve your image, and give you the time you need to get the company back under control."

"And then? What is my new fiancée going to say when I thank her and show her the door? Because that's exactly what I'll do. I have no intention of marrying Amanda Harper, or anyone else."

"You don't have to marry her," Cora said. "Engagements are broken all the time. Maybe Amanda won't like *you* once she gets to know you."

"Or maybe we'll fall madly in love and live happily ever after? I appreciate your multilayer scheme, Ma, but this is more than I'm willing to do to indulge the tabloids. Or your hunger for grandchildren. Sorry. I'll figure out a way to handle this problem on my own."

Cora exhaled impatiently. "This is the perfect solution, don't you see? And Amanda is the obvious choice. She's a family friend, not an outsider. She understands this world."

"Her *father* is a family friend," Jake said. "Amanda is just a twenty-one-year-old kid. She may or may not understand what she'd be getting herself into. When Skye's manager called me to arrange our first date, Skye understood perfectly well that it was about business. It wasn't supposed to be personal, but look what happened."

"It must be terrible to be so irresistible, darling," Cora said dryly.

Jake ignored her. "Let's say that I do use Amanda Harper to build myself a new reputation as a born-again family man. What if she starts believing the hype?"

"That wouldn't happen," Cora said stubbornly.

"I wonder. I see a lot of agendas involved with this plan of yours, and several of them conflict with mine."

"Jake . . ."

"I'll tell you what else I see. Myself, in three months, being forced to choose between either marrying a woman I don't love, or facing another nasty public breakup *and* the loss of Harry Harper, my friend and most loyal board member. Not a pretty scenario, is it?"

Cora sighed. "All right," she said. "I surrender. But you have to admit, it was a good idea."

"Maybe. But to pull it off, we'd need a young, good-looking woman with a sterling reputation, no desire to use the press for her own purposes, and no interest in actually marrying me. We might be able to find a candidate at our local convent, but when you remember that she'd also need a talent for lying and deceit, it starts to look dicey. I don't know anyone who . . ." He broke off, startled. Unbelievable as it seemed, he actually did know someone who fit that bill.

"What?" Cora asked.

Jake frowned. Molly Shaw was more than attractive enough to make a believable fiancée. And he knew firsthand that she had a knack for lying and deceit. With her secret life as Sandra, and her associated paranoia about publicity, she was highly unlikely to start giving interviews à la Skye Elliot. And based on the way yesterday's encounter had ended, he felt safely able to say that she did not want to marry him.

"You're thinking of someone," Cora said eagerly. "Who?"

"Someone who would never agree to do it," he said. "Even if I decided to ask her. I'm not convinced that we need to take such drastic measures."

Cora looked frustrated. "Well," she said, "let me know when you are convinced. I just hope that by then, it won't be too late."

CHAPTER 17

At nine A.M. on Saturday morning, Jake was back in his office at the villa. He had just finished breakfast on the terrace, and was attacking his e-mail inbox. He had almost a thousand messages waiting for reply or deletion, and that was only a week of backlog.

The phone rang. The villa had five lines, including a satellite link, but his private number was the only one that went directly to his desk without being answered by Cora's staff. He picked it up. "Yes?"

"It's me," said Susan Horowitz, his executive assistant. "Good morning. I'm sure that it's much nicer weather where you are, but I don't want to hear about it."

"Susan," Jake said. "It's Saturday. Don't you have a personal life?" It was an old joke between them, and he knew for a fact that she did. Her ability to balance marriage, motherhood, the minute details of his business schedule, and a significant chunk of the rest of his life said a lot about her natural level of efficiency.

"Listen," Susan said. "I just got a very strange phone call from Ed Thatcher's office at Atlas. His assistant tracked me down at home—I don't know how, and it's creepy to think about it—but the thing is that Ed wants to talk to you. Now. They gave me a number to call to connect you."

"Why?" Jake asked warily. He didn't know Ed Thatcher personally, and he didn't want to. Ed was CEO of Atlas Group, Berenger's main competitor. They were by far the largest hotel and resort group on the planet, and also operated a line of luxury cruise ships.

"Don't know," Susan said. "They didn't say."

"Shit," Jake muttered. Recently, Atlas had been swallowing smaller companies like a lion gulping down chunks of bloody meat. When an interviewer on CNBC had asked Ed about Atlas Group's latest acquisitions, Ed had chuckled and said that the current market prices of those companies had made it look as if the NYSE was having a fifty-percent-off sale, and he just loved to shop.

"Do you want me to stall? I can tell them that I can't find you."

"No," Jake said. "I'll talk to him. Put me through." He had a bad feeling that he knew what this was about, and if he was right, he needed to confirm it immediately. Berenger stock had dropped again on Friday. If Ed Thatcher was calling now, on a weekend, just days before Christmas, it was not to wish Jake a happy holiday. It was to make him the Christmas goose.

Moments later, Ed was on the line. "Jake," he said as genially as if they were old friends. "Hear you're at Gold Bay. Nice place. Good reputation. Enjoying the sun?"

"Not at the moment," Jake said. "I'm indoors. How are you, Ed?"

"Fantastic," Ed said. "I'm on the eighth hole at Crandon Park, how about that? Great cell phone reception here. You can hear me okay?"

"I can hear you fine," Jake said. He could hear everything, including the unspoken message. You did not contact a business acquaintance from the golf course unless you intended to make the point that you were powerful enough to ignore protocol.

"Great," Ed said, "great. Jake, I know you're a busy guy, so I won't keep you long. You know, I've always admired you; I like what you do at Berenger. You've got some fine properties. Well run."

"Thanks," Jake said. "What's on your mind, Ed?"

"Well, I'll tell you. I've been keeping an eye on Berenger's market value, and frankly, you folks are getting down to a place where Atlas would be interested in buying. I thought I'd give you a call, see what your thoughts might be on that."

My thoughts? Try this: You'll see me dead before you take my company, you goddamned pirate, Jake wanted to say, but he didn't. He knew Ed Thatcher by reputation. If Atlas Group wanted Berenger, they would first try to make a friendly deal. Friendly was cheaper for everyone, involved fewer lawyers, took less time, and allowed management to play golf together after the close. But when friendly didn't work, the gloves came off and people stopped smiling. Jake had no intention of selling, so if Ed Thatcher was serious about acquiring Berenger, he would need to launch a hostile takeover attempt.

"It's an interesting idea," Jake said calmly. The words felt like the vilest profanity in his mouth. He owned twenty-five percent of Berenger's stock—a huge amount, but not enough to block the sale if Atlas attacked. The only thing he could do right now was stall. The longer Ed thought that a friendly deal was possible, the longer Jake had to find a way to fight him off. But it was now a matter of a week or two, at most. "I'll need a couple of days for internal meetings, and some time to get the information together before we discuss it officially."

"Sure, of course," Ed said. "You talk to your people, do

what you have to do, and then we'll get together. How about next week?"

No problem, Jake thought. *Would that be right on Christmas Day, or would the day after be soon enough to suit you?* He was going to have trouble getting the relevant people together when half of them were gone for the holidays, and Ed knew it. Jake suddenly suspected that Ed also knew him, knew that he would rather die than sell, and this "friendly" offer was a paper sheath for a very sharp sword.

"Next week sounds fine," he said. "I'll send Oliver Arias, my COO, to Atlanta to meet with your team."

"Looking forward to it," Ed Thatcher said. "Good to talk to you, Jake. You take care, and enjoy your holiday. Don't spend too much time indoors. Life is short."

Fuck you, Jake thought as he hung up the phone.

He sat silently for a few moments, staring at nothing, and then made a decision. Cora's words from the previous day had been more prophetic than either of them could have guessed, and he was now officially convinced that it was time for drastic measures.

"I don't know what I'm going to do about that girl," Elaine muttered to herself. It was just before noon, and they were having another mostly silent breakfast in Cottage Five. Molly had already given Carter and Elaine a rough description of what had happened during her conversation with Jake the previous day, but Carter hadn't been satisfied with her version and kept pestering her with questions until Molly finally told him to leave her alone. He sat, frowning pensively, gnawing on a blueberry muffin.

"Are you talking about Ingrid?" Molly asked.

"Yes," Elaine said. She broke off a piece of toast and

spread marmalade on it. "That unscrupulous parasite has her completely in his power. It's appalling. To think that she would abandon a perfectly good husband, on a whim! That girl has all the sense of a potted petunia."

"Did he *specifically* say no to the idea of the book?" Carter asked suddenly. "Or was your impression that he just needed more time to think about it? Because if he didn't specifically say no, it could mean yes."

"I'm pretty sure that it didn't mean yes," Molly said.

"You didn't leverage the ruins," Carter said accusingly. "You were too nice. That's not how guys like Jake operate. You have to play hardball."

"It's not as if she were just a girlfriend," Elaine lamented. "Or a mistress. She was a *wife*. She had it all, and then she just threw it away. Does she think it's easy to find a man like Michael? And then get him to the altar?"

Molly's head was starting to hurt. She put down her coffee cup and rubbed her temples. It was their last day at Gold Bay, and so far, it had not been anything close to an enjoyable vacation. She thought that she would go down to the beach and try to relax, and not think about how much money she had spent on this trip. Letting Carter and Elaine pay the bills might not have been such a bad idea after all.

There was a knock on the door, and Carter looked up. "The muffins are here," he said. He had called five minutes ago for an additional basket. Carter liked to eat when he was depressed. He stood up, walked to the door, opened it, and yelped.

Molly jumped up, her napkin falling to the floor, and turned to see what had happened. Her eyes widened and her heart suddenly thudded in her chest when she saw Jake standing in the doorway. He looked equally alarmed, and was staring at Carter, who was staring back at him.

Quickly Carter composed himself. "Excuse me," he said,

backing away from the door. "We weren't expecting you. Come in, come in. I see that you have my folder of clippings. That's great, that's great. You've been looking over my work?"

"Molly left this at the villa yesterday," Jake said, holding out the manila folder. His eyes met Molly's, and she felt a flush of warmth in her cheeks.

"Yes," Carter said, waving it away. "I know. It's for you. Did you see the profile I did on Donald Trump for *Esquire*? I think I really captured the spirit of the man. We can sit down and discuss—"

"Actually," Jake said, "I'm here to see Molly."

A calculating look crossed Carter's face. "Molly is very busy with her research on the old plantation," he said. "You probably didn't hear her latest news about the *proof.*"

Jake raised his eyebrows at Molly. "What proof?"

"Historical documents," Carter exclaimed, moving to stand between them. "Very official. Very old. It looks like that plantation really did belong to Betty Mary."

"Bonny Mary," Molly said through her teeth.

"We just learned that the documents are in the archives of the . . . National Piratical Society," Carter said, and shrugged ruefully, giving Jake a wouldn't-you-know-it look. "Obviously, we should have looked there first. Hindsight. Ha!"

Jake was still focused on Molly, who folded her arms against her chest defensively. She couldn't imagine why he was there or what he wanted.

"I need to talk to you," he said. "Alone."

"Why?" Molly asked. As far as she was concerned, they had nothing more to say to each other.

"Oh, these existential questions are so pointless," Elaine said cheerfully from behind her. "Go right ahead, dear. Seize the day. Take your time."

It was quickly becoming clear to Molly that going out for a private talk with Jake Berenger—unpleasant as that might be—was better than staying in Cottage Five with two lunatics. She pretended not to see Carter winking significantly at her as she walked past him to join Jake.

"I've never heard of the National Piratical Society," Jake said as they left the cottage and began to stroll along the winding path that led to the main building.

Neither had Molly, but she had no intention of admitting that. "Carter was being hasty," she said. "It's only one of a few possible leads. Why did you want to talk to me?"

He stopped and looked down at her. His gaze moved over her as if he were appraising her. Molly felt a fluttering sensation in her stomach. His mouth curved slightly, as if he was privately amused by something.

"Everything you told me about yourself was true," he said. "You teach at Belden College. You have a reputation as a rising star of academia, and you've published an impressive list of research papers in notable scholarly journals. You also wrote a critically acclaimed book about eighteenth-century seafaring women. Very politically correct. I'm sure that the liberal establishment loved it."

Molly felt wary. "I didn't tell you all of that."

"No," he said. "I spent the past two hours researching you. That all came off of the Internet. That's not all I learned, though. Your credit is good, you have no criminal record, and your neighbors in Belden say that you're quiet, hardworking, and nice."

"What?" Molly sputtered. "You called my neighbors?"

"Not personally. I have people who handle that kind of thing for me. Mrs. Edith Olsen, who lives in the apartment above yours, says that you never play your music too loud, and that you haven't had a boyfriend in more than a year."

"Mrs. Olsen is deaf as a post! She wouldn't notice if I

blew up the microwave. And she doesn't know a damn thing about my personal life. I happen to have plenty of . . ." Molly stopped herself. "That's beside the point. What do you think you're doing, having your people investigate me? How dare you?"

He laughed. "Didn't you and your friends do the same to me? I also learned that you have a famous father. I had no idea that you were Stanford Shaw's daughter."

"Oh, my God," Molly said, and pressed her hands to her mouth, feeling as if her heart had just stopped. "You . . . your people, I mean . . . they contacted my father?"

Jake shook his head. "No. I know who he is, though. I heard him speak, years ago, at a White House luncheon. He seemed very well educated."

"What's this all about?" Molly demanded. "You don't need to investigate me—you already know more about me than you should! Let me remind you that you promised that you'd keep my secret. I'm not threatening you over the plantation ruins, whatever impression Carter just gave you. I've washed my hands of the whole thing, and it's on your conscience now . . ."

"What if I told you that I won't start demolition of Dyer's Fortune until April?" Jake asked. "That's three months from now. Would that give you the time you need to find your proof—if it exists?"

Molly looked suspiciously at him. "You told me that postponing such a large project would be very expensive."

"Yes," he said. A smile touched the edges of his mouth. "It would. You have no idea how much this is going to cost me."

"Then why would you do it?"

"As part of a bargain. I need your help, and I'll give you more time at the plantation in exchange. If you turn up your proof before April, then obviously I'll have to relocate the golf course. It's a risk for me, but I'm willing to take it."

"You haven't told me what you want from me," Molly said.

"It's interesting. If you overlook the business about *Pirate Gold*—which no one but you or I ever need to know about—then your public image is as angelic as mine is devilish."

"So?"

"So I have a proposal for you. But first, I want to confirm something. Do you have any interest in marrying me?"

Molly thought that she had misheard. "What?"

"Do you want to marry me?"

He was mocking her. Molly didn't know what his point was, but she knew that she didn't like it. "No," she snapped. "Definitely not. I don't even want to be having this bizarre conversation with you."

"Great," Jake said cheerfully. "That's exactly what I thought you'd say. So how would you feel about a three-month engagement?"

"I need a cold compress for my head," Elaine said. "I feel dizzy. Carter, call the butler. No—wait. Don't do that. Get a napkin, pour cold mineral water on it, and bring it to me. Not too wet."

"But—" Carter protested.

"Quickly! *Vite, vite*!" Elaine exclaimed, and Carter scurried toward the kitchen. She sat down, fanning herself with a copy of French *Vogue*. "Molly," she said, "we're going to need more details, dear. How exactly did this happen?"

"Not yet!" Carter shouted from the kitchen. "Wait for me! Where are the napkins? I'm coming back! Wait for—"

"In the drawer by the sink," Elaine called impatiently. "Molly, sit down," she said, patting the cushion next to her on the couch. "What did he say? Start from the beginning."

Carter sped back into the room, holding a wadded-up, dripping linen napkin, which he slapped into Elaine's hand. Ignoring her look of annoyance, he sat down in the chair opposite the couch and fixed Molly with an intent stare. "Okay," he said. "I'm ready now."

"Would the two of you please calm down?" Molly asked. "I thought I made this clear. He doesn't want to *actually* get married. He wants someone to pretend to be his fiancée for three months. It didn't make much sense to me. He said something about his company's image being very closely tied to his own image, and that he needs to raise his stock price because of some emergency situation, and he thinks that making his personal life look more stable is going to help. It's all just a big ruse."

"What emergency situation?" Carter asked.

"He didn't tell me," Molly said, "and I didn't ask."

Carter looked disappointed. "You should have gotten the details. It's obviously a business crisis—I could get some mileage out of that, even if I don't come away with anything else from this trip. Did he say anything more about the book?"

"No," Molly said. "He only wanted to talk about his own plan."

"It's clever," Elaine said thoughtfully. She folded the wet napkin and began to dab her wrists and forehead with it. "He's a very intelligent man. This is exactly the sort of news that would make headlines after his breakup with Skye Elliot. It certainly is unconventional, but if his public image really is so closely linked to the company's image—and I assume that he knows what he's talking about—then it just might work."

"Do you think he read my clippings?" Carter persisted. "Because I think my talent speaks for itself. Tell him that the book isn't the only possible project. I'm flexible. An interview would be enough. One interview. His first ever. Exclusive rights. Yes! When are you talking to him again?"

"I'm not," Molly said. "I told him that I wasn't interested in helping him, and since we're going home tomorrow, I doubt that I'll ever see him again."

"*What?*" Carter gasped. "But . . . Molly, how could you?"

"Oh, damn," Elaine muttered. "I might have known. Doesn't anyone under the age of forty have any sense?"

"Are you crazy?" Carter demanded. "You can't say no. Don't you understand what this means? Three months inside the world of Jake Berenger? The material! The scoop! Look, I'm sure it's not too late. You can change your mind. Call him. Call him now."

"I'm not crazy," Molly said defensively. "And I'm not going to call him. How could I agree to do something like that? It would completely disrupt my life."

"Molly, dear," Elaine said. "A little disruption is not necessarily a bad thing. We need to have a talk about the fact that handsome young billionaires don't come knocking on a girl's door, proposing marriage, every day of the week."

"He didn't propose marriage!" Molly said. "Isn't anyone in this room listening to me? He proposed a fake engagement. That's different."

"A fake engagement can be leveraged into a real one," Elaine said. "You may not know this, but men are lazy. They don't like to leave home unless they have to. Achieving close proximity is half the battle."

"I can't believe this," Molly said. "You're telling me that after three months of having me around, Jake might decide to marry me because he's lazy and I would be *convenient*?"

"Yes, if you're clever about it," Elaine said. "The man is forty years old, and he needs a wife."

"But I don't *want* to marry him. I don't even like him."

"Dislike means nothing," Elaine said firmly. "I could name several lucrative, long-term relationships where the two people involved actually loathe one another."

"Don't tell me that," Molly said. "I don't want to know. Anyway, spending the next three months pretending to be Jake's fiancée would get in the way of my teaching schedule. I'd have to live with him, and—"

"Live with him!" Carter howled. "The opportunity! The access! Give me the Sandra wig, *I'll* be his fiancée. I love him. I'd make a beautiful bride."

"No, you wouldn't," Molly said. "And there's a confidentiality agreement involved, so neither you nor I could ever publish a word about it."

"Those agreements don't always hold up in court," Carter said.

"I don't care," Molly said. "I spent the last year of my life hiding from the press, and I have no intention of now becoming part of someone else's PR campaign."

"But—" Carter said.

Molly shook her head. "I don't want to talk about it. Remember when you said that even if nothing else worked out, we'd still have enjoyed a week at a five-star resort?"

"Yes," Carter said gloomily. "I remember."

"Good," Molly said. "Because I'm going to change into my swimsuit, and then I'm going down to the beach to try to pack a week of enjoyment into the rest of today. Are you coming with me?"

CHAPTER 18

Molly's parents still lived in the house where they had raised her, a blue and cream Victorian on the edge of the tiny town of Belden. They had bought it as newlyweds, more than forty years earlier, when Stanford Shaw had arrived to take his position as the youngest member of the Belden College history faculty. The house had seemed too large for just a professor and his wife, but the Shaws had planned to fill it with a dynasty of brilliant, successful children.

It was the only time—to Molly's knowledge—that Fate had ever dared to cross her father. She was an only child, born after ten years of failed attempts, and so the responsibility for filling the house with awards and achievement had fallen entirely onto her shoulders. She had never questioned this duty, or wondered about the limitations of her father's definition of achievement.

It was December 31, and the Social Sciences' New Year's Eve party—traditionally hosted by her father and catered by her mother—was in full swing. It was the usual crowd of professors, their spouses, the dean, his wife, the department secretaries, their spouses, and a handful of diehard students who had stayed on campus for the holidays and wanted everyone to know it. It was just before ten P.M. and most of the guests were tipsy on spiked eggnog, except for Professor

Crump, who—as he had done every year for as long as Molly could remember—had consumed half a punch bowl of grog and passed out on the couch under the mistletoe. He was snoring gently, and someone had put a Santa hat on him. Molly knew from experience that most of the group would vanish before midnight—the older faculty home to bed, the younger faculty home to relieve the babysitter, and the students to the local pub. Professor Crump, widowed for the past five years, would spend the night on the couch and have New Year's breakfast with the Shaws in the morning.

Molly had never liked or disliked the party; it was just something that happened annually, like her dental checkup. It was the same every year, so she had assumed that it would always be the same, in perpetuity. She had never considered the possibility that she herself might change, even if the party didn't.

"I can't believe how different you look," Rachel Feinstein kept saying whenever the crowd circulation brought her close to Molly, which was by then three times more often than Molly would have liked. Rachel was Molly's age, had been hired shortly after Molly, and was "Preparation H," as the academic community admiringly described someone with both an undergraduate degree and a doctorate from Harvard. She and Molly had been rivals from the moment that each laid eyes on the other's curriculum vitae. Only one of them was likely to be offered tenure at Belden, and they both knew it.

The fight for academic dominance was getting ugly. Rachel's area of expertise was Elizabethan England, and for the past year she had been attempting to prove that Shakespeare's plays had actually been written by his sister. It was a shameless publicity ploy, and unfortunately it was working. Rachel's research had made headlines in the popular press and had just earned the department a large grant from a private foundation called the Society for Revisionist Herstory.

"You bleached your hair," Rachel said smugly. "It looks much lighter. It's almost blond."

"It's caramel," Molly said. "Not blond."

"And your dress . . . I've never seen you look so . . ."

"Yes?" Molly asked.

"Fashionable," Rachel said.

"Thank you," Molly said, although she knew that it wasn't meant as a compliment. She was wearing a black cashmere dress with long sleeves and a plunging V-neck. Elaine had picked it out a few days earlier, during a shopping trip in Chicago. She had also guided Molly toward a black push-up bra that Molly wanted to hand over to the Belden Physics department, because it seemed to create matter where there was none.

Her new look caused even more of a stir than she had expected. Her haircut and color raised stunned eyebrows, and the bra and dress unleashed a rumor that she had actually been in the hospital the previous week, getting breast implants. There was also talk that she was having a torrid affair with a graduate student. Professor Crump told her in slurred tones that she looked like Hedy Lamarr, then spilled a cup of grog on her.

Her father had pointedly avoided saying a single word about her appearance, but her mother had pulled her aside and whispered that she looked beautiful. Molly had hugged her, and then asked her who Hedy Lamarr was.

"I heard that you just got back from a trip to the Caribbean," Rachel said, staring suspiciously at Molly's chest.

Molly nodded. "And I heard that you turned up new evidence that Shakespeare kept his sister locked in the attic while she worked."

"That's not true," Rachel said. She looked upset. "Who told you that?"

Molly sighed. "Nobody. I was joking."

"Oh. What were you doing in the Caribbean? Research, I assume? Do you have a new project?"

"No," Molly said. "Actually, I was vacationing."

"You're joking again," Rachel said. "I can tell. You do have a project. What is it?"

"Oh, okay," Molly said. "You're right. I have a project, and it's big. Very big, but I can't tell you what it is. Sorry."

Rachel frowned. "Why can't you tell me?"

Molly made a show of looking covertly from side to side. "Because," she said in a low, dramatic voice. "It would expose you to terrible danger. There is a *lot* of money involved."

She smiled mysteriously, then slipped away into the crowd, leaving Rachel to wonder what she'd meant. Molly didn't know either, but it had sounded good. It was funny—until that moment, it had never occurred to her that despite her colleagues' professed disdain for money, most of their time was spent obsessing over ways to get it, in the form of various grants and cash awards. Scholarly recognition was nice, but it was Rachel's big grant that had earned her an invitation to a personal lunch at President Dickerson's house. Molly had eaten a peanut-butter-and-jelly sandwich at her desk that day and thought about downloading a virus onto Rachel's computer while she was gone.

Interesting, Molly thought. The world was in better focus these days, and it wasn't entirely due to her new contact lenses. It seemed that she had uncovered part of her brain along with half of her chest, and she was beginning to understand things that she had never understood before. Slowly, she made her way through the crowd, heading for the front door. She had had enough for one night, but she felt good. Tired, and a little shaky, but with her new bravado intact. She waved to the various people who were staring at her, and slipped through the doorway into the cold, clear air of the approaching New Year.

New Year's Day was hot and sunny at Gold Bay, but Jake was too exhausted to enjoy the weather. He had spent the past week more or less living on his Gulfstream jet, shuttling back and forth between Antigua, Miami, and New York City, having emergency meetings with his senior executives, the company lawyers, and the Berenger board, as they worked to develop a strategy to block the hostile takeover by Atlas Group. So far, he had managed to avoid going to Atlas's corporate headquarters in Atlanta by delegating the job to Oliver Arias, who had a cooler head. Jake could handle a phone conversation with Ed Thatcher, but he knew that if he looked the man in the eye, Ed would see through him in a second. So far, they had stalled Atlas by feigning interest in a friendly deal, and by leveraging the excuse of the holiday week to keep meetings and negotiations crawling forward at the slowest possible pace.

But tomorrow was January second, and that tactic would no longer be viable. The stock price hadn't dropped any further, but it hadn't gone up, either, and at Berenger's current market value, the company was a sitting duck. It had not—to say the least—been a pleasant holiday.

After Molly Shaw had refused his proposal, Jake had briefly reconsidered Cora's suggestion that he use Amanda for their PR campaign, but his instincts warned him off. Amanda wasn't the right person for the job. Molly, on the other hand . . .

She was perfect, damn it. She had an image that the press

would love—he could see his PR department directing the Cinderella story like a feature film: "Small-Town Teacher Swept Away by Big City Prince." It was all hype, of course. He was no prince, and Molly was no small-town teacher, but people seemed to like stereotypes in their headlines.

He exhaled, frustrated. It might be time for another try. By now, she had had more than a week to cool off and reconsider the idea. It was very possible that she was now regretting her haste in rejecting his offer. She might even be hoping that he would call her to negotiate. He swiveled his chair to face his computer and logged into the Gold Bay reservations database. Molly's contact information wasn't there, but Carter McKee's was, and that was all Jake needed.

"You!" Molly Shaw exclaimed. "What do you want?"

"Happy New Year," Jake said. She didn't sound very pleased to hear from him. Maybe a week wasn't a sufficient cooling-off period.

"How did you get my number? It isn't listed."

"I called your friend Carter. He gave it to me."

"Did he," Molly said grimly, and Jake imagined dire consequences for Carter McKee.

"Are you always this friendly on the phone?" he asked.

"I'm friendly when I have a reason to be. But you rank just below telemarketers in my caller hierarchy. That person that you paid to ask about me . . . do you know what he said when he called my neighbor, Mrs. Olsen?"

Uh-oh, Jake thought. "What?"

"He told her that he was from the FBI! He said that he was investigating me, but it was too classified to talk about. She's eighty-seven years old, and she's sure that it must be something to do with drugs, because all the young people are on drugs these days. Now she won't speak to me, and she's been slipping 'just say no' pamphlets into my mailbox. Thanks a lot."

"Sorry about that," Jake said.

"Sure you are. Why are you calling me?"

"I wanted to discuss the offer I made before you left Gold Bay. Now that you've had some time to think it over, I wondered if you might have reconsid—"

"No," Molly said.

Jake exhaled slowly, reaching for his patience. "I don't know why your neighbor thinks you need those pamphlets. I've never met a woman as good at saying no as you are. Will you at least let me finish?"

"No," Molly said again. "I'm not interested. I don't want anything to do with you, and that includes talking to you on the phone."

"This is crazy," Jake exclaimed. "You're the one who tricked me. You're the one who was stalking me—you and your friends! If anybody here has a right to be angry, I do. But I'm trying to make you a new offer. If you'll spend the next three months posing as my fiancée, I'll give you until April at the old plantation, and I'll add a cash payment to the deal. How about—"

"I don't need your money," Molly said. "Use it to hire someone else. The new semester starts in two weeks, and I have a full teaching load scheduled."

"You told me that you were planning to write a book about Mary Morgan," Jake said. "I thought that you academics were always looking for new research projects. What about 'publish or perish'? This would be better for your career than spending a semester teaching."

Molly was silent for a long moment, and Jake hoped that he had stumbled onto something. Finally, she spoke.

"Would you be willing to sign a legal document stating

that if I find proof in the next three months, you'll turn the Morgan plantation into a museum?"

Jake did a quick mental calculation of odds and costs. Rezoning the golf course would cost more than he wanted to spend, as would polishing up the old site to make it safe for tourists. He didn't like the idea of being legally required to do either. But there was always the chance that the plantation hadn't belonged to Mary Morgan, or that Molly would be unable to prove that it had. His top priority was to keep his company out of Atlas's hands. If he couldn't manage that, whatever happened at Gold Bay in three months would be a non-issue. For him, at least.

"Yes," he said. "I'll sign a document stating exactly what you just said. Three months. If you have proof by then, I'll make it a museum."

"And you'll start the Mary Morgan Foundation to maintain and preserve the site."

"The *what*?"

"I'll be honored to accept the position of executive director," Molly said. "Thank you so much for thinking of me."

"I don't believe this," Jake said, annoyed. "All right. Fine. I'll do it. Now will you—"

"And you'll give Carter the first interview about the engagement. He gets to break the news."

"No. My PR people will break the news. That's not negotiable."

"What about Carter?"

Jake hesitated. He didn't like Molly's friend, and he had no desire to see the man again, much less to spend time talking to him. But it would be pointless to stall the deal over that. There wasn't a reporter on earth who he did want to talk to, but he no longer had a choice. "One interview," he said. "Sometime after the news has been released. He can peddle it wherever he likes, but that's the most I'll agree to. All right?"

"That sounds reasonable," Molly said.

Jake felt a surge of relief. "Great," he said. "It's settled, then. You'll do it."

"No," Molly said sweetly. "Sorry. I told you, I'm not interested."

"What? Then why the hell were you—"

"I was just wondering if you were getting desperate."

"God damn it," Jake snapped. "I'm not desperate. You aren't the only woman I know. There are plenty of others—"

"So I've heard," Molly said.

"—who would be happy with a cash payment and some media attention. They wouldn't ask me to build them *museums*, and set up *foundations* . . ."

"Wonderful," Molly said. "I hope that you and they have a very nice engagement. Good-bye, Jake."

She hung up on him, leaving him sitting there, staring in stunned disbelief at the silent receiver in his hand.

CHAPTER 19

On the morning of January fourth, Molly was awakened by the sound of the phone. She groaned and rolled over to squint at the clock. It was a little before eight A.M., not early by her usual schedule, but classes didn't resume until the middle of the month, and she had been celebrating her vacation by lounging in bed until nine.

Who would be calling at this hour? Even Carter knew better than to bother her before eight. He had been phoning for the past two days, after Jake had made the brilliant move of asking him for her number.

On the fourth ring, her answering machine picked up. Molly lay dozing under her comforter, feeling too warm and snug to move. The machine beeped, and then she heard her mother's voice, fluttering with anxiety.

"Molly? Are you there? Your father and I . . . we're just so shocked. We can't believe the news, and we don't understand why you didn't tell us. Your father heard about it from the neighbors when he was out for his morning walk . . ."

What? Molly frowned and lifted her head to listen.

"It's all over the newspapers! I heard that it was on the front page of *USA Today*. Oh, honey, everyone is talking about it, and they're calling us to ask about you. We don't know what to think . . ."

Molly sat bolt upright in bed, feeling as if her heart had jumped into her throat and cut off her air supply.

This can't be happening.

Jake couldn't have gone ahead with his plan without her consent. He couldn't have been crazy enough to announce the engagement to the press, thinking that such a move would maneuver her into a position where she would have no choice but to play along. Could he?

She lunged for the phone. "Mom?"

"Molly!" Her mother sounded almost tearful. "I'm so glad you're there. Ginny Goldman told me that she saw it on *Good Morning, Milwaukee*! I can't believe that we found out like this."

"It's not true, Mom," Molly exclaimed. "I swear, it's all a mistake."

"Your father is so upset that he can't speak. He wouldn't eat his breakfast, and now he's locked himself in his study."

"Mom, listen to me. Tell Dad that it's a lie. I am not engaged to marry Jake Berenger, no matter what he's been saying to the press. He's crazy, and he's trying to force me to cooperate with a plan to—"

"What?" Mrs. Shaw said, confused. "Engaged? To who? A crazy person? Oh, honey, I don't understand any of this. But I'm so glad to hear that it's not true. I knew it. I knew that there had to be some kind of mistake. Of course you would never have written that awful novel *Pirate Gold*!"

Model? Princess?
You'd Never Guess by Looking at Her!

An anonymous source has revealed the true identity of Sandra St. Claire, the author of the international best seller and cult phenomenon novel Pirate Gold. *Rumors and misinformation—apparently started by the marketing department at Leighton House, Ms. St. Claire's publisher—have depicted the mysterious author as everything from a top model to a member of a European royal family, but the* Enquirer *has confirmed that Sandra St. Claire is actually the pen name of Dr. Mary Margaret Shaw, a professor at Belden College in Wisconsin. Dr. Shaw was not available for comment . . .*

Molly's mother had been wrong when she said that the story was on the front page of *USA Today*. It was not. It was on the front page of the Life section, inside. It was also in the *Chicago Tribune*, the *New York Post*, and the *National Enquirer*. After that, Molly had stopped looking.

In each case the article was brief, said something similar in tone, and was accompanied by Molly's faculty photo from the Belden Web site, showing her sitting stiffly at her desk, rows of books lining the walls behind her. Her hair was flat and muddy, and the light of the flash reflected off of her glasses and her colorless face, giving her a deer-in-the-headlights look.

After her mother's phone call, Molly had thrown on her clothes, wrapped herself in her new black wool coat, and rushed to the Belden bookstore, which was connected to the coffee shop where she went every morning to pick up her daily double latte. Her newspaper-and-caffeine stop was a normal part of her routine, and for one moment, as she stepped into the warm and crowded building, it seemed as if nothing had changed.

Then, someone saw her.

Conversation ceased abruptly, silence moving in a wave through the store like a fast-spreading virus, and Molly found herself standing just inside the front door, staring into a sea of stunned faces.

"Professor Shaw!" cried Jessica Wong, one of Molly's Intro to British Colonial History students from the past semester. She was working behind the register, and a tabloid newspaper was open on the counter in front of her.

Molly looked around, trying to control the surge of panic rising from her stomach. Her heart thudded, and she felt dizzy. It was just like one of her dreams, but it was really happening. There was Kay Grotsky, from the Economics department, standing by the magazine rack, staring at her. There was Christopher Polk, from her senior seminar, holding an espresso and staring at her. There was Professor Sommers, her father's friend, with Mrs. Sommers, and Mike Kennedy from English, and—*Oh, God*, Molly thought—Rachel Feinstein, clutching the *New York Post*, staring at her. Everyone in the bookstore, everyone in the coffee shop—everyone in Belden, Wisconsin, as far as Molly could tell—had frozen in midsentence and stopped to gawk.

Molly took a deep, shaky breath. *Dead Professor Walking*, she thought. And she had been nervous about causing a stir with her new dress and haircut. Her nightmare had just come true, and there was nothing to do now but march forward.

Up, up, dear, said Elaine's voice in her mind. *And smile. You're being watched.*

Molly lifted her chin, squared her shoulders, and smiled at the crowd as if she didn't have a care in the world.

"Good morning," she said into the silence. "I hear that I'm in the news."

David Fowler, the Dean of Faculty at Belden College, had a corner office in the main administration building, a sandstone mansion that had once been the home of Alfred Pottsworth Belden, the railroad tycoon whose foresight and funds had created Belden College in 1872. The decor in Dean Fowler's office had changed little from the original Victorian scheme, and over the fireplace hung a copy of the famous oil portrait of the venerable A. P. Belden himself. He glowered down at Molly as she approached one of the leather armchairs facing the dean's desk. Behind the desk was Dean Fowler, wearing the same expression.

"Professor Shaw," he boomed. "Sit down."

Molly sat. It was eleven A.M., and she was still numb from the shocks of the morning. She had stayed at the bookstore long enough to ascertain the extent of the leak, then fled back to her apartment. Five messages were waiting on her answering machine, and one of them was from Dean Fowler, requesting that she come to his office immediately.

"You've seen this, I assume?" The dean pushed the *USA Today* article across his desk toward Molly. "And this. And this."

More papers followed, including the *Daily Star*, which had helpfully supplied a voluptuous sketch of the imaginary Sandra St. Claire to contrast with the real-life Molly Shaw. Molly glanced at it and winced.

"Our Public Relations Office is being besieged with calls from reporters asking about you, Dr. Shaw. If anyone tried to contact us for another reason—to discuss our press release about Janet Heinrich's recent National Science Foundation grant, for example—I doubt that they would be able to get through."

"Oh, dear," Molly said. "I'm really very sorry about all of this. I'm sure it'll die down soon . . ."

"Let's hope so," said the dean grimly. "In the meantime, President Dickerson has decided that we will not comment on this matter. Our public relations staff is not accustomed to working with the *Globe*, the *Star*, and the *Enquirer*. This is not the sort of publicity that we want for Belden College."

Molly nodded.

"Professor Shaw," the dean continued, "I've known your father for thirty years, and I consider him a personal friend, which is why I supported your application for a position here at Belden. The Shaw name is a famous name, and an honorable one. It is a name that your father has linked to scholarship of the highest quality. I consider his name and his reputation, like that of Belden College itself, to be sacrosanct. I had hoped—no, I had *expected*—that you would carry on that tradition of excellence."

Molly's hands were knotted together in her lap. She stared down at them, feeling miserable, saying nothing. What could she say? Dean Fowler was right. She had embarrassed herself, her father, and her school. The papers had all made a point of mentioning that she was a professor at Belden College, and the daughter of the famous historian Stanford Shaw. Some had reported it simply as fact, others had used the opportunity to mock Belden's arrogant, elitist reputation.

The dean sighed, shaking his head. "Professor Shaw, I've known you since you were a child. Your father has always been very proud of you. Why you would do something like this to him, to us—"

"Excuse me," Molly said suddenly. "But I didn't do it *to* anyone. I did it for myself. It had nothing to do with anyone else. That was why I used a pseudonym. I never meant for it to become public."

"That may be so, but the scandal is only part of the problem. Your novel was more than six hundred pages long. Having written several books myself, I know that such a large project takes a great deal of time. It would have been wiser to spend that time doing work to benefit the academic community—work that does not require a pseudonym. Your choice does not reflect the Belden College Principles."

"I know the College Principles," Molly said stubbornly, "and I live up to them. I've been producing academic work, and I'm a good teacher. I get some of the highest marks on campus on the student evaluations. Even my father doesn't score as well as I do."

"Students enjoy showmanship," said the dean. "But this is not a popularity contest, Dr. Shaw. This is not *American Idol*. We at Belden want our faculty to show absolute commitment to their academic research. Someone whose strength is primarily in teaching would be better suited to a state university, where she would need to hold the attention of a lecture hall filled with football players."

Molly recoiled. "Am I being fired?" she asked.

"No," said Dean Fowler. "I would never do that to your father. It would kill him. But I have an obligation to the school, as well. You're free to finish out the academic year with us, Dr. Shaw. But your tenure review is coming up in May, and I feel that I should tell you now that you are unlikely to be offered a long-term position at Belden College."

Molly walked slowly across the quad. The day was overcast, and the sky and the snow were a similar shade of dingy gray-white. Salt crystals crunched under her feet, and the air was sharp and cold. She felt as brittle as the thin layer of ice that coated the snowbanks. *You are unlikely to be offered a long-term position . . .*

She hunched as she walked, tensing as the wind slipped inside her coat and chilled her. The fingers of her right hand were red and raw. In her haste that morning, she had forgotten her gloves, and she couldn't put her hand in her pocket because she was carrying the pile of newspapers from Dean Fowler's office. "Take them," he had said, looking pained. "Please."

On top of the pile was the *National Enquirer*. Coincidentally, the cover story was an interview with Skye Elliot. "I Told Jake to Get Lost Because I Knew He Was No Good," screamed the headline. In the bookstore that morning, Molly had glanced at the story, which consisted of Skye explaining that she had broken up with Jake Berenger because she had sensed that he was in a personal and professional decline. The cover featured a photo of Jake next to Skye in happier times, now depicted with a jagged cartoon rip down the center of the picture.

For the first time in her life, Molly felt a kinship with Skye Elliot. *No good, indeed*, she thought darkly. *He did this*. It wasn't as if there were any other suspects. Carter would never betray her, and Molly had believed Elaine when she said that she was not the kind of person who deliberately ruined lives. Molly's agent, editor, and publisher had nothing to gain by suddenly shattering the Sandra myth, and that was the extent of the inner circle. Obviously, Jake had been the so-called anonymous source. He had exposed her secret to the papers. But why?

Sheer malice was one possibility—he was paying her back for her refusal to help him. But that didn't seem like Jake's style. He was calculating and shrewd, and if he had decided to destroy her life, it wouldn't be for fun, it would be for profit. His own profit. He knew—because she had told him—that she might lose her job if the truth about *Pirate Gold* became public. He must think that forcing her into a desperate position would make her reconsider his offer.

But why hadn't he bothered to threaten her first? If he had told her that he would expose her unless she went along with his plan, she would have had no choice but to agree. It would have been much simpler. This scorched-earth strategy did conceal Jake's identity as the villain, but it was also a big gamble. How could he be so sure that she would turn to him now?

It was a mystery, but Molly didn't care about the details. She would turn to Jake, all right. As he had obviously guessed, she didn't have anywhere else to go. She didn't want to stay at Belden, to be patronized and pitied for four months before she was officially kicked out of the club. And he had made sure that she had nothing left to lose by cooperating with his scheme. But the game was not over—in fact, it was only beginning. Just like the pregnant Mary Morgan, Molly Shaw had a secret trump card, and she intended to pull it out when Jake least expected it. She was going to make him very sorry that he had ever dared to interfere with her life.

Susan Horowitz buzzed Jake in the executive conference room at Berenger headquarters in Miami. "Sorry to disturb you," she said, "but I have Molly Shaw on line four, and you told me that if she ever called, I should—"

"Put her through," Jake said, standing up. "I'll take the call at my desk."

He excused himself from the meeting and walked through the connecting door into his private office. He had seen the news about Molly that morning, after Cora called to tell him about it. Sonny Carmichael had phoned her to ask if she'd had something to do with the leak. Cora, horrified, had denied any involvement, but Jake had heard the same question in his mother's voice.

"I didn't tell them," Jake said. "You swore me to secrecy, remember? I wouldn't do that to you, or to Sonny."

"I didn't think so," Cora said. She sounded distressed. "But I'm not sure that Sonny is convinced, and I don't blame him for being suspicious. A week after he told me the secret, it's all over the news. It's very embarrassing, Jake. I feel terrible."

"Why? It's not your fault. You didn't do anything wrong."

"I know, but it's such strange timing. Molly Shaw must be very upset. I know all about that school of hers, and how snobbish they are. This won't go over well at a place like Belden."

"How do you know that she didn't leak the news herself?" Jake asked. "Maybe she was tired of anonymity."

"Only if she was also tired of her professorship," Cora said. "And she didn't seem to be. Poor thing. I think she's probably having a very bad day."

"Molly Shaw can take care of herself," Jake said dryly. "Believe me, I know."

But the Molly Shaw on line four sounded very different from the confident woman who had recently told him to take his engagement offer and get stuffed. Her voice was subdued, as if she had gathered her remaining strength just before she called him.

"You saw the news this morning?" she asked.

"Yes," Jake said. "I didn't think that the photo looked much like you." *To say the least.* Apparently, she had been telling the truth when she said that the dowdy professor character really was her. Or, had been her until recently. Jake couldn't imagine why a woman as attractive as Molly would want to hide behind such unflattering hair, clothes, and glasses, but she obviously had her reasons. He paused. She didn't sound good at all. "Are you all right?" he asked.

"No. This morning, the dean more or less told me that I wouldn't be offered tenure at Belden. I'm free to finish out the school year, but that's it for me."

"I'm very sorry," Jake said. "If my opinion matters, I think they should be proud of you. It's great publicity for the school."

"They don't seem to agree."

"Then they're a bunch of clueless snobs." In Jake's opinion, any school that considered a best-selling novelist a liability was so far removed from the real world that it ought to wither up and die.

Molly was silent for a moment. Then she said, "Well, I know who did it. Who leaked the news, I mean."

"Who?"

"One of my colleagues. She saw the book galleys sitting on my desk last year, and I'm sure that she's the one who told the newspapers. She's very competitive, and I guess she decided to get rid of me."

"I wouldn't have guessed that people were so ruthless inside the ivory tower of Academia," Jake said. "Sounds more like my world."

"Does it? Well, you might be surprised to learn what we academics are capable of."

"What are you going to do now?" Jake asked. "Finish the year?"

"They expect me to stay. A single semester at Belden is a lot better than nothing, and I suppose I should be grateful for it. Anyway, it wouldn't be very ethical of me to abandon them just before classes start. They would have to scramble to find someone to cover my teaching schedule."

"So you're staying."

"No," Molly said. "I'm leaving. Let them scramble. I'm tired of being good, and I'm not going to hang on for four months, hoping to be redeemed. That's why I'm calling. I was wondering if your offer is still open."

That was exactly what Jake had been hoping to hear. This news leak might be trouble for Molly, but it was a lucky break for him. "It's still open," he said.

"Will my sudden . . . notoriety be a problem?"

"A *problem*?" he repeated. It was an amazing question, reflecting how utterly brainwashed she had been by her community. "No, your notoriety is an asset. Unlike your dean, I consider media interest to be a valuable tool. This adds a whole new dimension to the story. It's going to be very useful."

"Of course," Molly said slowly. "That makes sense."

Jake thought that he heard a sudden chill in her voice, but a moment later it was gone, replaced with businesslike briskness.

"I want to make sure that my terms are clear. I won't do this unless you agree to sign a legal document stating that you'll turn the plantation into a museum."

"If you find proof in three months."

"Right. And the Mary Morgan Foundation? And my directorship?"

"We've already been through this. Proof first, then your museum and foundation. We'll draw up a legal document defining 'proof' in a way that's acceptable to both of us. I'm impressed to see that the change of circumstances hasn't weakened your spine, Professor."

"I'm not desperate," she said stiffly, having interpreted his tone as mockery. "I don't need money, so the circumstances don't matter. Either we do this my way or we don't do it."

"That was meant as a compliment," Jake said. "I really am impressed. You negotiate like a pro." Would she also accept defeat like a pro if her proof never materialized? He wasn't so sure about that, but if luck stayed on his side, he would find out in three months.

He heard her take a breath, as if she were preparing to dive from the high board. "Okay," she said. "We have a deal. I'm yours. What do you want me to do?"

"I think it would be best if you came back to Gold Bay. That way, we can control your media exposure. Unless you'd rather stay in my Miami condo and face the paparazzi every time you leave the building."

"No," Molly said immediately. "I don't know how to handle that kind of thing. You'll need to brief me on exactly what to say, how to say it, and when to say it. This is not familiar territory for me."

"Don't worry," Jake said. "I'm not going to send you out there alone or unprepared. Can you be ready to leave tomorrow?"

"I'm ready to leave anytime, starting now."

"Good. I'll send my plane for you. Are you close to an airport?"

"Yes, but I have one more request."

Christ, Jake thought, annoyed. The woman wouldn't quit. He hoped that she wasn't about to throw in a deal-killer at the last minute. "What?"

"I'd like you to send a helicopter to bring me to the airport."

That was all she wanted? He shrugged. "Sure."

"Thank you. There should be enough room to land it on the Belden College quad."

"What?" Jake said, surprised. "On the quad? Are you serious?"

"Very serious. Can you do it?"

He began to laugh. Now he understood what she wanted, and why. "It would be my pleasure, Professor," he said. "It won't be easy, but I think I can talk my pilots into it. A very large, very loud Berenger corporate helicopter will come up from Chicago and meet you tomorrow in the middle of the Belden College quad. I guarantee that your departure will not go unnoticed. Does noon sound good to you?"

"Yes," Molly said. "Noon would be perfect."

CHAPTER 20

The heat from the studio lamps was making Molly perspire. She was sitting on a beige couch next to the interviewer, and everything immediately surrounding her was drenched, almost drowned, in relentless incandescence. Just beyond the lights was the man with the television camera. Molly had been instructed to look at the interviewer, not at the camera, but her peripheral vision caught the glassy shine of the lens. If you looked into the lens, you could see a dot of darkness in the center of it, like a blood vessel channeling away your recorded image. It was no wonder, Molly thought, that some primitive tribes still believed that a camera could steal your soul. Her own was feeling very loosely attached these days.

"Now tell me," said the interviewer, "was it love at first sight?"

"Yes," Molly said. "The moment I laid eyes on Jake, I knew he was the one."

The interviewer exhaled impatiently. "No, you didn't," he said.

She blinked. "But—"

"Ken, stop the tape. Molly, remember the message. You need to stay on message. Don't improvise. I gave you the answer to that exact question forty-five minutes ago."

"You did? Oh. I don't—"

"You fell in love with Jake *after* you got to know him. The real Jake Berenger is very different from the public image. You fell in love with the real man, the family man underneath the playboy image. You look blank, babe. Is this ringing any bells?"

Molly nodded. "I remember now. Sorry. May I have a glass of water? It's very hot in here."

The interviewer assessed her condition with a glance. "Kill the lights, folks," he said briskly. "We're going to take a break. Somebody get our girl a drink—she's fading."

The spotlights went out with a startling pop, plunging them momentarily into darkness, until someone opened the curtains and natural sunlight flooded the room again. They were at Gold Bay, in the basement of Cora Berenger's villa, which normally served as a screening room. But the comfortable armchairs had been moved out and audio/video equipment moved in to create a makeshift television studio for the purpose of giving Molly a crash course in media performance. The camera was recording onto videotape, which Molly would soon be studying together with her new coach, Tom Amadeo, the man who had just been posing as a talk-show interviewer. He was in his early fifties; tall, burly and intense, with a clipped black beard speckled with gray, and piercing green eyes set under bushy brows. A former television producer, he had started his own PR firm at about the same time that Jake had started Berenger. Cora had explained to Molly that as a longtime friend, Tom had been the logical choice to run the unconventional campaign that he had immediately dubbed "Operation Family Man."

Someone handed her a glass of ice water. She took it, drank it straight down, and asked for another. She had been at Gold Bay for four days, and had been doing this kind of training for two of them. She didn't mind—she was grateful to have a distraction to keep her from thinking about what had happened in Belden. She didn't like to think about it, because when she did, she felt a strange numbness that disturbed her. She knew that she should be angry, but she wasn't. She was just numb, as if she didn't care.

"Feeling better?" asked Tom Amadeo. "Ready to get back to work?"

He had a boundless energy that made Molly feel feeble by comparison, and his goal was to arm her with a ready answer to any question that she might be asked "on the record." The news of the engagement had already been released to the press, right on the heels of the outing of Sandra St. Claire, and the size and tone of the resulting headlines had pleased Jake, Tom, and Cora very much. Skye Elliot was refusing to comment, her sudden silence an indicator that she was "busted and disgusted," as Tom put it.

To Molly's surprise, the sudden publicity had caused the sales of *Pirate Gold* to jump, lifting the paperback to number two on the mass-market best-seller lists. Her agent e-mailed her to say that he humbly apologized for all of the times that he had scolded her for refusing to promote the book, because he now understood that she was some kind of Zen master of publicity who knew exactly what she was doing. A national book-signing tour had nothing on an engagement to a celebrity billionaire. Plus, her hair looked great. And what about that sequel?

Despite having her name and photograph (a new and improved version created with the help of a stylist, a hairdresser, a makeup artist, and a lighting specialist, all of whom had been awaiting her when she arrived at Gold Bay) plastered all over the news, Molly hadn't yet come face-to-face with a single reporter. Jake had been the one handling the media so far, as well as dealing with a "serious business issue," as Cora cautiously described it. As a result, Molly hadn't seen him at all. She was being flown to Manhattan to meet him on Saturday, where she was due to be "launched," like a book or a ship, at the opening of the new Berenger Grand hotel on Fifty-sixth and Fifth. The Grand was a New York landmark, but it had slumped into disrepair until Berenger acquired it. They had closed the hotel fifteen months ago for a complete renovation, and the reopening was expected to be one of the major social events of the year. The Operation Family Man team had agreed that it would be an ideal venue for the press to meet Jake's fiancée.

"Tom, Molly needs a *real* break," said Cora Berenger from the periphery of the room. Molly looked up, surprised. She hadn't realized that Jake's mother was there. Cora had been supervising the proceedings since Molly returned to Gold Bay, and this was not the first time that she had stepped in to rescue Molly. Molly had become convinced that Tom Amadeo was able and willing to work twenty-four hours a day, neither eating nor sleeping, and that without Cora's intervention, he would have demanded the same from her.

Tom looked annoyed. "Not yet, we're behind schedule. We still need to cover"—he checked his clipboard—"Wedding Date questions, Do You Feel Like Cinderella questions, and Are You Intimidated by Famous Ex-Girlfriends questions."

"That may be so," Cora said pleasantly, "but it's teatime."

Ten minutes later, Cora and Molly were sitting under the bougainvillea arbor on the terrace, drinking tea and eating the small sandwiches that Molly had enjoyed during her week at the resort. Tom had surrendered without a second protest, which was no surprise to Molly. It had taken only one day at the villa before she realized who was in charge at Gold Bay. Jake might be at the helm of Berenger Corporation, but Cora was Queen of the Island, and woe to anyone who forgot it.

Molly liked Cora Berenger's stately dignity, her down-to-earth sense of humor, and the fact that she didn't have the surgically sculpted look that was so common among women of her social class. Cora wore her own face, lines and all, with an old-world elegance that made her seem more attractive and more formidable. She was the absolute opposite of Molly's anxious, submissive mother, and Molly was fascinated by her.

Cora poured her a fresh cup of tea and offered her the plate of sandwiches. "You were starting to look pale in there, my dear. I admire Tom's work ethic, but he forgets that normal people need to rest. He doesn't understand that teaching is like watering a plant. You have to regulate the stream, giving it time to soak in, or else it all overflows and you end up with mud." She smiled. "But you're a teacher, of course, so you already know that. Don't let Tom—or me—bully you. If you need a break, just say so. You're doing us a favor, after all."

"Not really," Molly said. "I think it's a pretty fair trade."

"Do you? All this work for a gamble on an island museum and the directorship of a small foundation? I hope that you don't mind my frankness, but is that really why you agreed to help us? It doesn't seem worth it."

"You're forgetting the impact on my book sales," Molly said. "Your son is single-handedly pushing me up the best-seller lists."

"Yes, I know. Did you expect that to happen? Forgive me, but you don't seem very . . . marketing-minded."

"That would be considered a compliment at Belden."

"But you're not at Belden anymore."

"No," Molly said. "I'm not. So I need to learn how to operate in the real world, and I thought that this would be good training. My anonymity was already gone, so I had nothing to lose by working with Jake, and I knew that the publicity would be good for *Pirate Gold*."

"Hmm," Cora said thoughtfully. "Well, that certainly was a bargain for us. Book sales or no, if I were you, I would have asked for something more concrete than a promise of a possible museum."

Molly smiled slightly. "Would Jake have agreed to the museum and the foundation if I'd made it an unconditional demand?"

"Oh, I don't think so," Cora said. "He's gambling, just like you are. He doesn't want to redo the plans for the golf course. It would be expensive for the company, and he would look very careless for not foreseeing the problem. That's the last thing he needs right now."

Molly nodded. She had guessed as much, despite Jake's early attempts to placate her by telling her that he had a soft spot for historical sites. Their last conversation at Gold Bay, when he had threatened to expose her as Sandra St. Claire if she tried to block the golf course development, had made his true colors very clear.

He had signed the agreement, betting that she wouldn't find proof that Dyer's Fortune had belonged to Mary Morgan. What he hadn't known was that she had already found it. She had two documents in her suitcase, courtesy of her friend at the British Library. The first was a copy of a marriage certificate dated 1722, joining one Mary Dyer to Captain Frederick Morgan of His Majesty's Royal Navy. Mary was sixteen years old at the time, and Molly now had a good idea of where she had picked up her sailing skills.

The second was an old will, dated 1749, in which Ephraim Dyer of St. Anthony's Parish, Antigua, did bequeath his lands and property to his "dear and affectionate" daughter, Mary, for her sole use and benefit forever.

Frederick's fate remained a mystery, but the connection between Mary Morgan and the Dyer name was clear. It had taken three pages of legalese to define "proof" in a way that satisfied Jake, who had made it as narrow and specific as possible, thinking that he was making a safe bet. But he had greatly underestimated the power of the academic network.

Molly could have warned him that the British colonies had been wonderfully efficient at record keeping and—with the exception of documents lost through fire, shipwreck, or other disasters—most of what had been written down in eighteenth-century Antigua now resided in various archives in London.

She didn't know when she would break the news to Jake, but she did know that she would enjoy his shock and dismay. He would look like a fool when he was forced to relocate his golf course. It wasn't exactly an eye for an eye, but it would be a satisfying blow.

"I still think that you should have been a little more practical, dear," Cora said. "That old plantation obviously means a lot to you, but Jake is a very stubborn man, and he always puts the company first. He won't give an inch on this, believe me. What will you do if you don't find your proof?"

Molly tried to give a guileless smile. "Well," she said, "if my plans for the museum don't work out, I'll still consider myself lucky to have enjoyed so much time at Gold Bay."

She saw a slight frown touch Cora's forehead, as if the older woman wasn't convinced. Molly did feel guilty for lying to her, but she had no choice. She could hardly confess to Jake's mother that she was planning to pay him back for the loss of her job and her reputation. The pieces were all in place, and she had Jake right where she wanted him. He didn't know it yet, but messing with Molly Shaw was going to turn out to be more embarrassing and more expensive than he had ever expected.

CHAPTER 21

Jake's apartment in the new Berenger Grand had been designed by Sir Harry Smythe, the famous British architect whose firm had handled the remodeling of the entire hotel. Spanning one-third of the forty-fifth floor, and reachable by its own private elevator, the apartment was an ultramodern loft-style space, with soaring glass outer walls buttressed by stainless-steel beams. Downtown Manhattan lay spread out below, and Jake's interior designer had worked hard to create a living space that echoed, but did not compete with the glittering magnificence of the city. The furnishings were modern and minimal, with leather and steel furniture, and textured area rugs that covered sections of the sandstone floor. The inner walls were decorated with huge black-and-white abstract prints, and most of the color came in dramatic splashes from tall arrangements of orchids.

It was all new, and had all been chosen, purchased, and arranged by Jake's staff, from the sheets on the bed to the soap in the bathroom to the shirts in the closet to the spatulas in the kitchen drawer. The lack of his own personal touch didn't bother Jake at all—his real home was in Miami, and this apartment was intended to be a showplace, not a cozy retreat. Besides, it was shockingly beautiful, and it amused him to open random drawers to discover what he owned.

"What the hell is this thing?" he asked, holding up a small gadget made of a cheap-looking plastic base attached by a hinge to a frame strung tightly with parallel wires.

Tom Amadeo squinted at it. "Cockroach torture instrument," he said.

"No, it's not. It's a hard-boiled egg slicer," said Molly. She was perched on the edge of a kitchen bar stool, trying to avoid crushing her gold taffeta gown. It was Saturday night, and downstairs in the ballroom the party was in full swing. They were due to make their entrance soon, and Molly was rigid with tension. Her hair had been styled into an elaborate updo, and a makeup artist had spent an hour painting her face into a seemingly airbrushed perfection. Technically, she was beautiful, but between her glassy-eyed expression and the overall stiffness of her dress and hair, she looked more like a department-store mannequin than a woman. Jake and Tom were doing what they could to amuse and relax her while they waited, and somehow they had all ended up in the kitchen.

"Okay, how about this one?" Jake displayed another mysterious-looking item.

"Cockroach juicer," said Tom.

"It's a garlic press," Molly said. A tiny smile touched the edges of her mouth.

"Forget about it," said Tom, shaking his head. "This is New York City. Sooner or later, it's all about the roaches."

Molly laughed, and Jake and Tom exchanged looks of relief. Jake was feeling more than a little uptight himself. The campaign's first week had been very promising, but this was the big night. Just as Cora had predicted, the news media had been delighted by the story of the playboy's taming at the hands of the professor, and the fact that the professor had been maintaining a secret life as Sandra St. Claire added extra spice to the stew. Molly's own notoriety suddenly rivaled Jake's own, and the ballroom was filled with people hoping to get a look at her. Berenger stock was up one point, and Tom had arranged for the *New York Times* to publish the first personal interview with Jake, a favorable profile called "Hospitality's Terrible Tycoon Comes of Age."

Operation Family Man was right on track, but so far, it had been under Tom and Jake's complete control. Now—by necessity—they were handing over some of the power to Molly. Tom insisted that she was ready, but she didn't look ready to Jake. She looked . . . unpredictable. If he had had any choice in the matter, he would have left her in seclusion at Gold Bay for the entire three months. They had been managing well with just her name and picture, but they couldn't afford to let the story get stale, so it was time to turn the volume up a notch. He needed to deliver the goods, and in this case, that meant newswire shots of the happy couple gazing lovingly at each other.

Molly reached up, patted the side of her head, then made a disgusted face.

"What's wrong?" Jake asked.

"They put so much hair spray on me that my head crunches when I touch it," she said. "I feel like a beetle."

"You look great," Tom assured her. "Just remember the message. What's the message?"

Molly sighed. "Jake Berenger is a Family Man. Jake is a more stable, more reliable person because of my steadfast devotion, and he only needed the Love of a Good Woman to convince him to settle down and abandon his wild ways."

"Good," Tom said, nodding approvingly.

"And Berenger Corporation is now a safe investment risk."

"Bad," said Tom, recoiling. "Sweetheart, I know that

you're just kidding around, and that you won't actually say that last part, right?"

Molly chuckled. "Buy Berenger stock today!" she proclaimed. "Buy low, sell high!"

"Jesus," Tom said. "I've created a monster."

"I see that you've relocated your sense of humor," Jake said to Molly. He wasn't amused. He was about to put his life into Molly Shaw's hands, and that kind of vulnerability did not sit well with him.

"And the stage direction?" Tom asked.

Molly stood up, smoothing her skirt. She smiled at Jake. "Adoring looks," she said, demonstrating one that was so syrupy that it made Jake feel sticky by association. "Loving pride. Hold Jake's hand whenever possible."

"That's right, babe. Think Nancy Reagan with Ronnie. Jake, you already know what to do." Tom checked his watch. "All right, kids. It's quarter to nine—time to roll this film."

He started toward the elevator. Molly was about to follow, but Jake caught her arm.

She looked inquiringly at him. "What?"

"Something important. Give me your left hand."

He reached into his tuxedo jacket pocket, pulled out a ring, and slipped it onto her finger.

"Oh," Molly said, staring at the stone. "That's huge. It's not . . . is it . . . ?"

"Real? Yes. It's a five-carat, d-flawless diamond. If the Berenger stock hits twenty by April first, it's yours to keep. You can consider it a thank-you gift for a job well done." *And a bribe to make it worth your while to do the job well.* The value of the ring was roughly equal to the payment that he had offered when he first proposed his idea.

Molly's hand was still suspended in the air, as if she were

mesmerized by the shimmer of the stone. "Good grief," she said. "Isn't it a bit . . . uh . . . flashy?"

"Not compared to some of the other rocks that you'll see tonight," Jake said. "Believe me, by ten P.M., you'll think it's understated."

"Let's go, lovebirds!" called Tom Amadeo from the elevator. "Chop chop!"

Molly started forward, but Jake stopped her again. "Wait," he said. "You understand that this is serious?"

She looked at him in surprise. "You're worried?" She seemed to be realizing for the first time that she had the power to destroy him with one careless sentence.

"No," Jake said. "I just want to confirm that you're ready. It's not too late to skip this event if you don't feel prepared."

"You *are* worried. I was joking about your stock. I wouldn't actually say those things in public."

"Good. It wouldn't go over well."

There was a strange look on her face. "Imagine that," she said. "You, dependent on me. If I were to make a mistake and expose your plan, you'd be ruined, wouldn't you? You could lose everything. Your job, your reputation . . ."

"Thanks for the reminder," Jake said curtly. "That was my point." He wondered if Amanda might have been the better choice, after all. Risking trouble with the Harpers was daunting, but at least he would know what he was getting himself into. Molly Shaw had more going on behind her amber-colored eyes than he understood.

"I won't make any mistakes," Molly said. "I could harm you intentionally, but why would I do that? I don't have any reason to want to ruin your life. Do I?"

"No," Jake said. He assumed that she was teasing him. He knew of no reason why she would want to destroy him, and several reasons why it would benefit her not to. That was why he was willing to trust her.

She smiled like the Mona Lisa. "Well, if you're sure about that, then you don't need to worry, do you? Your secret is safe with me."

The flashbulbs began to pop as Jake stepped out of the limousine. In a move choreographed by Tom for maximum impact, Jake and Molly had gone down in the private elevator, slipped out through a hidden back entrance, and gotten into the car, which had driven them halfway around the block to the main entrance of the Berenger Grand and released them at the foot of the red carpet. It was dark, but tall floodlamps threw a dazzling glow over the scene, illuminating the arriving guests for the benefit of the photographers and television cameramen massed outside. Closed-circuit cameras filmed each arrival's progress up the red carpet, transmitting their smiles and waves live to a giant screen suspended like a billboard above the main entrance. There was an identical screen and speakers inside the ballroom, allowing the partygoers to hear some of the noise from outside, and to enjoy the anticipatory excitement of knowing who was about to walk in. Celebrities and socialites enjoyed gawking as much as anyone in the crowd of spectators outside.

Velvet ropes and security guards held back the crowd of onlookers, who pressed forward hoping to glimpse a late-arriving movie star, or even to be selected for admission into the party. At the opening of the first Berenger hotel—the success of which was considered a textbook example of brilliant marketing—Jake had come up with the idea of having the security staff choose people from the crowd to invite inside. He had gone more for the glamorous and the glittery types then, because he had needed them, but the policy had changed as Berenger grew.

His staff was now instructed to choose without sticking

to any obvious category of person. Dressing fabulously or looking like a model was not necessarily an entry ticket. The staff always chose a few of those hopefuls, but they also knew to select apparently at random: a group of giggling teenage girls from NYU, a middle-aged couple from New Jersey, a freelance photographer, a cheerful octogenarian holding a sign that said "Pick Me! I'm Old and Bored!"

In actuality, the hundred people that the security staff now chose, checked, and admitted did fall into a very specific category, just not an easily identifiable one. They might not even be able to afford a room at a Berenger hotel, but they were the ones who fueled the celebrity industry. They were the people who read *People* and the *Star* and watched *E!* on TV. Their money and interest supported the world that Jake depended on, and he felt that he owed them. Plus, he was no fool. The policy ensured a huge crowd outside every Berenger event. The crowd drew the celebrities, who drew the media, who had helped build Berenger into a multibillion-dollar corporation.

Jake turned back to the car and extended his hand to Molly. As she had been taught, she pivoted on the limousine seat, swung her legs out, placed her feet on the curb, took his hand, and rose gracefully to a standing position beside him. He felt her body go rigid, and her fingers tighten involuntarily around his as the throng of journalists and spectators began to shout. Flashbulbs exploded from every direction, and he could hear the cameras shooting—an appropriate verb, because the sound was as rapid and mechanical as automatic gunfire.

Molly pressed up against his side, surprisingly close, and Jake guessed that it was not because of any prior instruction. The chaotic scene was more than she had expected. There was really no way to prepare someone to face the wall of paparazzi for the first time, and he didn't blame her for being alarmed. It wasn't so much a sea of photographers as it was an enormous cluster of impersonal lenses; huge, black, and gleaming, they were jammed together—seemingly piled on one another, in an alien mass of shiny, clicking circles.

Jake! Jake! Over here! When is the wedding?

Molly, look over here! Show us the ring!

Jake! Did you invite Skye to the party? What did she say about your engagement?

Molly! How did you catch America's most eligible bachelor? Was he dating you and Skye at the same time?

Molly looked at Jake, and he saw that although her mouth was smiling, her eyes were wide and frightened. He bent to murmur into her ear, aware that the cameras were capturing the apparent intimacy of the moment. "You're doing fine," he said. "The people out here are mostly freelancers and local press. We aren't taking questions from them now—we're supposed to talk first to the journalists waiting in the lobby. We'll stand here for a minute and then walk inside."

She nodded and they stood, posing hand-in-hand, turning from side to side to face the cameras on either side of the red carpet.

Molly! What name are you using for your next book?

Molly! Was Andre DuPre based on Jake?

It was time to move inside. Jake walked Molly forward up the carpet, past the photographers, and then saw something very unexpected. He should have expected it, as Molly should have, but judging by the look on her face, she was as surprised as he. Half of the people close to the velvet ropes were not hopefuls in evening dress. They were bundled in warm coats, as if they had been camping out by the front of the hotel all day, determined to secure their spots. They were holding books—paperback and hardbound versions of *Pirate Gold*, and they were waving them and calling Molly's name.

"I'll be damned," Jake said, reluctantly impressed.

"I think they want me to sign," Molly said in a small, astonished voice. "What should I do?"

Jake reached into the inside pocket of his tuxedo jacket, pulled out a gold-plated Berenger Corporation pen, and handed it to her. "Sign," he said. "I'll wait."

CHAPTER 22

The ballroom of the Berenger Grand was a soaring space of glass and golden sandstone that redefined the concept of Modern American Elegance, at least according to Sir Harry Smythe, who—as a Brit—claimed to have an impartial perspective on the subject. He was not impartial about his own work on the redesign of the hotel, which he described as "a groundbreaking marriage of classical architecture to a daring and prophetic vision for the future."

"Did you say marriage?" asked the gossip columnist for *Style Weekly*. "What do you think of Jake Berenger's fiancée?"

"I beg your pardon," said Sir Harry coldly, and Jake quickly stepped in. He had been standing just a few feet away, listening while an Associated Press reporter asked Molly about the engagement and her future plans. It was their third consecutive interview. Jake had monitored Molly's answers carefully at first, ready to intervene if necessary, but she had been parroting Tom's prepared quotes so perfectly that he had gradually relaxed and tuned out. Sir Harry was just behind him, also giving interviews, and the prickly Brit had a reputation for telling reporters that he was "unable to answer that question, because it is simply too stupid."

"Sir Harry hasn't met Molly yet," Jake said to the columnist. "He's been busy with a new project in Cairo."

Sir Harry nodded, gratified. "My design for the Baraka monument will reflect the Old Kingdom masterpieces of the fourth Pharaonic dynasty," he said, "and yet, it will be one more step in my epic journey to cast off the fetters of the past—"

Jake turned back to Molly. Sir Harry's nose was red, and he looked as if he had knocked back a few too many vodka martinis, but the man had delivered a damned good-looking hotel, and he had earned the right to orate.

It was almost ten P.M. and the ballroom was packed with people. Between Molly's impromptu book signing and the phalanx of journalists lined up inside the lobby, it had taken them an hour to progress from the limousine to the actual party. The opening was an obvious success, and after this last interview, Jake's plan was to make a pass through the crowd, greet a few key people, and then get out of there. Despite his regular presence at events like this—or perhaps because of it—he did not enjoy parties. The curious stares and the stultifying small talk wore on him, and he usually tried to escape once he'd achieved his objectives of chatting with any useful business contacts and being photographed with his date-of-the-moment.

"It was Jake's decision to settle down," Molly was saying to the reporter. "He wanted stability. He was tired of having the kind of life that distracted him from his commitment to Berenger Corporation."

Jake watched, pleased, as she delivered the message without a single misstep. She sounded a little wooden, but that was fine. The reporter was nodding and writing, and things seemed to be under control.

Tom Amadeo appeared suddenly on the edge of the crowd and beckoned to Jake. "Problem," he said. "There's a blonde over there telling the guy from the *Post* that she was responsible for introducing you to Molly, and he's writing it down like the Lord's own gospel."

"Where?" Jake asked.

Tom pointed. "There. I've seen her before—she's some kind of high-society matchmaker. Do you know her? If you don't, I'm having her tossed out of here on her skinny little butt."

Jake looked where Tom was pointing. It was none other than Elaine Newberg, wearing a black-and-white gown, opera-length gloves, and a pearl choker. Next to her stood Carter McKee in a rumpled tuxedo and a fuchsia bow tie. He was holding a wineglass in one hand and a microcassette recorder in the other. Elaine was speaking to the *New York Post* reporter, who looked much too interested in whatever she was saying.

"I know her," he said. "And him. They're friends of Molly's."

"Well, then, can Molly go over there and tell her friends to quit fucking with my PR campaign? They are making me very unhappy."

Molly was still talking to the reporter. It occurred to Jake that her friends had been at Gold Bay when he had made—and she had rejected—his first offer. She was bound by a confidentiality agreement now, but she hadn't been then, and it was very possible that she had gone back to her cottage that day and told them about his proposal.

Not good, he thought. If they knew the truth, then he was dependent on the discretion of a celebrity matchmaker and an ambitious journalist—neither one an acceptable security risk. Briefly, he told Tom of his suspicions.

Tom shrugged philosophically. "Okay," he said. "Damage control time. What's it going to take to keep them quiet?"

"I don't know about the woman," Jake said. "But I promised Molly that I would give the guy an interview."

"Can he write? Not that it matters. If he's satisfied with an interview, we're getting off cheap. He might even turn out to be useful, who knows? And if the blonde wants credit for the introduction, I'm willing to negotiate. Okay—your lovely fiancée is busy here, so how about you and I go over and say hello to our new friends."

"Mr. Berenger," said Elaine warmly as Jake approached, with Tom on his heels. "The redesign is absolute perfection. I keep an apartment in New York, of course, but I used to dine at the Grand restaurant whenever I was in town. Darling Henri always insisted on personally making me his white truffle risotto. How is he?"

"Retired," Jake said. Henri LeDuc, the Grand Hotel's executive chef, had been in the middle of one of his legendary screaming tantrums when he had collapsed from nervous exhaustion, falling facedown into a heap of freshly julienned carrots. He had returned to his native Provence to recover, self-medicating with foie gras and vintage Bordeaux, and Jake had replaced him with a young female chef from San Francisco, respected for her innovative Eurasian fusion cuisine and her lack of desire to abuse the kitchen staff.

Elaine clucked her tongue at the news. "Well, that explains the coconut prawns," she said. "Henri never approved of the frivolous use of coconut."

Tom cleared his throat impatiently, and Jake said, "May we talk to you for a minute?"

"Of course," Elaine said. She smiled meaningfully at the *Post* reporter. "Do excuse us."

They walked over to an unoccupied area near the doors to the inner courtyard, now sealed against the January cold.

"Does Molly know that you're here?" Jake asked. Somehow, he needed to find out whether they knew about Operation Family Man, and then, if they did, what it would take to buy their silence.

"Yes, but we haven't had a chance to speak with her," Elaine said. "She's been besieged with reporters. She does look a bit shell-shocked, which is no surprise after the trauma you put her through."

"She's doing well," Jake said vaguely. He didn't know what Elaine was talking about.

"You should be glad that she isn't holding your methods against you. Your plan is clever, though, and it seems to be off to a good start. I see that the stock is up."

Carter nodded enthusiastically, and Tom and Jake exchanged glances. That answered the first question. And for the second . . .

Neither of them had missed the stealthy movement of Carter McKee's thumb as it activated the microcassette recorder. Tom scowled at Carter and pointed to the small machine. "Off," he said. Carter grimaced and clicked the STOP button. Tom held out his hand, palm up, and wiggled his fingers. "Right here."

"But I'm with the *Chicago Tribune*," Carter protested.

"The *Tribune* isn't covering this conversation," Tom said. "Hand it over. You can have it back in five minutes."

Carter gave him the recorder.

"Okay, folks," Tom said. "Here's the deal. You two are Molly's friends. That's terrific. Friends of Molly are friends of ours, which is why we need to help each other. If we work together, we can make this a very good experience for all of us, if you get my meaning. *Capisce*?"

"Yes, indeed," Elaine said. "I have several ideas about how this campaign can be improved. When would you like to meet to discuss our strategy?"

"What?" Tom stared at her, taken aback. "No, no. What I meant was—"

Elaine patted him on the arm. "I don't mean to imply that I don't admire your work. You've done a good job so far, but your lack of expertise in certain areas is rather obvious. Fortunately, I know exactly what to do, and I'll be happy to advise you."

"Advise me?" Tom exclaimed. "*Me!* Do you know who I am?"

Elaine sighed. "Male vanity can be so tiresome," she said. "Of course I know who you are, Mr. Amadeo, but the ability to promote the careers of movie stars and basketball players does not necessarily qualify you to deal with the subtle complexities of *this* situation."

"Subtle . . . what?" Tom sputtered. "Listen, lady. I know who you are, too. I've seen you on *Oprah*, and I'll be goddamned if I'll let some Chanel-covered dilettante tell me that I'm not qualified to do my job."

"My gown is by Valentino," Elaine said. "Which delivers an entirely different message than Chanel. This is a perfect example of the problem. Just like a man, you're focusing entirely on the big picture and ignoring the details. You are trying to club the media over the head with your message, which was fine in the beginning, but you cannot beat people into believing that Jake has changed. One must seduce in order to persuade, and seduction is all about detail. Consider Molly's dress."

"What about it? I picked it myself. She looks great."

"No, she looks entirely wrong. Gold taffeta is too stuffy, and it doesn't suit her. She should be wearing chiffon. A pale color . . . sky blue, I think. It's not seasonal, but it would make her look fresh and angelic in the midst of all of this formal black."

Tom glared at her. "Gold is the Berenger signature color."

"That may be so, but Molly is not a Berenger mascot. Her hair is also wrong. It should be loose, not sprayed into a helmet. You dressed her up like a fifty-year-old political wife. I cannot imagine what you were thinking."

"Hah," Tom said triumphantly. "I knew it. You don't have a clue about this business. Making her look like a political wife was the whole *idea.* She looks stable and respectable. And elegant. She looks like a fucking grande dame of society. She's the antibimbo, which is exactly what we want. Babe, I have been doing this for twenty years. I am the king of marketing, and you are an *amateur.*"

Elaine gazed disdainfully at him, as if he were some kind of hairy barbarian. "Does she look like the love of Jake's life?"

They both turned to Jake, who had been hoping to stay out of the discussion. Tom was a pro, but Elaine had a point. His first thought upon seeing Molly that evening was that she looked like one of his mother's friends from Palm Beach. In his opinion, she had been much more attractive when she arrived in New York that morning, fresh off the plane from Antigua. She had been wearing a fuzzy cream-colored sweater and snug jeans, and he had been amused to see that she had a sunburned nose.

"Well?" Elaine asked Jake. "Does she?"

"No," Jake admitted. "I like women with less shellac on them."

"What the hell difference does that make?" Tom demanded, throwing up his hands. "This isn't about reality, it's about image. We have a message to deliver. Jake Berenger is a Family Man."

"Perhaps you should write your message on a sign and glue it to Molly's forehead," Elaine suggested tartly. "That would make it equally convincing. Right now the poor girl looks and sounds like a puppet, and every journalist I know is wondering if this is some sort of publicity stunt. I've been doing my best to help, but you need to show the world *why*

Jake Berenger fell in love with Molly Shaw, and why he is now changing his entire life for her. If you don't do that, no one will believe your message, and your whole campaign will be a failure."

Tom stared at her, speechless.

Elaine looked smug. "Thank goodness you came to me in time," she said.

Jake left Tom and Elaine together and made his way through the crowd toward the stage. It was a few minutes before ten, when he was scheduled to address the crowd with one of the welcome-and-thank-you-for-coming speeches that he had given so many times that he no longer bothered to prepare in advance.

Cal Kennedy, the manager of the new Berenger Grand, was already onstage with the mayor of New York. Jake greeted them, then stood, waiting while the jazz band finished the last song of the set. He looked out over the dense crowd, his eyes instinctively finding Molly. She was talking to another journalist, one who Jake didn't recognize, and who wasn't on the schedule. One of Tom's assistants stood nearby, waiting for her to finish. He was to escort her through the crowd and onto the stage for the final photo op of the evening.

She was speaking at length to this new reporter, a petite woman who was writing fast on her notepad. Jake wondered what she was saying, and why Tom's assistant was maintaining such an unnecessarily respectful distance. He was supposed to be monitoring the conversation so that he could intervene if Molly started to say something indiscreet.

He tapped his fingers against his leg. Tom's assistant

glanced at his watch, then at the stage. "Don't look at me," Jake muttered. "Look at her. That's your job."

He reminded himself that Molly knew what she was doing. He had supervised every word she said since they arrived, and she hadn't made a single mistake. But she had given brief, careful answers when he had been with her. Now unsupervised, she was suddenly holding forth as if she were at the head of a lecture class. What, exactly, was she talking about? He remembered her strange, enigmatic smile just before they had left his apartment. *I could harm you intentionally, but why would I do that?*

The band's final number closed with a blast of sound from the saxophone, and applause broke out through the ballroom. That was supposed to be Jake's cue to take the microphone, but he didn't. He had an uneasy feeling in the pit of his stomach. What had Elaine Newberg meant when she told him that he should be glad that Molly wasn't holding his methods against him?

The music and the last applause were dying away, and heads were turning expectantly toward him. He frowned. Molly was leaning toward the reporter. She was listening now, nodding, and Tom's useless assistant didn't seem to be planning to break up the conversation. Abruptly Jake faced Cal Kennedy.

"Can you do the welcome?" he asked.

Cal looked surprised. "Sure. I didn't prepare anything, but I could just—"

"Great," Jake said. "It's all yours. Excuse me."

He walked down the stairs at the side of the stage and quickly crossed the room to Elaine. Her back was to him, and he reached out and grasped her by the elbow.

She turned, and he beckoned her away from the group. "You said that I put Molly through a trauma," he said without preamble. "What did you mean?"

"I beg your pardon?"

"You also said that I should be glad that she isn't holding my methods against me. What methods? What trauma?"

Elaine looked stern. "That cannot possibly be a genuine question, Mr. Berenger. You know exactly what I meant."

"No, I don't. Explain."

She sighed. "I suppose that my willingness to offer my help has given you the impression that I approve of what you did to Molly. In fact, I think it was very ruthless. Necessary . . . perhaps. That's debatable. But—"

"Tell me what I did to Molly," Jake said through his teeth. "Now."

"You betrayed her to the press," Elaine said impatiently. "She lost her job because of you. It was very selfish—oh, damn, there's the society columnist from *Style Weekly* staring at us. She doesn't like me, and she's going to be wondering what's happening here."

"I didn't betray Molly to anyone," Jake said sharply. "Who told you that?"

Elaine gave a cheery little wave to the columnist. "Jake, dear, would you mind smiling a bit? It would be better to make this look like a cozy tête-à-tête . . ."

"Who told you that?"

"Molly did, of course. I admit that I was glad to see her leave Belden. Carter and I felt very strongly that she didn't belong there, but we agreed that she needed to make that decision for herself. Your interference was—"

"Interference!" Jake exclaimed. "I just said that I didn't have anything to do with it. It was some professor at Belden who blew the whistle on Molly. She told me so herself."

"Oh?" Elaine said. "How odd. That's not what she said to us. She's very sure that you did it. I suppose that she didn't confront you because she decided not to hold it against you."

Jake's guts went cold as he suddenly understood what was happening. Elaine was wrong; Molly hadn't decided to forgive him for his alleged crime. On the contrary, she had decided that the best revenge would be to wait until she was in a position where she could really screw him. Her mysterious statements in the apartment now made sense. He should have known then that something was wrong—he should have been alerted by the look on her face. She had learned what Skye Elliot had always known: that the media could be the most powerful weapon on earth. And just like Skye, Molly intended to use it against him. He had to stop her, if it wasn't already too late. He turned and pushed back into the crowd, heading for the spot where Molly had last been standing.

CHAPTER 23

Molly was talking to a female reporter from the *National Enquirer* when her peripheral vision caught the shape of a man with a camera approaching from the right. She began to shuffle stealthily, turning where she stood. The reporter looked surprised, but obligingly moved with her, and Molly kept talking, pretending that nothing unusual was happening. She had spent the past hour doing this weird revolving dance, trying to keep the photographers on her left, her best side, according to Tom. He had also instructed her not to eat anything, to prevent any sloppy shots of food halfway into her mouth. Champagne was permitted, because the glass served as a prop, and after consuming four glasses of Dom Perignon on an empty stomach, Molly was feeling increasingly talkative.

Tom had also told her to smile with her tongue pushed firmly against the back of her front teeth, a move designed to tighten a sagging chin. A week earlier, Molly had not known that she had a sagging chin, and as she forced another smile, her tongue aching with the exertion, she decided that ignorance had been bliss. Vanity—like fire—was useful in small amounts, but it had the potential to destroy you if it got out of control. Tom had taught her all of the tricks used by actresses and models to look good in candid photos, but between dutifully employing those tricks and delivering Tom's prepared answers, Molly was left with very little brainpower to focus on anything else—much less to enjoy the party.

When the reporter asked her about *Pirate Gold*, she was so happy to be released from the confines of Tom's script that she launched into an enthusiastic description of the latest adventures of Andre DuPre.

"And when does the sequel come out?" asked the reporter, scribbling down what Molly had been saying.

"The what?" Molly said, taken aback. She had been describing a story that existed only in her head.

The reporter looked curiously at her. "You don't think of the new book as a sequel?"

Molly hadn't even thought of it as a book. "Oh," she said, "a sequel. Yes. Of course it is." She smiled nervously. "I mean, what else would it be?"

The reporter said something, but Molly wasn't listening. She thought of all the time that she'd spent insisting that she wasn't writing another novel. She thought of how she'd made the resolution to focus solely on her academic work, because it was the proper thing to do. And all the while, she had been spinning the story in her head and covertly writing down the best scenes. Her own denial suddenly seemed ludicrous. She was indeed working on a sequel, and why shouldn't she? Everything was different now. The gods of Academia had evicted her from the Garden of Belden, and she had nothing left to lose by indulging herself. Surprised, she laughed. Was it really as simple as that?

An arm gripped her shoulders, solid as a plow yoke. Molly twisted, startled, and saw that the arm was attached to Jake. He and Tom had disappeared into the crowd a little while earlier, after spending close to an hour hovering nearby, monitoring her.

"Hi there," she said, clutching at him. She was slightly dizzy, and knew that she had better find some solid food before long.

"Jake," said the reporter, swiveling to focus on him with laserlike intensity. "Great party. Are you planning to—"

"Sorry," Jake said. His voice was neutral, but his arm felt like iron around Molly. "No time to talk. Excuse us."

Before Molly had a chance to say anything else, he was moving her away, walking her briskly toward the exit doors. Curious stares followed them.

"Where are we going?" she asked, hurrying along with him, trying not to stumble over the hem of her gown. Something about his stride and his silence suggested that all was not well.

He didn't answer, nor did he release her. They passed the marble reception desk with its towering arrangements of flowers, and approached the row of elevators.

"What's happening?" Molly asked. Still, he said nothing. There was a uniformed security guard next to the private elevator, who nodded to Jake and used his key to open the doors. They stepped in, the doors closed, and only then did Jake let go of her. Molly was surprised to see that his face was set into grim lines.

"*Your secret is safe with me*," he said coldly. "Very cute. Too bad I didn't catch the reference earlier."

"Huh?" Molly said.

"It's what I said on the day that I figured out that you were Sandra. You asked me not to tell, and I told you that your secret was safe with me. You repeated that back to me earlier this evening, before we left the apartment. What was that supposed to be, a warning? A test?"

Molly frowned. "This is so strange," she said. "I don't *think* I'm drunk, but I'm finding this conversation very hard to follow, so maybe I—"

"Why the hell didn't you talk to me before you decided that I was the villain? I would have told you that I wasn't the one who gave away your secret. I had nothing to do with it."

The elevator stopped, and the doors slid open into the apartment's entrance foyer. Molly walked out into the hall, her gown making a whisking noise as the hem brushed against the stone floor. Through the archway leading to the living room, she could see the wide glass windows and the lights of the city below.

Jake followed her. "Who was the reporter? And what did you say to her?"

"I don't remember her name," Molly said. "But she was from the *National Enquirer*."

"Great," he muttered. He strode past her into the living room and toward the bar, where he pulled a crystal highball glass from the rack on the wall and poured himself a straight shot of whiskey. He turned to face her again.

"Let me remind you that you signed a legally binding confidentiality agreement. Anything you said to the press will be evidence in court when I sue you for every goddamned penny you have. You should have done your homework before you messed with me, Molly. I am not a nice guy when I'm crossed."

Molly giggled. "You do seem cross," she said. "And it's true, you aren't being very nice." Now that she was away from the noise and excitement of the crowd, she could feel the effects of the champagne. The buzz, combined with the heady relief of having successfully handled the press, was making her giddy.

Jake set his glass down on the bar with a thump, and the amber liquid sloshed up to touch the rim. "You're drunk? I don't believe this."

"No, no." Molly said quickly. "Just a little light-headed, honestly. I was a very respectable fiancée. Now, what were you saying about suing me for every penny I have? I'm sorry—I'll be serious this time."

"This is a *joke* to you?" Jake demanded.

"I'm not sure," Molly said. "If I knew what you were talking about, I might have a better answer."

"I'm talking about the fact that you *think* you have a reason to want to destroy me. I know what's going on, Molly. There was no jealous professor at Belden who told the press about Sandra. You think I'm the one who told them. And you just paid me back in kind, didn't you? What did you tell the *Enquirer* reporter?"

"Oh," Molly said. Now she understood. Somehow, Jake had figured out that she knew the truth about what he'd done, and he had panicked, thinking that she would use the night's spotlight as her chance for revenge. It was a reasonable fear—she had considered the idea when it occurred to her earlier that evening. She had been shocked to realize that she actually had the power to hurt him in a way that had made her original plan seem about as painful as a mosquito bite. If she really wanted an eye for an eye, then exposing Jake's scheme to the press would be the way to do it. She had had the perfect opportunity when he had left her alone.

Jake was staring at her, and she was secretly glad to see him looking so tense. In her opinion, he deserved more than a few moments of agony, and she was in no hurry to ease his mind. "You're the one who should have done his homework," she said. "I spent my whole life working to earn that job at Belden. It was all I ever wanted, and then you came along and ruined everything. What made you think that I would just say, 'Gosh, that's a shame,' and then help you? Do I look like a human sacrifice? Maybe so, but I'm not."

"I didn't have anything to do with the loss of your job," Jake said. "My mother and I both knew that you were Sandra, but neither of us told anyone else, especially not the press."

"Oh, please," Molly scoffed, her temper rising. "Who else would have told them? Carter? Elaine? I don't think so. *They* are my friends. *They* care about me. You just saw an opportunity to use me . . ."

"Actually," Jake said, "a lot of people—including your friends—stood to gain from you leaving Belden and helping me. Your friend Carter gets his interview, your friend Elaine is taking credit for the introduction, your publisher gets to sell more books, your agent makes more money . . . stop me anytime. Why was I the only suspect?"

"This is ridiculous!" Molly exclaimed. "Of course it was you. You already threatened me once. I kept the secret for more than a year without any problem, and then, a week after I told you, it was all over the papers. My friends would never sell me out. You, on the other hand . . ."

"Why would I do that?"

"Because I wouldn't have helped you otherwise. And you said yourself that my notoriety would be useful."

"Yes, but that doesn't mean—" Jake began angrily, and then stopped himself. He took a breath, and said, "I hope you aren't expecting to walk away from this. You're looking at a lawsuit and public exposure like you never even imagined. You might hate me and want to see me ruined, but it won't be worth the price you'll pay."

"I don't hate you," Molly said.

Jake gave a short, humorless laugh. "Then God help me if you ever decide that you do."

"Oh, good grief. Look, there isn't any scandal. I was talking to the reporter about my next book. That's all."

He shook his head. "Nope. I don't buy it. She looked too interested in whatever you were telling her."

"Excuse me, but you aren't the only interesting topic

available for discussion. I was telling her about the sequel to *Pirate Gold.*"

"You were baiting me before we left the apartment. You can't tell me now that you weren't planning something."

She sighed. "I admit that I considered exposing the fake engagement. But I didn't do it."

"Why not? You had the chance. If I'd known what was really going on, I sure as hell wouldn't have sent you downstairs to meet the press. That should prove that I had nothing to do with outing you as Sandra. Why would I put my own neck on the block if I thought you had an ax and a reason to swing it?"

"You didn't know that I knew the truth," Molly said, but she felt a sudden flicker of doubt. "You thought you were safe."

"Believe me," Jake said, "that's not a risk I would have taken. I'll say it again. I did not give away your secret. You're going to have to look elsewhere for your villain."

He met Molly's eyes squarely, his jaw set. She looked back at him. In the novels she'd read, and even in the book she'd written, characters were always seeing the truth in each other's eyes, as if there were subtitles scrolling across their irises. But as she gazed at Jake, she saw only an unnervingly handsome man with a level stare and a grim look on his face. The truth, whatever it might be, was not going to present itself so easily.

"Why didn't you go through with it?" he asked.

Molly hesitated. The answer was tangled up in a complex mixture of feelings, and she wasn't going to try to explain it to Jake before she had sorted it out for herself. She lifted her chin slightly. "I don't know. I didn't want to."

"That's not a satisfactory answer," Jake said. "I want some assurance that I'm not gambling my entire future on your daily mood. You're in a position to do me a lot of harm if you decide that you do *want* to."

Molly didn't answer. She was troubled by his insistence that he had not told the press about Sandra. It wasn't that she had expected him to admit everything—that would be foolish, and Jake was no fool.

But now she was more confused than ever. There was no way to know if his denial was sincere. His words sounded heartfelt, but maybe she was just gullible. What did she know about Jake Berenger's heart, after all?

CHAPTER 24

Novelist Greets Fans at Berenger Bash

Molly Shaw, also known as novelist Sandra St. Claire and the fiancée of real estate mogul Jake Berenger, signed autographs for fans waiting outside the new Berenger Grand last night. Some had come from as far away as New Jersey in hopes of catching a glimpse of the mysterious author, who was sporting an enormous diamond on her left hand. Ms. Shaw's first novel, Pirate Gold, *a meaty and meticulously researched historical saga, was a runaway best seller . . .*

"Meaty," Molly said, thumping the *Post* onto the table in front of Jake. She sounded outraged. "Meticulously researched! Can you believe this?"

Jake stirred sugar into his coffee and glanced down at the article. "Sounds good to me. What's the problem?"

"Six months ago, they called it sleazy! What changed? Not the book, that's for sure."

"Two words," Jake said. "Tom Amadeo. He has a finger on every keyboard."

Molly shook her head in disbelief. "But that's crazy. Isn't there any kind of objective reality?"

"Sure. The people who actually read your book, liked it, and told their friends to buy it. Other than that, it's all hype. But that's the way the world works."

"Apparently so," Molly said. "If Napoleon Bonaparte had had a better publicist, he'd probably be known as a visionary who brought codified laws to Europe, instead of as an egocentric dictator."

Jake grinned. "A nice guy, old Napoleon. Just a family man, underneath it all."

"Right," Molly said dryly. "Like you."

They were having breakfast at a round glass table tucked into the corner of Jake's living room. The two outer walls were made of floor-to-ceiling glass, giving the impression that the table was perched on the edge of a cliff.

Jake was trying to shake off a feeling of vertigo. He wasn't sure whether the sensation was brought on by the view or by Molly's presence. The innocuous tone of the morning news reports had confirmed that she had been telling him the truth last night. She hadn't leaked the story. As a result, Jake was breathing a little easier. Operation Family Man was turning out to be very much like windsurfing on a blustery day—lots of forward momentum and an exciting ride, coupled with the constant threat of capsizing. And he had been sailing in very deep water lately.

"I've got some work to finish this morning," he said to Molly. "But we'll be leaving for the airport at two. I'm going to Miami, but the plane will take you to Antigua, and the resort helicopter will meet you there. I'll be back at Gold Bay early on Friday."

Molly nodded. "I'm already packed. I hung that taffeta dress in the closet."

"You're welcome to take it," Jake said. "It's yours."

"Oh," Molly said. "Is it?" She cast a glance down at the *Post* article, which was accompanied by a photo of her signing books outside the Berenger Grand. With the sprayed hair and the conservative gown, she bore an uncanny resemblance to Ambassador Pamela Harriman—in her later years.

"I think I'll leave it," she said, and Jake could hardly blame her. She put her napkin on the table and stood up. "I'm going out for a while. I'll be back before two."

Something about her manner caught Jake's attention. "Where are you going?"

Molly seemed startled by the question, as if she hadn't expected him to ask. "Oh, nowhere," she said. "Nowhere important, I mean. I just thought I'd do some shopping."

"Sounds good," Jake said, looking curiously at her. Her tone was a little too bright and casual.

"On Madison Avenue," Molly added. "I thought I'd walk over there and look at the stores. And then I'm meeting Elaine for lunch at La Grenouille."

Jake nodded, but a prickle of alarm moved through him. She was lying. He didn't know why he was so sure, but he would have bet money on it.

"No need to walk," he said, watching her. "Take a hotel car. We have one on standby for you."

"The limousine? Oh, no. I can't ride around town in a stretch limo. I'll feel ridiculous. Really, it's fine—"

"We have other cars. Take a sedan. The driver can handle your shopping bags for you."

"That's not necessary. I wasn't planning on buying much."

"Even so, La Grenouille is too far to walk."

She looked dismayed. "I'll just get a cab—"

"Why bother, when we already have a car for you?" *And a driver to keep an eye on you*, he added silently. *Or is that the problem?* He was getting a bad feeling about this. He remembered Molly's animated conversation with the *Enquirer* reporter and wondered if he had been too quick to relax and sound the all-clear.

"Right," Molly said. She looked frustrated. "Of course. It makes much more sense to take the car. I'll stop by the front desk on my way out and arrange it."

"No need," Jake said. "I'll call while you're in the elevator. The driver will meet you in front of the main entrance in five minutes."

Molly's smile did not reach her eyes. "How thoughtful," she said. "Thank you."

"Glad to help," Jake said pleasantly. "Enjoy your morning."

Ten minutes later, Molly left in a Lincoln Town Car with a Berenger staff driver at the wheel. Following closely—but not too closely—was another car whose passenger, "Big Rick" Rubio, a six-foot-four, three-hundred-pound member of the Berenger security staff, had been instructed to keep an eye on her and to report back at regular intervals.

Jake was at his desk when the first call came. He was not at all surprised to hear Big Rick confirm that Molly had not gone shopping. She had headed uptown, all right, but not on Madison Avenue. Instead, her driver had made a beeline for Central Park West, and within a few minutes, she had been dropped off at . . . the museum.

"The *museum*?" Jake repeated. "What, the Met?"

"The American Museum of Natural History. She got off on Seventy-seventh. I'm outside right now. You want me to follow her in?"

"Yes," Jake said, frowning. Either Molly had been overcome by a sudden desire to see dinosaur bones, or she was up to something. "Stay close to her. Call me if she meets anyone."

It wasn't long before the phone rang again. Jake had been staring down at a pile of legal documents, reading the same paragraphs over and over without processing the words.

"She's with a guy," Big Rick said ominously. "Still at the museum. They're at a table in the fourth-floor café."

"Short guy? Brown hair? Bow tie?"

"Nope. Tall. Light hair, no tie. Good-looking. They're talking, seem pretty friendly."

"What do you mean, friendly?"

"Sitting close. Looking into each other's eyes. She kissed him when she saw him."

Jake stiffened. He had assumed that Molly was sneaking off to a secret meeting with a journalist, but what if this was something else entirely? What if she was in the middle of a romantic liaison? The Natural History museum wasn't his idea of a steamy setting, but maybe it was a professor thing. He suppressed a sudden feeling of outrage. True, Molly wasn't actually his fiancée, so her personal life was none of his business, but she was hardly anonymous. She might think that she was free to go out on a date, but after all the recent publicity, there was a very real chance that she would be recognized.

"Great," he muttered. Molly was too green—she didn't know how to play the game at this level, and it was his own fault for not warning her. If she and her friend got too cozy, they were likely to end up on the front page of tomorrow's *Daily News*.

"Now he's taking notes," Big Rick said.

Notes, Jake thought, baffled. Who was this guy? A reporter? A boyfriend? Both? It made no sense.

"You want pictures?" Big Rick asked. "I've got a camera."

You and everybody else. "No," Jake said. "Definitely not. But stay with her. I'm coming over."

The American Museum of Natural History covered four city blocks, and was made up of an eclectic mixture of architectural materials and styles, from pink granite to red brick, from neo-Gothic to futuristic. Jake had never been inside, but he guessed that the museum was probably on the Berenger Foundation beneficiary list. Cora had a soft spot for educational enterprises.

He took the elevator up to the café on four, and immediately spotted Big Rick. In a Sunday crowd made up mostly of the under-twelve age group, the bodyguard's massive frame and bald head were somewhat conspicuous. The fact that he was also wearing mirrored sunglasses and an earpiece didn't help. He was sitting at a small table by a window with a coffee cup in front of him. Some of the parents glanced uneasily at him, but others seemed to assume that he was a museum guard. One woman, dragging a kicking toddler by the hand, stopped to speak to him, and Big Rick pointed toward the ladies' room with a nonchalance that suggested that this was not the first time he'd been asked.

Molly and her friend were at a table in the middle of the room, and Jake headed straight toward them. It was likely to be an awkward situation, but at the moment his priority was security, not elegance.

Molly's eyes widened, and she suddenly stopped speaking mid-sentence when she noticed Jake approaching. Her mouth stayed slightly open for a moment, and then thinned into a tight line as she began to scowl.

Jake pulled out an empty chair and sat down. "Hi," he said. "Sorry I'm late. Glad to see you started without me."

Molly's friend blinked at him for one surprised moment. Jake stared back, sizing him up. He had sandy hair and blue eyes, and he was broad-shouldered, but skinny.

Weak, Jake thought with sudden satisfaction. *I could take him in a fight, no problem.* He wasn't planning to brawl in the middle of the museum café—it was just a matter of establishing the order.

The man looked uneasy, as if he could read Jake's mind. Molly looked as if she planned to throttle Jake at the first available opportunity. "I knew it," she muttered through her teeth. "I *knew* it."

Big Rick had been stretching it to call this guy good-looking, in Jake's opinion. He wondered what Molly thought she was doing, kissing someone so skinny. He would have expected better judgment from her, but there was no accounting for taste. Not that he cared, anyway. She could kiss any loser she wanted to, but she had damn well better do it in private next time.

He shook the man's hand, making a point of squeezing a little harder than he should have. "Jake Berenger," he said. "And you are?"

"Oh, yes, of course, I know," the man said with a pained look as he retrieved his hand from Jake's grasp. "Nathan Van Peebles. I was at your opening last night."

"Great," Jake said. "In what capacity?"

"Supplicant," Nathan Van Peebles said earnestly. "I try to go to as many of those events as possible. It helps me catch up with our top donors. I hope I don't sound too pushy if I say that I'd love a chance to tell you about some of our new programs."

"Programs," Jake repeated, nodding vaguely. Who was this Peebles person? And what kind of name was that, anyway? There was a little notebook open on the table in front of him, and Molly's e-mail address had been jotted down in neat block letters. Below that were a few messier notes that Jake couldn't read.

"Nathan is the director of the Natural History museum," Molly said in a chilly voice. "That's this building, where we're currently sitting, in case you don't know."

"Thanks," Jake said. "I saw the sign on my way in. And how do you two know each other?"

"Nathan was a student of my father's at Belden," Molly said.

"Among other things," Nathan Van Peebles said. "Molly and I have quite a history together."

Jake raised his eyebrows inquiringly. "Oh?"

"Oh, yes," Nathan said. "We dated for a while, but—"

"Casually," Molly interjected.

"Yes, of course," Nathan said. "And then—eight years ago this month, in fact—was the night that Molly made me the happiest man in the world."

"Good Lord," Jake said.

Nathan Van Peebles smiled fondly at Molly. "I'll never forget it. We were at her parents' house in Belden. I had no idea what was in store for me, but Molly had been planning the whole thing for weeks."

"You don't say," Jake said.

"It was the first time I'd ever felt anything so powerful," Nathan said dreamily. "The only time, in fact. Once is enough for a lifetime, of course."

Jake turned to stare at Molly. He knew from personal experience that she was a great kisser, but it was hard to imagine that anyone could consider one night enough for a lifetime.

Molly exhaled impatiently. "He's talking about *love*," she said. "Love at first sight. Eight years ago I introduced Nathan to—"

"Lisette," Nathan Van Peebles said. "The most wonderful

woman on earth. She was Molly's college roommate. Now she's my wife."

"So why didn't you just *say* that you were meeting your friend for coffee?" Jake demanded later. "What was all that about shopping and lunch with Elaine? Why lie? Who cares?"

They were in the Hall of Ornithischian Dinosaurs, wading through a sea of schoolchildren. Shiny brown bones loomed around them, arranged into hulking shapes.

Nathan had gone, promising to give Molly's love to Lisette, who was away on a business trip and would be glad to have Molly's new e-mail address. Big Rick had been sent back to the Grand.

"You care, obviously," Molly said. "I didn't feel like telling you the truth and then needing to convince you that Nathan was just an old friend and not a reporter. Shopping seemed like a simpler explanation. And I was right. I saw the look on your face when you sat down. You almost broke Nathan's hand! He plays the violin, you know. You can't just squeeze him like that."

"I don't know what you're talking about," Jake muttered.

"And I *knew* that you were going to send someone to watch me. Listen, Jake, where I go and what I do is none of your business! I—"

"It's my business if you're a threat to me," Jake said. "Just last night you were amusing yourself with the idea of ruining my life, remember? And today I'm supposed to trust you? No way, babe. I'm keeping an eye on you, so get used to it."

"Hmm," Molly said. "Do you know who Howard Hughes was?"

"The tycoon? The one who almost married Ava Gardner?"

"Among others. He was a control freak who used to send his people to spy on whatever Hollywood starlet he was dating."

"What about him?"

She gazed levelly at him. "He died alone and insane, if I remember correctly."

"So? What does that have to do with me? This isn't about jealousy, damn it!" A nearby mother gave Jake a disapproving look, and he lowered his voice. "This is about security. You can go off and meet anyone you want, just do it discreetly. And stay away from the press."

A group of children passed them, and Jake moved out of the way, putting his hand on the stegosaurus's leg.

"No touching," said a guard.

"Sorry," Jake said. He dropped his hand, stepped sideways, and almost tripped over a stroller, earning a dirty look from the man pushing it. Regaining his balance, he turned and bumped into an elderly couple.

"Sorry," he said again. "Excuse me." He turned to Molly, who was pressing her lips together, trying—unsuccessfully—not to laugh. He seized her by the arm. "Get me out of here."

The elevator was jammed with people, crushing them against the back wall of the metal box. Jake folded his arms and stared forward at the ground-floor button, which glowed on the panel like a beacon of freedom.

"You look surly," Molly remarked. She was pressed up against his side, by necessity, and it was more distracting than he wanted to admit.

"I hate crowds," he said, looking down at her. Even in the warm dead air of the elevator, he could smell the faint sweetness of her perfume. It tickled his nose in a pleasant way. He associated that particular scent with Molly in her Sandra St. Claire guise, and it brought back vivid memories of the day that he had kissed her. She had apparently adopted Sandra's perfume for long-term use, which didn't bode well for Jake's peace of mind.

The elevator stopped on the third floor and disgorged half of the group. They were immediately replaced by a fresh surge of bodies, and Jake exhaled slowly as the doors slid closed again.

He wondered what kind of kiss Molly had given her friend Nathan. A polite peck on the cheek? A friendly brush of lips against lips? Surely not more than that, even if they had once dated. What did "casual" mean to Molly? Something less, Jake hoped, than the steamy invitation that she had surprised him with at Falcon's Point. If she had ever kissed Nathan Van Peebles like that, they would certainly have been lovers. No normal man—under normal circumstances—could resist that kind of offer.

The elevator stopped on the second floor, and Molly began to push toward the open doors. "Hey," Jake said, startled, and followed her. "This is the wrong floor . . ."

She turned to look at him as the elevator doors slid shut behind them. "For you, maybe. Not for me. You don't think that I met Nathan here just because I like the café food so much, do you? I'm not ready to go yet."

"I am," Jake said.

"So?" Molly shrugged. "Go. I'm not stopping you."

She wasn't, but something else was. He had come to the museum in the Berenger limo, but he had left the hotel in such a hurry that he had forgotten his cell phone. Given the traffic outside, it was likely that the driver had gone off to find a quieter spot to wait, and now Jake had no way to contact him.

"I can't," he said. "I don't have a ride. I need to go back with you."

She looked surprised, then amused. "Take a cab," she said.

"I can't do that, either," he muttered.

"Why not? Are you too rich to use normal transit?"

"No," Jake said, annoyed. "Too poor. I don't have my wallet, either."

Molly began to chuckle. "I'd be glad to loan you ten dollars," she said. "Or you could just come with me. I'll only be here for another hour or so."

"What are you doing?"

Still grinning, she pointed to something behind him. He turned and saw a huge red banner displaying a skull and crossbones, along with large type reading: "Buccaneers! A History of the Caribbean Pirates."

"Special exhibit," Molly said. "The director of the Antigua museum was one of the consultants, and he told me to be sure to see it while I was in town. It's been getting great reviews. People love pirates."

"I hate pirates," Jake said, with feeling. Caribbean or corporate, in his opinion they could all go to hell. As a category, they were making his life as difficult as that of any eighteenth-century sea captain.

"Yes, and crowds," Molly agreed. "I remember."

"Listen, about that ten dollars . . ."

She shook her head. "I'm rescinding my offer. Since you were so determined to follow me to the museum, I think it would be good for you to stay and learn a little more about Caribbean history. It's relevant to your top resort, and who knows? You may even develop a new appreciation for Mary Morgan."

Despite Molly's best efforts as a tour guide, Jake did not discover any new affection for Bonny Mary Morgan. He was interested to learn, though, that the real name of the pirate Blackbeard was Edward Teach or—according to some documents—Thatch. It seemed grimly appropriate.

"Blackbeard was known for weaving hemp into his beard, then setting it on fire during a battle, so his whole head would smoke and glow satanically," Molly said. "He was one of the most feared and hated pirates of all time. He allegedly made a prisoner eat his own ears once."

Jake nodded. "That sounds like Ed, all right."

Molly looked puzzled, so he explained the situation with Ed Thatcher, Atlas Group, and the potential takeover.

"How odd," Molly said. "Does he have black hair? Does he wear brocade?"

Jake shook his head. "Nope. Gray hair, and he wears madras golf pants with embroidered ducks."

"No," Molly said, looking appalled. "Not really."

"Yes," Jake said. "I'm telling you, the man is pure evil. Blackbeard didn't run a line of cruise ships, did he?"

"I don't think so," Molly said. "He had a fleet of ships, but I'm pretty sure that none of them had shuffleboard courts. I'll check that with my sources, though."

"Thanks," Jake said. "If you could uncover some kind of outstanding arrest warrant from the eighteenth century, you could save me a lot of trouble."

Molly laughed. Her eyes were warm and approving, and Jake couldn't help grinning back at her. They stood like that for a long moment, gazing at each other, and Jake realized that the feeling rising in his chest was anticipation. Molly Shaw was difficult and often incomprehensible, but she was also the most interesting woman he had met in a long, long time. His eyes dropped to linger on the curve of her mouth.

"I want to know something," Molly said. She was looking at him as if she, too, had just stopped being aware of the crowd surrounding them. "That day, when I was dressed as Sandra . . ."

"Which day?"

"The one when you . . . I mean, when we . . ." She frowned. "You know."

Jake thought that he did know what she meant. If so, it was provocative to hear that Molly had also been thinking about their encounter at Falcon's Point.

"Why did you kiss me?" she asked in a sudden blurt.

He raised his eyebrows. *"Why?"*

"If you thought I was from the press, kissing me was about the last thing you should have done. It was reckless, but you're usually very deliberate. So why did you do it?"

Jake wondered what she expected him to say. That he had been overcome with lust for the seductive Sandra? That he had been curious to see the professor's reaction? That Molly's mouth had simply been as appealing then as it was now? If anything, the question should be why had he kept kissing her, long after he'd made his point. She was right—despite his image, he wasn't generally a reckless person. He had too much to lose to risk it with foolish behavior, and molesting a tabloid journalist—as he had believed her to be at the time—was foolishness writ large.

"I wanted to see if you lived up to your padding," he said finally.

Her cheeks reddened, but she held his gaze archly, with a boldness that seemed forced, almost experimental. "I see. And did I?"

He nodded. "Yes. Definitely." He paused for a moment, watching her color deepen. If Molly wanted to play games, he was more than willing to join in. He reached out and touched her mouth, feeling the softness of her lips against his index finger. "But too briefly."

She looked shocked, and the boldness fell away from her face like a mask dropping. Her mouth opened slightly under his touch, and Jake lightly traced the arc of her lower lip before pulling his hand back.

"We should go," he said. "We have a plane to catch."

CHAPTER 25

"That woman is impossible," fumed Tom Amadeo, pacing up and down the length of Cora Berenger's terrace. Molly and Jake were sitting at the table, drinking tea and coffee respectively, and watching Tom rant. He had been at it for ten minutes now, ever since Elaine had left the villa.

"How the hell am I supposed to work with her breathing down my neck?"

It was Saturday afternoon, one week after the Berenger Grand opening, and Elaine and Carter had just returned to Gold Bay to be reinstalled in Cottage Five. Over the next few days, Carter would be taping an interview with Jake as part of an extensive profile that he had already sold to *Vanity Fair*. Carter had told Molly that the editors at the magazine were so impressed with his work and his connections that they were considering offering him a position as a staff writer. It was a world above the *Tribune*, and Carter was high with excitement.

Tom had surveyed Carter's work, spoken with him at length, and then given him the official nod of approval. Tom liked Carter, specifically Carter's willingness to do exactly what Tom told him to do, and he made no secret of the fact that he was pleased to have Carter on the Operation Family Man team.

Elaine was another story. She had arrived with two trunks of clothes and accessories that she deemed "more suitable" for Molly, and then had inserted herself into Friday morning's planning meeting. Worst of all—according to Tom—she had even had the nerve to make friends with Cora Berenger, who agreed that marketing Molly would be a useful way of improving Jake's image by association.

By necessity, Tom was coldly polite to Elaine, but as soon as she was out of hearing range, he let loose.

"Whose show is this?" he demanded, then answered his own question without pausing for breath. "Mine! Does the New York Philharmonic have two conductors in the orchestra pit at the same time? No! I don't work with amateurs. I especially don't work with bleached-blond, fashion-fixated, multiply-married socialites who think they know something about my business, but don't."

Elaine's latest sin was that she hadn't consulted Tom before she contacted another one of her myriad ex-sisters-in-law, this one being an assistant producer for *Good Morning, America*, which Elaine said would be a perfect venue for Molly to be interviewed about her book and—of course—Jake. She had already taken the liberty of discussing the idea with Molly's agent.

"Has she done this before?" Tom asked the air in front of him. "No. Have I? Only for twenty years! Remember Russell Hayes, the Chicago Bulls center who got caught in Vegas with the eighteen-year-old twins? They called me in, and now he's doing Pepsi commercials. I did that. I told the world that Russell Hayes was a Family Man, and the world listened."

Tom had been doing a lot of histrionic complaining, but despite what he said, he seemed to have resigned himself to the situation. On Saturday morning, Molly had caught him staring at Elaine, pinching his beard as he did when he was deep in thought. His pensive look quickly became a scowl as soon as he realized that Molly was watching.

"Ow! God damn it!" Tom stopped pacing and started hopping. He had just stubbed his toe. He limped over to the table and sat down next to Jake. "Let me tell you," he said. "I am not at all surprised that that woman can't keep a husband."

"Actually," Molly said, "it's been the husbands who can't keep her."

"Hah," Tom said forcefully.

Molly glanced at Jake, who shrugged philosophically. She had learned from quizzing Cora that Tom was a confirmed bachelor with a history of dating starry-eyed marketing interns fresh out of college.

"Oh, Tom," Cora had sighed, shaking her head. "Oh, dear. He gets older and older, and the girls just stay the same. I remember a dinner party I gave in New York last year. I made the stupid mistake of calling his date Amber, which was the name of the girl he'd brought to my *last* party. I was so embarrassed, but nobody even batted an eye. It turned out that this one's name was also Amber."

Tom and Jake had arrived late on Thursday night, and although Tom had been scheduled to fly back to Manhattan on Friday after the meeting, they were now well into the weekend and he was still occupying one of the villa's guest rooms. Molly hadn't been able to resist inquiring about his extended visit, and he had muttered something about not wanting to give that woman the impression that he was leaving her in charge.

Cora was highly amused by it all. "He'll have to go home sometime," she had said to Molly at breakfast. "He has a business to run. We'll see what happens."

Molly had spent the week writing. It was a novelty to work so openly, sitting at the table under the bougainvillea vines, and not worrying one bit about prying eyes. Cora's butler brought her tea and sandwiches whenever he decided that she was looking weary, and she was producing pages at a respectable rate. It would have been an idyllic situation, but two worries were lurking on the edges of her mind.

One was that her father had phoned on Wednesday morning and left a message requesting that she call him. It was the first that Molly had heard from him in weeks—her outing as Sandra St. Claire and her departure from Belden had come and gone with no reaction but a stony silence from the Shaw household. Molly was uncomfortably aware that the mature reaction would be to call home and make the first attempt at reconciliation, but on further consideration of the idea, she had decided that maturity was overrated. The truth was that she was too terrified to pick up the phone. She was sure that she could feel an icy wave of disapproval seeping across the two thousand miles separating Gold Bay from Belden.

She'd had an e-mail from her mother, reporting breathlessly that Stanford had refused to speak or to come out of his study for several days following Molly's dramatic helicopter departure. On Wednesday, however, he had put on the herringbone tweed suit that he had acquired during his sabbatical year at Oxford, and then marched off to an extended meeting with Dean Fowler and President Dickerson. Stanford wouldn't say what had transpired, but Mrs. Shaw hoped that a compromise had been reached. She also hoped that Molly would write and tell her a little bit about this Jake Berenger person, who didn't seem like a very nice man, judging by the things Mrs. Shaw had seen when she looked him up on the Internet.

So far, Molly had not been able to summon the nerve—or the desire—to call her father back, but every day that she delayed made the discomfort worse. At some point, she knew, she would have to face the inevitable.

The other problem plaguing her was that Jake had hijacked her brain. She kept catching herself remembering the way he had looked at her when they were standing together in the museum. All he had done was run one finger lightly over her mouth, but that tiny gesture had released a tidal wave of longing inside her.

Molly was no innocent teenager, though, and she knew an extremely unwise attraction when she felt one. Diligently, she set about curing herself, as if a crush were similar to a head cold. Instead of bed rest and chicken soup, she tried to ward off the illness by focusing on Jake's flaws. She reminded herself that he had done her a bad turn, that he was unscrupulous and untrustworthy, and that she would enjoy his misery when she produced her Mary Morgan proof and triumphantly demanded her museum. Unfortunately, she was somehow able to acknowledge all of that and still think about how good it had felt to kiss him, and how much she wanted to do it again. The opportunity had not presented itself, though. Jake had not made a single move toward her since returning to Gold Bay, possibly because Molly had been making a point of always keeping her laptop nearby, opened in front of her like a portable castle wall.

Tom sighed heavily. "Am I the only one who finds that woman unbearably smug?" he asked.

Jake nodded. "She doesn't bother me."

"Me either," Molly said. Elaine could be pushy, but she seemed to be insisting that Tom allow Molly to be herself, instead of trying to mold her into yet another caricature. Molly was touched by her unexpected advocacy. Her opinion had gained some ground over the past week, as it had become obvious from the tone of post-party news stories that Tom's canned message hadn't quite done the job. The *New*

York Times had come through with the positive profile of Jake, and Tom had wangled a Larry King interview and an upcoming *Fortune* cover story, but it was not enough. The general press remained skeptical about Jake's credibility. "A Timely Shift in Strategy?" asked the *Washington Post* archly, referring to the engagement. Skye Elliot had finally rallied and informed the *Daily News* that she knew that the engagement was only a publicity stunt, because Jake had tried to convince her to do it first. The fact that her latest story contradicted everything she'd said a month earlier didn't seem to bother anyone.

Molly had been wondering what Jake thought of Elaine's idea of putting her on television. After what had happened at the Berenger Grand opening, she suspected that he might feel more inclined to lock her in a closet for the next two months. He had said very little in Friday's meeting, although admittedly it had been difficult to get a word in edgewise while Tom and Elaine were arguing. Cora had watched the whole thing as if it were a comedy act, occasionally speaking up in support of one point or another. Molly had become distracted by the pressing question of whether or not she even *wanted* to be on television, and Jake had simply stared through the window with a remote expression.

Looking at him in the bright daylight, Molly could see dark circles under his eyes. She had noticed on Friday morning that he looked tired, and the previous night's sleep—or the lack thereof, in his case—had not helped. She had seen light leaking through his curtains at two in the morning when she had awakened and gone to get a glass of water.

"You're working too hard," she said. "Can't you take a break?"

"Nope," he said. "Not yet. Later, maybe."

"What's going on? More business problems?"

"The same business problems. And now I have the added pleasure of doing two or three interviews a day."

"Hey," Tom said. "No whining. You hired me, chief. Keep on going, and one of these days you'll learn to love it."

It was a topic that Molly had wondered about for a long time. "Why did you spend such a long time refusing to give interviews?" she asked Jake. "Carter told me that you hate the press. Is that it?"

"No," he said. "That's not the reason."

"Then why?"

"I don't know. I didn't want to."

"My friend is being too modest," Tom said. "He figured out his strategy years ago. I call it 'present, but unavailable.' He's always near the spotlight, but he never gets overexposed. And he never looks desperate for attention, which is a killer. It wouldn't work for everybody, but it works for him."

Molly looked curiously at Jake, and saw that he was shaking his head. "That's not the reason, either," he said.

Tom looked surprised. "Huh? So, then . . . ?"

Jake pushed back his chair. "*The scars of others should teach us caution*," he said, and stood up. "Excuse me. I have a phone call to make."

He walked away, leaving them staring after him, startled.

"What was that about?" Tom asked finally. "Who was he quoting, Yoda?"

"I'm not sure," Molly said. "But I think he was answering our question."

"Oh, yeah? Then *I* think we'd better cool it with the interviews until he catches up on his sleep. If he starts throwing out random weird shit like that on CNN, I'm going to quit and let that woman take over."

CHAPTER 26

On Sunday, after Molly had gone down to the resort to see her friends, Cora mentioned to Jake how much she had been enjoying her company at the villa.

"She's a wonderful houseguest," Cora said. "She's polite, she cleans up after herself, she chats with me at breakfast, and in the afternoon she sits there for hours, tapping on her computer. My goodness, I remember Skye, and all of her demands—special low-carbohydrate meals from the chef, her favorite brand of bottled water flown in by helicopter because she doesn't like the taste of Evian, the personal hairstylist, those dry-clean-only bikinis . . . she nearly wore out my staff. Amanda wasn't much better, to be honest. Compared to them, it's almost as if Molly isn't even *here*."

Jake didn't agree. Molly was very definitely there, in his opinion. He had a constant peripheral awareness of her whenever they were in the same room.

"I would have expected some emotional drama, at least," Cora continued. "The poor girl's whole life has been turned upside down, and it must be terribly stressful. I still don't understand why she agreed to do all of this with no more compensation than the possibility of a piddly little island museum. It's so odd."

Why, indeed, Jake thought. That was the billion-dollar

question. He and Molly had not discussed the issue of her ex-professorship since the previous weekend in New York, but as far as he knew, she still believed that he was the saboteur of her lifelong dream of scholarly bliss.

Cora was stunned when Jake filled her in on the behind-the-scenes events of that night. "Good heavens," she said. "Do you mean to tell me that she blames you for the loss of her job?"

"Afraid so."

"And you seriously think that she's considering exposing the fake engagement as her revenge? It would explain her motivation for helping us, if you could call it that . . ."

"I don't know," Jake said. "She had a chance to do it last weekend. But she didn't."

Cora frowned. "How Machiavellian this all sounds! I can't imagine Molly doing something so malicious. She doesn't seem like that sort of person."

"Let's hope she isn't," Jake said. "Because hoping is about the only thing we can legally do. I've been looking into it, and we're more vulnerable than you want to know."

"What about the confidentiality agreement?"

"It's only a deterrent, and not a very effective one if she doesn't care what it costs her to destroy me. If she breaks the agreement, we can take her to court to prevent her from making any profit from it. And we could probably recover some damages, but obviously, money isn't the issue. The real damage would already be done. We'd have a snowball's chance in hell of stopping the story if Molly decided to tell it."

"Oh, dear," Cora said. "I'm rethinking my support for putting her on television. Is there any way that we can keep her away from the press until we have a better idea of her intentions?"

"Not really. She's an adult woman, and a celebrity in her own right. We can't hold her prisoner here, unfortunately."

"She doesn't seem very eager to leave. Or to seek out publicity. That's a good sign, isn't it? You saw her on Friday when Elaine brought up the idea of putting her on television. She looked reluctant, which hardly suggests that she wants a venue to expose you."

"Maybe. We'll see."

Cora sighed. "Yes, I suppose we will. In the meantime, is there any way to find out who did leak the information about Sandra? That would solve the problem."

Jake nodded. "Believe me, I'm looking into that, too."

Molly found it very strange to be sitting in Cottage Five again. The weather was as tropically bright as ever, the cottage was the same, and Carter and Elaine were the same. It was almost as if it were still December, and the recent events at Belden had been some kind of terrible dream. She almost expected to look down and find herself wearing pink platform sandals.

"What did you do with the Sandra gear?" she asked Elaine. Carter was out on the deck with his laptop and his microcassette recorder, transcribing the first of the tapes of his interview with Jake.

"Oh, it's all in a box at home," Elaine said. "I suppose I should give it to Goodwill. Carter took the wig because he thought he could sell it on eBay, but his cat developed some sort of romantic attachment to it, and that was the end of that. You know how he feels about his cat."

Carter's cat was burly and striped, and had already lost half of one tufted ear by the time that Carter adopted him from the local animal shelter. He didn't like Molly, but it wasn't personal. He didn't like anyone, including Carter.

"It's just as well," Elaine remarked. "Anyone willing to buy a used wig from someone like Carter should be protected from themselves."

Elaine was in a cheerful mood after one of her many sources of information had forwarded the news that Ingrid Anderson would be returning to Gold Bay at the end of the week. She would be there for three days, doing a swimsuit photo shoot for French *Vogue*, and Elaine knew a perfect opportunity when she saw one.

"I've already called Michael," she told Molly. "He's flying in on Thursday morning, and then we'll put an end to this One True Path to Joy foolishness."

"What about Rama Guru?" Molly asked.

Elaine smiled. "He won't be here. He never goes to work with her. By the time he hears that she's gone back to her husband, it'll be too late. That freeloading karma quack is going to have to find himself a new supermodel, because this one is mine."

"But what if Ingrid doesn't *want* to be reunited with Michael?" Molly asked. It seemed to her that Elaine, of all people, should be considering this as a serious possibility.

"Nonsense," Elaine said briskly. "The girl is confused, that's all. I've arranged everything. A romantic candlelight dinner in a secluded spot, with roses, poetry, a violinist, and a little something from Tiffany's. Michael has very clear instructions about how to handle this. It can't possibly fail."

Molly wasn't so sure, but she refrained from commenting.

Elaine leaned back against the sofa. "Have you been working on your book?" she asked.

"Not for the past few days," Molly said. She had found it extremely difficult to concentrate since Jake arrived. And, as if one disturbing man wasn't enough of a distraction, her father had called again that morning and left another message. She had been trying to ignore all thoughts of home, but she couldn't put them out of her mind entirely, and the Belden catastrophe lurked menacingly around the edges of her consciousness. She knew that she couldn't delay the confrontation much longer.

"I'm sure that it's busy at the villa," Elaine said. She casually inspected the tip of one perfectly manicured nail. "I suppose that Mr. Amadeo is still hanging around?"

"No, he finally went home," Molly said. Tom had left that morning, after a private meeting with Jake.

"Oh," Elaine said. She sounded surprised and slightly miffed, which made no sense to Molly. She would have thought that Elaine would be glad to have Tom out of the way.

"He'll be back on Thursday," she said.

"Will he?" Elaine said coolly. "Hmm. He'll probably be on the same flight as Michael then. I doubt I'll have much time to spend advising him next weekend. I do have other commitments you know."

CHAPTER 27

Jake had planned to fly back to Miami after dinner on Sunday night, but he made the mistake of sitting down at his desk to read through some paperwork, and by the time he looked up again, it was past eleven P.M. His room was dark but for the light of the desk lamp and computer screen, and the house was silent.

His jet was standing by at the Antigua airport, and if he left now, the Gold Bay helicopter would get him there before midnight, when the airport closed. He would be back home in Palm Beach by three A.M., and his first Monday meeting wasn't until ten. It wouldn't be a perfect night of sleep, but it would suffice, if he hurried.

His eyes felt hot and scratchy, and he reached up to rub them. He didn't feel like hurrying. He also didn't feel like getting into a helicopter, then a plane, then a car before he finally made it to bed. Staying at the villa was much more appealing, and if he left early the next morning, and went straight to work from the airport, he could easily make his meeting. It wasn't a difficult decision. He made a quick phone call to let the pilots know that the plan had changed, and then stood up, stretching, and realized that he was hungry.

The kitchen was on the bottom floor of the villa, a significant hike from his room. The hallway was dark, but as Jake approached the main staircase, he saw light coming from Molly's room, down the hall. Her door was ajar, and as he paused at the top of the stairs, he could hear the faint sound of her voice. He couldn't make out what she was saying, but her tone was different, higher, as if she were upset.

It sounded as if she were on the phone, but with whom? And why did she sound so unhappy?

He hesitated for a moment, then moved cautiously down the hall toward her door, listening as her words grew more audible with each step.

". . . sorry that you had to go through all of that," she was saying. "I never wanted you to feel humiliated in front of your colleagues. I know how much your reputation means to you, but I really don't think that my actions reflect on your—"

Another moment of silence. "It doesn't matter. It's too late, anyway. I made the choice to write the book, and they made the choice to fire me."

She paused, listening, and Jake heard her take a sharp breath. "I don't agree," she said in a shaky voice. "I worked very hard on *Pirate Gold*, and it's not fair to call it trash. The history was accurate, and a lot of people liked it. I think that the next one will . . . Yes, I . . . I am writing another one. What? No, I won't be using my real name."

Jake leaned against the wall, shocked by what he was hearing. Molly sounded like a stranger; someone entirely different from the confident and funny woman that he knew. It was clear that he should leave and pretend that he had never heard any of this disturbingly raw conversation, but he couldn't make himself move. He found that he was angry. Whoever Molly was speaking to seemed to think that they had the right to denigrate her, and he couldn't imagine why she didn't just tell the person to go to hell. She sounded barely able to stand up for herself, and he hated the unfamiliar submissiveness of her tone.

"But I *do* share your values," she was saying pleadingly. "I work hard, and I care about doing my best, and I try to be a good person. I know that this isn't the life that you wanted for me, but it's the life I have now, and I'm . . . proud of it. I want you to be proud of me, too."

She listened. "I see," she said at last. Her voice was low and brittle. "Well, give it some time, and maybe you'll feel differently later."

More silence, and then, "I can't talk about Jake. Yes, I understand that it was a shock for you, and you don't know what to tell people, but I'm not going to discuss it. Well, you've read the papers, haven't you? That's all there is to it . . . what? *What?* No, of course I'm not *pregnant*!"

Jake ducked his head, suppressing a snort of laughter.

The caller seemed to have said something that pushed Molly over the edge, because her voice sharpened suddenly, and she said in a breathless rush, "Well, if Jake is a shallow, publicity-seeking playboy, and I'm an embarrassment to you and Belden, then we must be perfect for each other! I'll send you photos from the wedding."

She slammed down the phone, and Jake exhaled silently, relieved by the restoration of the familiar Molly. He began to sneak away, taking care not to make the wooden floor creak, but he hadn't gone more than a few cautious steps before he heard a new sound that stopped him in his tracks.

It was a choking noise interspersed with moist sniffles, and it was unmistakable. Molly was crying. Her sobs were muffled, as if she were holding something up to her face to stifle the noise, but her gasps were coming faster, and they sounded increasingly ragged. Jake froze, deeply alarmed, and turned to stare at the mostly closed door, wondering what to do. In his experience with weeping females, tears were usually a tactic, but in this case they were private and not directed at him. He remembered his father's funeral—the only time he had ever seen his mother cry. After a week of supernatural calm, she had suddenly broken down and begun to sob, making rough, primal sounds of grief that had terrified him.

Molly's tears were more controlled, but in them he heard an echo of that same sorrow. She was crying as if she had lost someone or something that she thought she couldn't do without. It was unbearable to Jake, and without considering how he would explain himself, he stepped forward and knocked on her door.

All sound inside the room stopped abruptly, as if someone had flicked a switch. There was a rustling noise, and the sound of footsteps pattering across the floor, and finally Molly's voice said tremulously, "Who is it?"

Jake pushed on the door, which swung open. Molly was now on the far side of the room, standing in front of the open window. She was wearing a thin white pajama top that fell to the middle of her thighs, and her legs were bare beneath it. The only sound in the room was the soft crash of waves against the cliffs below the open window.

"Are you all right?" Jake asked. It was a stupid question, because she obviously wasn't, but it was the best he could do on short notice.

She sniffed slightly and pressed her nose against her raised hand. Looking up again, she cleared her throat. "What? Yes, of course. I'm fine, why do you ask? I was just reading. I was about to go to bed. It's getting late. What are you doing here? I thought you left hours ago."

Jake blinked, taken aback by the sudden torrent of words. "I decided to stay the night," he said. He wondered if he should back off and leave her alone. It seemed boorish to confront her when she clearly wanted to hide the fact that she had been crying. But he didn't go. The disturbing sound of her sobs still lingered in his ears.

"Who was that on the phone?" he asked.

She recoiled. "What? When?"

"Just now. You sounded very unhappy."

"You were listening to my conversation?"

"I was walking by your door, and I overheard a few words." It wasn't strictly true, but it wasn't exactly a lie, either. He had overheard a few words . . . a few hundred.

"Why were you walking by my door?" Molly asked suspiciously. "There's nothing at this end of the hall but guest rooms. And I'm the only guest here now."

"Right," Jake said. "I was . . . coming to talk to you. I wanted to know if you needed anything from Miami. I'm leaving early tomorrow morning, but I'll be back on Friday, and if there's anything you want me to bring you . . ."

Molly gave him a strange look. "Thanks," she said. "A chocolate bar and some clean socks. It's tough to be out here in the wilderness without any of the basic comforts."

"Chocolate with almonds or without?"

She ignored the question. "It's almost midnight. If you wanted to offer courier services, you could have called me tomorrow. You do have the phone number for this house, don't you?"

"Oh, for God's sake," Jake said impatiently. It was too late, and he was too tired to play verbal fencing games with her. "Fine, I listened to your conversation. You were talking to your father?" From the content of the call, and from what Jake remembered of the pompous Stanford Shaw from the White House luncheon, he seemed like the most likely candidate. And it was only ten P.M. in Wisconsin.

Molly didn't answer. She folded her arms against her chest and turned her head to stare through the window. The moonlight glazed her profile, and Jake saw a damp shine on her cheek.

"You were crying," he said.

"I was not."

"Right," he said dryly. "My mistake. So if I leave you alone, are you going to start not crying again?"

Apparently, she wasn't even going to wait that long. She sniffed and reached up to swipe at her eyes. "Go away," she said miserably.

For some reason that Jake didn't understand, Molly's shrewish temper didn't bother him at all, but the sight of her with a tear-tracked face and her body slumping in defeat made him want to shake her until her fighting spirit reasserted itself.

"Your father is a self-centered blowhard," he said.

"What?" She was so surprised that she looked fully at him.

"It's true. You were kinder to him than he deserved. He should be proud of you, and if he's not, then he's as narrow-minded as the other snobs at Belden College."

"You don't know what you're talking about," Molly said indignantly. "He's famous. He has two Pulitzer Prizes and the Medal of Freedom."

"He also has a daughter who has every right to refuse to speak to him again. I hope his prizes keep him company when he gets old."

"He is old," Molly said. "He's not that bad, really. He spent last Wednesday morning trying to talk the administration into taking me back."

To whose advantage? Jake wondered. It might make Stanford Shaw feel better to have his daughter securely back in her high-octane professorship, but anyone who knew Molly ought to know—and care—that Belden was the wrong place for her. "What did the administration say?"

"They said no." She pressed her lips together for a moment. "He told me that he felt like a beggar, and that I put him in a humiliating position."

"That's ridiculous. Did you ask him to go to them?"

"No. But he wanted to help me."

"Sounds to me like he wanted to help himself. And he's upset because they didn't defer to him, so he's trying to blame you for his wounded ego. Not very nice."

She didn't say anything, but he saw her staring at him, her eyes luminous in the moonlight.

He shrugged. "I could be wrong, of course. After all, what do I know? I'm just a shallow, publicity-seeking playboy."

"Oh," Molly said. "I'm sorry about that."

"No problem. I've been called worse."

"I can't tell him that the engagement is a sham . . . he wouldn't understand. But he isn't very happy about the prospect of me marrying you, either."

Jake feigned shock. "What, I'm not the son he always wanted?"

Molly's mouth curved reluctantly. "No. But it's looking like I'm not the daughter he wants, either."

So we're perfect for each other. She didn't add that, but he could still hear her voice in his mind.

"You've been playing a lot of roles," he said. "For your father, for your friend Carter, and now for me. It seems like a lot of trouble. It might even make it hard for you to remember who you really are."

"It does," Molly said. "You should know, Mr. Playboy-Billionaire-turned-Family-Man. You spend more time and money on your image that I thought was possible. Who are *you*, really?"

Jake shrugged. "Depends on who you ask. Skye Elliot

would tell you that I'm a drug-addicted narcissist with a commitment phobia."

"And what would your mother say?"

"That I'm a nice boy with workaholic tendencies."

"You're not a drug-addicted narcissist," Molly said. "That much I know. But I wouldn't say that you're a nice boy, either."

He laughed softly. "No. And what would you say, Molly? If I asked you? Don't tell me I'm a Family Man—save that for the press."

She gazed at him for a moment, considering an answer, and Jake saw that she had taken the question seriously. He hadn't intended it that way . . . or had he? The dim light and the intimacy of the setting gave an edgy intensity to the scene, and ever since he had come into her room, he had been very aware of the shadowed curves of her body under the thin shirt.

"I would say . . ." she answered finally, slowly, "that you are the only man . . ."

Jake watched her, curiously.

She paused to think. "Yes," she said, "definitely the only man who I ever . . . ever . . ."

He waited as she searched for words, and found himself staring at her, caught by the intensity of her eyes.

"You are the only man," Molly said finally, "who I ever kissed while wearing a blond wig and a double-D bra." She grinned at him, looking very pleased with herself.

"I'm glad to hear that," Jake said calmly. "And how many men have you kissed while wearing only a pajama top and no underwear?"

Her grin vanished. "Hey," she said sharply, and cast a sudden, anxious glance down at her lower half, and then back at the bright moonlight coming through the window behind her. "Wait a minute . . . you can't—"

"I couldn't actually tell," Jake said. "It was just a guess."

"Oh, very funny," she said.

"So, how many?" he asked.

"What?"

"How . . . many . . . men?" Jake repeated, stepping forward.

Molly looked at him, startled. And then her expression changed, and her lips parted slightly, and he knew that she understood.

"Lots," she said, her eyes never leaving his. "So if you want to distinguish yourself . . ."

"I'd better make it good," he said, and pulled her into his arms.

Jake knew from the moment that Molly came to him—her hands sliding up his chest to lock around the back of his neck, her mouth meeting his with the fierce hunger that he remembered—that the night was unlikely to end with a kiss.

And it didn't. Her pajama top and his own shirt were soon discarded, and when he felt the softness of her naked chest pressed against his, he knew that he was lost.

Molly clung to him so tightly that his belt buckle left a mark like a brand on her stomach, and she kissed him as if she, too, had been holding on to the memory of that afternoon at Falcon's Point. The rest of Jake's clothes followed his shirt onto the floor, and he and Molly tumbled onto the bed, tangled together, awkward and laughing with the urgent excitement of the moment.

Jake took certain challenges very seriously, and from Molly's ardent response over the ensuing hour, he thought that he had indeed managed to distinguish himself.

Later, they lay entwined with the white cotton sheet, enjoying the warm night breeze and the novelty of lying quietly in each other's arms.

"I wanted to ask you something," Molly said. Her voice had a warmth that Jake had never heard before, but liked very much. "What did you mean yesterday, when you talked about the scars of others teaching us caution? You were quoting someone."

Jake nodded. "Saint Jerome. I stumbled across the line a few years ago, and it always seemed like good advice."

"Is it? Whose scars made you cautious?"

"My father's," Jake said. It was not his ideal conversation to have after an hour of amazingly good sex, but he had barged in on Molly's own family problems, so he probably owed her a little disclosure in return. "He was a commercial developer in Miami, and one of his partners got caught in a crooked land deal with a state senator. The investigation lasted months, and it was a media circus. The papers printed everything they could find that made Dad look sleazy, including details of an old affair that my mother wasn't very happy to learn about. Dad was basically a good guy, but the stress and the shame just broke him. He had a stroke at the office, and died in the hospital a couple of days later. They cleared him posthumously of all charges."

"I'm very sorry," Molly said seriously. "Your poor mother."

Jake nodded. "It was a bad time. Most developers—even big ones—are living on their next loan. The whole house of cards collapsed when Dad died, and we lost everything. I had to quit school, and my girlfriend, who I wanted to marry, decided that the 'for richer or for poorer' clause didn't really work for her."

Molly chuckled, suddenly. "Oops," she said.

He grinned. "Yeah, oops is right."

"Did you love her very much?"

"I thought so. But I was twenty, so what the hell did I know? It was just as well. I started Berenger Corporation a couple of years after that, and then for a long time I was too busy for a wife. She probably would've gotten fed up and left me anyway."

"So you held a grudge against the media?"

"Not a rational one. They're just people trying to sell newspapers, after all. But after I saw firsthand how they could suddenly go for your throat, I never felt like making personal contact."

"Until now."

"I still don't feel like it," Jake said. "But I do what I have to do. The company is my first priority."

Molly snuggled against him and yawned.

"It's late," he said. "I should go back to my own room."

"Should you?"

"Or I could stay here." He was warm and comfortable, and didn't feel inclined to move.

She nodded agreement. "That's a better idea."

"I have to leave at dawn, though."

"That's fine," Molly said. "Tiptoe on your way out, have a good trip, and I like my chocolate without almonds."

CHAPTER 28

On Monday morning, shortly before Jake's plane landed in Miami, Atlas Group publicly announced their hostile bid to acquire Berenger Corporation for the price of eighteen dollars and fifty cents per share, roughly two dollars more than the stock's value at the time that the news broke. Ed Thatcher had grown tired of stall tactics.

Berenger stock jumped a point as the market reacted to the news, but then leveled off, reflecting a general opinion that Atlas's takeover attempt would be successful.

"Berenger's business is in trouble," Ed Thatcher announced to the press, who replayed the clip throughout the day. "Time is not on their side."

Jake had been expecting it sooner or later, but he had hoped for later. Operation Family Man was starting to show results, and the stock had been creeping slowly upward over the past two weeks. The campaign was working, but not quickly enough.

He canceled his morning meeting and spent the day doing live and taped interviews for the cable news channels, reacting to Ed's comments and repeating the same message over and over for each network. "Berenger has weathered the economic downturn better than our competitors, and we're poised for a strong comeback as the economy recovers. Atlas Group's offer undervalues the company assets, and we advise shareholders to reject it."

He was still at headquarters at ten P.M., finishing up a discussion with the inside directors, and by the time that the group dispersed, his voice was almost gone. His head ached, and he couldn't remember the last time he'd eaten anything. He was due back at the office at six A.M. for a live broadcast on CNBC's *Wake Up Call*, which was likely to kick off another fifteen-hour workday.

Somehow, he managed to drive himself home. He did not have live-in staff, preferring to fend for himself after hours. One of the housekeepers had left lasagna in the refrigerator for him, and he cut and ate a square of it cold, too hungry to bother with the microwave. He fast-forwarded through his voice mail, noting that he had messages from Tom, Molly, Susan, and his mother. None of them sounded like emergencies. Tomorrow, if he was lucky, he would have time to deal with personal business, but at that moment, the only thing he cared about was sleep.

By Wednesday, Molly was disturbed to have heard nothing at all from Jake. It wasn't that she suddenly expected him to start writing ballads for her just because they'd slept together, but she would have appreciated a quick phone call to say hello. She found herself growing more and more anxious that she had misinterpreted the level of passion between them that night—it was a painful possibility that the intensity she'd felt had been one-sided. If that was so, she knew that she would not be the first—or the last—woman to have made a fool of herself over Jake Berenger.

Cora had been behaving oddly for the past two days. Jake's mother was not psychic, as far as Molly knew, and neither did she have hidden cameras in the villa's guest rooms, so there was no way that Molly could explain why she thought that Cora knew—or at least suspected—what had happened on Sunday night. She also appeared to know that Jake had not returned Molly's Monday afternoon phone call, because she was making a heroic effort to explain Jake's behavior, as if she were an ambassador for a foreign and inscrutable king.

"The timing of this takeover bid is so frustrating," she said as they sat together on the terrace, eating breakfast. "The PR campaign was just beginning to have an effect, and a few more weeks of progress would have lifted us out of the danger zone. Atlas does want Berenger, but not at any price. If the stock had just made it to nineteen . . ."

Molly was not a regular watcher of television, and she had never developed a newspaper-reading habit, so she had not known about Atlas's hostile bid until Cora told her.

"It might still get there, though, right?" Molly asked hesitantly. To her embarrassment, she knew very little about business, and investment lingo did not come easily to her tongue. "And then, they'll go away."

Cora sighed. "Or raise their bid, but I don't think they'll do that. I'm afraid that it will be more difficult to lift our stock price now that Atlas has gone public with the offer. Jake is going to have to convince the market that Berenger is worth more than Atlas is offering, and he'll have to do it soon. This is a real crisis, my dear. Jake is under terrible pressure right now."

It was a pretty legitimate excuse for not calling, Molly had to admit. But it still didn't relieve her fear that her feelings for Jake were unrequited. It also didn't keep her heart from jumping with anxious hope whenever the phone rang.

On Thursday, Molly confided some of her concerns to Carter. He was a last resort—she would have preferred to talk to Elaine, but Elaine was in a frenzy of planning and preparation for the reunion of Ingrid and Michael. Michael had arrived on the morning helicopter from Antigua, a flight that—contrary to Elaine's prediction—had not delivered Tom Amadeo.

"Well, I'm glad to be spared his company," Elaine said loftily. "But I suppose the reprieve won't last. He'll probably be flying in with Jake, like he did last week."

"I don't think so," Molly said. "Jake is coming from Miami this time, not New York."

Elaine pursed her lips. "Hmm," she said, and refused to discuss it any further.

What Carter lacked in insight, he made up for in attentiveness. He sat eagerly forward in his chair, his eyes barely leaving Molly as she spoke and he listened. Molly was not in the habit of discussing her emotions with Carter or anyone else, but she was feeling needier than usual, as if she had a bad case of PMS. It was a relief to vocalize some of her worries, although it would have taken truth serum to force her to confess to sleeping with Jake. That was too personal to discuss. But she did finally admit to having a crush on him.

Carter nodded knowingly. "Totally normal," he assured her. "Nothing to worry about. You've been immersed in a world of dazzling glamour, and you've . . . uh . . . been dazzled by it. When this is all over, and you come back to live in Chicago, you'll be fine."

"I'm fine now," Molly said. That wasn't true, but she hoped that saying so would hasten the process.

"It's not Jake you're attracted to," Carter explained. "It's the glitter and the gold, the heady aura of excitement, the rush of a thousand starry moments within the rarefied world of the wealthy."

"Oh," Molly said. "I see." Carter had been talking like that ever since he started working on his article about Jake, which he was billing as an "unprecedented glimpse into the mind and heart of America's most enigmatic magnate."

She didn't bother to argue, but privately she thought Carter was off the mark. Her only starry moment so far had been at the Berenger Grand party, and while it had been fascinating from a sociological standpoint, she had found it exhausting and not much fun. Most of her time was still spent with her laptop, just as it had been in Belden. Lately, she had been happiest when she was absorbed in her work . . . or when she was with Jake.

"He's not the kind of man that you can allow yourself to get emotionally involved with," Carter said. "He's a player. He only cares about his business, and he'll never settle down. You have to use him, take what you can from him, and then get out. That's what he's doing to you, isn't it?"

"I don't know," Molly said, disturbed. "Maybe."

"Definitely. But here's the question. How much is the ring worth?"

Molly blinked. "What?"

"The ring. You still have it, right? It's payment, right?"

Molly wasn't wearing the "engagement" ring that Jake had given her. The band was slightly too big, and the weight of the stone made it flop around on her finger, which annoyed her when she typed. Plus, she just didn't like it. The sight of it depressed her, for some reason. The diamond seemed as oversized and as emotionless as the role that she was supposed to be playing.

"It's in Cora's safe," she said. "I only get to keep it if the Berenger stock hits twenty by April first. It's meant to be a bonus."

Carter shook his head. "You really should have talked to me before you negotiated this, Molly, but since you didn't, it's lucky I'm here to help you now. The ring—*if* you get to keep it, and that's a big if—is probably worth a quarter of a million dollars. Do you know how much you could get from selling your story to the tabloids?"

"I can't," Molly said. "I signed a confidentiality agreement."

"I told you that those don't always hold up in court," Carter reminded her. "You'd need to get a lawyer, and there might be a little fight, but you could win. And the publicity would be incredible. I'll work with you on it, of course. I'll make a deal to write the articles myself, under my byline, but we'll split the profits."

"Carter, I can't," Molly repeated, feeling anxious. "It would ruin Jake's life."

"Why not? He didn't have any qualms about ruining yours, did he? He should pay for that, one way or another."

Molly had an uneasy feeling in her stomach. She wondered if her unwillingness to exact a real revenge meant that she was a wimp. She had returned to Gold Bay intending to pay Jake back, but even at the outset she had known that forcing him to create a museum and a foundation was hardly going to destroy him. Cause him some embarrassment, yes. Cost him more money than he wanted to spend, yes. But it wouldn't come anywhere close to bringing him down. In truth, her plan wasn't really to revenge herself. It was to assert herself, to show Jake that she, too, could be devious and clever, and that he had better think twice before he underestimated her again.

"Molly," Carter said urgently, "this is a golden opportunity. You don't get many of these in life, and you can't let it slide. This isn't about being nice, it's about winning! It's about getting what you deserve."

"What do you think I deserve?"

"Compensation for your pain and suffering. More than you can get by selling that ring."

"And what about Jake?"

Carter smiled slightly, but his eyes were sharp. "If he was careless enough to put you in a position where you can win at his expense, then he deserves to lose, doesn't he?"

Just then the front door opened, and Elaine swept into the room. She stood facing them, breathing hard. She was holding an enormous bunch of red roses wrapped in white tissue paper, but she did not look happy.

"This is a catastrophe!" she exclaimed. She dropped the bouquet onto the table. "He's *here*!"

"Who?" Carter asked. "Who's here?"

"That *man*. He's come to mock me and ruin my plans."

"Oh, you mean Tom," Molly said.

Elaine exhaled impatiently. "No. Would the two of you please focus on the issue at hand? I'm talking about that bald-headed swindler. Rama Guru! He arrived on the boat with Ingrid and the group from French *Vogue*."

"I thought you said that he doesn't go to work with her," Molly said.

"He doesn't," Elaine said. She sat balefully down in an armchair, crossing her legs and tapping one foot on the sisal rug. "But he's here this time, and that can only mean one thing. Someone warned him about my intentions."

"He had a vision of danger while he was meditating," Carter said. "He saw you waving a Tiffany's box at Ingrid, luring her away from the Light . . ."

"Oh, Carter, be quiet," Elaine said. "I'm trying to think. The reunion is supposed to take place tomorrow at sunset. I found a secluded spot with a wonderful view, and the Gold Bay staff is going to have dinner waiting there. It's all arranged, and Michael is in his room writing poetry at this very moment."

"Michael writes poetry?" Carter asked curiously. "He doesn't look like the type."

"He isn't the type," Elaine said. "I told him to do it. I gave him a rhyming dictionary and bookmarked the pages for 'devotion,' 'love,' and 'passion.' It would have been perfect, but now I'll have to find a way to separate Ingrid from that accursed guru, which won't be easy. He'll be watching her like a hawk. How *utterly inconvenient.*"

"I know how you did it before," Carter said with a glance at Molly.

"Oh, no," Molly said. "Not again." She had ended up spending an hour walking the beach with Ingrid's guru the last time Elaine needed someone to divert him. She had kept his attention by telling him that she was having problems with her boyfriend, Dwayne, who she thought might love her only for her body and not her mind. Rama Guru had been a very sympathetic audience, and had spent the time asking increasingly detailed questions about her sex life. It had been more than enough for one lifetime.

"You won't need to distract him for more than a few minutes," Elaine said. "The meeting place is very remote, and if we can sneak Ingrid away without him seeing, he won't know where she's gone."

"What makes you think Ingrid will sneak anywhere with you?" Carter asked. "I don't think she likes you very much, actually."

Elaine gave him a chilly look. "I beg your pardon. The poor girl is very confused right now."

"I can't do it, anyway," Molly said. "We don't have the Sandra outfit."

"That's true," Elaine said, frowning. "Drat. I wonder . . . if I have my housekeeper rush the Sandra box to the post office . . . international overnight would get it to Antigua by tomorrow, and the Gold Bay shuttle could pick it up . . ."

"You're forgetting about the wig," Molly said.

"The wig!" Elaine looked at Carter. "You still have the wig, don't you?"

Carter looked dubious. "Well, technically yes, but . . ."

"The wig that now belongs to Carter's *cat*," Molly said indignantly. "Remember? I'm not sharing a wig with a cat."

"We'll have it sent, anyway," Elaine said. "We'll only use it as a last resort. I'm sure that we can find a new one before tomorrow evening."

"Where?" Molly asked.

"At the concierge desk," Elaine said firmly. "The Gold Bay staff is famous for their ability to accommodate unusual requests. Last year they brought in a tiger for the Maharajah of Marabai. I don't know why he wanted it, but they found him one in less than twelve hours. And then he needed to have its claws painted with Revlon's Jungle Red. If they can do all of that, I don't think a platinum wig will be much of a challenge."

CHAPTER 29

Jake arrived back at Gold Bay at one A.M. on Friday morning. The villa was dark, and he made his way to his room without seeing anyone other than Cora's butler, who had waited up for him.

He woke at nine, then showered, shaved, and dressed with more care than usual, expecting to see Molly at breakfast. She wasn't there, though, and Cora said that she had eaten early and left the villa.

He pretended not to care, but he was disappointed. He had been waiting for the weekend, using thoughts of Gold Bay as a talisman to ward off the stress at work. Now that he had returned, though, he knew that sun and surf were not what he had been wanting. Atlas's offer and the resulting chaos had demanded all of his energy and attention, and although he hadn't been able to afford a single distraction, Molly had never been far from his thoughts. He caught himself picturing her face when he should have been paying attention to a meeting. When he tried to read the weekly reports, he found his mind drifting away, remembering Sunday night. When he spoke to the television cameras, and delivered his relentless pep talk to the Berenger shareholders, he wondered if she might be watching.

He spent the morning and part of the afternoon wandering restlessly around the villa, reading the newspapers and watching birds swoop over the terrace. He kept one eye on the driveway, waiting for Molly to return, but she didn't.

Finally, frustrated, he went to find his mother in the greenhouse, where she was repotting one of her beloved orchids.

"Molly? I told you, she's gone down to the resort," Cora said, tucking fuzzy green moss around the newly settled plant. "She's helping her friends with some kind of scheme, and I don't think she'll be back before dark. I get the impression that she has plans tomorrow, also."

"What? But I'm leaving on Sunday morning," Jake said. "I have to fly to New York."

"Do you? Well, say hello to Tom for me."

She seemed to have missed his point. "I had to rearrange my whole damn schedule to come back here! And now I'm hardly going to see Molly at all."

Cora gave the orchid a generous misting of water. "You might catch her at breakfast tomorrow," she said. "If you get up early."

"I don't want to just 'catch her at breakfast,'" Jake said, annoyed. "I've been waiting all week to see her."

His mother looked up from the flower. "Have you? My goodness, I had no idea. I'm sure that Molly didn't, either, since you didn't bother to call."

Jake narrowed his eyes. He sensed a female conspiracy. "I was busy," he said. "You might not have noticed, but there have been problems lately."

"I know that, my dear," Cora said, suddenly serious. "And I made sure to explain to Molly that you are very distracted and under terrible stress, and that she shouldn't judge you by your actions right now. She's being very good about it, but her confidence is a little fragile, and not hearing from you after Sunday night was—"

"Hold it," Jake said sharply. "How do you know about Sunday night? Molly told you?"

"Molly doesn't confide in me," Cora said. "You left your belt in her room. I saw the maid bringing it out on Monday morning and drew my own conclusions, which you've just confirmed."

He looked at her, half amused and half exasperated. "This is why I usually stay in Miami on the weekends," he said. "I'm too old to have my mother monitoring my sex life. Do you have a point to make, or are you just reminding me that you always know everything?"

"I do have a point," Cora said. "I'm concerned about this, Jake. Molly has done well so far, but I'm worried about her ability to handle this situation with the necessary amount of sophistication. Especially if you start indulging yourself at her expense."

"What?" Jake exclaimed. "Wait a minute, you think I seduced her? No, no. That's not how it was, believe me. She—"

"Stop," Cora said. "I *don't* always know everything, and I don't want to. You were the one who was so concerned about Amanda falling in love with you that you rejected her as a candidate for this PR plan. What makes you think that Molly isn't vulnerable? What makes you think that she won't also be wounded when this fake engagement ends and you tell her thanks and good-bye?"

"Molly's not in love with me," Jake said, shocked by the very idea.

"Oh?" Cora said.

"You have no idea what you're talking about. You said yourself that she doesn't confide in you."

"Oh, for heaven's sake. My dear, listen. I've become very fond of Molly, and I don't want to see you break her heart."

"Her *heart*," Jake repeated.

Cora shook her head. "The differences between men and women will never fail to amaze me," she said. "No matter how long I live."

"Are you trying to tell me to stay away from Molly?" A suspicion came to him. "Are you the reason she's avoiding me? Did you arrange—"

"No, of course not," Cora said impatiently. "Molly's avoiding you because you didn't call her, and she doesn't know what to think about you. I said that her confidence was fragile. And I'm certainly not telling you to stay away from her. I'd prefer the opposite, but it's your life, and I'm not going to meddle in it."

"Since when?" Jake asked dryly.

"Accidental passion is fine, and sometimes these things just happen. But if you do continue this involvement, *don't* do it thoughtlessly. Pay attention. Make sure you know what you're doing, and why."

She was right, and Jake knew it. "I should apologize for not calling."

"That would be a good idea, dear."

"I'll go down to the resort and find her. Which cottage are her friends in?"

"Five," Cora said, and hesitated. "Jake, I really don't mean to meddle in your affairs. It's just that this one is important, and I would hate to have it ruined by carelessness or foolish mistakes."

"I understand," Jake said. She had justifiably reminded him of something that he should never have overlooked. "Point made. I need to handle this situation more carefully. It would be stupid to give Molly an entirely new reason to feel vengeful."

Cora sighed. "That's not what I meant," she said. "But it's a start, I suppose."

"*Magnifique!* So sexy! Eeengrid, *bebe*, turn zees way, now be like ze kitty cat and show me ze claws. *Miaou!*"

Ingrid Anderson twisted sideways and crooked her fingers at the photographer, a wiry man in tight jeans. She was wearing stiletto heels, a leopard-print bikini, and a diamond choker. Her hair was wildly teased, and her eyes had been painted with black kohl. Next to her, a well-oiled male model in a loincloth embraced a stuffed giraffe and pouted sulkily at the camera.

"It's a very artistic shoot," Elaine said to Molly. "French *Vogue* is so avant-garde. That's Pascal Thibault behind the camera . . . the man is a genius."

"Uh-huh," Molly said. The genius in question was now making growling noises and wiggling his hips at Ingrid, who didn't seem to think that any of this was odd.

The photo shoot was taking place on the pool terrace, half of which had been cordoned off for the afternoon. They had just arrived at the scene, and they were standing behind the bulk of the crowd of spectators. It was late afternoon, and the shoot would be over as soon as the light faded. Elaine's plan was to swoop in as the *Vogue* group dispersed, using Molly to distract Rama Guru while she approached Ingrid.

To that end, Molly was experiencing an episode of fashion déjà vu. Luckily or unluckily, depending on your perspective, the old wig had arrived by helicopter that morning, along with the rest of the Sandra gear. It did look slightly the worse for wear—the hair was matted, and the nylon cap was crushed, as if a heavy weight had been sitting on top of it for several weeks.

"He sleeps on it," Carter explained as Molly looked askance at the blond tangle. "That's all. There's been no improper activity."

Elaine had managed to return the wig to a reasonable state, and had sprayed it generously with Chanel No. 5 to drown out the faint odor of cat that still lingered after two washings. Molly was now wearing it, along with a pink stretch minidress, the pink platforms, and all of the old padding. The blue contacts had gone missing, and so Molly was using her own clear contacts, with Elaine's sunglasses to conceal her eyes, just in case Rama Guru remembered what color they had been.

"Where *is* he?" Elaine muttered, scanning the area. "He must be here somewhere . . . if he suspects anything, he would never let her—aha!"

She had spotted him standing off to the side, inside the roped-off area, but out of the central buzz of activity.

"Perfect," Elaine said. "They'll be finishing up at any moment, and then there will be enough hubbub for me to pull Ingrid aside, provided that he isn't looking. Molly, dear, go now and start talking to him. Try to lure him away. Carter is waiting just beyond those trees, and I'll send him back to rescue you when Ingrid and I are safely away."

Molly edged her way through the crowd, earning her own share of curious looks. When she drew near to where Rama Guru was standing, she exclaimed loudly, "Oh, my goodness! Mr. Guru, can it really be you?"

He turned and saw her. A gleaming white smile spread over his tanned face, and he held out his hands in a gesture of welcome. "Sandra. *Namaste*."

Molly stepped over the ropes, letting the minidress hike up higher on her thighs. "I just can't believe it," she said.

"What an amazing coincidence that you and I would both be back at Gold Bay right now."

Rama Guru's eyes moved over her. "Coincidence?" he said. "Oh, no, my child. There is no such thing as coincidence. Our karma has brought us together again. This moment was meant to be." He glanced around, frowning slightly. "And your friend, Mrs. Newberg . . . is she here, too?"

"I don't know where she is," Molly said truthfully. "But I really, really, need to talk to you. Could we go somewhere more private?"

He hesitated, glancing over at the photo shoot. Pascal the photographer was shouting something in French, and Ingrid was now holding the giraffe. Rama Guru frowned, but he didn't move. Molly had assumed that Elaine was just being paranoid when she insisted that someone had warned him to stay close to Ingrid, but now it did seem as if he suspected something.

"I need to talk to you about Dwayne," Molly persisted. "He doesn't love me. I think he's just using me . . . for sex. And not the normal kind, either."

Rama Guru's eyes widened. "Tell me more," he said. "So that I may cleanse your soul of this pain."

"First I tie him up," Molly said improvising. "Then I go to the kitchen and bring back a huge jar of marshmallow fluff, and a spatula . . . and then . . ."

Rama Guru's attention was now riveted on her. His mouth opened slightly. "And? Yes?"

"I'd rather discuss this in private," Molly said firmly.

It was the closest thing to frustration that she had ever seen on his normally serene face. "Perhaps," he muttered. "Perhaps . . . Ah. Yes. Come with me."

He led her toward one of the poolside cabanas, now being used as prop storage for the photo shoot. Molly had a moment of uncertainty, wondering if this was a bit too private, but it seemed safe enough. There were plenty of people around, and if a problem developed, she could always yell.

The cabana was made of heavy canvas, closed on three sides but open toward the pool. It normally contained only a few lounge chairs covered in white terry cloth, but that day it also held a rolling rack of bikinis on hangers and several large stuffed animals that had not made the final cut. Molly saw a three-foot tiger, and thought of the Maharajah of Marabai.

"Here, my child," said Rama Guru, clearing a space for her on one of the padded lounge chairs. "Sit here, and I will listen."

Molly sat, wondering how long she was going to have to keep this up. Outside, the music had stopped, and it sounded as if the shoot had ended.

Rama Guru was watching her eagerly, and she sighed, trying to think. It was hot, and she was feeling distracted. "I'm sorry," she said. "This is . . . so difficult for me."

"You come back from the kitchen," he prompted.

"Right," she said. "And then Dwayne . . . uh . . . he says . . ."

"What are you wearing, Sandra?" he interrupted.

"What?" Molly asked, confused.

"During this abnormal activity. What do you wear?"

Molly's mouth opened slightly with outrage. She was becoming very glad that she had agreed to help get Ingrid away from this letch. "I don't wear much," she said. "Obviously. Marshmallow fluff is extremely sticky."

He looked surprised, and she realized that her tone had been too sharp. "My child," he said reproachfully, "clinging to your pain will only prevent you from finding the Way to the Light."

"I know," Molly said. "And I haven't even told you yet about the leather gloves, and . . . the eggplant, and . . . and the turtle."

"Turtle?" Rama Guru echoed. He finally looked disturbed, which was a relief to Molly. "Oh, Sandra," he said. "You are deeply in need of my help. I will need to guide you through an Insight Meditation, to awaken the Spirit within you."

"What do I have to do?" Molly asked.

"Nothing, my child. Just sit quietly and close your eyes."

She closed her eyes and heard the rustle of his robes as he stepped forward to stand in front of her. Startled, she looked to see what he was doing. He stopped a few inches away, then lifted off her sunglasses. Quickly Molly squeezed her eyes shut again.

"We are One, Sandra. I will reach out with my chakras to awaken yours. You may feel the touch of the Spirit, but focus only on your breath."

It sounded suspicious to Molly, but she kept her eyes closed and breathed, thinking that if she felt any touch—from the Spirit or otherwise—she was going to punch Rama Guru in the nose and leave the hapless Ingrid to her fate.

But nothing happened. She sat, listening to the crew talking in French, hearing the sounds of equipment being moved and dismantled. She hoped that Elaine would be quick, and that Carter would make haste to find her as soon as his sister had gone off with Ingrid.

"Sandra . . ." sighed Rama Guru. "Do you feel the Spirit?"

"Yes," Molly lied. "I sure do."

"Do you feel the Ultimate Unity? Does it bring you joy?"

"Oh, yes."

"Great joy?"

Molly was about to affirm that it did when she suddenly

heard footsteps by the front of the cabana. There was a gasp, and then a scream split the air.

"Pig!" shrieked Ingrid Anderson.

Molly's eyes flew open, fast enough to catch Rama Guru jerking his hands away from her chest, his fingers still curved as if he had been gripping two grapefruits.

"Hey!" she snapped, suddenly realizing what had been happening. She hadn't felt a thing under all of the Sandra padding, and Rama Guru apparently had had no idea that he was feeling up four inches of foam rubber.

"I knew it!" Ingrid cried. "Baroness Von Reinholz warned me about you! I should have listened!"

Molly agreed with that. Angrily, she grabbed the nearest object—a stuffed tiger—and whacked Rama Guru with it. He jumped backward, holding up his hands defensively as Ingrid stomped into the cabana toward him.

"Ingrid, my child," he said hopefully, and looked at Molly. "Sandra . . ."

Ingrid threw a scornful glance at Molly, then paused, surprised, and looked again. "Sandra?" she said. "Sandra St. Claire?"

"No!" Molly said quickly. Rama Guru might not read the papers, but it was too much to hope that Ingrid didn't. The last thing that Operation Family Man needed was to have wild rumors flying around that Jake Berenger's fiancée was trysting with a guru in a Gold Bay pool cabana. "You're thinking of someone else. I'm not—"

"Yes, you are. I remember. You were here a few weeks ago, but then your picture was in the news, and you didn't look like this. You had brown hair, and your name was actually—"

"Molly! Is that you?"

Molly gasped, stiffening at the sound of the familiar voice. *Oh, no*, she thought, horrified. *Not Jake. Not now. Oh, please.* She glanced wildly around, searching for somewhere to hide, but it was too late.

Jake appeared in the doorway. He took one look at her, and stopped short. He stood, staring at her, with disbelief on his face. "*What?*" he said.

"Hi there," Molly said weakly, reaching up to pat the wig. "What brings you to the party?"

"I've been looking for you," he said. "And then I heard your voice." His eyes moved over her, noting the pink shoes, the skintight dress, the inflated chest, and the platinum hair. Then he looked at Rama Guru, who was investigating the back wall of the cabana to see if there was a way to escape through the canvas.

Jake folded his arms against his chest. His mouth tightened into a grim line. "*What,*" he repeated slowly, enunciating with cold precision, "the *hell* . . . is going on here?"

CHAPTER 30

A brief, frightened silence descended on the cabana after Jake's demand for information. There was a buzz of urgent French outside, and Molly saw various members of the *Vogue* crew—alerted by Ingrid's shrieks—staring through the open flaps of the cabana.

"What ees zees!" Pascal the photographer appeared on the fringe of the curious crowd and shoved his way through. "Eeengrid," he exclaimed. "*Chérie!* Why do you scream?"

Ingrid was still trembling with fury. "He's a cheat!" she said, pointing at Rama Guru. "And a liar. He told me that I was the only woman who could know Ultimate Unity with him. But then I came in here to change out of my bikini, and I found *them* together . . . sharing their chakras!"

Molly winced, feeling sordid. Jake's expression seemed to darken. "Listen," she said to him. "I can explain."

"Not here, you can't," Jake said. He strode forward and grasped her by the arm, pulling her to her feet. "We're leaving."

Just like old times, Molly stumbled in her shoes. She squawked and grabbed Jake to steady herself. "No, wait! Where's Elaine? She's supposed to be with Ingrid. And then Carter was going to come and rescue me—"

But he hustled her out of the cabana, to the sound of

Ingrid hurtling a shrill stream of abuse at Rama Guru, who was protesting weakly.

"It's not what you think," Molly protested as they hurried across the terrace, although she actually had no idea what Jake was thinking. "We had a plan. Elaine and Carter—"

"A plan?" They reached the spot where he had parked the Jeep. Ignoring the curious stares of the people nearby, he opened the passenger door for Molly, then came around the car, climbed into the driver's seat, and started the engine.

He cast a sideways look at her as they drove away. "This seems like a good time to tell you that I have serious doubts about your taste in friends."

"Oh," Molly said, dismayed. "But this wasn't their fault. We were trying to reunite Ingrid and Michael, except that I don't know what happened to Elaine. Did you see her?"

"No."

The breeze picked up as Jake headed up the road toward the villa, and Molly inhaled gratefully. She felt hot and flushed, and the heavy Sandra makeup was making her itch.

"My job was to distract Rama Guru," she explained. "So that Elaine could slip away with Ingrid."

"I'm sure you were very effective," Jake said. "What does sharing karmas involve, exactly? And why do you need to hide in a cabana to do it?"

"Chakras," Molly corrected. "We were sharing chakras. You don't think that I was actually trying to seduce Rama Guru, do you? That's ridiculous!"

"Sure," Jake said. "Of course. How could I imagine that you would dress up like that and try to seduce someone as part of a stupid plan invented by one of your friends?"

"Oh," Molly said. "Hmm. Well . . . what do you care, anyway? You didn't even bother to call me!" Gathering steam, she drew herself up indignantly. "I waited all week to hear from you, and your mother did her best to explain that you were just too *busy* to call, as if *that* made it okay . . ."

Jake pulled the car over to the side of the road and cut the engine. Startled, she paused. For a moment, the only sound was the rustle of the wind in the trees, punctuated by the cries of birds. Molly waited, but Jake didn't say anything. Instead, he stared straight ahead, drumming his fingertips on the steering wheel and frowning, as if he were working through a math problem in his mind.

Finally, he turned to her. "This is going to sound pretty lame, but it's the truth. I don't know why I didn't call."

"You're right," Molly said. "That does sound lame."

"I wanted to give you a good explanation, but I don't have one. All I can say is that it was a terrible goddamned week, and I thought about you every day, even though I tried not to."

"How nice. Thanks."

He looked frustrated. "Look, I don't know how to say this. You're in a separate compartment in my head. I'm not the same person here, with you, that I am out there, and this past week it was too dangerous to mix the two. I had no choice—I couldn't afford the distraction. I thought that if I just waited, I could come back . . ."

Molly was silent. She knew something about keeping separate lives in separate mental compartments.

"But I should have called," Jake added. "Next time, I will."

"Next time," Molly repeated. Was that how it would be, then? A series of steamy weekends until they parted company in April?

"Unless you want to come with me, that is."

"Where?" Molly asked, startled.

"New York. I'm leaving on Sunday morning."

"Oh. Do you need me for another event?" She hadn't

made a single public appearance or spoken to a single journalist since the Grand opening two weeks ago, and she guessed that it was no coincidence. Tom and Jake had decided to keep her away from the press. Molly didn't mind—she didn't like interviews any more than Jake did. But if he wanted to reinstate her as an active player in the PR program, she needed more than a day to prepare.

To her surprise, Jake was shaking his head. "There's no event. I have meetings in the city, and I'll be taping some television shows. That's all."

"But if there's no event, why do you want me to come?" She bit her lip, knowing that he was unlikely to say what she wanted to hear.

"I'll be busy," Jake continued. "You can work, or shop, or go back to that museum, whatever suits you. But I'll try to take an evening off so that we can go to dinner and the theater."

"For a photo op," Molly said, her heart sinking.

"No," he said, "for fun, if you don't mind traveling all that way for one night on the town. Now that I think about it, it doesn't sound like much of an offer."

"I wouldn't say that," Molly said. "It sounds like an adventure. I have a soft spot for those, in case you haven't noticed."

He chuckled, and reached out to brush a strand of platinum hair out of her face. "Sandra St. Claire rides again. You're a very unusual woman, Molly."

"Not boring?" Molly asked hopefully.

"Definitely not. I don't think I've spent a single boring minute with you. You could stand to be a little less interesting, in fact. Just a humble request."

Her eyes met his. "What about keeping things separate? Won't I be a distraction?"

"Oh yes," Jake said. "You sure will."

"Maybe you'll just have to learn to deal with it."

A dry smile touched his mouth. "Maybe so. And if that's the case, I've got no time to lose. Right now, I hardly know what to do with you."

"Do whatever you want," Molly said. "It's worked for you so far. Why change your strategy now?"

He laughed softly. "Good point," he said, and reached for her. Molly's hands slid up his chest as he pulled her to him and began to kiss her, holding her as if he never wanted to let her go.

"Take this damn thing off," he muttered against her mouth, his fingers tangled in the blond wig. "And burn it." He tugged at it.

"Ow," Molly said, wincing. "Wait, you can't do it like that—there are pins . . ." She began plucking pins out of the wig, dropping them on the floor of the Jeep. He watched as she pulled it off and shook out her own hair. "There. Is that better?"

"Yes," he said.

Before long, Molly had been divested not only of the wig, but the padding, the enormous Sandra bra, and all of her carefully applied lip gloss. She had also discovered that the front seat of a Jeep was not a comfortable spot for a make-out session.

"How are your chakras?" Jake asked.

"Cramped," she said, adjusting her position. The gear stick was digging into her hip.

"Do you want to go back to the villa?"

She shook her head. "No, I have a better idea. Do you remember when you accused me of starting games that I couldn't follow through?"

He looked intrigued by the teasing note in her voice. "I remember. Why?"

"You were wrong. I always follow through. And I believe

that you and Sandra St. Claire—or whatever is left of her—have some unfinished business to attend to at Falcon's Point."

To Jake's surprise, there were three cars parked in the clearing just below the steps to Falcon's Point. He had occasionally encountered a guest or two up at the overlook, but this appeared to be a tour group. Or a party, he thought, as they drew closer. One of the Jeeps had a stack of insulated metal boxes in the back, the kind that the kitchen used to keep food warm. Another Jeep was empty, but littered with petals and bits of greenery, as if it had been used to transport several large floral arrangements. There was a young man sitting at the wheel of the third car, and as Jake pulled up next to him, he saw that it was Brett, the staffer who had done a less-than-ideal job of babysitting Molly in December.

"What's going on?" he asked Brett.

The young man shrugged. "I don't know. I drove him up here a while ago. I'm supposed to wait until he wants to leave."

"Who?"

"Mr. Delafield. It was supposed to be dinner for two, but so far, he's the only one."

A staff butler was coming down the stairs, walking very carefully and balancing a white confection that looked like a miniature wedding cake. He looked surprised when he saw them. "Sir," he said to Jake. "I was just going to put this back into the cooler. It's melting in the heat."

Molly inhaled sharply, and Jake looked at her. She was staring at the tiny cake. "Oh, dear," she said. "I think I know who's up there. How long has he been waiting?"

"More than an hour, madam," said the butler.

Molly shook her head, muttered something that sounded like "Elaine," and "secluded spot," then started up the stairs. A moment later, Jake followed.

Falcon's Point looked very different than it had the last time Jake had seen it. Now, tiny lanterns were strung through the trees, and they glowed faintly, still eclipsed by the warm light of the evening sun. A table had been set up in the middle of the clearing, covered with a white cloth that spilled extravagantly over its sides and onto the ground. Masses of white, pink, and red rose petals were scattered over the ground like soft confetti, and a fluffy bouquet of flowers was arranged on the table, flanked by two fat white candles that had burned halfway down, puddling wax onto the linen.

A man in a tuxedo sat on a rock. He was holding a violin in his lap, and he appeared to be asleep. Molly walked up to him. "Excuse me," she said. "Are you . . . Michael?"

The man opened his eyes, blinked at her, and then focused on Jake, who was standing just behind her. He looked startled, then quickly jumped to his feet and began to play "Moon River."

"Oh," Molly said. "I guess not. Do you know where he went?"

The violinist swung around, using the tip of his instrument to point toward the vegetation near the edge of the cliff.

Molly gasped. "What? Oh, my God!"

"Who's Michael?" Jake asked, moving fast to keep up as Molly hurried toward the trees. He did not like the look on her face. There was a rock wall at the edge of the drop-off, intended to keep clueless tourists from plunging to their deaths, but it wouldn't do much to thwart a determined jumper.

They took the path through the scrubby trees and burst out into the area before the wall. A man stood there, his back to them as he stared out into the air over the vast cliff. He was leaning on the wall, his shoulders hunched despairingly.

"Stop!" Molly cried. "Michael, wait!"

The man straightened up and turned, and Jake saw that he was holding a cell phone to his ear. He waved one hand impatiently, gesturing for them to be quiet. "God damn it," he said into the phone. "Don't give me that obstruction of justice shit. I deleted those e-mails because they were old! Company policy requires regular file cleanup, and you can tell that to the feds."

He snapped the phone closed and glared at them. "Who the hell are you? Where's my wife?"

"You're Michael?" Molly asked, looking slightly stunned. "Ingrid's Michael?"

"No, I'm Batman. Look, babe, I've been waiting here for hours. Where's Ingrid? Where's that Newberg woman? What do they expect me to do, stand around all night listening to a penguin playing lounge music on the violin? I'm getting eaten alive by bugs."

"I . . . don't know where Ingrid is," Molly said. "She finished her photo shoot, but then there was a little problem . . ."

Jake remembered the scene in the cabana. "I don't think she's coming," he said.

"Yeah, I pretty much figured that out." Michael shook his head, disgusted. "Whaddya do? I wrote poetry for her, and *still* she stands me up. That's it. I quit, and that Newberg woman is going to be hearing from my lawyers. Do you know how much this goddamned dinner is costing me?"

"Don't worry about it," Jake said. "I'll make sure that it doesn't go on your bill. We're sorry that your Gold Bay experience wasn't more satisfying."

Michael looked surprised. "You work here?"

Jake nodded. "You could say that."

The other man smiled for the first time. "Great. That's great. Thanks, sport. I appreciate it. Listen, since I'm taking off, why don't you and the young lady enjoy the evening? Hate to see all those flowers go to waste. There's a bottle of vintage Dom Perignon, too." He winked. "Don't worry, I won't tell the boss."

Jake grinned. "Gosh," he said. "Thanks."

"What I don't understand," Jake said later, after they had dined on lukewarm beef Wellington and wedding cake, then sent the violinist and the rest of the staff back to the resort, "is why you let your friends involve you in these crazy schemes."

"Oh, please," Molly scoffed. She'd had two glasses of champagne, and she was feeling giddy and relaxed at the same time. The sun had dropped below the horizon, and the sky had turned from salmon pink to a melting dark apricot. The tiny lanterns bathed the clearing in a glow like moonlight, and so far, there had been no sign of whatever bugs had been eating Michael Delafield alive. "What about your scheme? You can hardly call Operation Family Man a normal business strategy. You should be glad that I'm so agreeable."

Jake shrugged. "At least I didn't make you wear a wig. How did your friend Carter talk you into the Sandra project?"

"I owed him a favor, but that's not really why I agreed to help him. I spent two years at Belden trying to get rid of any part of me that didn't fit the mold of Perfect Professor, and I was sick of it. The idea of coming here, of pretending to be someone totally different . . . it sounded like a vacation from myself. I think I needed one."

"And now?" Jake asked. "You've had your vacation. Do you wish that you were back in your old life?"

Molly could see the candlelight flickering in his eyes. "I can't ever go back to my old life," she said. "Why do you ask? Are you hoping to hear me say that I'm glad? Would that ease your conscience?"

He exhaled a short breath. "I don't have a guilty conscience. I was just curious. You seem happy now, but I didn't know you before. All I saw was how you reacted to your father, that night on the phone."

Molly hesitated. This topic had been on her mind for the past week, ever since that terrible conversation with Stanford. "I am happy," she said, slowly. "It's interesting. Before Dean Fowler told me that I wouldn't be offered tenure, he said that my choice to spend my time working on *Pirate Gold*—instead of my academic research—didn't reflect the College Principles."

"I can guess what those are," Jake said. "Principle One: Do what you're told to do, not what you want to do."

"I think I was supposed to want to work on my research," Molly said. "But I didn't. I wanted to write novels. I argued with the dean about it then, but recently I've been wondering if he was right. The Belden College Principles don't seem very compatible with the Molly Shaw Principles."

Jake looked curious. "And those are . . . ?"

Molly smiled. "Never leave a glass of champagne half empty," she said, and held hers out to him.

"Words to live by," Jake said. He reached out with the bottle and refilled her glass. The foam rose to a rounded dome over the rim, then settled. "What's next?"

"Never share a wig with a cat."

He grinned. "I'll keep that in mind. Any others?"

"Always keep your eyes open when men in white robes offer to awaken your chakras."

"I'm not sure that applies to me," Jake said. "But here's one that does. Never listen to short men in seersucker suits who tell you that I prefer voluptuous blondes."

"Oh," Molly said. "I like that."

"Here's another one, then," he said, leaning forward. His steady gaze held hers, and a shiver of excitement ran through her. "Never spend time talking if you could be doing something better."

"Like attending to unfinished business?" Molly murmured. She stood up and came around the table to him. He pulled her down into his lap and began to kiss her hungrily, his tongue hot against hers. Molly slid her hands up under his T-shirt and ran her palms over the flat ridges and curves of his chest, loving the feel of soft skin over hard muscle. She grabbed the shirt's hem and lifted it, pulling it over Jake's head and off, with some help from him.

It was almost dark now, but the glow from the lanterns reflected softly off of his golden skin. The sight of him gave Molly a moment's pause, as she suddenly wondered what on earth she was doing here, in a tropical clearing, dizzy with champagne, kissing a man like this. But it was not the kind of situation that called for scholarly analysis, or logical thinking of any kind. It demanded action, and Molly was very willing to oblige.

One of Jake's hands was gripping her thigh, sliding upward, pushing the tight spandex hem of the pink minidress higher and higher. Molly looked into his eyes, biting her bottom lip, and saw his mouth curve knowingly as he read the anticipation on her face. He pulled his hand away . . . and they both jumped, startled, as the dress snapped back into place with an audible crack.

Molly stiffened, but Jake began to laugh. He stood up, easing her to her feet. "Nice dress," he said. "What is it, some kind of chastity protection system? You'd never guess by looking at it."

"It's a tease," Molly said. "Like Sandra."

"Let's get rid of it before it takes one of my fingers off."

"What if someone comes?"

"Then we'll hide in the bushes and sic the dress on them," Jake said. "But don't worry. It's dark, so we'll see headlights long before anyone gets this far."

"I can't believe I'm doing this," Molly said as she wriggled out of the dress. She had already left the Sandra bra—and most of its contents—on the floor of the Jeep, and now she was wearing only a tiny scrap of a bikini that covered less than Eve's fig leaf. "I've never been naked outdoors before."

"Never?" Jake asked. "Not even to swim?" He put his arms around her, and she shivered—though not with cold—as her nipples pressed against the bare skin of his chest. His hands slid down to grip the backs of her thighs, pulling her snugly up and against him.

"Never," Molly whispered against his mouth as he bent his head to kiss her again. She could feel the warmth of the tropical night breeze against her whole body. Crickets had begun to trill in the bushes, and their song seemed to be pulsing in time with the beat of her heart.

With an effortlessness that surprised her, Jake bent and hooked one arm around her waist and another under her knees, and scooped her up. She gasped, clutching at him, as he stepped backward and sat down in the chair again, with Molly cradled against him. His mouth moved down to taste the hollow at the base of her throat, and Molly tipped her head back, staring upward. The stars were coming out in a glittering profusion, so abundant that they blurred together like a smear of frost over the inky sky.

She slid one hand up the nape of his neck and knotted her

fingers into his thick hair. "I have a new Molly Shaw Principle," she murmured.

He lifted his head to look at her, his eyebrows raised inquiringly.

"Never be the only one naked outdoors," she said, sliding her other hand down to fumble with the button at the waistband of his khaki shorts. Jake laughed softly, low in his throat, and pulled his arm out from under Molly's knees, reaching around to assist her.

"I'll do my best to comply," he said seriously. "Because I'm starting to think that I want tenure."

CHAPTER 31

"And then Ingrid told the guard that she didn't know me!" Elaine exclaimed. "They detained me for fifteen minutes, until they understood that I was a personal friend of Mr. Berenger. But by then, their apology was *totally* inadequate." She put down her fork and dabbed at her lips with her napkin.

It was early on Sunday morning, and Molly and Jake were due to leave for New York at noon. Molly had come down to the resort to have breakfast at the cottage with Elaine and Carter and to hear the story of what had gone wrong with the previous day's plan.

The trouble had begun when the photo shoot ended. Molly and Rama Guru had been ensconced in the cabana, and Elaine, seizing the chance, had tried to step over the ropes to approach Ingrid. But a security guard had stopped her, then held her for questioning after Ingrid airily claimed that she'd never seen Elaine before in her life.

"I have never been more offended in my life," Elaine said darkly. "That girl is too much of a fool to deserve my help. I have a reputation to maintain, after all."

"At least she's not Seeking the Light anymore," Carter pointed out. "You did a good deed. Let your heart be warmed by that."

Elaine glared at him. "Thank you, Carter, but I don't find much consolation in that, and neither does Michael."

What had happened, according to Elaine—who had been released by security and arrived at the cabana only moments after Jake dragged Molly away—was that Ingrid had informed Rama Guru that his betrayal meant nothing, because there was another man who truly loved her, in a genuinely spiritual way.

Elaine had known a perfect opening when she saw one. "Yes!" she exclaimed. "That's right. And guess what, dear. He's here, waiting for you."

"Who is?" Ingrid had asked.

"Michael, of course. He's come to take you home."

"I'm not going back to Michael. I need a sensitive, artistic man. Michael is boring."

"But he's been writing poetry for you," Elaine protested. "It's very sensitive. 'My love/is a dove/it flew over the ocean/to prove my devotion' How about that!"

"I don't care. Pascal is the only man I want."

"What? *Him*?" Elaine gasped, staring at the photographer, who winked at her.

Ingrid had then informed Elaine that she was already studying French so that she would be able to speak it with their baby, who was due in August. At that point, Elaine had washed her hands of the whole affair.

"Seems to me that Michael is actually taking it pretty well," Carter remarked.

"What?" Elaine snapped. "Don't be absurd. The man is devastated."

"If he was so desperate to have Ingrid back, then why did he bring the divorce papers with him?"

"Carter, you have no understanding of how an intelligent businessman's mind works. He gave it his best. He wrote poetry for her, for heaven's sake. But if she's going to be completely unreasonable, then Michael can't be blamed for having a backup plan."

"He sure did. Who would have guessed that that guy in the plaid shorts was his lawyer?"

Elaine pursed her lips. "It's just as well that it's been wrapped up quickly."

Carter nodded. "I'll bet Michael thinks so, too. I saw him talking to Brooke Metzner on the beach last night."

"What?" Elaine's eyes widened. "Brooke is here?"

"Not anymore. She was on the ferry back to Antigua with Michael. She had a lot of luggage."

Elaine was barely listening. "She's been on the hunt for a rich husband for ages. I arranged a date between her and that ill-fated heir to the Wallabee Chicken fortune last year, and it looked good for a while, but you know what happened to him. Oh, this is very interesting news. I'm going to call her right now and find out what happened. Excuse me."

She left the table.

"And so it continues," Carter said. "Ingrid has escaped my sister's web of intrigue, but Michael never will. Not unless his stock takes another dive, that is."

"I have to go, too," Molly said. "I'm supposed to meet Jake at the heliport."

"Not yet," Carter said quickly. "Have some more coffee. Elaine and I are flying back to Chicago tomorrow, but I'll be in New York on Wednesday. I've got a meeting with *Vanity Fair*. Do you want to get together for lunch?"

"Sure. Are you staying at the Grand?"

"No, the Plaza. Call me. After that, who knows when I'll see you again?"

"In April," Molly said. "When all of this is over."

Carter bent down to fumble in the canvas beach bag sitting by the foot of his chair. "I have something for you," he said.

He straightened up again, holding a wadded-up green sweater, which he plopped onto the tablecloth. Molly frowned at it, wondering why he wanted to give her his old sweater, but then he handed her a copy of the latest *Time* magazine, opened to a half-page article featuring a picture of her—one of the early publicity shots that had been taken when she arrived at Gold Bay. "Have you seen this?" he asked. "They describe you as a 'literary sensation' who single-handedly revived the market for historical sagas."

"Yes," Molly said. It was one of a number of pieces that Tom had placed in major magazines, and Cora had already shown it to her. The "interview" had been taken from her conversation with the Associated Press reporter at the Berenger Grand opening.

"I'll bet you're glad you agreed to fake this engagement," Carter said. "The publicity has been very good for your book sales."

Molly glanced at him curiously. His expression was neutral, but she thought that she'd heard a slight edge to his tone. If so, she could hardly blame him for it. Carter had always been hungry for fame—much more so than she was. She knew that he was happy for her, but it couldn't be easy for him to stand on the sidelines and watch her achieve what he so desperately wanted for himself. He was doing a heroic job of concealing his feelings, though, and she was touched by his effort.

She reached across the table and squeezed his hand. "Carter," she said, "thank you. You're a good friend."

He looked surprised, then began to blush, to her amusement. "I want the best for you, Molly," he said. "I truly do. That's what friends are for."

"I know. We'll have a good time in Chicago when this is

all over," she said, trying to ignore the knot in her stomach at the thought of Jake fading out of her life forever. By now, she knew how it would happen. There would be no drama, no breakup announcement. Just a gradual slowing down of available news. It would all be done carefully and quietly, handled by Tom, who would keep it under the media's radar until some point in the future when it was already obvious to everyone that she and Jake were no longer a couple.

"Will you be glad?" Carter asked. "When this fake engagement is over, I mean?"

"I don't know," Molly said. "In some ways, yes. I'm tired of lies and deception, for anyone's sake. I'm done with that. I'm going to live on my own terms for a change." That much, she knew. She was ready to abandon the dutiful daughter, the tense academic, the tottering bombshell, and the cardboard fiancée. The only person left standing in April would be the real Molly Shaw, for better or for worse.

"What happens if Atlas Group acquires Berenger before April? Does the plan end early?"

"I don't know," Molly said. "I guess so. We haven't talked about it."

"What if the stock price doesn't go up fast enough, and Jake decides that he would get better publicity if you two really got married?"

"What? That's ridiculous."

"But just hypothetically speaking, if he asked you to do it, would you? Marry him?"

"No," Molly said. The sunny sparkle of the morning suddenly dimmed, and she felt a twist of pain in her heart. "I couldn't actually marry Jake. I don't mind pretending to be engaged, but there's only so far I'm willing to go to help raise the Berenger stock price, and that seems a little extreme."

Carter grinned suddenly.

"What?" Molly asked.

"Nothing," he said. "I'm just glad to hear that."

She looked curiously at him. "You are? I would've thought that you would tell me to go ahead with something like that. Think of the access . . . the inside scoop . . ." She was teasing him, but he didn't smile.

"Molly," he said, "I'm trying to be helpful. Your crush on Jake is affecting your brain, and it's my duty to help you regain your perspective."

"What do you mean?"

"I mean, be smarter. Make this situation work for you. You know that Fox news show, *Inside Edge*? They would pay big money for a story like this."

"No way," Molly said.

"We could do it together," Carter persisted. "A live appearance on the show, to break the story, and then a deal with one of the tabloids to tell the details. I'll write the story and arrange the whole thing, then we'll split the money, sixty-forty, in your favor, naturally—"

"No," Molly said again, sharply. "I'm not going to betray Jake."

"Betray?" Carter echoed. "Hello! If he were some poor innocent, I'd agree with you, but he's not a good guy. He deserves everything that he's got coming to him. He's *using* you, Molly. You're just a tool to him—a strategy for his own success. He doesn't care about you, so why not use him right back?"

Molly stood up. "I have to go," she said. "Have a good trip home, and call me when you relocate your morals."

"Wait, wait," Carter said quickly. "So the money doesn't matter to you. What about justice? What about your job at Belden? Have you forgotten what he did?"

"Of course I haven't forgotten," Molly said. She reached down and ran her finger over the rim of her juice glass. "I just . . . don't feel angry about it anymore. I think he did me a favor, in a strange way. It was for the best."

Carter looked dismayed. "But—"

"What's the matter with you?" she asked, exasperated. "You've been telling me for *two years* that I should leave Belden. And you were right. I should have listened."

Carter exhaled in a long, audible breath. "As your friend, Molly, I have to tell you that it's really hard to help you when you keep refusing to act in your own interest."

"You don't understand," Molly said.

He looked reproachfully at her. "Are you really going to become Jake's sacrificial lamb, just because you have a little crush on him?"

"No, but it's not—"

"I thought you were tougher than that."

"I am, but—"

"And I thought you were living only for yourself now."

"I *am*," Molly said impatiently, "but—"

"So how can you justify letting Jake get away with—"

"Because I'm in love with him!" Molly shouted. "That's how! I keep trying to tell you that it's not just a crush. I'm in love with Jake Berenger, so stop asking me to destroy his life. I can't do it! I won't."

"Oh, no," Carter said. He looked horrified. "No, no. This is not right. You are *not* in love, Molly. Remember what we talked about? The glitter, the gold? The dazzle? This is temporary! Not real! You were the one who said that Jake is a shallow playboy, remember? You said that I should pick someone more worthy to write about."

Molly was quickly becoming very sorry that she'd ever said anything. "Carter, please calm down. I'm trying to get over it, okay? Pretty soon I'll be back in Chicago, sitting at Java Jerry's with you. Everything will be fine."

"Not if you don't wise up," Carter snapped. "You don't

know as much about him as I do. I talked to all of the ex-girlfriends, remember? They were *all* in love with him! And he used them, just like he's using you, except that he didn't cost them their careers."

"He hasn't cost me mine, either," Molly said wearily. "I'm a novelist now, *remember*?"

Molly sat with Cora Berenger on the terrace while they waited for Jake to finish packing.

"I'm glad that you're going with Jake this time," Cora said. "A trip to New York is much more civilized than spending the week climbing around on those old ruins at Dyer's Fortune. I worry about you when you're up there, dear. You could break your ankle."

"I'm very careful," Molly said. "You know, there's danger in the big city, too. I could get mugged."

"Not at the museum, you can't," Cora said. "You see? I know all about you." She chuckled. "I'm trying to imagine Skye Elliot at a museum. Or climbing around on an unrestored historical site, for that matter."

"She did it for *Revenge of the Mummy*, didn't she?"

"Hardly. They used a stunt double for anything that involved more effort than drinking champagne. I believe that Skye's standard contract entitles her to half a million dollars compensation for every broken nail."

"You're kidding."

"Well, yes, but I do know that all of her jungle scenes were filmed on a sound stage in Hollywood. Believe me, my dear, you are very different than the sort of woman that my son used to associate with."

"Is that good or bad?" Molly asked.

"Good," Cora said firmly. "But you're causing loyalty

problems for me. I'd like to see you get your Mary Morgan museum. How is the research going? Any luck?"

"Some," Molly said vaguely. Cora was not the only one plagued by loyalty problems. She still hadn't broken the news of her proof to Jake, and she was increasingly unwilling to do so. She never would have expected a conflict between her obligations as an historian and her personal feelings, but despite her commitment to preserving the Morgan site, she was reluctant to hurt Jake in any way. She was delaying, trying not to think about it, hoping that by April, the Berenger stock would recover to a point where the Atlas takeover was no longer a threat and Jake's own position was more secure. In that case, the relocation of the golf course would be a costly inconvenience, but not a serious blow.

"Are you still planning to write a book about Mary?" Cora asked curiously. "Jake said that you wanted to write a novel about her life."

Molly was surprised by the question, but then remembered saying that to Jake weeks ago, on the beach, during one of her Sandra routines. She had only been ad-libbing, of course, trying to needle him.

"I was actually thinking about doing a nonfiction book," Molly said. "A biography, but an exciting one. It would be hard to write a boring book about someone as dramatic as Mary."

"Good idea," Jake said from the doorway, and they turned to look at him. He was wearing a suit and carrying a black leather garment bag. He walked toward them and draped the bag over the back of a chair. "Write a book that will get made into a movie, and then we'll expand Gold Bay to keep up with the tourist demand to see Bonny Mary's old house. Hell, I'll use the other side of the island to build a pirate theme park. I might be willing to negotiate on this museum after all."

Cora nodded. "And Molly will become even more famous, of course. Those terrible people at Belden will come crawling to her, begging her to come back to Wisconsin and start a pirate research center . . ."

Molly laughed. "Or maybe not," she said. "But that's okay. It'll be an interesting project."

"Yes, if that son of mine doesn't get in your way," Cora said. "Jake, it would be terrible if we knocked down the old plantation and then found out later that it really had belonged to Mary."

He regarded her with mock irritation. "Whose side are you on?"

Cora turned to Molly. "He's stubborn, but I'll do what I can to persuade him to postpone the demolition date, if it comes down to that."

Jake cleared his throat. "Time to go," he said abruptly. "Molly, where's your suitcase?"

"I gave it to the butler," Molly said. She stood up and kissed Cora on the cheek. "Thank you," she said to the older woman.

Cora squeezed her hand. "Don't worry, dear, I do have some influence."

"More than I do," Molly said lightly. "I couldn't get him to budge beyond April first."

"The first?" Cora looked puzzled. "No, that isn't right. They aren't even scheduled to begin until the middle of April, and I think we might be able to push that date back a few weeks, if you need more time— Oh! My goodness. Are you all right?"

Molly had just stepped backward and knocked over Cora's teacup. It rolled off of the table, spraying both of them with brown droplets, and then shattered on the terrace's stone floor.

"That's going to stain," Cora said, clucking her tongue at

the sight of Molly's shirt. She pressed the wireless button to summon the butler. "No, no, dear, don't worry about the cup. Just leave it, and go and change. I don't want you to be late."

Molly's face was red. "Wait," she said, "I think I must be confused. Do you mean—"

Jake took her by the arm. "We need to get going," he said.

Molly balked, still facing Cora. "You're talking about pushing the start date back a few *more* weeks, right? Because it's already been pushed back to April." She glanced at Jake. "Right?"

"No, dear," Cora said cheerfully, and Molly heard Jake exhale hard. "The April date has been set for months—almost a year. You have to arrange these things far in advance for big commercial projects, especially in remote locations." She looked curiously at Molly, then at her son. "Oh. Did I say something wrong?"

Jake was rubbing his forehead as if his head had suddenly started to ache. "Look," he said to Molly, "I can explain . . ."

"I don't believe this," Molly said. "Your *generous concession* to postpone the demolition until April . . . the one that you used to persuade me to help you with your PR project . . . it was a *lie*? You were scheduled to begin in April all along?"

"Jake," Cora said disapprovingly.

He threw an exasperated glance at her. "Excuse us," he said, and walked Molly into the living room.

"You have no idea how much this is going to cost me," Molly quoted, glaring at him. "Does that sound familiar?"

"Vaguely," he said.

"It should. You were right—I had no idea that it was going to cost you nothing. Nothing! All that talk about the expense of delaying such a huge project for my sake, and how you were willing to take the risk if I would help you in exchange . . ."

"It didn't cost you anything, either," Jake pointed out. "The end result is the same. You have until April to locate your proof. What difference do the circumstances make?"

"A lot of difference! I've been helping you in good faith, and all you gave me in return was a false sense of your own willingness to compromise. You tricked me."

He nodded. "I did. That's true, and I apologize. But I haven't lied to you since the very first day, when I met you at the ruins. I admit to doing it then. I don't lie to my friends or my family, but you were a stranger that day. If I told the truth to every stranger who asked me questions, I wouldn't have made it very far in life. Except maybe as a priest."

"I don't know how you can face me and say that," Molly exclaimed. "You lied when you proposed your scheme! You told me that in exchange for my help, you would postpone the demolition of Dyer's Fortune until April—"

"No. That's what you heard, but not what I said. I was very careful. I said that I would give you until April to find your proof. You assumed that I meant that I was postponing the demolition, and I admit that I didn't bother to correct you."

"Oh, clever you," Molly said. "And I didn't bother to ask for details. Well, you shouldn't feel too pleased with yourself. One of these days, I might have a little surprise of my own."

He raised his eyebrows, but she didn't elaborate. Whether he had lied or not wasn't the point. It was another example of his willingness to manipulate her to suit his own ends, and Molly felt a fresh surge of anxiety. She wondered if she had been too hasty in dismissing Carter's assertion that Jake cared more about his own agenda than he did about her. She had begun to believe otherwise, but what if she was wrong? She had fallen in love with him, but what if that had been his intention? No doubt he preferred to have her gazing doe-eyed at him rather than worrying about her stabbing him in the back.

Jake held out his hand to her, and she took it, studying his face. She could see nothing but sincerity in his eyes. "Forgive me," he said. "I would have told you the truth at some point. I honestly didn't think it mattered that much. We have a history of playing games with each other, don't we? But they've always been harmless."

"Exposing me as Sandra wasn't harmless," Molly said. "I lost my job, and even if I don't want it back, it was still a rotten thing to do."

Jake's mouth tightened, and he seemed about to say something sharp. But then he stopped. "I thought we were beyond that by now," he said. "Does this mean that you're still looking for a chance to pay me back? You're right, that wouldn't be harmless."

Molly shook her head. She felt miserable, suddenly. "I just want to forget about the whole thing," she said.

"That makes two of us," Jake said. Gathering her into his arms, he held her snugly, and she hugged him, feeling the crisp white cotton of his shirt against her cheek. The smell of cologne and laundry soap and warm male skin surrounded her, and she wished that she could stay forever in the protective circle of his arms.

But she couldn't shake off her apprehension. Abraham Lincoln had said that the only reliable way to get rid of your enemies was to turn them into your friends. What if Jake saw a tactical purpose in going one better than that? It wasn't impossible, but Molly couldn't bear to think about it.

CHAPTER 32

Jake had always liked New York City. It was exciting and dynamic; arguably the most interesting spot on earth. Cracking the Manhattan market had been a longtime goal for him, finally achieved by the acquisition and renovation of the new Berenger Grand. Now that his company had a strong presence in the city, he felt for the first time that he belonged there.

His apartment at the Grand was still so new that he had only used it on two previous trips. He remembered the first time that he had stayed there, alone in the echoing rooms. He had known intellectually that the place was beautiful, but had felt no emotional warmth for it, or any real pleasure in being there.

Molly had changed all that, though. Her presence had turned the apartment from a piece of walk-through sculpture into something that felt like a home. He liked waking up in the morning and seeing her asleep next to him, tangled in the covers, her hair spread out over the pillow. And he liked returning at night, knowing that she would be there. They spent Monday and Tuesday nights lingering over late dinners from room service, talking until the last of Jake's energy began to fade.

They were supposed to be in town until Thursday, but on

Wednesday afternoon Jake found that he was in no hurry to leave. Despite the ongoing stress of the potential takeover, and the fact that his schedule was booked from eight to eight every day, he was happier than he had ever been in his life.

Molly seemed happy, too, but he could feel a slight remoteness in her that seemed to be an aftereffect of their argument on Sunday. Several times, he caught her watching him with an intent expression, as if she were trying to read his mind. He didn't know why his mother's disclosure had affected her like that—to him, the semantics of the April date were a minor issue. Molly had perceived their agreement as a win-win situation until Cora had spoken up and changed her perspective. And it was only that: a matter of perspective. None of the facts had changed. Her reaction made no sense to him.

He left work early on Wednesday, with the intention of taking Molly to dinner at Madrigal, one of the newest Manhattan hot spots. She had met with her agent that afternoon, to discuss contract negotiations for the *Pirate Gold* sequel, and Jake hadn't forgotten his promise to take her out for a night on the town.

When the elevator doors opened and released him into the foyer of the apartment, he heard the telephone ringing. He hurried forward and picked up the extension in the butler's pantry.

"Jake!" It was Tom Amadeo. "Finally. I've been tracking you all over the goddamned town! Didn't you get my messages?"

"No. I had a meeting with our bankers, and now I'm back here. What's going on?"

"Big fucking trouble, that's what," Tom exclaimed. Jake had never heard him sound so agitated. "You were right, I can't believe it. I didn't think she'd do it, but you were absolutely right."

"What?" Jake asked sharply.

"Molly. She sold you out. Damn it! I'm sorry to have to tell you this. She went to the media with the story, and I just got a call from *Inside Edge*. They're breaking the news about the fake engagement tomorrow."

"Impossible. They're bluffing."

"No, they—"

"They've got nothing! You know there's been speculation about the engagement being a PR stunt. They're trying to get something out of us—it's a trick. Tell them no comment."

"Molly talked to them."

"She wouldn't do that," Jake said, but he felt a sudden tightening in his throat. "Not anymore. They're lying."

"That was what I thought, too, until they sent over the tape."

"Tape?"

"Yeah. It's just a couple of cuts from the interview she gave them, but it was enough to convince me that this is all for real. If she's talking, there's nothing we can do."

Jake tried to breathe. He felt as if a cold wave was breaking over him, crushing him toward the floor. "I don't believe it," he said. "Whoever you heard on tape isn't Molly."

"It's her," Tom said. "It's unmistakable."

"No! I know her voice better than you do. You have the tape right there? Good. Play it for me. Put it on the phone. Now."

"Yeah, okay. Hold on," Tom said. He put down the receiver. There was silence for a moment, and then a fumbling sound, and then a voice came across the line, slightly muffled, but clear enough.

"I'm tired of lies and deception, for anyone's sake. I'm

done with that. I'm going to live on my own terms for a change."

It was Molly. Jake's stomach clenched. The voice cut off suddenly, and the tape played three seconds of scratchy silence, then:

"I couldn't actually marry Jake. I don't mind pretending to be engaged, but there's only so far I'm willing to go to help raise the Berenger stock price."

He heard a click as the recorder was switched off.

"That's all they sent," Tom said, back on the line. "Just a sample. Listen, I've been threatening them. I told them that it wasn't Molly, and that the whole story was an outrageous lie, and that they would never book another one of my clients again if they fuck me like this, but they didn't even hesitate. They're going ahead with it."

Jake said nothing. He couldn't speak. Molly had betrayed him. She had wanted revenge, and she was about to get it. Not only would her disclosure cost him his job and torpedo the Berenger stock price, but he would also become a target for any ambitious attorney who wanted to try to make a case for the fake engagement as stock fraud. Leaking the story to the *Enquirer* on the night of the Grand opening would have done the job, but Molly had been smarter than that. By biding her time and exploring her options, she had managed to find a deal that offered both revenge and money.

"Molly's still at Gold Bay?" Tom asked.

"No," Jake said. "She's here."

"Here? What, in New York? Okay, I'm getting it, I'm getting it. That might be why the producer sounded so cocksure. He hinted that they had an inside source to put on the air tomorrow—he probably meant *her*."

"Sounds likely," Jake said. He felt numb.

"If she wanted money, she would have approached you before she did this, but maybe we can still reason with her.

She might have a price where revenge doesn't seem worth it. If we can get her to back away from this, we might be able to buy some time for the lawyers to stop *Inside Edge* from breaking the story. It'll be messy, but it's our best shot. Do you know where she is? Can you track her down?"

"Easily. Judging from the sound, she's in the shower."

There was a stunned silence on the other end of the line. "Wait," Tom Amadeo said. "*Your* shower? She's right there, in your apartment? Jesus, I didn't know she was staying with you. That girl is running a dangerous racket. What does she think she's doing?"

"I don't know," Jake said. "But I'm about to go and find out."

"Don't do anything stupid. Be cool. Calm."

"I am calm."

"Call me as soon as you have any information."

"All right."

"You sound a little too calm," Tom said suspiciously. "Are you sure you're okay? Do you want me to come over there?"

"I'm fine."

"Just a thought—if anybody at Fox owes you a favor, now would be the time to use it. And one more thing . . ."

"What?"

"Please," Tom said fervently, "if we get through this, don't piss off any more academics, okay? Those people play for keeps."

Molly peered at herself in the bathroom mirror where she had rubbed a spot clear of steamy fog. She was leaning over the sink and holding a pair of tweezers, trying to extract one stubborn hair from the place where her eyebrow wanted to be. Sandra's tweezed arches had been one of the elements of the character that she had decided to keep, but maintenance was turning out to be a constant struggle.

Jake had putty-colored towels in the bathroom, a novelty for Molly. They were painfully sophisticated, a dull grayish brown, but not really to her taste. She didn't think that they were to Jake's taste, either. Who but an interior decorator would ever choose towels that looked dirty even when they were clean? Nonetheless, they were the only towels available, and she had knotted one around her torso and fashioned another into a turban over her wet hair.

She was so focused on her tweezing that she didn't hear Jake appear in the doorway behind her.

"Getting ready?" he asked.

Molly jumped, startled, and dropped the tweezers into the sink. She had a glimpse of him reflected in the mirror, leaning against the open doorway, his arms folded against his chest.

She turned, remembered the towel on her head, and pulled it off, letting her wet hair tumble around her shoulders. "Hi," she said. "You're early."

"Am I? I think I may be late, actually," he said, and Molly realized that he was not returning her smile. He just stood there, staring at her, his face expressionless.

"Is something wrong?" she asked, concerned.

"I wonder what you're getting ready for, exactly," Jake said. "Dinner with me tonight? A television appearance tomorrow night?"

"Are we going on television?" Molly asked. He was acting very strangely, and she was getting an uneasy feeling.

"What I can't understand," Jake said, "is how someone who hates me so much could hide it so well. Every time you looked me in the eye . . . were you actually thinking about how you were going to destroy me? Maybe you didn't have to hide it. I didn't notice a damn thing. I was in love with you."

Molly's mouth fell open. "What, *was*?" she gasped. "What do you mean, was? Why didn't you tell me this before it was . . . *was*? You were in love with me, and I missed the whole thing?" Her knees suddenly felt wobbly. She stepped backward and sat down on the edge of the bathtub.

"Let me tell you a little bit about what you've done," Jake said coldly. "Your vendetta isn't only going to hurt me. It's going to hurt every Berenger employee and every shareholder. You've been angry with me because you think I ruined your life? If our stock crashes because of this scandal, you'll have ruined the lives of thousands of people, none of whom ever did anything to you. But you didn't think about that, or maybe you just didn't care."

"What scandal?" Molly demanded. She raised her hands to her mouth in sudden horror. There was only one scandal that she could think of, and if that had somehow happened, it was no wonder he thought she was behind it. "Jake! Is someone printing the truth about the engagement?"

"Someone is *telling* it," he said and his eyes were full of blame. "You. I just heard a tape of your interview. Tom played it for me."

Molly stared at him. "But I haven't given an interview in weeks! Not since the Grand opening. Where did Tom get this tape? How do you know it was me?"

"You think I don't know your voice when I hear it? Let me refresh your memory. *'I'm tired of lies and deception. I'm done with that. I'm going to live on my own terms for a change.'* Very admirable, Molly. And you sure as hell are doing it, aren't you?"

All of the air rushed out of Molly's lungs, as if someone had just kicked her in the chest. "I said that," she whispered. She had said it recently, but not in an interview. Not in any situation that she thought was an interview, at least. She remembered Carter's wadded-up green sweater, plopped so casually down on the breakfast table. It would have been easy for him to conceal his microcassette recorder in the folds.

"Oh, no," she said in a small voice. "No. Why?"

Frantically, she tried to remember what else she'd said that morning. He had been asking her a lot of questions, and like a fool, she had answered. She had talked about the engagement, she knew. She didn't remember exactly what she'd said, but obviously it had been enough.

"It's *Inside Edge*, isn't it?" she asked, already knowing the answer.

"How much are they paying you?" Jake asked.

"Nothing! You have to believe me. I never talked to them. What you heard . . ." She stopped. She didn't know what he had heard. Parts of that conversation, but not the whole thing. She had told Carter that she wouldn't agree to talk to the press. She had told him that she was in love with Jake. Carter must have edited the tape and sent the news show only the parts that seemed to support the "inside" story that he was telling. His betrayal was overwhelming, and Molly felt weak with the shock of it.

And then, in a terrible flash of clarity, she realized something else. She took a trembling breath and looked Jake in the eye. "Tell me one thing," she said. "Jake, it's critical that you tell me the absolute truth right now. Was it you who told the press that I wrote *Pirate Gold*?"

"No," Jake said stonily. "It was not."

Molly pressed her hand to her mouth and nodded. She believed him. Tears welled up in her eyes. "Of course you didn't," she said. "I've been so stupid, and I'm so sorry. This will seem like a strange time for me to tell you this, but I've been in love with you, too. I still am."

Jake recoiled. He didn't speak for a moment. Finally, he said, "You have a strange way of showing it. Here's my offer, Molly. Two million dollars. Tell your friend at *Inside Edge* that you invented the whole thing as a joke and you won't be appearing on the show. My lawyers will take it from there."

"I don't want money," Molly said urgently. "I'm not going on the show. I was never planning to—I didn't even know about it. Jake, that tape . . . whatever you heard . . . it was edited. It's not an interview. Carter taped me during a personal conversation, and he's the one selling the information to *Inside Edge*."

Jake shook his head. "Sorry," he said. "I'm not that gullible. Your friend Carter might also be involved in this, but that doesn't make you innocent. You two have a history of cooking up schemes together, and he couldn't pull this off without your help." He paused, and then a humorless smile touched his mouth. "I just thought of something interesting. Remember last Sunday, when you told me that I shouldn't feel too happy about having tricked you over the construction at Dyer's Fortune, because you would have a surprise for me, one of these days?"

"Oh, my God," Molly groaned. "No, listen, that wasn't—"

"Consider me surprised," he said coldly.

"I was talking about the sugar estate! That's all. I found the proof that it belonged to Mary Morgan."

"Great," Jake said. "Hand it over to Atlas. They'll own it in a few weeks. They might be interested."

The phone rang with the special sound that signaled the in-house intercom. Jake stepped into the bedroom to pick it up, and Molly took the opportunity to dash into the dressing room for her clothes. She put them on quickly, shaking out her wet hair, and then grabbed her coat and bag.

"Going somewhere?" Jake asked as she returned to the bedroom.

"Yes. I'm going to prove that I had nothing to do with this story," Molly said staunchly. "And I'm going to stop it. Who was that on the phone?"

"Tom. He's coming up in the elevator." Jake regarded her with narrowed eyes. "He's worried that I might do something unethical to keep you off the air. Make sure you say hello to him on your way out—it will ease his mind."

CHAPTER 33

Downstairs in the lobby, Molly stopped by the bank of public phones and called Carter's room at the Plaza Hotel. She had already called him that morning and left a message asking if he wanted to meet for lunch. He had never returned her call, though, and now she thought she knew why. He had been too busy stabbing her in the back.

He picked up on the second ring. "Hello!"

"Carter?" Molly had to make an effort to keep her voice sounding normal. "Hi, it's me. I was wondering if you want to go out and get a drink."

"Molly! Sure, yeah, I just finished with my meetings. Sorry about missing you for lunch—I have something big going on. Very big. I'll tell you about it later. Do you want to meet in the lobby bar?"

"I'll see you in a few minutes," Molly said.

The Plaza Hotel was only a short taxi ride from the Berenger Grand, and when Molly walked into the crowded bar, she saw Carter sitting at a corner table, holding a snifter of something that looked like cognac.

"Busy day?" she asked, sitting down.

He nodded.

"What kind of meetings did you have?"

"Oh," he said vaguely. "*Vanity Fair*, a couple of others . . ."

"*Inside Edge*?"

He looked startled, then wary. "Well . . ."

"Don't you dare lie to me, Carter," Molly said. "I know what you did."

"Oh," he said, as if he were a schoolboy who had been caught stealing candy. Then, to Molly's shock, he grinned at her. "Okay, so I thought it would be a good idea to approach them, right? Just to gauge the interest level, to see what the offer would be. No commitments, though—"

"They're breaking the story tomorrow," Molly said through her teeth. "How does 'no commitments' fit into that? Don't try to tell me that you don't know about it. You taped me. You betrayed me!"

"No, no!" Carter said quickly. "I didn't betray you. We're splitting the money, just like we talked about. They're paying half a million for the story, and another two-fifty if you agree to do an in-depth interview next week. It's the best deal we're going to get, believe me. This is big! I know you had mixed feelings about going public—"

"*Mixed feelings!* I never had mixed feelings—I said no! How dare you do this, Carter! How *could* you? I trusted you. I thought you were my friend."

"I am your friend. I know you're upset, and this is a little bit of a shock, but it's the best possible move, I'm telling you. I'm trying to look out for you. Otherwise, you'll walk away from this fake engagement with nothing, and that isn't fair. It isn't right."

Molly fought back a wave of furious tears. The crowd of people around them made it necessary for her to keep her composure, which was exactly why she had wanted to meet Carter in the bar. In private, she might have tried to strangle him. It was not her safety that Tom Amadeo should be worrying about—it was Carter's.

"You aren't looking out for me at all," she said. "You never were. You only care about yourself. That's why you told the press that I was Sandra St. Claire—it wasn't Jake who wanted to force me into agreeing to the fake engagement, it was you! You wanted the *access*, the *scoop* . . . you didn't care that you ruined my life in the process."

"But I didn't ruin it," Carter said. "Right? You never belonged at Belden, you said so yourself. But you weren't getting any closer to figuring that out; you were miserable, wasting your time clinging to the idea that you had to be an academic. I helped you figure out that you were really meant to be a novelist."

"You helped me?" Molly repeated. She felt sick. Was he lying to her, or had he really deluded himself into believing that he had acted in the name of friendship?

"I know it was painful for a while," Carter continued, "but it was the right thing to do. You're happy now! You should thank me. Not just any friend would have the integrity to risk the whole friendship to help you. I did, and it worked, right? So you should realize that you can trust me now. I know what I'm doing with *Inside Edge*. This is the right decision."

"It is not," Molly said. "And it wasn't your decision to make. None of the things you did ever had anything to do with my wishes. Even if I was making mistakes, it was my life! They were my mistakes! You had no right to interfere."

"I made it better," Carter said sulkily. "I don't see why you're mad at me."

"Because I almost did something terrible to Jake because of your lies! And then, when I refused, you went ahead and did it yourself. You're going to destroy him, Carter! How can you justify that? He never did anything to you."

Carter looked uneasy. "I told you, he's fair game. You're too emotionally wrapped up in the situation to have a clear perspective, but I do. He's using you. He doesn't love you, and he's not going to—"

"How do you know?" Molly demanded. She felt a hot surge of misery in her chest as she remembered what Jake had said. He had loved her. And now he believed that she had betrayed him. "How do you know that he doesn't love me?"

"Because you're not his type. I spent months researching him, remember?"

"Carter, I want you to stop the story. Call *Inside Edge*, and tell them that it was all a mistake."

"I can't do that!"

"You have to do it."

"No, no, Molly. You don't understand. In this business, you don't just hand someone a huge story, then grab it back. This is my whole career, this is everything. I have to go ahead with it. They're already getting the leaders ready—'Tonight on *Inside Edge*, a shocking exposé of the truth about Jake Berenger, America's most controversial billionaire . . .' "

Molly exhaled slowly, trying to keep calm. She had to think clearly, had to come up with a way to stop him. "Is Elaine helping you?"

"Her?" Carter looked annoyed, as if his sister were a sore point. "I didn't even bother to ask. She's obsessed with the idea of getting you and Jake married. All she thinks about is her own reputation. Elaine is totally self-centered."

Molly didn't even try to respond to that. She was just relieved to hear that Elaine was not also in on the scheme. There was only so much betrayal that she could handle in one day, and she already felt past her limit.

"Molly, listen," Carter said. "You're all mixed up, and

you don't know what's best for you, just like when you were at Belden. This deal is really good, and in April, when you're back in Chicago with me and Elaine, you'll be glad that you didn't just let Jake Berenger walk all over you. This is how the world works, believe me. You have to be strong, and take advantage of people who would do the same to you."

Molly stared numbly at him. He couldn't use that argument to explain why he was taking advantage of her, so he'd told himself that he was helping her. It was an astonishing rationalization for his own ambition and ruthlessness.

She hesitated, as if she were mulling over his words, and then made herself nod slowly. "I don't know . . ." she said, feigning confusion. "Maybe you're right . . ."

"I am!"

"They would really pay more for an interview with me?"

"Definitely. And that's just the beginning. We can sell the detailed story to one of the tabloids, and then do a string of interviews, live, print, you name it. Molly, this could be *big*!"

It was an indicator of Carter's level of self-delusion that he didn't question her sudden change of heart. And why should he? He had convinced himself that his plan was a great idea, so it would be easy for him to think that he had convinced her, too.

"Carter, wouldn't it be even bigger if I went on the show with you tomorrow? And broke the story myself?"

His eyes widened. "It would be huge. You'd do that?"

Molly forced herself to smile at him, although her heart felt heavy and sad. *So many losses, in such a short time. So many changes, and so many things that turned out so differently than I ever expected.*

She nodded. "Yes. I'll do it."

"They're going to be blown away," Carter cried gleefully.

He slapped the table, and his drink jumped. "I told them that I wouldn't be able to deliver you until next week."

"Well," Molly said. "Here I am."

After Molly left Carter in the bar, she went to the Plaza's reception desk and paid for a single room at the hotel. Her luggage was all at Jake's apartment, but she didn't think it would be a good idea to go back there that night. She had her purse and her wallet, and she could manage without much trouble until the next day. If her plan worked, then by tomorrow night Jake would know that she had never meant him any harm. And if her plan didn't work . . . Molly pressed her lips together. It was a frightening prospect. If it didn't work, she didn't know how she would ever face him again.

She took her room key and went straight upstairs in the elevator. In the room, she sat down on the bed, picked up the phone, and called Elaine at home in Chicago.

"Molly, dear," Elaine said warmly. "How nice to hear from you. Are you still in New York? How is Jake?"

"Not good," Molly said. Briefly, and with as little emotion as possible, she explained to Elaine what Carter had done. There was a horrified inhalation on the other end of the line.

"*No,*" Elaine exclaimed. "He hasn't!"

"He has."

"That snake! How could he? You do know that he's only my half brother? Oh, I cannot believe that he would do something like this." Elaine paused. "Hmm," she said. "Actually, on second thought, I can believe it. But my shock is not the issue at hand. My dear, this is a crisis situation. Carter must be stopped."

"I agree," Molly said. "That's why I'm calling. I need your help."

CHAPTER 34

"And we'll tell you the shocking story behind hotel tycoon Jake Berenger's recent engagement to professor-turned-best-selling-novelist Molly Shaw. Was it really true love? Or did something else motivate the handsome billionaire's very public announcement that he was finally settling down? Join us, *tonight*, for an exclusive live interview with Molly Shaw, and get the real . . . *Inside Edge*."

"Feels like a funeral home in here," Tom Amadeo said gruffly. "Do you mind if I turn on some lights?"

"Go ahead," Jake said. He didn't care one way or another. A funeral home seemed like an appropriate atmosphere, since he was about to become a dead man.

It was just before eight P.M., and they were in Jake's apartment. Tom had been pacing the floor, and Jake was sitting on the couch and staring at the enormous plasma television screen mounted on the wall. A group of dancing oranges was singing about a new juice drink, but in a few moments, *Inside Edge* would go live.

They had spent the day trying to stop the story, and had been spectacularly unsuccessful. The show's producers had brushed off the lawyers' threats, and Jake had been unable to get through to Sandy Kertzman, the president of Fox television, who had never ignored his calls before. It all added up to one clear message: They had something good, and they knew it. The identity of that good thing became very clear with the first trailers for the upcoming show.

Molly.

The show's opening montage of busy newsroom shots filled the screen, and Jake felt a wave of nausea. Even at that moment, he couldn't quite believe what she had done. Last night, after Molly and Tom had both gone, he had lain awake in bed, going over the scene in the bathroom. He had replayed it again and again in his mind, analyzing it logically, emotionally, any way that might give him more information. He had almost believed her when she insisted that there had been no interview, and that she had had nothing to do with the news show. She had sounded so horrified, and so sincere.

Jake had finally fallen asleep at two A.M., but it was a restless sleep, and he was awakened by even the slightest noise as he subconsciously listened for the sound of the phone. But Molly didn't call, and he woke early, with a splitting headache.

As the day passed, and they learned that Molly would indeed be appearing on the show, it became obvious that everything she had said had been a lie. Her intention had clearly been to escape from the apartment after Jake had discovered her betrayal. She had been in a tight spot when he had cornered her in the bathroom, and she would have said anything, including confessing love for him, to get out safely.

By six P.M., Jake and Tom had finally conceded defeat. Tom had begun working out an aggressive plan for damage control that involved discrediting Molly in every possible way. He intended to cast a shadow on her morals, her personal life, her past relationships, even her sanity. Jake was simply too numb to think about it. He sat, watching the screen, feeling like a condemned man.

It should have been a day of celebration. That afternoon, in a moment of stunning irony, Jake had gotten a call from Oliver Arias, who reported that all of the recent publicity had caused Berenger room reservations to surge. Bookings were up twenty percent, a stunning increase for a still-shaky market. The company would be having an outstanding fiscal quarter that significantly exceeded the forecasts. When Jake delivered the earnings results in two weeks, it was almost a certainty that the stock price would jump to a point where they were no longer vulnerable to Atlas's hostile offer.

Operation Family Man had succeeded.

Oliver had also wanted to propose a plan by the marketing department to develop a *Pirate Gold* weekend theme package at the Miami and Key West Berenger hotels, but Jake had not been in the mood for that discussion.

The opening music stopped. Tom paused in his pacing and moved to stand behind Jake like a sentry, his hands gripping the back of the couch. "O-kay," he muttered. "Let's get this over with."

The camera cut to a close-up of the anchorman. "Welcome to *Inside Edge*," the man said, gazing levelly at the camera. "I'm Drake Daniels. Tonight: a bizarre conspiracy revealed. In this era of corporate greed and wrongdoing, the public demands the answer to one overwhelming question. How far would an embattled CEO go to secure his own success? Would he lie to his employees? To the press? To the American people? The answer . . . may shock you."

Clips began to roll of Jake and Molly together at the Berenger Grand opening, along with a voiceover describing the surprise engagement of the celebrity billionaire to the professor-turned-novelist.

". . . years as a confirmed bachelor, the playboy mogul has been associated with the most glamorous and desirable women in the world . . ."

The inevitable medley followed, photos and film from the past ten years, of Jake with a succession of beautiful women, posing on a succession of red carpets. The clips went on and on as Jake watched silently, surprised by how few of those glittering dates he actually remembered. It was like watching pictures of a stranger who looked just like him, someone who had been having much more fun than he recalled having.

"Wow," Tom said suddenly. "Who's that?"

"Anjalika Devi," Jake said. "Miss India 1993." He had liked Anjalika. They had been introduced by a mutual friend and had dated for a few months, but there had never been real chemistry between them. She was married now, to a British surgeon, and they had two sons.

". . . rumors of an engagement to actress Skye Elliot were crushed when the couple parted on bad terms in October, a result, says the Academy Award-winning actress, of Jake's unwillingness to give up life in the fast lane."

The pleasant face of a plump, middle-aged woman appeared on the screen, with a caption reading Dr. Judith Brightman, author of *Casanova Complex: Men Who Can't Commit.*

"These men have a terrible fear of intimacy," she said earnestly to the camera. "This problem usually has roots in a dysfunctional childhood relationship with the mother."

Jake raised his eyebrows at the screen, hoping that Cora was not watching. She would not be amused.

" . . . But then, in a shocking twist just three weeks ago, Jake Berenger announced that he planned to marry Dr. Molly Shaw, also known as Sandra St. Claire, the author of the best-selling historical saga, Pirate Gold. *There was*

speculation that the very public engagement was an attempt to improve the troubled tycoon's image . . ."

A recently recorded interview with Skye Elliot began to roll. She was in the garden of her Malibu home, with softly filtered sunlight playing on her blond hair. "In my opinion, this engagement is definitely a publicity stunt. I know Jake better than anyone, and I guarantee that he'll never get married. He secretly hates women. Anyway, Molly Shaw isn't his type."

And then a clip from an interview that Jake had given just the past week. He had been at Berenger headquarters in Miami and—as orchestrated by Tom—the news crew had filmed Jake and the interviewer walking slowly down a hallway, where the walls displayed huge photos of the various Berenger properties. "I've waited years to find the one woman I loved enough to marry," Jake was saying to the interviewer. "Molly Shaw is that woman, and now I have only two priorities in my life: my family, and the continued success of Berenger Corporation."

Jake turned his head, feeling a stab of pain and anger. *More irony*, he thought. At the time he'd said that, he had meant every word.

The camera returned to live feed of Drake Daniels. "Two priorities?" he asked, looking very grim. "Or, perhaps, only one. Here with us in the studio is Molly Shaw. Welcome, Molly. Also joining us is *Vanity Fair* staff writer Carter McKee."

The camera pulled back to reveal Molly and Carter seated in chairs next to Drake Daniels. Molly was wearing a soft blue suit that looked suspiciously like something that Elaine Newberg would have picked out. She had not been wearing it last night when she fled the apartment, and she had taken nothing then but her coat and purse. Carter

McKee had apparently brought it to New York as part of the pre-arranged plan.

He stared at Molly as the camera zoomed in on her face. She looked beautiful, intelligent, and tired. There was a weariness around her eyes and mouth that suggested that she had not slept well. A last-minute attack of conscience? If so, it hadn't been strong enough to keep her off the air.

"Molly, this is a story that the viewers would like to hear first from you," said Drake Daniels. "Tell us the truth about what Jake Berenger asked you to do."

Molly nodded, and looked into the camera with the practiced ease of someone who had undergone hours of Tom's media training. "This is difficult for me . . ." she said.

Nope, Jake thought coldly. *You don't know difficult, babe. You just wait.*

"I know that people are questioning Jake's motives for announcing this engagement. I was told to stay quiet and go along with the plan, but I couldn't do that. I think that the public has a right to know the truth."

"Go ahead," said Drake Daniels. Carter McKee was on the edge of his seat, almost twitching with excitement.

Molly took a deep breath. "I'm here to admit to everyone that the rumors are true. I . . . I *am* pregnant."

There was a stunned silence, and Jake saw Carter's face freeze. The camera cut to Drake Daniels, who also appeared to be speechless.

"What the hell?" Tom exclaimed, straightening up from where he had been slumping over the back of the couch. *"What?"*

"I don't know," Jake said, staring at the screen.

"What is she *doing*? She's not pregnant!" Tom stopped suddenly, as if something had just occurred to him. "Uh, I mean . . . is she?"

"It's not impossible," Jake said, doing a quick mental calculation. "But even if she is, she wouldn't know it yet."

"I'll be damned," Tom said. "Well. I didn't know that you two were . . . uh . . . huh."

Molly was speaking earnestly to the camera. "Jake wanted to keep it a secret until after the wedding. He thought that the tabloids might start saying that he was being forced into this marriage. But the truth leaked out anyway, and sure enough, people started questioning his motives for deciding to settle down. I wanted to come on the show tonight to tell everyone that it was absolutely his decision, and that he asked me to marry him *weeks* before we had this wonderful news. We've moved up the wedding date so that it will be as soon as possible. We're very happy, and we'd like to thank all of the people who wrote to offer us their congratulations."

"Molly," said Drake Daniels, "surely you know that there have been other, more serious rumors about this engagement. Rumors that accuse Jake of arranging it with the intention of deceiving the public in order to raise the Berenger stock price. Do you have a response to that?"

Molly looked surprised and slightly hurt. "What a funny idea. When other businessmen decide to get married and start a family, it's considered very normal, isn't it?"

"Did Jake Berenger ever ask you to participate in a fraudulent engagement for publicity purposes?"

"Of course not," Molly said, smiling now, as if she were indulging in a little joke. She waved her ring for the camera, and the studio lights caught the glitter of the diamond. "This certainly isn't fraudulent. It's Cartier!"

Drake Daniels gave a tight smile that did not reach his eyes. "Yes," he said. "But—"

"Oh," Molly exclaimed. "I have one more announcement. I wanted to tell my readers that my new novel, *Caribe*, the sequel to *Pirate Gold*, will be released by Leighton House in July!"

The camera cut to a full-screen shot of Drake. "Thank you," he said. He seemed to be clenching his teeth. "The real story on Jake Berenger's engagement . . . and Molly Shaw's new novel. You heard it first right here, on *Inside Edge*. Up next: Is your veterinarian overcharging you for pet medication? A hidden-camera exposé."

The show went to a commercial break.

"Unbelievable!" Tom exclaimed. He was pacing again, going back and forth behind the couch. "You can turn it off—it's over. They won't put her back on the air. Why the hell did she just do that? Why would she give them an interview and then screw them like that, on live television?"

Jake clicked the remote, and the screen went dark. He had a tightness in his throat that made it difficult to speak. "She told me last night that she never gave them an interview," he said. "She told me that Carter McKee taped her secretly, then edited the tape and used it to help sell the story to *Inside Edge*. I thought she was lying."

"What!" Tom exclaimed, stopping in his tracks. "Are you serious? If that's true . . ." He stared at Jake for a moment, then started to laugh. "Yeah. Okay. I get it now. I get it. Jake, my friend . . . Molly didn't betray you, she betrayed Carter McKee. I think I can explain what happened. That girl saved our asses."

"Explain," Jake said. His heart was beating fast.

"Carter McKee sold the story to the network, and they were going to break it tonight, using him as the inside source. But then—last night, I'm guessing—Molly told him that she would go on the show to tell the story. That sounded great to the producers, who put her on, but then she didn't say a damn thing! You saw her—she stonewalled them. She was good, wasn't she? I taught her that."

"Why didn't they play the tape?" Jake asked.

"Because," Tom said happily, "they couldn't! There was no interview, so the edited tape was all they had, and taping Molly without her consent was illegal. Even the lowest tabloid show wouldn't be stupid enough to put that on the air."

"Carter McKee can still tell the story."

"He could," Tom said. "But who's going to believe him? He's got no proof, and after what Molly did, his credibility is zero. He looks like a liar, or worse—a nutcase. I don't think that *Vanity Fair* is going to be taking his calls, either. That young man is destined for a career in the tabloids—he'd better start polishing up his application for a job at *The Weekly World News*."

Tom's cell phone rang, and he picked it up. "Amadeo."

Jake reached up to scrub his face with his hands. He felt shaken, as if he had just run through a burning house and somehow come out only slightly singed.

"Aha," Tom exclaimed accusingly into the phone. "You! I'll bet that you were—what? Of course I saw Molly on the show! Did you know about this? When? Oh, yeah? And you didn't bother to call me, did you! Damn it, woman, you have some nerve. Jake? He's right here. Yeah, I'm at his place—we were both watching. Why?"

He listened, and Jake saw a surprised look on his face. "I'll be damned," he said, and listened again. "No kidding. Okay. Hold on."

He turned to Jake. "It's that woman," he said.

"I guessed," Jake said dryly.

"She's downstairs in the lobby. She says that she's been trying to get through to you for twenty minutes, and that your security people are very rude."

"She called to tell me that?"

"No, she wants to come up. She has . . . well, you'll hear it. Okay for me to go down and get her?"

"Fine," Jake said. It didn't surprise him to hear that Elaine Newberg was in New York. He had long since concluded that he was doomed to be dogged by her wherever he went. He hoped that she would finally prove herself useful by telling him where to find Molly. He had a feeling that she would know.

Unable to sit still any longer, he stood up, walked to the window, and stared out. With the exception of the darkened rectangle of Central Park, the lights of the city stretched as far as he could see. It was enormous, this city, and well able to hide one woman, especially one who did not want to be found. Molly would have left the television studio by now, but to go where? Back to the Grand? To another hotel? The airport? Gold Bay? Belden? He didn't know what she was thinking, where she was going, or when he would see her again. The uncertainty was maddening, and it made him want to pace the floor, swearing like Tom.

He heard the chime of the elevator, and moments later, Elaine swept into the room. "Jake, dear," she said briskly. She was wearing a swirling black wool cape trimmed with fur, and clutching a large, shiny crocodile handbag, which she plunked down on the coffee table. She looked at him, and shook her head. "It's been a dreadful two days, I know. I am so terribly sorry about all of this. I had no idea that that shameful brother of mine—half brother, actually—was intelligent enough to cause so much trouble."

"What brings you to New York?" Jake asked, feeling persecuted.

"A desperate cry for my help, of course," Elaine said. "I should tell you first that I don't make a habit of breaking and entering. But I do make an exception for crisis situations, and I know an interesting young man named Fabrizio who can work magic with a deadbolt lock. We went to Carter's apartment last night and retrieved something that Molly asked me to find and give to you."

She reached into her bag and pulled out a small cassette player. "The original tape," she said dramatically. "Proof that there was never any interview!"

"I already know that," Jake said impatiently. "I don't need to hear the tape. Do you know where Molly is?"

"Yes, but first, this—"

"I don't care about that. I have to talk to Molly. She said something very important to me last night, and I thought it wasn't true, but now . . . Look, I need to find her. Where is she?"

"Jake, dear, if you'd just be patient—"

"I can't be patient," Jake exclaimed. "Tell me where she is!"

Elaine sighed. "She's on her way here, of course. But the traffic is bad, so it will be a few more minutes. In the meantime, if you'll just listen to this tape, I think it will explain everything that you want to know."

CHAPTER 35

After the taxi dropped Molly off in front of the Berenger Grand, she hesitated on the steps, huddling in her coat and staring apprehensively up at the hotel's sandstone and bronze entrance. People streamed past her in both directions without giving her a second glance, and she could hear the blare of taxi horns and the shrill notes of the doormen's whistles behind her.

She had not been nearly so nervous in the television studio. She didn't know what to expect—didn't know, even, if she would be allowed upstairs to see Jake. If everything had gone according to plan, Jake would have seen the show, and Elaine would have played him the real tape, and he would know that she had never been a part of Carter's scheme. But Molly had had a lot of recent experience in the many ways that plans could go wrong.

Elaine had arrived on the early morning flight from Chicago, and at ten A.M. they had proceeded to Madison Avenue to find an outfit for Molly to wear on television. At first, Molly had objected to the idea of spending the morning shopping, on the grounds that it seemed inappropriate to focus on fashion in the middle of a crisis, but Elaine had prevailed.

"One does not win any points for public slovenliness, however earnest it may be," she said with a critical look at the black sweater and wrinkled pants that Molly had been wearing since her escape from Jake's apartment the previous evening. "And you won't be doing Jake any favors by appearing on television looking like a bag lady, dear. We'll go to Rosalind, my personal shopper at Bergdorf. She'll have just the thing."

Molly had eventually given in, but she had drawn the line at a professional blow-dry and makeup application. She didn't want to look too polished. Elaine might think that she was being silly, but if Jake watched the show, Molly wanted him to see a hint of her real feelings on her face, like a coded message of sincerity, meant only for him.

Molly had expected to have to explain herself to the security staff before they would call up to Jake's apartment, but—to her surprise—Tom Amadeo was standing by the reception desk, scanning the crowd as if he were looking for someone.

She approached him warily, and then he saw her. He grinned and strode forward. Her heart jumped.

"Did you see the show?" she asked him anxiously.

"Ha!" he exclaimed. "Did I see it! Listen, babe, you were pretty good, but next time you need to remember to turn a little more toward the camera. And no fiddling with your hair—it distracts attention from the message. Nice job with the book plug at the end, though. They didn't want to let you get that in, but it's like I told you, you've got to be *assertive* with these people."

"Did Elaine . . . ?"

Tom chuckled. "She did. She's up there right now. She is a piece of work, that woman." There was an admiring twist to his mouth.

Molly felt weak with relief. "And Jake?"

"Let's go upstairs," Tom said.

Tom talked nonstop during their ride up to the apartment, giving her a detailed analysis of exactly what she had done right—and wrong—during her first official television appearance, but Molly barely heard him.

Finally, the elevator stopped and released them into the foyer. Molly hurried toward the living room, her heart beating so hard that she could hear it in her ears.

"The thing is," Tom was saying, following right behind her, "when you're improvising live on camera, you've gotta be concise. Hit them straight up with the message, then give them a few facts to back it up, then . . ."

For the first time, he seemed to realize that Molly wasn't listening to him.

Jake and Elaine were standing by the window, and Molly had the impression that they had been talking until they were alerted by the elevator chime. Jake looked tense and uncertain, but the relief on his face when he saw her was unmistakable. Molly breathed in softly, feeling a lump in her throat.

"Molly, dear," Elaine said, hurrying forward to embrace her. "I thought you were wonderful on the show, and I'm glad that you remembered what I told you about powdering your forehead. Even a star shouldn't shine under the studio lights."

"That's true," Tom agreed, "plus I was telling her that thing about the three-quarter angle that you and I talked about. Jake, back me up on this. The question is—"

"Mr. Amadeo," Elaine said.

Tom frowned. "What?"

She gave him a meaningful look. "I would like you to take me downstairs for a drink."

"Sure, the jazz band starts at ten, so we can—"

"Now."

"Oh," Tom said awkwardly. "Right. Come on . . . uh . . . Elaine. Let's go down to the bar." He offered her his arm, she took it, and together they left the room.

Molly and Jake stared at each other for a moment, and then Molly said softly, "You don't look like you slept much last night."

"I didn't," he said.

"I thought that if I called to tell you that I actually was going on the show, it would just make things worse. I thought you'd hang up on me."

"I probably would have," Jake said. "But I would have been wrong. You killed their story."

She nodded. "I think it's really dead, too. You don't have anything more to worry about from Carter. Or me. I . . . can go away quietly, if you want."

"No," Jake said. "That's not what I want. But tell me one thing, just so I'm sure. You aren't really pregnant, are you?"

"Oh," Molly said, feeling her face getting warm. "No, I don't think so. I hope you don't mind that I said that. I know it isn't the kind of thing that anyone should lie about, but I needed something dramatic to say to distract everyone, and I couldn't think of anything better. I guess it puts you in an awkward position, since you'll eventually have to explain where your fiancée and child went, but I think we can manage it. We could just say that it was a mistake with the test . . ."

"No," Jake said again, firmly. "I'm tired of lies and deception. Aren't you? You said so on that tape."

Molly nodded warily. "Yes . . ."

"So, there's only one thing to do. Make it true."

"What?" she whispered.

"Make it true," Jake repeated. "All of it. Will you marry me, Molly?"

A lump had formed in her throat, and she could hardly speak. "For real?" she asked, finally.

"For real. I love you, and I waited all my life to find you. I'm not giving you up in April, or ever."

She nodded. "Okay," she said. He reached out, and she ran forward into his arms, burying her face against his chest. He held her so tightly that the breath was almost squeezed out of her, and she could hear the sound of his heart, beating as fast as her own. "I love you, too," she said, her voice muffled against his sweater. The secure warm solidity of him loosened something inside her, and she took a deep, shaky breath, feeling hot tears rising in her eyes.

"Molly?" Jake said as she trembled against him. He pulled back and looked down at her. "What's wrong?"

"I'm sorry," she said. She swiped at her eyes, blinking away the prickle of moisture. "It's been a very complicated two days."

"I'm sorry, too," he said. "For everything. Especially for not giving you the benefit of the doubt. Did you see Carter after the show?"

She nodded. "He was angry. He told me that if I was going to be so stupid and unreasonable, there was nothing more he could do to help me. He said that I was on my own from now on, and good luck to me."

"Just as well," Jake said. "If his scheme collapsed on top of him, he can only blame himself."

"I don't know about that. Carter is pretty good at blaming other people. I just wish . . ." She stopped, and sighed. "I feel like I lost something, but I think it was just an illusion of friendship, not an actual friend. Carter kept telling me to live on my own terms, but he really meant that I should do things his way. It started to fall apart when I actually started thinking for myself. I wish that I'd guessed earlier . . ."

"It's not your fault," Jake said.

"It is. I should have known. What if I'd listened to him? What if I really had gone to the press, looking for revenge? I considered it!" She shook her head, horrified by the thought.

"But you didn't do it," Jake said. "All you did was trap me into a legal agreement to build you a damn museum. And I know you well enough to be sure that you won't let me out of it, even if you do love me."

He didn't sound as if he minded all that much. Molly began to smile again as her eyes moved over his face. His eyes, his mouth . . . they were all familiar to her now, and she thought that she would never grow tired of looking at him. "Aren't you the one who told me that you feel strongly about the preservation of cultural heritage sites?"

"Oh, I do," Jake said dryly. "Believe me, I feel very strongly. Just do me a favor, and write that best seller about Mary so I can at least use her to promote the resort. It's my island now, and she should earn her keep."

"I'll try," Molly said. "Now, about that pirate theme park . . ."

He silenced her with a kiss that was surprisingly tender, as if they now had the time to enjoy a gentler passion. It felt to Molly like a promise of the years ahead.

Later, when she was feeling breathless and half melted, she remembered something. "Jake, do you think that we should go and find Tom and Elaine? Or would it be better to leave them alone together?"

"We should find them," Jake said. "They were almost on a first-name basis when they left. God knows what could happen next."

"They'll be surprised to hear about the new plan. I don't think anyone expected Operation Family Man to be quite so successful."

"They should have seen it coming," Jake said. "Then

again, everyone knows that I only like voluptuous blondes. And you could never fall in love with a shallow, publicity-seeking playboy."

"That's true. Considering that I'm not your type, and you're not mine, do you really think that we should settle for each other?"

"Sounds risky," Jake said. He laughed softly and took her face in his hands, gazing down into her eyes. "But I'm willing if you are."

Molly nodded. "The engagement has already been in the newspaper," she said. "So I guess we'll just have to do the best we can."

About the Author

Melanie Craft studied archaeology at Oberlin College and the American University in Cairo, Egypt. She has been a sales clerk, a bartender, a safari driver, a pastry chef, a cocktail waitress, a housecleaner, and—through it all—a writer. *Man Trouble* is her third novel. She and her husband live in Woodside, California. For information, please visit her web site at www.melaniecraft.com.

THE EDITOR'S DIARY

Dear Reader,

Love comes in many disguises. But sometimes love comes while you are in disguise. Just ask Eliza Merriweather and Molly Shaw in RULES OF ENGAGEMENT and MAN TROUBLE, our two Warner Forever titles this May.

Julia Quinn calls **Kathryn Caskie**'s Regency-set first novel, **RULES OF ENGAGEMENT**, "a delightful debut" and Eloisa James raves "clever, frothy and funny—an enthralling read." So hold onto your muslin skirts, this one's going to blow your stockings off! Eliza Merriweather has no desire to get married. But her two scheming aunts Letitia and Viola have other plans. They've enlisted the help of an old military guidebook called "Rules of Engagement' to secure her offers of marriage. After all, engagement is engagement no matter the context. But Eliza, a worthy adversary, has hatched a scheme of her own. She's persuaded Magnus MacKinnon, a Scottish earl, to pose as a suitor to discourage other callers. Before long, Magnus's brogue sends shivers down her spine and his kisses make her heart race. Could what began as a lark blossom into real love?

Journeying from the wiles and the guiles of the ton to the warm sun and the gentle surf of the Caribbean, we present **Melanie Craft**'s **MAN TROUBLE**. *Romantic Times* called her "a fresh new voice" and the praise couldn't be more well-deserved. Dr. Molly Shaw is leading a double life. By day, she's a history professor on the tenure track and by night, Molly is bestselling romance author Sandra St. Claire. These parallel lives never intersect . . . until a journalist friend asks her to pull off the story of the century: transform herself into billionaire playboy Jake Berenger's perfect woman to get the inside scoop. But Jake is anything but an innocent victim. In fact, his reputation as a ladies' man is so overexposed that his business is suffering. His only solution is a radical makeover into a family man. And for that he needs the perfect wife. Could she be right under his nose, hidden beneath Sandra St. Claire's sexpot act and her spandex? It looks like there's trouble brewing in paradise!

To find out more about Warner Forever, these May titles, and the authors, visit us at www.warnerforever.com.

With warmest wishes,

Karen Kosztolnyik, Senior Editor

P.S. The temperatures are beginning to rise so treat yourself to some ice cream and these two reasons to relax: **Sandra Hill** pens a spicy contemporary about a woman who's on the lam from a loan shark and discovers that she's still married to a man she thought she divorced years ago, in **CAJUN COWBOY**; and **Edie Claire** delivers the poignant tale of a woman who inherits half a mountain inn and a tangled web of untruths she must unravel before she can claim a love that was **MEANT TO BE**.